“Scott Shachter’s *Outside In* is a funny and ... intriguing genre of ‘jazz fantasies’. ... Ellison among others, *Outside In* ta... interaction and abstraction as a fast-s... ineffable questions of identity, ambiti... even the nature of reality itself.” —H... of the *Jazz Journalists Association* and author of *Future Jazz,* and *Miles, Ornette, Cecil: Jazz Beyond Jazz.*

“*Outside In* is an up and down love story and an intriguing fantasy from inside the jazz world—all narrated by the main character, Shawn. ‘Playing’ Shawn is professional saxophonist Scott Shachter, a storyteller who makes you want to know what will happen next.” —Ira Gitler, distinguished jazz historian and producer, and author/editor with Leonard Feather of *The Biographical Encyclopedia of Jazz.* His other books include *Swing to Bop* and *Jazz Masters of the Forties*

“Scott Shachter’s *Outside In* travels a literary orbit similar to Douglas Adams or Kurt Vonnegut, rocketing through such disparate worlds as jazz music, zealot gangsters, elder-care facilities, schizophrenic painting, extra-dimensional dog planets, even the Holocaust. By turns hilarious, provocative, surreal and inspiring, it’s a comic, cosmic journey through the meaning of reality and beyond.” —Steve Armour, Hollywood screenwriter and celebrated New York jazz trombonist

“A fascinating, unsettling, enjoyable journey. Scott Shachter’s writing is exceptional--clear, creative and captivating.” —Joel Leach, past president of the *International Association for Jazz Education* (IAJE)

“The boundary between creative genius and madness is often an unnervingly thin and permeable one . . . *Outside In* explores that mysterious frontier . . . through a talented New York City saxophonist who can’t get out of his own way . . . Shachter’s story has humor and heart, and will give the reader much to chew on.” —*Fearless Reviews*

“Five stars! Humorous, insightful, imaginative and full of metaphors. And very romantic.” —Ted Nash, featured soloist with *Wynton Marsalis and the Jazz at Lincoln Center Orchestra*

"A tremendous jazz novel. Funny yet also sad and profound—and always engaging. You're hooked right from the first sentence." —Walt Weiskopf, renowned saxophonist with *Steely Dan*

"A stunning jazz book, from a player's side, and extremely funny . . . Ambitious, insightful and hilarious. A real achievement. Shachter walks a very fine line here, pairing the loftiest, fantastical human heights with some deep human suffering. It would all be too much if it wasn't hilarious at every turn. It's at its best when most adventurous, most risky, and in those moments, which begin subtly and then take over the book, this novel is absolutely spectacular. I loved it." —Andrew Sterman, featured soloist, *Philip Glass Ensemble*

"This wonderful debut novel blends the zany, unpredictable life of the New York freelance musician with an Ignatius P. Reilly-esque world of near insanity. Throw in a bit of surreal fantasy and the result is utterly engaging and page-turnable. As a musician, avid reader and fiction writer myself, I assure you this book does not disappoint on any level. Read it!" —Belinda Whitney, concertmaster, *Knickerbocker Chamber Orchestra*

"This book captured me from the very first sentence and I simply couldn't put it down until I finished it . . . The music came alive . . . Fantastic, highly recommended." —John Cipolla, president of the *International Clarinet Association* and *Associate Professor of Music, Western Kentucky University*

"Scott's new novel is brilliant . . . A fun read and right on point in the 'real' world of the professional musician. It's a must read for all, musician or just music lover." —John Moses, New York's leading freelance clarinetist

"An exciting and thought provoking ride inside the mind of a potential genius who will achieve this potential if he embraces his true self. Musician or not, we can all relate to this inner questioning of ourselves. Will we be okay if we do exactly what we want with our true talent? A thoroughly inspiring, funny and beautiful read." —Marc Phaneuf, Broadway woodwind veteran

OUTSIDE IN

A Novel

SCOTT SHACHTER

Printed in the United States of America

Cover art and design, interior design by Lisa Sloane
www.lisasloanedesign.com

Published by Starbeat Press

First Edition: 2013

I have enormous gratitude for my writing teacher, Steve Armour, who like Wendell Rice in this novel, taught me how to create from my most genuine voice. I honor my stepdad, George Weiss, for his sweet encouragement, my mother, Jaqueline, for teaching me to strive for excellence, and my father, Sam, for making me believe I could do *anything*.

I dedicate *Outside In* to my wife, Lisa Sloane, whose love is what holds me here, and whose designs of the cover and words are what make this novel look so beautiful (*and who wouldn't have finished the design unless I'd sworn to dedicate the book to her*).

TABLE OF CONTENTS

PART

CHAPTER 1

Jellybeans

I'D NEVER LOOKED into the eyes of a lunatic before. Like most New Yorkers, I'd always avoided the time bombs wandering the streets. But it was just days since Carole broke up with me, and I felt scattered. I was perched on a teetering stage ten feet above the pavement when the most disturbing person I'd ever seen shouted at me from the crowd—and I couldn't look away.

Ignore the bastard, I told myself. Concentrate. The saxophone is all there is. Just play with the rhythm section and you won't see him; you'll even forget you ever knew Carole. It didn't matter that I had to wear an orange ruffled shirt three sizes too big or that our supersonic speakers were bludgeoning the crowd with our jazz or that I was standing on a one-story float wobbling up Sixth Avenue. It wasn't Carnegie Hall. It was just a stupid parade—the 1999 Sixth Avenue Street Fair—but it was one of the best gigs I had going, and I needed it. I needed every gig. Yet as if I could afford to trash them all, I blew one dissonant solo after another, each more reckless than the last.

I couldn't help myself—not with this lunatic shouting at me. And not after losing Carole. Solos were the moments I felt most alive, when I'd hold nothing back and sense the whole world nodding with me, the air shimmying, the stars flickering with every note. Infinite possibilities would gush over me, as if from some cosmic wave. Every artist has their fantasies, and I didn't dare tell a soul about mine. I was just a typical sax player and composer, with one little quirk: I could blow the wildest avant-garde jazz and escape anything, even a broken heart.

That whole afternoon I'd struggled to keep my playing in line, especially since I was only a sub on the gig. But as I started my long solo in "A Night in Tunisia," the lively bass, drums and keyboards inspired me into my freest-blowing style, and that's when I noticed the huge man in clashing shades of red, yelling at me, elbowing toward me through the crowd, the whites of his eyes bugging with shock or fury or something too crazy to imagine.

Maybe he's just mad at the soundman, I thought. We *all* wanted to kill the soundman—for driving us to wear earplugs. Or maybe he's outraged by the fifteen minutes we spent on "New York, New York." I'm outraged *too,* I wanted to yell—but don't blame *me*. Blame the city power brokers strutting alongside us. Blame our ass-kissing leader for forcing us to pander to them.

As the huge red maniac shoved people out of his way, his bald head flashed in the sun. His gray beard, like a squirrel's nest, along with his bulging eyes made him look like a medieval executioner. But his red baseball jacket was more for a little boy. And underneath his red bell-bottom jeans, his red high-top sneakers were untied, laces flapping.

He paused to holler at me again as policemen angled toward him through the crowd. Not even the man in red, who would ultimately impact my life like no one else, could make me put down my horn to hear what he had to say. This was my *solo,* after all. And I'd sacrificed far too much just to get hired for the Sixth Avenue Street Fair.

HALF MY LIVING came from babysitting nine and ten-year-olds in the form of private saxophone lessons—the other half, from the gigs no one wanted: gazebos, pep bands, junior high productions of *Bye, Bye, Birdie*. My best-paying job, about once a month, was at The Mediterranean Club, an empty banquet hall in Bensonhurst, Brooklyn. Here a handful of brawny, armed men in silk ties and pinky rings would hire combos to play mellow tunes while they smoked and whispered in the shadows. A stressful gig—but everyone, even your average sociopath, needs music.

My jazz was too severe, friends would say. And they were always wondering if there was something wrong with my horn. It required a discerning audience, I'd tell them. Without mentioning any cosmic waves, I'd tell them the music was just a natural outgrowth of the jazz tradition, the ultimate in musical liberty—as American as the Declaration. And the only way I wanted to blow.

Two clubs that paid as little as possible welcomed my version of freedom. Den of Dread, a gothic nightclub in the East Village, featured grunge and every kind of alternative noise. Everything in the Den of Dread was about death. Death posters. Death tablecloths. Death fixtures. Even the waitresses looked fresh from the morgue.

My other jazz gig was in a bar in the lower Bowery. Sober people went there on their way to somewhere else. The rest got plowed while they listened to jazz that was "out." It was The Out House, and had no trouble living up to its name.

But I wanted more than this. I wanted to create a new sound. All my life I'd been listening to Bird—Charlie Parker. On the alto saxophone he was God declaring the great truth: Music is more than pleasant sounds. Real music is a link to Heaven and Earth and all the subtle places in between. And when I first heard Julian "Cannonball" Adderley, I no longer had a choice. I'd *have* to play the alto. It was everything. The alto was my religion, and Bird and Cannonball sat atop the pantheon.

Of course, I'd never anticipated the hundreds of "new-sounding" saxophone players arriving in New York every day. There were thousands of us and we were everywhere. Even mailmen and parking attendants raced home after work to practice their groundbreaking be-bop. It was hard to get a gig, and my early years in New York were spent moving from one cheap and cramped sublet to another—my best job, cleaning cages for a veterinarian.

By the time I'd acquired a roster of private students, I was also playing in every jam session and rehearsal band in town. It was what jazzers were supposed to do. But I kept scaring everybody with my avant-garde. No one recommends you if you scare them—unless it's to someone they hate. I needed to tone it down.

On one session at a nearby club I waited with twelve other horn players for a chance to blow a solo with the rhythm section. One virtuoso after another played smooth and soaring music. My turn came after a tenor player named Bjorn, who'd glided through the brisk chord changes to "Cherokee" like he was just getting warmed up. He ended his last chorus and eased away. As the pianist, bass player and drummer continued comping the changes, I sidled between them with my alto. They were playing so fast, my foot couldn't come close to tapping their beat. Stick to the changes, I told myself. This is tonal bebop. Form is king. Make them love you.

But my mind blanked. I forgot whatever I knew about "Cherokee" or anything else. Bjorn had played five glistening choruses and stolen all my notes. As I stumbled out of my second chorus, a heavyset alto player from Panama edged me aside like a bug in his way, and proceeded to blow almost like Cannonball.

This was ground level of the jazz world, and I wasn't going to get a single gig if I couldn't at least temper my free jazz and showcase the time-honored styles expected of me. In other words, I had to compromise. But all too often—when it came to my solos—nothing, not even a thin wallet could hold me back.

THE MAN IN RED frantically waved his arms, demanding the same thing over and over, but between my earplugs and the din from our speakers I couldn't understand a word. Pushing and elbowing, he bullied his way through the thick crowd, toward the float, toward me. A policeman hustled in front of him, the man in red now less than twenty feet away.

Maybe he hates my playing, I thought. He wouldn't be the only one. But even my worst critics were never *this* enthused. Hey *asshole*, I wanted to yell back, *you* try blowing a horn on a stagecoach. Luckily, "A Night in Tunisia" and its spicy chords were enough to draw me back to the crisp groove of the rhythm section. It wouldn't last long, though. Again and again the man in red would flail his arms while barking at me with those bugging eyes—and throw me off. Why *me?* I couldn't stop wondering. But I'd claw my way back into the music—thanks to Carole. Rejection brings out the dogged rage in a musician. Maybe, I thought, I should get her to come to all my gigs and tell me she's moved on—just to keep the heartbreak absolutely fresh.

~~~

I MET CAROLE at Forest Hills Hospital. I was in a trio performing for the patients—ninety minutes without a break and very little cash. It was the best gig I ever had. Carole Bonner, the bright-eyed attending nurse with a bashful smile, never left my side. Would you like to take a break, Do you need water, Can I get you a sandwich, Wouldn't you like a better chair? She didn't even blink at my two older comrades. That's how I met Carole, and for one year we delighted in each other—until the week before the Street Fair.

For most of our relationship we'd lived in our separate places and busy separate lives—hers busier than mine—and it was easy to stay in the glow of new love. I'd visit her snug West Village apartment, where she'd cater to me like I was an ambassador—elegant china, scented candles, appetizers, gourmet meals, all knocked out in the time it would've taken me just to locate the stuff in my cupboards. Carole was slim and quick, and had snatched my heart.

"We had to discharge a six-year-old today with Type 1 diabetes," she'd say softly while she shredded cabbage, "just because his insurance ran out." Now she was basting a chicken. "Kamal was his name. We saved his life. Do you know what it's like to save someone's life? There's nothing, nothing better, no words to describe it," she'd say, stirring a saucepan and two pots. "But the boy still needs us. He can't stand up without fainting. His father died; his mother works two jobs. I can't stop worrying about him." She'd pause to take me in, and unwind with a big sigh, gazing at me with her chestnut eyes for a long moment—a look no one and nothing else could ever live up to.

"My daddy used to play the cello," she'd say. "He was so happy then. We all loved it when he played. But he couldn't make a living so he gave it up. You're so lucky, Shawn, your whole life is music. No pills, charts, sick people. I talk too much, don't I?"

"Your voice is like Bird to me," I'd say.

"I'm making you a surprise dessert," she'd say, sliding something into the oven. "Where's your next gig? You're either playing private parties or those disgusting dives. Wait till you taste this dessert. And the casserole.
~~~

A musician should eat well . . . Hello? Are you composing again? You're so spacey. I hate that. You're never completely *here*. You're making up a song right now, aren't you?"

"I was thinking of my latest piece, the one I wrote for you. I can't wait for you to hear it."

"Avant-garde?" she'd say. "I don't know if I'm ready for that. When we met you were playing show tunes—sounded so wonderful." She'd dice something and flick it into a saucepan. "I like music you can hum to, or at least tap a foot."

"Each piece is its own world," I'd say. "Just think of it like that."

"Maybe that's why your head's always in the stars," she'd say, shaking her head. Then she'd smile. "While everyone else is just hanging on, you're creating your own little heavens."

She's the one, I thought. When she hears my tunes it'll be "forever." I prodded her to join me in one of those disgusting dives and taste the avant-garde I loved so much.

"Oh, I can't go in that place," she said. "What was that, the Dead of Dead?"

"Den of Dread," I said.

"That's the place; I'm scared to even pass by it on the sidewalk."

"Well, what about The Out House?" I said.

"How can you work there? It's so sleazy."

"I know. At least the bartender now *tries* to break up the drug deals."

"It's awful, Shawn," she said. "I'm just not sure I'm ready for it—The Out House and the avant-garde. Will you play any show tunes?"

I shook my head.

"If I go," she said, "you better not ignore me."

"There are only three rows of tables. The whole time I'll be playing just to you. It's great; you just have to be open. Think of it simply as spontaneous, free expression overlapping a web of competing structures."

"What? Oh. Sure. Okay . . . "

AS THE LEADER of my Out House twice-a-month gig at twenty dollars a man—I took twenty-five—I was so thankful to find a pianist, bass player and drummer willing to play my originals, I'd never considered their personalities. They despised each other. They despised the gig. And in spite of how much I featured them, they despised me too. They assumed I was somehow cheating them—a corporatist for The Out House.

It took twelve minutes to walk from Carole's quaint section of the Village to the more neglected streets of the Bowery and The Out House, where I escorted her to a front-row table. My guys were already setting up, and as usual, grumbling at each other.

I introduced Carole, and she smiled and waved from her chair. She'd hoped her V-neck and jeans would camouflage her, but they only accentuated her smooth curves. The guys flashed their grins, checking her up and down.

I hopped onto the bandstand, and we opened with my bow to Stravinsky, a modal funk groove with layered meters I called, "The Blight of Spring." Within the first minute I was blowing an avant-garde solo that lasted most of the set. I usually shared solo time with the guys but I wanted so much to impress Carole, to validate her confidence in me. I was celebrating her with my horn, but she looked pale.

At the break I joined her and asked what was wrong.

"Are you aware that while you're playing," she said, "your guys behind you are cursing at each other?"

"They've got mental problems," I said. "Are you enjoying this at all?"

"Shawn," she said, examining her drink, "was that one of the pieces you said took months to write?"

"Absolutely. And I was thinking of you the whole time I wrote it."

"Thinking of *me?*"

"Could you hear the layers of fours against sixes?"

"I never knew a saxophone could sound so loud."

"Well, my music gets very free," I said. "This next set should be more fun. We're doing the piece I wrote for you, our premier of 'Finger Muscles.'"

The intertwining rivers of notes and superimposed harmonies of "Finger Muscles" demanded at least a week of rehearsals, but there was no money for even one, so we winged it to honor my girlfriend. I counted it off and within a minute the drummer was abusing me: "Where are we now; what fucking tempo do you want; stop and count it off again; I'm leaving if you don't stop this thing." The piano player kept trying to jump to the Beguine section while the drummer never got out of the seven-eight, and I was convinced the bass player had the wrong tune on his stand. Even I got lost after ten minutes, but my music was my drug and I couldn't stop blowing more and more "out." Then a guy with oily hair and a long earring leaned all over Carole, whispering in her ear. I put down my alto and flew to her table.

"She's with me, buddy," I said into his face. "Back off." The earring guy slunk away as I nodded to Carole, leapt back onto the bandstand, and continued my solo.

It was my finest moment of the night. She could hate the music, but at least I'd stood up to the weird earring guy. I'd have to get points for *that.*

I picked up the tempo, daring my guys to keep up. The drummer threw his sticks down, and folded his arms. The club emptied out. When we finished, the guys left so fast, the last note was still fading as they dashed for the subway.

The bartender was busy cleaning up. Carole had one hand on her head, the other on her stomach.

"I'm sorry," I said to her. "We were pretty bad tonight. I'd ask you to come next week, but we might not sound any better."

"My stomach hurts," she said.

"I felt a little queasy too when that bum threw up all over the bar."

She kept her hand on her stomach, her eyes shut.

"I wish the bartender hadn't waited so long to clean it up," I said.

"Did you know that everyone was talking the whole time you were playing?"

"Well, things weren't clicking tonight. My music is out, but not *this* out."

"The table behind me was dealing heroin," she said.

"I'll never do this to you again," I said. "Well, not for a few weeks until we've rehearsed."

She blew her nose. "What were those goose sounds in the last piece?"

"Oh, I was trying for a double E. Didn't quite speak."

"We should go now," she said. "I'm very tired."

"Sure, we've got tomorrow off. We'll sleep in, relax, your stomach will ease up; we'll have brunch at Berry World."

She didn't say another word until I'd walked her home.

"It's not working," she said from her stoop.

"What's not?"

"I'm so confused," she said, shaking her head. "I grew up with Brahms . . . and 'Music Man.'" She asked me to go. That was five days before the Street Fair.

"I'm still confused, Shawn," she said when she finally returned my calls, the morning of the Street Fair. "You and I have always been so comfortable; we could always talk about *anything* . . . well—except for your music. You deserve someone who understands your music."

"No I don't," I said.

"Yes you do."

"No, I don't care. Sometimes my music . . . well . . . it can sound really *crazy*—even to me. There, I said it. Can't I still see you?"

"Shawn, your music is your whole life. I love you, but . . . I've moved on."

FEEDBACK SHRIEKED from the speakers, snapping me back to my horn and Sixth Avenue. In my daze I'd leaned too close to the microphone. The rhythm section lit into double-time infusing new life into the last chorus of my solo. Three policemen had corralled around the man in red. Ah, I thought, the creep is busted. Lunatics are just a part of the fabric of New York—like sirens.

But the man in red broke free from the surprised policemen and rushed the float. He grabbed a railing on the right side and held on, just yards below where I stood. My solo regressed into yelps and howls—"A Night in Tunisia," an avant-garde scream. The flatbed crawled at two miles an hour; if only the driver would floor it, I thought. But the man in red was climbing, now groping for the lip of the stage, for the electrical cables, for anything that could prop him up. Layers of glitter and roses flew as he ripped the "We *LOVE* New York" banner to the street.

Between the band and all the equipment I could hardly move an inch.

I looked behind me for help. The bass player was drunk, the drummer had his eyes closed, the keyboard player was lost in concentration, and Danny James, our leader and so-called trumpet player—no longer scowling at me for playing outside the key—was examining his trumpet as though he could find the missing valve that had held him back all these years. No one was aware or concerned about the danger climbing toward me. I turned my head around, still blowing into my horn, only to stand face to face with the man in red. His mouth twitched. His hands shook in a spasm, bumping the bell of my saxophone, and he shouted into my face. I stopped playing. Over and over he shouted the same thing. If this is how it's going to end, I thought, if he's going to kill me, I have to know why. I yanked out my earplugs. I stared into his frenzied eyes, and with just a few words—words I now know were not meant for my "normal" ears—the man in red jarred my grip on reality.

"Jellybeans!" he yelled. *"Jellybeans! Yellow, red, and green jellybeans!"*

CHAPTER 2

Sheepshead Bay

I SAT ON MY COUCH, listening to Bird, but I couldn't enjoy it. Bird—I couldn't enjoy *Bird*. I turned on the Yankees. I lived minutes from their stadium and for the first time I didn't care who won. In the Bronx this was a sin. All I could think about was the man in red risking it all to tell me about his jellybeans. Why pick on me, I thought, and during my solo? This was more than a wacko in love with his candy. This was a lunatic desperate to rave to me about his jellybeans because *my music made him think I'd understand.*

My free jazz *was* a bit unhinged. It had shocked Carole. Why couldn't I just give it up? It didn't fit my personality at all. *I* was low-key, soft-spoken, downright bland. Carole used to love the way I could make her relax. But that was because I was *dull*. In the subway people fell asleep on me. In fact, without a saxophone in my hands, I was so normal no one noticed me.

Normal. But how could anyone so normal hear music in imaginary cosmic waves? So far, my jazz career was going *really* well—as a magnet for the city's lunatics. What were next? Little green men? Demons waving Tootsie Rolls? I got very tense. Then I blamed Carole; this was *her* fault. She'd dumped me over my highly original music, and now I was paranoid. For two days I hid in my apartment, obsessing: "My music is not for maniacs. I'm fine, I'm not crazy just because my solos are crazy. My music is not for maniacs . . ."

I was too jittery to pick up a saxophone. I had to get out of my gig with the Lehman College women's lacrosse pep band—even though I loved watching the girls run up and down the field. And I canceled my students. I was sure my ten-year olds would lose what little zeal they had for music if they saw their teacher trembling.

I vowed to forget Carole, to obliterate her from my mind. In the meantime, I distracted myself with CDs and movies while I sat by the phone, leaving messages on her machine.

The phone rang. I knew she'd call back. She can't believe she broke up with me for such a silly reason, and wants to see me right away. "What the hell was all that shit you were playing on 'A Night in Tunisia?'" a gruff voice asked. It was Danny James.

His tone worried me, not because I respected his opinion—I didn't. He was a lame trumpet player and a singer with unfounded confidence who lorded over his sidemen. No, his tone worried me because I needed the gigs. His quintet played everything from weddings to cruise ships, and paid double my ordinary jobs. He used ace musicians like the regular sax player, Freddie Cavanaugh, who was too busy to cover all the work. A sub for Freddie could make a living taking care of his leftovers. Danny's pianist, Tommy Meehan, was my friend from the old neighborhood in Philadelphia, and he got me on the sub list. As the fifth-call sub I managed to work with them just enough to know my avant-garde leanings could make any one gig be my last.

"Sorry about that solo," I said, still quivering. "Something came over me."

"What the hell were those goose sounds?"

"Oh, I was trying for a double E . . . Didn't you see the red nutcase screaming at me about his jellybeans?"

"Parades always bring out the squirrels," Danny said. "Still no excuse for playing shit."

"I thought—I thought he was going to kill me. You—you didn't see him poking at me? I guess the cop pulled him off the stage while you were checking your trumpet for holes."

"You're on thin ice, Shawn. Listen, I got something in three weeks: June 5th, seven to ten. Anniversary party in Brooklyn—Sheepshead Bay. You open?"

"I should be able to move my fingers by then . . ."

"What? What the hell was that?"

"I'll be there."

AFTER YEARS OF ONE-ROOM SUBLETS, I'd found an affordable one-bedroom managed by a super who'd said, as far as he was concerned, "Practice all you want." Home at last. It was on the third floor of a six-story brown and tan speckled brick, close enough to Bronx Park to escape the bustle. The North Bronx world of machine shops, auto bodies, markets, pubs, corner toughs and schoolyard superstars from families of all colors, generated plenty of saxophone students and more than enough grit to fuel my modern compositions. Finally I had my own apartment and a chance at a normal life—the life of a working class jazzer. Of course, I'd never asked about the neighbors.

New York apartment life destroys whatever myths you have about your independence. Cheap apartments are scarce, and people cling to their spaces no matter what their neighbors do. It couldn't have been easy for mine, living next to a sax player, but they found ways of getting even.

Daylight hours were divided in two: From sun-up till mid-afternoon my downstairs neighbor, Lloyd Fetterman, who worked nights for a car service, rattled the floorboards of my apartment with a robust snore that paused only for phlegm-filled snuffles. From mid-afternoon till early evening my upstairs neighbors, the Mendez family, or families—it would be years before I'd know which—sounded like they were playing full-court basketball with five or six teams at once. Occasionally the two shifts would overlap and I'd get it from both apartments at the same time.

When my hands steadied enough to play again, I hated everything I played. And I could barely hear myself over the Mendez kids and Lloyd's snore—and his wife's broom. Because my practicing threatened Lloyd's sleep, Muriel Fetterman would pound her broom on their ceiling—my floor—following me around my apartment wherever I played. Only one thing could make her stop. Muriel's pudgy hands were on a number of direct-sales schemes, so I was always buying her off with soaps, hairbrushes and cosmetics I could never use. But this time I couldn't spare the cash. Maybe my music *is* a pile of annoying shit, I thought. Why can't I just stick to bebop? Or simple standards and show tunes, for God's sake? Right now Carole would be sitting in my lap—no doubt sleeping—but at least she'd be in my lap.

My life was caving in. I left another message on Carole's machine, then fled the building, took the subway to Penn Station and boarded a train heading south to meet with the only person who could straighten me out.

WENDELL AND I hadn't talked in so long, it was a shock to learn he'd been languishing in a Philadelphia hospital. There was nothing special about his room—no flowers, no cards, no audience of fans or students. But he wasn't alone. Someone else lay behind the curtain, coughing, hacking, the whole time I was there. The heavy smell of antiseptics and urine made me want to run away. But when I saw my favorite teacher Wendell Rice dozing in a thicket of tubes and IVs, his frail, black body withered and tied to machines, I dragged a chair to his side.

It had been a dozen years since I'd seen Wendell, my last day in Philadelphia. Even as I was saying goodbye, he was still teaching me, handing me a sheet of paper with a long list of names on each side. "We covered a lot of ground," he said, "but we never had a chance to go over these folks." One side listed twentieth century composers with notes on what to listen for in their music. The other side catalogued jazz soloists from the late sixties on up, with similar notes. "They're more complicated than the people we studied," he said. "I don't even *like* some of it, but you got to start listening to them, get to know them, if you want to be a complete musician."

I hung on to that list. Beyond the names and careful notes, it was Wendell's way of saying, You can do it—if you keep your mind and ears open. As I sat by his bed, I pulled out the faded, crumbling piece of paper scotch-taped at every crease, and remembered what it was like to have someone believe in me.

His eyes opened. He saw me and cracked a huge smile. "Hey," he rasped, "what a *surprise*. Been way too long. You're looking great."

"You remember me, Wendell?" I said.

"You? Of course I remember you. Yeah, you look great. How are the kids?"

"Uh . . . I don't have any kids."

"Right, right," he said. "You don't get to see them."

"No, I mean it, Wendell. I don't have any kids."

"Right. I guess Pearl got custody."

"Pearl?"

"Your wife."

"I'm . . . not married. I had a girlfriend, but that didn't quite—"

"Well, how's the truck? You still trucking for Acme?"

"I . . . never had a truck. I don't even own a car."

"So what happened—Pearl and the kids get the truck?"

"No . . . no truck, Wendell."

"Oh. Well, you look great anyway."

"Thanks . . ."

"Yeah, your big rash is all cleared up."

"Uh, I never had . . . "

Wendell's eyes shut and he was out again. I should leave, I thought, but how could I? A master was lying there. A life that had shaped everyone around him had dwindled down to tubes and machines in a shared, smelly hospital room.

TOMMY MEEHAN AND I were sixteen when he urged me to study with his piano teacher. "Wendell Rice," he said, "is the best be-bop piano player in Philly, and he's got a ton of sax students, students on every horn."

In those days traveling to Mr. Rice's house was an act of bravery. Not only did he live two busses and a train away, but his small single home was on the outskirts of one of the roughest ghettoes in Philadelphia. Yet when I walked down his block, the faint sounds of his piano tickled the air and always made me feel safe. His music was an oasis.

"*Shawn,*" he greeted me on the first lesson, "call me Wendell, come on in, put your case down, make yourself comfortable, can I get you some tea, how was your commute, did my neighborhood scare you, it's not so bad, really, most folks here are *good* people," he said all in one breath.

"I was a little scared," I said. "When I was walking from the train—"

"Needn't worry. Folks round here see an instrument and they know you're coming here. No one messes with *my* students." It didn't matter to Wendell that I was white, Jewish, in high school, or anything else, just that I came to study jazz with *him.*

The Steinway occupied half his living room. Shelves stretched to the ceiling, spilling over with albums and music books. And scattered on the floor were old lamps, toasters, and gadgets too rusty to recognize.

"They're from Roy," he said. "Plays trombone and works in a junkyard. He don't have money to pay for lessons, and I don't have the heart to throw it all out . . . Say, you need a lamp?"

Wendell was a gentle, slight man with thick bifocals, a false front tooth and a smile that welcomed you like family. He had worked with the biggest names in jazz, but for him, nothing mattered more than teaching. He could inspire anyone, even when he was critical. "Well, today it sounds like you got no time and no feel," he'd say, "but we'll get it going. Listen to me play it. Get the swing inside a you. Internalize—don't analyze." Then he'd play his piano, swinging with such light virtuosity it sounded like he had six hands. He taught me to improvise, and to carve my own style.

After a year of his lessons I thanked Wendell with the finest praise my high school mind could think of. "You're a much better teacher," I said, "than the moron I had before. I mean, this guy was a disaster, a real—"

"No, no, Shawn," he said, his smile gone, "don't let the mean thoughts in. Once in, they don't go. No end once they get a hold a you, Shawn. See, everybody's got problems. But you and me—we get to play *music.* Not everybody's so blessed. For all those folks with their problems, we get to make the world a more beautiful place. Nowadays I never let a mean thought cross my mind—bout nobody."

"Okay," I said, "but I'm not bitter. It's just that you never met this moron."

"You're not hearing me, Shawn. I'm teaching you how to be happy. You can lose everything—except the one thing God put inside a you, the thing that makes you special. That one thing fills my music. It's all that counts,

Shawn—putting the one thing in the music." His smile returned. "Find the one thing; find it, Shawn, so the Heavenly Voice can sing through *your* voice—like it has for musicians since the beginning. I know you've got it; I hear it. But *you've* got to hear it."

I graduated high school and went to a community college, but my real focus was on Wendell's lessons. "Music is music," he'd say, "whatever name you call it, but you got to learn *why* something is beautiful." He assigned me hours and hours of classical music listening; then at the lessons we'd dissect the composers' styles. At the same time, he was loaning me jazz records, pushing me to transcribe and memorize the solos. Though I got my degree, Wendell Rice was my education.

At the very least I owed him this visit, but what was the point if he was unconscious? As I stood up to go, I reached between the tubes and touched his arm, and in his sleep he began to mumble. I leaned in.

"Heart," he moaned.

"Wendell?"

". . . Heart . . . won't work . . . dotes . . . so many dotes . . . "

"I'll get you the nurse," I said. I hustled out the door. No one was at the nurse's station, and I hurried back. He was still at it. I didn't know what to do or if I should do anything at all. I found the call-button and pushed it over and over.

"Heart . . . dotes and dotes . . . won't work."

"Where is the damn nurse?" I said.

"Without heart, the dotes you play won't work."

"The notes?"

But that was all he had to say.

I left wondering if he was delusional—or still teaching me. I'll come back in a few weeks, I thought; it'll go better. In less than one he was dead.

LOSING WENDELL ON TOP OF LOSING CAROLE made me a mess. But sometimes a musician can play through the grief. June 5th, my next gig, was now a week away, and I had plenty of what Wendell meant by "heart"—if he'd meant anything at all. In between my private teaching I practiced more than ever.

I could play louder than Lloyd's snores and even match the Mendez kids' earthquake. The broom pounding started up, but this time I was ready for Muriel, buying whatever was on sale—Mary Kay eye pencils. I'll give them to Carole, I thought, if she ever picks up the damn phone.

My next-door neighbor to the west, Galicia, a professional psychic, as she called herself, was quick to strike back. "You must stop that God-awful instrument," she said. "The cards have spoken, and you're doomed if you ignore them." A more creative tack than broom pounding but just as offensive.

Galicia had five cats, at least one always roaming the halls. And she wore so many dangling medallions, earrings and bracelets that when she moved, her tall, shapely frame jingled like wind chimes. Whenever we heard the jingles, we'd dash into our apartments because any neighbor she could corner would get a reading.

"As I predicted," she said to me, "your big rash is all cleared up."

"Uh, Galicia, I never had a—"

"Listen to me: If you persist in your present course, the cards say you'll lose everything."

"But if I have nothing already," I said, "can it . . . work in reverse? Will I start to get things?" I always left her mystified.

My new neighbors to the east were the Dixon family, black churchgoers dominated by the father, Colfield, 260 pounds of muscle and neck. They'd been in the building only a few days and I'd yet to meet them. After practicing many hours one day, I went for my mail in the vestibule. Colfield charged down the stairs, straight to me.

"Shawn Lewis!" he yelled, shaking my hand and cracking my knuckles. "I'm overjoyed to meet you. Colfield Dixon." He leaned into my face. "*Tongues*," he whispered. ". . . Right?"

The exit door was six feet away, but leaping for it because the man just whispered "Tongues" in my face, could seem hostile—especially on our first meeting.

"I knew it," he said. "You're one of us."

I sidestepped toward the exit.

"That wild stuff you was playing today," he said, "you might a been playing the saxophone—but you was speaking in *tongues*, right?"

I slowly nodded Yes. He looked almost as crazy-eyed as the man in red.

"I knew it. My wife thought you was just honkin some noise, but you was with the Spirit. I never heard a musical instrument do the tongues."

I continued the slow nod as he kept talking.

"You should check out our church on 235th Street," he said. "But I'm sure you got your own church already . . ."

I kept nodding. His breath smelled like old tires. He was asking me about my minister now. What did I play today? I've got to remember so I never do it again.

". . . Tongues is a funny thing. Lot a people don't believe in tongues. But I know it when I hear it . . ."

When was the last time I ate tongue? I wondered. I'd cut out red meat—oh, unless it's offered free at a gig. At gigs musicians eat like they just got out of prison. Caterers could pile whipped cream over shoelaces and the band would fight over it. But still I don't think I could eat tongue.

". . . I need a good Christian neighbor. Would you join my prayer group?"

I earn so little, I look forward to the free meals at gigs. Still, I don't think I could eat—Did he just ask me to join his prayer group? I should tell him I'm Jewish.

". . . Good, Shawn. Wednesday night, then. I'll pick you up at seven."

I always found an excuse for not getting together with Colfield. It wasn't just the prayer group. I wasn't ready to believe my "crazy" music was anything more than ordinary, freedom-loving American inspiration—cosmic waves or not. But you can't lie to your next-door neighbor—or yourself—forever.

THE GIG WAS FAR: Sheepshead Bay—well over an hour by subway. Seven to ten, Danny had said.

I put on my tux, slid the alto into its form-fitted case, packed the sax stand, microphone, folding mike stand and walkman in my shoulder bag, and boarded the #5 train. It was a long ride to Lower Manhattan where I would change to the Brooklyn train, the B, so I sat back, put on headphones, and drifted into Miles Davis's *Kind of Blue*—the greatest sextet ever assembled, including Coltrane on tenor, Cannonball on alto.

You couldn't listen to *Kind of Blue* without feeling soulful and pensive at the same time. Wendell considered it the jazz bible and had made me transcribe most of the solos. I worried about Wendell. Does he know I'm thinking about him right now? Where is he? Is my teacher now nothing? Oblivion? Cannonball was blowing a solo and it sounded like the juice of life. How did he capture all that joy and energy with just an alto, a mouthpiece and a reed?

Lost in my beloved Cannonball, I barely noticed my stop in time. I gently pushed away the bag lady asleep on my shoulder, and darted out as the doors closed. I waited in the subway station for the B with nowhere to sit and nowhere comfortable to stand. Thirty people were already there, all staring at me like they were calculating what they'd get for my instrument once they knocked me out. I would've done anything to blend in, but the tux was a bull's-eye, and everything I carried with it looked priceless. These were just my work clothes, yet somehow the weathered black gleam could still fake the sharp look needed for a New York society band.

The B screeched up to the platform, and I raced to a seat. In seconds my headphones were playing the Bartok string quartets, and I fell asleep dreaming of female cellists playing for me alone in a thorny meadow, their naked legs wrapped around their celli, their arms bowing passionately.

"Sheepshead Bay!" the conductor shouted, wrenching me out of my meadow, and off the train, now elevated. I walked down the stairs, searching my pockets for the address: 271 Denwood Street, Apt. 1, Sarah and Arnold Bell.

A gig in someone's apartment meant the band wasn't likely to get a meal. It wasn't yet 6:30, so I bought a tuna sandwich at a deli while I took in Sheepshead Bay. I strolled with my case and shoulder bag past humble wood-frame houses and low-rise apartments, tree-lined streets bathed in the calm salt air, while I wolfed a tuna sandwich that reminded me of wet socks.

On Denwood Street a crowd of white-haired seniors massed on the patio of a three-story redbrick with terraces. Gold tinsel and yellow balloons swirled above the entryway around the iron numbers 271.

I was no longer early. I needed to squeeze through a crowd of old people who'd finished moving aside for anyone years ago and weren't about to do it again for a mere saxophone player. I wiggled through them as delicately as I could, through the open door to Apartment 1, a jutting shoulder bag and a saxophone versus walkers and canes. "Hey, where's the fire," people shouted, and "Look out, here comes the band!" I couldn't see through the mob to find the guys but I followed the sounds to the far corner of the room: a bass drum tuning, an electric keyboard setting its controls. And then I saw the bass player hovering over his bass fiddle, drinking a cocktail. Danny James was arranging the microphones, his tanning-booth tan looking orange under the track lights, his toupee, slightly ruffled.

"Hey Shawn, where were you?" Tommy said. "They served us five courses, man: wild salmon, roast potatoes, avocado salad, fresh baguettes—"

"Stop, Tommy. I ate," I said, as the wet-socks tuna backed up a few inches.

"Oh, too bad. There won't be another shot at the food. No breaks—the gig's continuous."

Young caterers in bow tied white shirts and black pants flitted around with hors d'oeuvre trays for the incoming guests, who looked between the ages of seventy and a hundred, some alert, some barely clinging to life. The guests seized the chairs gracing the walls, their prize for getting in ahead of the pack. Though the rectangular living room was almost as big as a warehouse loft, we were crammed into the far corner, watching the space quickly fill.

Danny waved for me to hurry and set up. He gathered me to his right, in front of the drums, my right elbow close to the living room's brick wall. Now he could keep an ear on me and make sure I didn't play anything out of line. God forbid I should graze the avant-garde. He liked his music safe.

I positioned my microphone while the caterers cleared the hardwood floor in front of us for dancing, as more and more elders streamed into the apartment, drowning out Tommy's keyboard warm-ups with boisterous Brooklyn and Yiddish accents. Yellow balloons bobbed along the fifteen-foot ceiling. Disturbing, framed abstracts cluttered the walls—in between them, slivers of gold tinsel. In the center of the brick wall, above an antique fireplace draped a shining gold banner: "Happy Golden Anniversary, Sarah and Arnie!"

Carole and I will never have one of these, I thought. I felt hopeless. I wondered if there were Jewish monasteries. At least there I'd get credit for being celibate. Then I noticed a curvy, bow tied brunette serving a cheese plate to a hunched man. No rings were on her fingers, and for the moment I forgot about monasteries.

"Freddie's extra hot these days," the drummer said to Tommy about the genius I was subbing for. "What a cat. Never ceases to amaze."

"I know," Tommy said. "Even on the lamest tunes Freddie sounds hip."

"You catch what he did last night on 'Body and Soul?'" the drummer said.

"Yeah, outrageous," Tommy said.

"Here we are on some kid's Bar Mitzvah, and Freddie blows note-for-note The Hawk's original solo, then perfectly works in his own thing at the end."

"Yeah, he's the best."

Why the hell did I have to sub for "the best?"

"Fellas," Danny said, facing us, his thick toupee still mussed, "this is a golden anniversary. Old people. Very old." Then he looked at me. "That means nothing loud, nothing challenging on the ears, okay? No free jazz, no avant-garde, no Downtown. Understand, Shawn? Tonight we're fox-trots, ballads, bossas and swing tunes. Ready? Shawn, 'Body and Soul' in Db. Take the intro, Tommy."

Why "Body and Soul," of all tunes? Another chance for them to wish Freddie could make all the gigs. But there was no time to worry. Tommy's intro was through, and I started blowing the melody. The guests got quiet, many of them covering their ears. There was even a mass retreat to the kitchen, the back end of the apartment. But most stood there watching me, unsure whether to join the retreat or leave now. A few started to dance. The rich melody stirred me to close my eyes, forget the brunette caterer, Carole or Freddie Cavanaugh, and fill each note with a soft, true sound.

SCREEEECH. An offensive scraping noise much louder than a saxophone with a rhythm section destroyed the sweet illusion. In the middle of "Body and Soul" some asshole was violently dragging their chair across the hardwood floor. I opened my eyes, and my lungs collapsed. I couldn't play another note. Less than two yards in front of me, staring into my eyes, was the man in red.

CHAPTER 3

The Anniversary Gig

HIS MOUTH TWITCHED. His gray beard gleamed with drool. Every thirty seconds his hands shook. And his bulging eyes fixed on me like a wild animal who's cornered his prey. A floppy orange-red beret sat on his big bald head. His red high-top sneakers were worn and blotched, the laces untied. A scarlet T-shirt, too tight on him and buttoned to the collar, was flecked with stains. His pants were pajamas—fire-engine red. I didn't want to think about the stains on those.

I couldn't understand how he got there. I'd been watching the crowd wedge through the doorway. I would've noticed *him*. Yet no one was alarmed. Maybe they *were* alarmed but posing as calm so not to arouse him—like with a grizzly bear. A SWAT team could be on its way.

"Who told you to stop playing?" Danny said. He leaned his orange face in close. "What's a matter with you?"

This is no coincidence, I thought. The psycho's been following me.

"Play!" Danny shouted. "We're coming up on the bridge—play!"

Is this about his jellybeans? *I'll buy you some new goddamn jellybeans,* I wanted to yell.

"Hello?" Danny said. "Spaceman? 'I'm in the Mood for Love,' the bridge! Play!"

Or, I gulped . . . is this lunatic here because of my jazz?

Three jubilant couples danced in front of us. Oblivious, I thought. Everybody is so oblivious, living in their own little shells, unaware of the slightest things going on around them.

That's when I realized I was frozen, not breathing, and Danny's orange face had been inches away, trying to get my attention. I couldn't play a note, and I couldn't explain why. My lips wouldn't move.

"You want to play games?" Danny said. "Want me to call another sax player?"

The man in red looked angry.

"Can't you *see?*" I blurted out. "Can't you see what's going on here?"

"Tommy'll finish the tune," Danny said. "Pull yourself together. Next time I tell you to play, play or go home."

I tried not to look at the man in red. Every time I did, he was staring at me. I had to get out. But I was boxed in. I'll grab the alto with one hand, I thought, straight-arm Danny with the other—that part would be all right—then plow through the dancers. Their tumbling bodies would block the man in red long enough for me to slip out the door.

The man was squirming in his chair now, mumbling things: "The Tenth, yes, absolutely the Tenth. Outside. Absolutely. They don't understand. No one understands. No one understands. Even *he* won't understand . . . "

Whatever was aggravating him, I didn't know how he could blame *me.* But if he cut my throat and left, this crowd would still be dancing and smiling. Our bandleader would hold the door for him.

In fact, keeping the party alive was Danny's talent. He'd blurt out a warbly trumpet solo and sing in almost every tune—convinced he was Frank Sinatra—but music was not his strength. He had skillful sidemen, and he knew how to please his rich clients. Tonight was all about "mellow." "'My Funny Valentine,'" he announced. "C minor."

If the man in red attacked me, at least someone would notice the silences in "My Funny Valentine" while the sax player was bleeding. But as I played, he got quiet and settled back in his chair. When Danny started singing, the man in red squeezed his bug eyes into a wince.

When it was over, Danny said: "'Blue Skies,' E minor. Shawn, improvise the first chorus." I did as I was told, managing to stay within the swing era for eight bars, but soon I was tumbling into the avant-garde—I couldn't help myself. I could feel Danny's ire without looking at him. But the man in red had calmed, folded his big-boned arms, and grinned. As Danny started to sing and I laid out, the man squirmed in his chair and glowered at Danny. When I improvised behind Danny's vocal, the man settled back again. The more I played, the more the man in red seemed to listen.

I tried an experiment: I riffed as loud as I could behind Danny's vocals. The man in red smiled and swayed in his chair.

At the end of "Blue Skies" Danny switched off his mike and leaned into my face. "Pull yourself together, you shit. You're subbing for *Freddie Cavanaugh*."

The head caterer handed Danny a note, and our leader threw back his shoulders, turned euphoric, and smiled wide into the microphone: "Kind ladies and gentleman, please take a glass of champagne and let us toast our celebrities of the evening—Sarah and Arnold Bell. Happy Golden Anniversary!" The honored couple emerged from the center of the crowd, and Danny turned to me. "'Anniversary Waltz,'" he said coldly. "1–2–3."

I played while everyone watched the couple dance—everyone except the man in red, who sat and watched me.

Arnold Bell danced with proud, heavy steps, his stomach jutting out through his white dinner jacket, his left hand holding his wife's hand and a lit cigar. Sarah Bell, in a glittering blue gown, floated so gingerly through the waltz, it looked like Arnold was all that kept her from drifting away. The crowd kept backing up to give them more room as Sarah glided and Arnold stomped over the wood floor.

When the dance ended, they kissed, and the apartment resounded with cheers and applause. Arnold then stepped up to Danny's microphone, and with a husky, Yiddish accent, announced, "I want to tank everybody who comes!" He paused, glancing at each of the many guests, and then his wife. "This a very special night. I have specially to tank my wife Sarah, who witout her, there no golden nothings." Everyone clapped, even the curmudgeons who were hiding in the kitchen to get away from the music.

But the man in red was unfazed. Arnold handed the microphone to Sarah.

"You are our dearest friends in the world," she said without a trace of an accent. "We love you with all our hearts." Then softly: "Your support has meant everything, everything to us . . . Let's now honor our son, our angel. Come, Jimmy."

She smiled and gestured to the man in red.

He stood abruptly, his chair flipping over, and he hugged and kissed both of them at the same time.

Their *angel*? This changed everything. I let out the longest breath. No psycho had been following me after all. The air, full of booze and salmon, smelled sweeter, the guests looked less gnarled, the waitresses cuter. Even Danny seemed a hair less repugnant. I felt free, liberated. I started laughing.

"Kind ladies and gentleman," Danny said, smiling, showing lots of teeth, "your dinner is now being served." Two buffet lines speared toward the kitchen while Sarah and Arnold ushered their son to a table by the fireplace.

I couldn't stop laughing.

Danny switched off his mike. "You've been playing like shit; why are you laughing?" he said to me. "I'm taking a break. Do some bossa novas and ballads."

I was still laughing.

"Real funny," he said. "It'll be *real* funny when I forget to mail your check. Now play *soft and mild*—none of that free jazz bullshit."

Danny left for the bar and took our bass player, Joe Terry, with him. Joe, middle-aged, black, and aloof when he was sober, was one of the finest bass players in the city. He never said much, his face never showed much, but you knew when Joe was unhappy on the gig. He'd get plastered. And tonight Danny encouraged it.

I called the tune, "Quiet Nights." I played while I watched Sarah and Arnold drape a smock over Jimmy as they all sat down. But Jimmy quickly stood up, and hustled back to the chair only five feet from me.

I traded solos with Tommy, his delicate, piano lines flowing like a brook made of jewels. My childhood friend's career had never stalled. I could only wonder whatever happened to mine.

The drummer, Gus DaLucci, all arms and legs, tapped a sparkling bossa nova groove. Gus rarely spoke to me; it annoyed him that I wasn't

Freddie Cavanaugh. His annoyance annoyed *me*—my momentary cheer now gone.

Soon, Sarah and Arnold followed Jimmy, bringing chairs of their own. And directly in front of me the anniversary couple parked on each side of their son, his clashing reds shielded with a stain-flecked, white smock.

While Tommy, Gus and I churned out anesthetic dinner tunes, I found myself roiling at the leader and the drummer, and took it out with angry squeals in "Blue Bossa." Danny, splashing his cocktail all the way from the bar, rushed over to me.

"I said *soft and mild*," he said. "The old farts'll choke on their dinner, you idiot." He hadn't noticed the clients sitting right below him.

"Who you talking about?" Arnold said, standing to face him.

"You should take a nice, long break," Sarah said to Danny. "The drinks are on us. But please, make sure your bass player joins the others. I miss his sound when he's not there."

"Of course, Mrs. Bell," Danny said, smiling, "whatever you please."

"Just for your information, Mr. James," Sarah said, "we 'old farts' include a former congressman, several retired members of the New York Philharmonic, a half dozen highly decorated veterans, as well as many others whose accomplishments certainly exceed those of the average bandleader."

Danny's jaw dropped.

"Our son likes your saxophonist," she said, stroking Jimmy's arm. Jimmy was now staring above my head, muttering about quadrants and loops and links. "Go on, young man," Sarah said to me, "play."

Our leader, shocked, miffed and a little tipsy, motioned for Joe Terry to join the trio, then shuffled back to the bar. The few gigs I had left with the quintet had just evaporated.

"Hey Shawn," Joe said, now properly medicated, "where you been hiding? I never heard you blow like that before."

"Yeah, man," Gus said, nodding. "Yeah, man" was the most Gus had said to me in two years.

Most of the guests were either in the buffet lines or sitting with their plates in their laps. But my audience didn't care about the food. They only wanted to hear me play. So I led the band through the swing era—Benny

Goodman, Duke Ellington, Count Basie, with an occasional avant-garde touch. Released from Danny's cold grip, the music warmed into a swinging conversation, and soon people were cramming the dance floor to see if they could remember the jitterbug. The more infirmed still hid away from the band, but a large clique of elders was now jumping.

In spite of his twitches, Jimmy swayed and bounced his feet to the rhythm. After a few minutes Sarah and Arnold could no longer avoid the attentions of their friends, as several pulled them away, and my devoted audience shrank back to one.

I wanted to please the jitterbuggers, but I'd never had the use of such a great rhythm section happy to play whatever I called. I couldn't resist calling be-bop tunes, and the dancers ran out of steps. Still, no matter what I played, Jimmy's yellow-tooth smile couldn't have been wider. When we moved through my favorite Thelonius Monk tunes—which were practically all his tunes—I soloed in every direction, from blues to free-form grunts and growls. Occasionally a couple would try and dance and wind up tripping over each other. People started saying their goodbyes. But the client's son was still there, hollering, convulsing in approval, and that was all the encouragement I needed. I quieted my sound and listened.

"Jellybeans . . . jellybeans . . . jellybeans . . ."

Then he stood and wiggled to the beat, waving his arms above his head as if he were signaling an airship. I stretched backward as far as I could, almost brushing Gus's ride cymbal. Tune after tune Jimmy waved and gyrated to the rhythm. If it wasn't for the grin I would've thought he was having seizures. Gus was so lost in his polyrhythms he didn't seem to notice. And Joe, sailing on piña coladas, may have noticed but didn't care. Only Tommy looked agitated.

By 10:00 almost everyone had left. I'd been playing without a break for two hours—exhausted, but at last I felt like a musician.

Sarah asked Jimmy to sit, gently guiding him down to his chair. Then she approached me. "It's been years since I've seen Jimmy behave like this."

"I'm sorry," I said. "I'm not sure what I'm doing to cause—"

"Don't be sorry. I'm sure you've noticed that our Jimmy is . . . well, special."

"Really?"

"He usually hides in his room," she said, "especially when we have guests. Oh, and he's very critical about music. But you—Shawn Lewis, yes? Your playing . . . "

She paused as her son, gesturing with both hands, mumbled toward the brick wall. "Loops," he said in a low voice. "The loops and links are dazzling. Yes, very dazzling indeed. Does the Sheml know?"

"You must excuse him, Shawn," Sarah said. "Jimmy . . . well, he's his own man."

Danny slid over to Sarah. "We're-done-right?" he said as one word.

"Actually," she said, "I'm glad you asked. We'd like the band to play longer. We'll pay overtime. But for you, Mr. James, feel free to take another break."

Fine, he said, and returned to the bar. The last of the guests said goodbye while the caterers packed up. I scanned the room for the curvy brunette.

"Now you're here only for us," Sarah said. "Only for Jimmy. He loves your music—the freer, the better. So go for it." The Bells sat in front of me again.

All these years in New York, I thought, and my one true fan is a lunatic who yells, "Jellybeans!" Tommy snuck beside me. "We should get going," he whispered. This is getting way too weird, and I've got a long trip home."

"I know," I said, "but they're paying *overtime*. I don't know when I'll get to work with you guys again. Did I mention the overtime? Let's play some Coltrane."

I called "Giant Steps" while Sarah and Arnold caressed their hulky, excited middle-aged son. The curvy caterer sauntered behind them, twinkling at me. She was leaving. She stood and waited. What could I do? I was in the middle of "Giant Steps," for God's sake. She waved goodbye, the last of the caterers.

It was just the Bells and us. We played "A Love Supreme" and "Resolution" and flew into the avant-garde for another thirty minutes until Jimmy had fallen asleep in his chair—and our gig was over. Jimmy's parents guided him through the living room to a doorway between the front entrance and the kitchen. "Thanks for sticking with me, guys," I said to Tommy, Gus and Joe.

They thanked me for choosing excellent tunes.

While I gathered my saxophone and equipment, Sarah tapped me on the shoulder. "When you're packed up," she said, "we need to speak to you." Arnold stood behind her. They looked solemn, no smiles. "It's important," she said. "We'll be in the kitchen, okay? Please, it's very important. We'll wait for you in the kitchen."

Joe had already left. Gus was making back-and-forth trips with his drum kit to his double-parked van. And Tommy hoisted the now-hammered boss—his carpool—up from the bar. "I guess I'm driving," Tommy said to him.

Already it had been a night of too many surprises. I didn't need any more from the Bells. Every part of me ached for my couch, a piece of cake and a nice *Star Trek* to forget all about psychos. After Tommy and I settled Danny into his car, I would've snatched my things and run for the subway. But the leader might not forgive his least favorite sideman for upstaging him, and the surest way to get paid was to stay on the good side of the clients. I dragged myself back to Apartment 1, and into the kitchen.

CHAPTER 4

The Offer

THEY POKED AT THEIR LEFTOVERS with furrowed brows, deep in conversation, and didn't hear me coming. "All I'm saying is it doesn't hurt to ask," she said to him.

"Whole ting is crazy, crazy," he said to her.

"On every little thing you fight me."

"What fight? The whole house is you. You see anyting a mine anywhere?"

"Well, that's because you'd leave your big fat underwear—"

I cleared my throat, and they both looked up from their food.

"You wanted to see me, Mrs. Bell? Mr. Bell?"

"Call me Sarah, please."

"And I'm Arnie. Have a seat." They motioned to the chair across from them.

"Thank you for coming to talk to us," she said.

The bright kitchen fixture was like an interrogation lamp, glaring off their eyeglasses and the white formica table. Arnie's jacket was off, his shirt open, his huge stomach ballooning his undershirt. Sarah sat tall and poised, though the cold light magnified the wrinkles and bags under her eyes.

"It's about Jimmy," she said. "He's had a rather hard life. If you don't mind my asking, how old are you?"

"Forty," I said.

"Jimmy's 49, but I imagine he's seen much less of the world than you have. He . . . he keeps to himself."

"A big understatement, that was," Arnie said.

"Jimmy stays in his room except for meals," she said. "You only saw him tonight."

"We see every day," Arnie said.

"We had to give him up for many years, too many years. He was so unhappy. We were all unhappy." She studied my eyes for sympathy, but I didn't know where she was going.

"Music has always been vital to us," she said. "I want you to know, Shawn, Jimmy is an artist in his own right. He's very discerning, especially about music."

"Look," Arnie said, "we love him all the way, but let's face it: Boy's crazy."

"I'd like to be able to speak to the young man without the constant interruptions," she said.

"A break in the flood, she calls an interruption," he said.

"Tonight we had planned a string quartet," she said, "friends of mine—quite excellent. But everything changed when I took Jimmy to the street fair and we heard your band. The fair was just my excuse to drag him out of his room. Anyway, the band was deafening, but when Jimmy heard your saxophone, he pulled away from me. He shoved through the bodies, toward the noise. Do you know why?"

I shook my head.

"To get as close to you as possible," she said. "We got into an awful mess with the police."

"I told you," Arnie said. "We should've kept that nurse to keep an eye on him. Built like a tank, this lady."

"Does he usually get this excited about music?" I asked.

"He used to," she said. "Years ago. But even then—not like this."

"But what about the other musicians in the band?" I said. "They're much better . . . much better known than I am. Why me?"

"I don't know," she said. "I'm not much for jazz, but Jimmy would have risked his life to get on that moving band car. Whatever the reason, I decided right then, your quintet would play our anniversary party.

Fortunately, your group was available."

"That's right," Arnie said, "and even if it makes no sense, for Jimmy we do lots of strange tings."

"But, I'm not a regular in the group," I said. "I'm just a sub, and here I am playing your anniversary. It's what you wanted but it's all an accident."

"No accident," she said. "I told that leader of yours that you needed to be the saxophonist or there was no deal."

"That's all there was to it?" I said.

"Oh, he protested," she said. "Said you weren't the usual guy, that he had players who were famous or something, but I told him, it had to be the same band that played the block party."

"Wow. Thanks. Would you like to be my agent?"

"Well, now we come to the point of our little discussion," she said.

"We want you should play for us—just you," Arnie said.

"I wanted to ask him that," she said to Arnie. "Is it too much to ask that you let me get a word in edgewise?"

"Edgewise?" he said. "Sarah, your tongue is a steamroller."

"Anyway," she said, rolling her eyes, "would you be willing to play for us, for Jimmy, say, once a week. For a fee we can negotiate. How are Sunday afternoons?"

"You want me to come here by myself every Sunday?" I said. "No band?"

"That's it," Arnie said.

"Solo saxophone every Sunday," she said. "We'll feed you dinner. It would mean so much to Jimmy. How does one hundred-twenty dollars sound—cash?"

"That's—that's okay," I said. "But don't you want me with a band? It'll make more sense with some accompaniment."

"I'm sure you're right," she said, "but Jimmy only wants you. I happen to know that a serious musician can make music with a full symphony or all alone. Would you like to think it over or check your book?"

I checked my gig book, the blank pages glaring like fresh snow. The only Sunday gigs were in August—with Danny's quintet. I thumbed slowly through the pages as though they were jammed with work. "Hmm," I said, "how many Sundays are we talking about?"

"Well, let's see how it goes," she said. "If it works out like we hope, every Sunday from now on."

Who ever gets offered a gig from now on? I thought. I'd have to skip those Sundays in August. But those gigs are gone! Danny won't want to see my face again. "I'd be delighted to play for you every Sunday until further notice," I said. "You're my best audience anyway." They were my only audience, but I left that out.

"Oh wonderful," Sarah smiled, relieved.

"Fantastic," Arnie said, and shook my hand, mangling my tired fingers.

"I hope you don't mind," she said, "but one of our friends taped some of your jazz tonight to play for Jimmy later on."

"No, I don't mind. You just gave me a steady gig; why should I mind?"

"Then you won't mind us taping you when you play on Sundays?"

"Whatever you need to do," I said. Sarah got up and shook my hand, then embraced Arnie. Their eyes were misting, they were so overjoyed. No one had ever been overjoyed at hiring me before.

The parents seem relatively normal, I thought, as they kept shaking and shaking my hand. But below all the smiles, I shivered. I'd just agreed to work every Sunday for the man in red. I had to—for the money, yes, but I couldn't escape the crazy feeling this was where I belonged. Music needs an audience, and I *had* to play for the only one who loved my music—even if he was a psychopath.

CHAPTER 5

A Cappella

I HAD TO PREPARE for my new gig, but how do you tame a big-boned lunatic for 150 straight minutes with just a saxophone? I pored through reams of music: No, this one's too atonal—this one's too hard—this one's too boring without a 65-piece orchestra. Or at least a pianist.

I decided to toss him every style I knew. If he didn't like my bebop, I'd give him Mozart. In between my private students I practiced every available minute.

Colfield retaliated, cranking his gospel music until the walls shook. This drowned out Lloyd Fetterman's snore, but Lloyd's wife Muriel attacked with the broom again. The Mendez kids, stomping like a battalion, added to the cacophony. I bought more detergent from Muriel. At least I could keep her quiet.

One night on my way to emptying the garbage, Galicia caught me in the hall.

"You mustn't!" she said, her orange nightie swinging slightly open.

"Wh—what?" I said.

"You mustn't embark on this dangerous path."

". . . Huh?" If I pretended to look at her chin while concentrating on my lower peripheral vision, then without her knowing it I could peek through the nightie.

"I'm sorry," I said, looking up. "Did you say something?" Despite the over-forty witch doctor vibe, she had an astounding body.

"I did another reading about you," she said.

I put the garbage bags down—for the sake of cleavage.

"You're in grave danger," she said.

"Without a doubt," I said.

"The cards say you must get out of the music business—immediately."

"This is about my practicing, isn't it?"

"You're in *danger*." Two cats, tails high in the air, wandered out of her open doorway. "The cards say your latest thing—whatever you're doing—will destroy you."

"What latest thing?" I said. "Teaching the Tamsy twins?"

"No, it's all this noise you're making for a new job or something. What in the hell are those goose sounds?"

"My double E isn't speaking very—Galicia, everybody else just tries to have me evicted. If you want me to stop, why don't you—"

"This new job will lead to your *ruin*. It's in the cards."

The threat didn't scare me. Galicia's body scared me, inspiring thoughts way beyond neighborly.

I couldn't afford to listen to her anyway. Without the Danny James gigs, my best-paying work was now once a month on the stage of the massive, empty Mediterranean Club, playing tunes for a handful of thugs meeting in the back. Izzy, their tattooed lieutenant, would hire me to lead a loud rhythm section while he'd stroll the room. He'd let us play a few minutes, then run up to the stage, signaling us to stop. Minutes would pass and he'd signal us to start again. And on and on for hours. No one but Izzy spoke to us: "Top-notch starts and stops, fellas."

I needed a gig where the music mattered, even to just one person.

I INHALED DEEPLY the bay air as I approached the Bells' redbrick building. Kids played stickball on the street between the oak trees and parked cars. It reminded me of the old neighborhood in Philly, of carefree days long before the burdens of paying rent or blowing a perfect solo—or performing for a lunatic. Arnie greeted me like he'd known me for years, led me down the hallway to Apartment 1, through their living room and to the fireplace along the brick wall. In front of the fireplace stood a music stand and a chair—with another chair facing it only a few feet away.

"Where's Jimmy?" I said.

"It's all right," Arnie said, "you play."

A merging of mouth-watering scents—chicken, vegetables, a maple syrup dessert—saturated the apartment. I dropped my things, including my oversized bag of music, and used my foot to stealthily slide the other chair further away. Sarah, wearing a yellow apron, slipped from the kitchen to welcome me as cheerfully as Arnie had, and urged me to start as soon as I was ready.

There was no sign of Jimmy, but I played anyway, a simple blues. I noticed a large fluffy sofa sat where the quintet had been; a stereo and TV had replaced the bar. Abstract oil paintings—framed specks and splats that crowded the walls—made me dizzy if I gazed for too long. Perhaps they made the Bells feel cultured, I thought, but they couldn't be more annoying.

Jimmy exploded out of his bedroom. He was quick but heavy-footed with a jerking, haphazard stride. In a red T-shirt and red sweatpants each covered in stains, he scraped his chair back to its original spot—closer to me—and sat with a thump.

Fat, burly and wild like a mountain man, he would've alarmed anyone even without all the red clothes. Crumbs dappled his beard while his twitching mouth contorted his face, and whenever his arms shook, I jumped. Worst of all were the bulging eyes.

He sat on the edge of his chair a yard from my horn, studying me. His mouth was open. He raised his hands and spread out his fingers as though he were feeling the air around me. My stomach lurched. Stare at the horizon, I told myself. I focused on the dining table yards behind him while he mumbled. More jellybeans.

After the blues I played some standards—fixing on each melody, then blowing a little avant-garde around it. After a while I reached over to shake his hand. "Hi, Jimmy. My name is Shawn."

He turned away, mumbling to the wall, "Oh yes, jellybeans. Number ten outside, I think, don't you, don't you? Yes, I agree, the tenth outside indeed."

"Is there anything you'd like me to play?" I said, slowly pulling my hand back.

He looked baffled. His mouth broke into another chewing spasm.

"Okay," I said. "How about Scott Joplin?"

I played "Maple Leaf Rag," weaving some free jazz around the ragtime, and he sat with his head back, his eyes on the ceiling.

After the last note he muttered, "Jellybean rainbow."

He wants "Over the Rainbow," I figured, but can't speak without saying the word "jellybean." I played the melody four times. His blank stare never changed.

Meanwhile, Arnie was stretched out on the sofa, wearing headphones, glued to the Mets game, and Sarah, still in her apron, was dragging a chair to sit next to Jimmy. "Keep going, Shawn," she said.

"What should I play?" I said to her. "I asked Jimmy for a request, but—"

"Play whatever you want," she said. "But play your best. My boy hears everything."

"What do you mean, 'everything?'"

"Every little nuance; he hears all of it."

I played a Handel transcription, blowing some jazz at the end. Jimmy sat like a statue and said nothing.

"He likes it," Sarah said. "He wouldn't be here, out of his room, if he didn't. But I prefer the Handel when it's played on flute or recorder like it was meant to be—and without the jazz."

"You're familiar with Handel?" I said.

"Of course," she said.

Arnie, freed from his headphones, was now arranging a microphone and mike stand. "We gonna tape you now," he said.

Jimmy turned around, his back to us, and whispered, "Yes, yes, yes, indeed. But I think the seventeenth forms the link. We must tell the Sheml."

I looked at Sarah, then at Arnie—no change in demeanor. I would ask no questions, not yet, at least.

While Arnie returned to his game and Sarah to the kitchen, for the next two hours I recorded on their cassette deck. Jimmy swooned in his chair or held bizarre poses, all the while mumbling more of the same. Twice he stood up to dance, waving his arms above his head.

At 5:30 I thanked Jimmy for listening. He looked at the floor, laughing, muttering, "Jellybeans. The tenth indeed, absolutely the tenth. Historigantic."

"Dinner's ready!" Sarah called. Arnie wrapped Jimmy in the smock.

As we stood around the table, Jimmy leaned down to kiss his mother and father each on the cheek, then used the same serving spoon to taste the steaming casseroles of chicken stew, kugel, and succotash. He then thwacked lavish globs onto his plate before returning the server that had been in his mouth back to one of the casseroles, his smacking lips spraying the air around him. Sarah and Arnie never flinched. The embroidered linen, the three-piece bronze candelabra, the bone china, the home-cooked dinner—none of it jibed with the presence of a red bigfoot.

I thanked Sarah over and over. It was an easy gig—decent pay and the food, delicious. The tricky part would be pretending Jimmy wasn't the most disturbed person I'd ever met.

The three of us chatted and ate while he stayed in his own world. Sarah apologized for not serving wine—some conflict with Jimmy's medication.

"Oh, I don't drink," I said. "I have to keep a grip on things—my compulsion, I guess. I just hate the feeling of, you know . . . *losing it* . . ." I glanced at Jimmy.

Sarah and Arnie wanted to know all about me. They were easy to talk to, and I couldn't hold back. I told them about my passion for the avant-garde, about Carole, even my deviant neighbors. I told them everything—except about Wendell; I couldn't talk about Wendell. They were perfect listeners but revealed little of themselves. When Jimmy splattered the tablecloth with stewed tomatoes, I jumped up to help.

"No, sit down," Arnie said, waving his hand. "Don't worry."

"Arnie's a dry cleaner," Sarah said.

"I don't understand," I said.

"Bell's Cleaners," Arnie said.

"You haven't heard of Bell's Cleaners?" Sarah asked me.

"He's in the Bronx," Arnie said to Sarah. "How's he gonna know what goes on in Brooklyn?"

"Why are you so snippy?" Sarah said.

"What snippy? The boy lives in the Bronx. Might as well be California."

"But Bell's Cleaners," she said. "Everybody knows Bell's Cleaners."

"In *Brooklyn*," he scowled. "Everybody in *Brooklyn* knows the hot spots."

"Anyway," she said to me, sighing, "Arnie owns three shops, all in Brooklyn."

"And soon I'm retiring," he said. "I'm seventy-five—time I relax!"

Jimmy finished his eating onslaught, cocked his head to one side and glared out the bay window behind the dining table.

Sarah removed from the oven a large pecan pie. She put a fourth of it on my plate, and I didn't object. Jimmy switched out of his pose long enough to assist Sarah in giving himself most of the rest of it while she and Arnie divided a sliver.

"Jimmy's usually more talkative," Sarah said, watching him assault the pie.

"Yeah, but mostly to himself," Arnie said.

"Would you not say things like that?" she raised her voice.

"You mentioned one of your friends had taped the quintet," I said, trying to calm things. "Did it come out okay?"

"There was too much crowd noise," Sarah said. "We're hoping Jimmy will listen to the tape we made today. We're counting on it."

I couldn't imagine why, but I had a better question: "Why does Jimmy talk so much about jellybeans?"

Arnie, sitting across from me, looked me in the eye, cleared his throat and leaned slowly toward me. "Boy's crazy," he murmured. "Told you that already."

"Arnie," Sarah said, "go in the living room. *Columbo*'s on."

"I still got pie," he protested.

"Shawn," she said, "Jimmy sees and hears things that aren't there. He has since he was twelve."

I felt a chill. "He sees . . . jellybeans?" I said.

"No one knows what he sees," she said.

"Jellybeans is someting good," Arnie said. "Who knows why?"

"There are many things we don't understand about our son," she said, smiling at Jimmy, "but I'm sure he has his reasons why he says the things he does . . . I hope we haven't scared you off."

"No," I said, "this is mild compared to my other gigs."

AFTER A WEEK of teaching kids who were more interested in the summer than the saxophone, a gig at Den of Dread and a wedding where I accidentally turned the first dance "Always and Forever" into an avant-garde free-for-all, I was thankful for Sunday and my dependable job in Sheepshead Bay.

When I arrived, Sarah and Arnie were on their way out the door, and my stomach buckled. *You can't leave me alone with the maniac,* I wanted to shout. He's out of control, unpredictable. That's the way of maniacs.

"Relax," Sarah said, chuckling, holding the door for Arnie. "As soon as you start making sounds, Jimmy will come out of his room."

"Excuse me?" I said. "Is it so . . . is it okay to—to leave me here alone with—"

"Don't worry," Arnie said.

"As long as you keep playing," she said, "Jimmy will be happy. We'll see you at 5:30."

"See me at," I said, ". . . are you sure you—is it safe to—"

"It'll be all right," she said, as they headed out the door. "He loves your music."

All right for *him,* I thought, for *him.* He won't go to prison. They'll gently transplant him to a funny farm—if he kills the sax player.

But my fear wasn't limited to physical violence. I couldn't help noticing the repulsive abstracts on the walls. For a moment they appeared to be moving, all of them trembling, the whole apartment trembling, as if the whole space was laughing at me. For one terrible, out-of-control moment I wondered if the "maniac" and I had far more in common than just music.

AS SARAH HAD PREDICTED, when I started to play, Jimmy bolted from his room and into the chair. For two and a half hours I played with my eyes clamped shut. I could hear Jimmy's dialogues and whoops, his creaking chair, his dancing, and I could feel the wind from his arms waving nearby.

Soon after 5:30 his parents returned with full shopping bags. Sarah gave her towering son a hug, and called us to dinner—take-out Chinese food. When I sat down, Jimmy was already shoveling through the egg foo yung and General Tsao's chicken, dipping and re-dipping his spoon into the little white boxes before I'd even had a taste. Irritated, I barked, "What's with all the red? Why do you only wear red?"

He stopped chewing, glanced in both directions as three ramen noodles dangled from his mouth. Then he tilted his head down.

"Why won't he talk to me?" I said. "I mean, if he supposedly likes me so much, why won't he . . . " A tear rolled down his cheek.

"Shawn," Sarah said, holding Jimmy's hand, "Jimmy is as sensitive to tone of voice as he is to music. Jimmy is sensitive."

"I'm sorry, I didn't mean to—"

"It's all right; you didn't know," she said. "We hope one day he'll be as comfortable with you as he is with your music."

Sarah then asked more questions about my life, diverting my attention away from Jimmy. And Arnie, with an elfin glee in his eyes, was always ready with a joke—this time about a famous parrot that spoke every language. English? someone asked the parrot. "Of course." French? "Oui." Spanish? "Si, senor." Yiddish too? The parrot shrugged: "Mit a nose like dis, vot you tink?" Even Arnie's worst jokes made me laugh. Everything he said sounded like a punch line.

Sarah would discuss the ballet, art exhibits, who was running for the local boards. When she talked she chose her words with care. Still, nothing seemed more interesting to Sarah and Arnie than what *I* had to say. After knowing them for only two weeks, I was already feeling loyal to the strangest gig I'd ever had.

Apparently, last week's tape recording had been a failure. "Jimmy didn't react the way we'd hoped," Sarah said.

"I'll play better next time," I said.

"That won't fix it," Arnie said.

"Maybe you just need a fancier mike," I said.

"No, it isn't that," she said. "He mangled the cassette."

"What do you mean?" I said.

"He stuck it on a lightbulb," Arnie said.

"What?"

"The cassette melted," she said. "Poor angel. He must've been trying to see the music."

CHAPTER 6

Blobs & Splatters

IF MY BUILDING'S washing machines hadn't been the best deal in the Bronx, I'd never go in the dark and airless laundry room in the basement. As it was, I always waited until my clothes gave me no choice. Then it was in and out, no dawdling in the linty catacomb.

On Wednesday I climbed down the four flights with my overloaded basket only to find Colfield Dixon standing there alone, dropping coins into a machine, his pecs busting through his T-shirt. I said Hello. He was mute.

He slammed his detergent box on the lid. He twisted the knobs like he wanted to tear them off. Everything he did popped an angry echo.

"You feeling all right, Colfield?" I said, quickly loading my clothes.

Silence.

I set the dials, turned it on, and was ready to race out of there when I heard him mumble, "I hate liars."

He turned to face me. I edged toward the door.

"Why didn't you tell me the truth?" he said.

"Uh . . . about what?"

"Stories. You made up a bunch a stories why you couldn't go to my prayer group with me."

"Really?" I said, almost at the doorway.

"One time you said you had a gig, but before I left, I heard you blowing your horn and you was still at it when I got back. Two weeks ago, when you said you was leaving for tango lessons, I heard the Yankee game through the walls. And last time you said you was playing over at the Bronx Loyal Order of Moose. I found out the Moose lodge uses only three musicians: two bagpipes and a ukelele."

"There's an innocent explanation for this, Colfield."

"Yeah, well, why didn't you tell me you was a Jew?"

"That's the innocent explanation."

"You don't play in tongues." In a flash he was between me and the door, his hands tensing into fists.

"I—I should've told you," I said, "you're right—but you seemed so happy with me, I didn't want to let you down."

"I got no problem with Jews . . . I *hate* liars."

I tried to move around him, but he blocked the exit. "You know," he said, "I bench press two a you every day."

"I . . . I . . ." I said, glazing my eyes, "I think it's the tenth, don't you? Yes, yes indeed, definitely the tenth, the tenth."

"Huh?"

"Loops and loops and links and loops," I said.

"What—what are you trying to say?" He squinted.

"Jellybeans, jellybeans, jellybeans. Red, yellow and green jellybeans!"

Colfield, still squinting, shifted out of my way, and I bolted from the laundry room. It was a desperate move, the only time I'd ever pretended to be crazy to get out of a jam. I must've been convincing. The strange thing was, even as I mimicked what I thought was Jimmy's nonsense, somewhere very deep down I knew what I was saying; I knew Jimmy's reality. A shudder ran through my bones. Nothing, not even Colfield's fists, could be worse than going insane.

ON SUNDAY Arnie and Sarah were waiting for me outside their building. "We'll see you at 5:30," they said, and took off.

Maybe they hired me to get a break from Jimmy, I thought, a hundred-twenty-dollar sitter who'll coax him out of his room for a couple hours.

Either way, I blew my horn, and he bounded into the living room. Since it didn't matter which music I chose, I closed my eyes for the two and a half hours and worked on my most challenging tunes, patterns and progressions. It was my chance to practice away from Muriel's broom and the Mendez kids—and get paid for it. Jimmy mumbled and hollered about loops and links and the usual jellybeans, but there was a new one: "Oh yes, we'll fly out tonight!"

When his parents returned with take-out Indian food, he swooped onto the cartons of tandoori chicken, paneer and vegetable curry, all with the same fork. The whole dinner he smacked his lips and muttered to the ether. Arnie lightened the mood with his curry jokes—awkward-stain jokes that must've been a hit with his dry cleaning pals. And Sarah asked why I chose the saxophone, why I came to New York, if I ever thought I'd have a family—all the juicy questions. I detailed every hurdle, every indignity, a perfect suffering-for-my-art routine. It was sublime.

But I had to know about the red clothes. "Jimmy," I said softly, "why do you only wear red?"

He mumbled for another few seconds, then glared at me. Then he grinned, turned away, and continued his mumbling dialogue.

"Likes red," Arnie said.

"It's all he'll wear," Sarah said.

"But why only red?" I asked.

"I'll bet Jimmy will tell you himself someday," she said.

"But," Arnie said, "you still won't know why."

THE FOLLOWING WEEK, again Sarah and Arnie left me alone with their son, but for the first time Jimmy was waiting for me in his chair when I arrived. I said Hello, and he grinned; he didn't look away. It was almost normal.

I closed my eyes and blew into the saxophone for a few minutes. Then I asked if he had a favorite tune or style.

He looked me in the eye. We stared at each other for almost a minute. Then he whispered, "Mr. Shawn Lewis style. Indeed."

I thanked him. I practiced my improvising for another hour, then took a short break. "Why do you only wear red?" I asked.

He grinned.

I played straight through for another half hour. At first he rocked to the beat in his chair, then he got up to dance, bellowing about jellybeans. I stopped. He stood motionless, waiting for the music.

"Where are the jellybeans?" I said.

He giggled, then doubled over with laughter.

At 5:30 Sarah and Arnie returned with an Italian feast: pizza, gnocchi, chicken parmigiana, salad and ice cream. By the time we got to the ice cream Sarah asked if I'd be willing to come three times a week for $360, including the meals.

"Great," I said. "Which days?"

"We can be flexible," she said. "It's official now: Arnie's retired. We sold Bell's Cleaners."

"Kaput," he said, flicking his hands in the air.

Jimmy, with tomato sauce and ice cream dappled over his beard and smock, lurched his chair back, and stood up. He removed his smock, growled a moist belch, looked at each of us and said, "Thank you for a most dazzling dinner, I go to my room now, thank you, thank you, good-night." What a specimen, I thought. But before I could decide he had a trace of decency, his arms jerked, tipping over the pitcher of iced tea, and he strolled away while we scrambled to blot up the river.

After we cleared the dishes, Sarah offered me wine. Of course I refused, still maintaining my control—as though the slightest thing could tip my world into chaos.

I'd been coming to Sheepshead Bay for a month and still had no idea what was really wrong with Jimmy. While Sarah and Arnie relaxed over the bottle of beaujolais, and Jimmy was safely in his room, now was my chance to find out. "What's—" I started to say. "What kind of illness . . . I mean, exactly what's going on with Jimmy?"

Sarah smiled, looking me straight in the eye: "What do *you* think it is?"

"I don't know," I said. "Am I prying?"

"Don't be silly," she said. "What do you think is wrong with our Jimmy?"

"Now Sarah," Arnie said.

"Well, the clothes," I said, "the talking to himself, that chewing thing he does . . . I mean, is he autistic, slightly mentally challenged? Am I prying? I guess there's nothing wrong with Jimmy you couldn't say is wrong with all of us once in a while. I should go now." I got up from the table.

"No, no, sit," she said, motioning with her hands. "You *should* know. In fact, I want you to know all about our Jimmy."

"All about what?" Arnie said. "Boy's crazy. What more do you need? We love the meshugana anyway."

"Isn't *Columbo* on?" she asked him. "Go in the living room so we can have a meaningful conversation."

He grumbled something as he got up and started for the other room. Then he turned to ask Sarah, "We still got to do the art tomorrow?"

"Absolutely," she said.

He grimaced and left for the sofa.

"We try to stay current," she said to me. "I have a special interest in the galleries, you know, the latest trends." She took a long sip of beaujolais, staring into space. If the abstracts hanging throughout the apartment were the latest trends, Arnie had all my sympathy.

A moment passed. Then she said, still staring vacantly, "We raised Jimmy to be *free*. It wasn't in us to be disciplinarians. But who would have dreamed he'd become such an . . . individualist?" She took another sip, removed her gold-framed glasses, and leaned back in her chair. "You only see Jimmy now, at 49, after years of being misunderstood. But he was an exceptionally talented, sensitive child. It's a crime his schoolmates never accepted him." She surveyed the paintings behind me and along the brick wall. "You could say, our society never accepted him. The drugs he was forced to take twisted him into what you see today."

Arnie returned for a bag of Oreos. "*Columbo*'s not on yet," he said.

"But Jimmy was in heaven," she said, "whenever I played the violin."

"You can play the violin?" I said.

"The best," Arnie said.

"Don't exaggerate," she said to him, waving her hand.

"I'm not," he said. "She was—"

"Shhh." Sarah held her finger to her mouth.

"Best violin in New York," he whispered.

"Far from it," she said.

"New York Phil," he said. "Tirty years, number one violin." He sat down, tore open a family-size bag of Oreos, and began chomping.

"Last chair of the first violins," she said with another dismissive wave.

"That's tremendous," I said.

"Number one," he said.

"You know he's tone deaf," she pointed to Arnie. He laughed as crumbs rained down his T-shirt. "Darling," she said to him, stroking his arm, "you're very sweet but you can't hear the difference between any two notes."

He laughed so hard, he started coughing, the crumbs sprinkling over us.

"The violin was my passion," she said to me, "from the old country."

"Which country?" I said.

"I don't play anymore," she said, "not since the arthritis."

"Which country?"

"Now Jimmy—he was a natural. Started violin at four. He had perfect pitch."

Arnie finished off the cookies, and left for the TV.

"It was Arnie," she whispered, "who helped Jimmy start painting. Yes, Arnie bought Jimmy his first set of watercolors, the oils, the canvases, everything. I've seen you admiring Jimmy's paintings. They're glorious, aren't they?"

My jaw fell open.

"I know, I agree," she said. "Cutting edge, really. The gallery owners are so pathetic. They don't see it. But one day they will." She nodded, scanning the paintings all around. "Jimmy became an artist when he could no longer hold the violin. It was the TD. The TD crushed him. It ended his violin playing and made everything a trial, even painting. But he's a committed artist now, and—"

"Excuse me—TD? What's—"

"Tardive Dyskinesia," she said, "a nerve disease—a side effect of the drugs, all the twitches and sudden shakes. It made his eyes bulge too. Did you know he used to weigh over 400 pounds?"

"Drugs for what?"

"Jimmy's problems started a long time ago. He was only twelve when he saw me having a nervous breakdown. That's too young to see your mother fall apart, Shawn. I went to the hospital and quickly recovered, but

Jimmy was never the same. Arnie dragged him to every expert." Then she whispered, "I think they got it wrong."

"Did you say 'nervous breakdown?'"

"Oh, I didn't leave the old country far enough behind." She poured herself the rest of the wine and took another long sip. "The doctors said Jimmy's personality had shattered; the chemicals in his brain had become radically imbalanced. He was now a 'disorganized' schizophrenic—liable to do *anything.*"

He *is* a psychopath, I thought; I *knew* it.

"They told us our boy was capable of murder, suicide, anything," she said, narrowing her eyes at me, "and he wouldn't even know it when he was doing it. But my son couldn't hurt a cockroach. They locked him in an institution and injected him with the strongest anti-psychotics to control his jumbled brains. And we lost him."

I can't breathe, I thought. Why did I bring it up? Why am I so nervous? I tried to relax, but just the thought of—of winding up like Jimmy . . . Why would I worry that just because my music is a little crazy, just because I'm driven toward the wildest, freest jazz on a wave without limits—*I could wind up like Jimmy*?

"The drugs stole his youth," she said. "He slept all day and gained weight. Still nothing stopped his hallucinations—his 'conferences.' The doctor upped the dosages, then used experimentals—two of which are now banned. Nothing stopped the conferences."

"Well," I said, standing up, blotting my forehead with a tissue. "Thank you for the three-times-a-week gig."

I hustled into the living room, grabbing my sax case.

"Don't you understand?" she said, following me. "The drugs shut him down but they couldn't shut down the voices he'd heard all along."

I'm fine, I thought. Not crazy just because my solos are "crazy."

"I'll call when I figure out my schedule," I said, angling for the door.

Arnie rose from the sofa. "I told him about the hospital," Sarah said to Arnie, "about the drugs. I think I scared him."

"It's nothing," Arnie said to me. "We give him a little drug now and then for the TD—not much. Calms it a little."

"It's been over ten years since they gave Jimmy back to us," she said. "Now he's loved and accepted. And he has his privacy. We weaned him from most of the medications. He still has his conferences; that won't ever change, but at least he's not sleeping all day. And he's *painting* again."

"You've done wonders," I said, as I opened the door.

"Shawn," she said, "when we got him out of the hospital he was numb, he was dead. It was the *music*—my violin playing—that woke him up. I played constantly for him until my arthritis took over, and—"

"He don't come out of his room," Arnie said.

"We've tried every therapy there is," she said. "We even tried group therapies, hoping he'd make friends or maybe meet a nice girl with similar—"

"He don't care about girls or friends," Arnie said.

"He has few inclinations," she said, "just the painting . . . and writing some gibberish in his notebooks. Oh, I'm sure it makes sense to him. But he stays in that room all day with the stereo and TV, writing and painting."

"He got his own batroom and shower in there," Arnie said.

"We're lucky," Sarah said. "He washes himself. He can fix simple meals and knows to turn off the burners. But he has no interest in other people. My friends from the orchestra used to play for him, until he preferred his room even to them."

Jimmy's door slammed open, and he charged at me with a square board. Drool dribbled down his beard, and with a huge yellow smile he pushed the board up to my face—a two-foot square canvas, oils still wet. It was offensive, the black and orange blobs and splatters shoved in my eyes. *Get your shit out of my face*, I wanted to yell. But like a Rorschach inkblot something began to form within the slop, a familiar image rising out of the splatters. I saw me, *my* image—a terrifying caricature of *me*—my hair, my nose, my mouth, even the clothes I was wearing. But my ears were enormous orange elephant ears. And I had no eyes.

I felt queasy and confused, somehow under its control. I couldn't stop looking at it even as it was shredding my mind. I had to get away. I stumbled into the hall and out the building. Sarah was right behind me.

"Are you all right?" she said. "You don't look well."

"My solos are normal," I said.

"Why didn't you take the painting, Shawn? He likes you very much if he's painting for you—"

"My music is very solid, very—very normal."

"Yes, Shawn, and there's something in it that's reaching him."

"How's Wednesday?" I said, my throat closing off. "Wednesday's open. Same time?" I backpedaled toward the stairs to the train, but she kept coming.

"When Jimmy hears your saxophone, it's like when *I* used to play for him. He's getting better, Shawn. He's going to be all right—if you keep playing for him."

"Train's over there; I better do that."

"You could be the difference," she said. "Because what if Jimmy isn't crazy after all? What if he's the genius and the rest of us are fools? What if the things he sees that no one else can see . . . are *really there*?"

I pulled myself up the stairs to the elevated.

"See you Wednesday!" she shouted.

CHAPTER 7

The Hero of Denwood Street

THE CAR AND PASSENGERS whirled around me as I tumbled to my seat. No one gets vertigo from a painting, I thought, even if the artist is a nutcase. This must be from the gnocchi. Never eat what you could use to caulk your bathtub.

After I switched to the #5 Train I fell asleep. I dreamed an orange elephant with no eyes was closing in on me. He was playing saxophone with his trunk—torrid bebop. We traded eights, and when *I* blew, I sounded like an elephant. I woke screaming, the other riders gaping at me, crammed as far away as they could sit.

Maybe it was Sarah's talk about 'shattered minds,' I thought, as I stepped off the train and down the dark sidewalk. I strode past shadowy figures loitering along an unlit construction pile, but they couldn't rattle me more than I already was. I walked toward my stoop around neighbors sitting on lounge chairs, enjoying the summer night. Some cake and a nice *Star Trek,* I thought. Tomorrow I'll feel better.

Sarah thinks her son is a genius—maybe in the jellybean world—but not in the world *I* know. And do I really want to get closer to *his*? "Boy's crazy," Arnie had told me more than once. I should quit the job.

But now it's three times a week. I could turn down Izzy's mob gigs. And I love the dinners—except for the gnocchi. She was just answering my question. When Jimmy ambushed me with his hideous painting, I overreacted, that's all. It's not *Sarah's* fault I hadn't realized the degree of my fear of insanity.

Every time I play the avant-garde, I choose to blow on that cosmic wave without limits—and go a little mad, just a little. What if I rode that wave and never came back? Wasn't it the madness in the music that scared Carole away? Or was it my passion for the music that attracted her in the first place? My mind was in a blender.

As I climbed the staircase to my apartment, I thought to myself, Quit them now or make a real commitment. I unlocked my door, and Galicia, wrapped in bear teeth and medallions, burst from her doorway. "You must quit that job," she said, holding cards high in the air while I ducked into my apartment. "The cards say—"

I slammed the door, but I was shocked by her timing. Could she be for real? Galicia? Wouldn't a genuine psychic have more going on than waiting behind her door to foist readings on her neighbors? And her advice was always so irritating. If I had listened to her, I'd have given up the saxophone years ago. I'd be living in Penn Station with a shaved head, handing out flowers. No, I needed to believe Galicia was wrong, dependably wrong. This would prove she was psychic after all—but in *reverse*. I had my answer: Keep the gig in Sheepshead Bay. It was exactly where I needed to be.

I RETURNED WEDNESDAY to find the Bells at their dining table with another couple, all of them laughing in a rowdy game of bridge. I set up, started to play, and Jimmy lumbered out of his room to the chair in front of me. The Bells and their friends rollicked on, unaffected.

Their friends had brought our dinner in Tupperware—tuna salad, fresh bread, a variety of cheeses. Jimmy pounced as usual, and no one seemed to care. We all made believe everything was ordinary—no psychos, no geniuses, no sinister paintings. Jimmy ate and mumbled while the guests talked for an hour about shoes.

On Thursday, while the Bells were playing bridge with a different couple, I arrived to find Jimmy dancing alone in the living room. He was getting bolder. On Sunday we had our first dialogue. "Blue jellybeans," he said, after I finished playing.

"Blue?" I said.

"The blue ones are new," he said.

The following Wednesday their doors were open, and I entered the apartment to roars of laughter. A tall, spry, white-haired man was entertaining Sarah and Arnie. His voice boomed and cut with a sharp delivery, his hands flailing in the air as he reenacted some humorous scene. Then he saw me and stopped himself. *"Aha,"* he said. "Sax man. I'm Henry, Henry Felder." He grabbed my hand and shook it.

I recognized him as one of the jitterbuggers at the anniversary party.

"I've heard a lot about you, son," Henry said. "We're all proud of you."

"Really?"

"Of course. You're working with the boy. I would've been here weeks ago but I've been out of town visiting family—which takes a lot a time when you've got three sets and a ton a grandkids, all a them spread out as far from the old man as they could run. That's right—three marriages. Hey, there would be more, but I've been . . . careful." He winked at Arnie and got a snicker. Sarah rolled her eyes.

"Hey, I'm 79; I'm entitled," Henry said to me. "Arnie says I don't look a day over 78. Come here . . ." He put his arm around my shoulder, led me away from Sarah and Arnie, and with superb timing, whispered the filthiest joke I'd ever heard. I liked him from the start.

Apartment 1 was Henry's second home. The Bells had many friends popping in during my two-and-a-half-hour sessions, but no one as often as Henry. He'd known them in the "old country." He'd helped plan their wedding. He even got Arnie started in the dry cleaning business. And at every stage of Jimmy's life he was the first one they turned to for advice and comfort.

It was easier to play for Jimmy when Henry was listening, not just because he'd tip me a five to blow some Ellington, but because he added an engaging and much-needed sense of "normal." Even Jimmy couldn't resist giggling at his comical "Uncle Hen." And Henry, always tolerant of

Jimmy no matter how much "the boy" carried on, never missed a chance to rave about the paintings, even the Elephant-With-No-Eyes canvas that was still waiting for me by the door.

"You know," Sarah pulled me aside one day, "Henry's not just our friend; he's a bigwig. He was Brooklyn borough president. And served in Congress—six terms."

"How did you meet?"

"That's a long story," she said. "Let's just say, we owe him more than we could ever pay back."

By August Henry was calling me The Hero of Denwood Street. I liked how it sounded—though Jimmy hadn't changed much. And there was nothing heroic about taking the money and the meals—and doing the opposite of whatever Galicia would have me do.

WHEN SARAH AND ARNIE added a fourth day to the schedule, I needed to make room by getting rid of my less desirable gigs—which were *all* the other gigs. The Latin band was ready to fire me anyway because their regular sax player would soon be on parole. The manager of The Out House was impressed I'd stayed as long as I had, especially after "that little E. coli flap." The only protest came from Izzy of The Mediterranean Club. "But no one starts and stops a band like you," he said. "Besides, where you going to work when all your fingers are broken?"

For now, I'd stick with The Mediterranean Club.

Tommy called to suggest I beg Danny James for another chance. "He loves it when people beg," Tommy said.

I told him I was finished with demeaning gigs, and bragged about my new job.

"Great . . . " he said, pausing. "It's great you got the work and the dinners, man. But you unloaded your jazz gigs just to play for the psycho in his parents' living room? Wait a second, man: Is it me or does this sound a little off track?"

Tommy had a point, but after all, I thought, he works all the time; he can afford to remind people of their ambitions.

~~~~~

BY LATE SUMMER Jimmy was getting more comfortable around me. His occasional one or two words during our sessions had now evolved into running commentaries, though most of them not to *me*. I couldn't tell who he thought the gibberish was for, or if he meant it all for himself.

Then came our turning point. On Wednesday, September 22nd, Jimmy was waiting in the hall for me as I arrived. "I'm so glad you came because I wanted to paint but my arms were acting up and I couldn't," he said, "and that made me sad so I was going to just watch TV but then I thought maybe some lovely mint chocolate chip but I ate two bags yesterday and dad wants me to lose thirty-five pounds so I didn't know what to do and felt bad and now you're here." He grinned, showing all his yellow, knobby teeth. I'd never heard him speak like that before.

"I'm glad to be here," I said, reaching to shake hands.

He ignored my hands and gave me a hug. I would've been moved if it wasn't for the dark glob that had transplanted from his beard and red shirt to my chin and jacket. I savagely wiped my face while he carried my instrument and music for me toward the fireplace arrangement.

After I scoured my case and handle with several wads of kleenex, I played an original Latin tune that featured the instrument's extreme low and high registers. He waited for me to finish, and said, "Purple and white jellybeans. But you didn't open all the loops."

I thanked him.

"Open the Earth Five loops," he said. "It would be dazzling, even historigantic, Mr. Shawn Lewis, if you could open *all* the loops when you play."

I didn't understand him, but after nearly four months of bleak communication, it felt like a breakthrough. Sarah and Arnie pulled up chairs around us.

I took out my orchestral excerpts—for Sarah—and improvised freely around themes by Debussy and Fauré. She was unimpressed, but after a while Jimmy declared: "Jellybean rainbows."

"Thank you," I said.
~~~~~

"You brought the rainbows but you still can't open the Earth Five loops."

Sarah and Arnie beamed. Sarah then excused herself to finish making dinner, but Arnie quietly stayed with us the rest of the session.

At dinner, Sarah and Arnie sat back, observing, while Jimmy, instead of disappearing into his own world, wouldn't stop talking—to *me*.

"I paint pictures," Jimmy said, food flying from his mouth.

I wiped my cheeks.

"I paint what I see and what I feel," he said, "and it all comes out just as I feel and see it, unless my arms shake and then it doesn't. So, I paint. That's what I do."

"Why do you only wear red?" I asked.

"You have to find your color, Mr. Shawn Lewis," he said, nodding vigorously.

"Why? What do you mean?"

"Colors are important, very important, yes, very important. Colors sing—like your sax sings. Colors can help—but colors can hurt. It's very important to find colors that help, like red is *my* color. It protects me. It protects me from . . ."

". . . From what?"

"You have to find your color because it might be red but it might not be red, like it might be yellow and then you would want to wear yellow and not red."

"Okay . . ." I said.

Arnie was glowing, and Sarah leaned over, whispering into my ear, "It's a miracle, a miracle."

After he ravaged the cheesecake, Jimmy stood up and said, "Thank you for a most lovely dinner, yes, a most lovely dinner. I'm going to lay down now and maybe later I'll paint for Mr. Shawn Lewis why I like red so much."

He left, and Sarah used her fresh-baked maple walnut cookies to entice me to stay with her and Arnie for the Yankee game.

"What's the miracle?" I kept asking them as we munched cookies around the TV. "Is it that Jimmy's talking?"

"No," she said. "That's the way he talks—with us, and sometimes with his Uncle Hen. The miracle is that he's talking that way with *you.* He's getting better. He's chosen a friend."

Sarah, Arnie and I thrilled to the Yankees clinching the pennant that night. Between the victory, the cookies, and the intimate conversation, I'd been ushered into the family. I'd won them over. I was the Hero of Denwood Street.

Of course, as far as I could tell, Jimmy was no better—only less shy, and shyness was not his biggest problem.

Am I a hero or a fool? I wondered. Every time I blow solos on the wave without limits to a man who lives every second without limits, I'm mingling in his world. I'm daring Madness.

CHAPTER 8

Carole

WHILE I WAS PRACTICING the next morning—timing my long tones to Lloyd Fetterman's snores—the phone rang, and all it took to make me nearly drop my alto was "Hello, Shawn." It was Carole. She said she missed me and wanted to meet for lunch.

I had so much to tell her yet I barely said a word. Lunch? Okay, fine, whatever. I pretended it didn't matter; she'd crushed me, after all. But I was delirious, so excited I even gathered the things I'd need just in case she wanted her heartsick ex to spend the night.

I brought my alto—for the Bells later that day—and my hopeful overnight bag to the hip Village café, Peppers. Carole, as radiant as ever, sat at an outdoor table, examining the menu. When she saw me, she smiled, that nervous smile that called attention to her lips and made me instantly forget the 139 days, four hours it had been since she'd said she'd call right back.

We embraced, but she pulled away.

"Are you all right?" she asked. "You look a little . . . confused."

"Uh . . . right . . ." I said. *Damn,* I thought, the pull-away hug.

"Sorry I missed your birthday," she said.

A dip in the pavement must've thrown her off balance.

". . . Well, happy birthday," she said, smiling, her lips still taunting me.

"Oh, fine, fine, my pleasure. You too."

"My birthday's next month."

"Right . . ." I studied the pavement. No dips.

Carole ordered a fajita salad while I buried myself in the menu, screaming to myself, *Damn the pull-away*. Was this her signal to back off? Why would she want to see me if she wanted me to back off?

"How are your students this year?" she said.

"Oh, it's my pleasure," I said to her, giving the waiter my order. "How are yours?"

"I'm a nurse, remember?"

"Right . . ."

"Shawn, did you mean to order the whole page of appetizers?"

She was just a shapely wisp but she had so much power. One pull-away hug and my world shrank into a snow globe.

"I think about you all the time," she said. "Are you taking care of yourself? Are you making the rent? Do you get enough work?"

"Terrific."

"Are you handling your bills? Do you use the tax organizer I gave you? You're so sweet," she said, chuckling, "you'd get pinkeye whenever you'd worry about missing a payment. Do you still—"

"Just great," I said, rubbing my eye. Two waiters crammed the table with my bowls of nachos, chile, guacamole, bean dip, corn chowder and beef tortilla soup.

"Shawn," she said, staring at her salad, "I'm sorry I hurt you."

"I got over it."

"I was hoping you'd say that."

I mumbled, "Once I could hold down solid foods." I played with my nachos. "The tax organizer was a help," I said. "This year I filed only two extensions."

"There's no one like you, Shawn. No one who understands me like you do, who'll listen to . . . you know, all my problems."

Our eyes met and I couldn't stop myself. "Carole, my life's a mess. I wake up confused; I go to bed confused. I haven't had a day without you that felt normal."

"I've missed you too."

"Why didn't you call me back?"

"Oh . . . I just couldn't." She poked at her salad. "I love that you care so much about your music. Reminded me a little of my dad . . . You were so cute, the way you'd get so wrapped up in your songs, you'd forget to eat. I could take care of you. Then . . . " She grimaced, her eyes down. "I—I heard your songs . . . "

"That was a bad night, Carole. But even on a good night, free jazz requires an open—"

"My stomach hurt for a week. But what do *I* know? Look, even if your work makes no sense to me and I can't relate to it and I get sick when I hear it, I still want us to be friends. Can you forgive me? Can we still talk?" She gazed at me, those big chestnut eyes.

"Of course." Those eyes could make me forget my name.

"I'm so relieved," she said. "It doesn't feel right for us not to be talking."

"You matter more than my work," I said. "Let's get back together. I love you." I reached between my soups and the guacamole to grab her hand, but she'd picked up her napkin to wipe her silverware.

"I met somebody," she said softly, her eyes down.

"You met somebody. Okay, well, I meet people all the time. See that waiter? We met ten minutes ago."

"His name is Mark. He's a doctor. He was after me for a long time, but you and I were together and . . . "

"My music drove you away."

"I got so sad after The Out House, and—"

"I promise," I said, "I'll never play my horn for you again."

"Let's just start fresh. I'd like us to talk like we used to." She asked if she could confide in me, if it would hurt me, and I said she could tell me *anything*. I'd always felt special when Carole shared her secrets. But I wasn't ready for this one.

"Mark can be a little cold sometimes," she said. "Everything will be going great, and then he'll shift to this quiet, superior mood that lasts for hours. I know he's under a lot of pressure—being a highly important doctor and all—but do guys get quiet like that when they're upset with you? I mean, it's nothing to worry about, right? You know me so well, I thought you could . . . give me the male point of view."

My male point of view was burrowing at the bottom of the snow globe.

"He's not sure he wants a family," she said. "But I don't want to miss my chance. I feel old." She was thirty-four and could have passed for twenty.

"He sounds like a turd," I said, sliding my chair back.

"That's not fair, Shawn."

"*I* could be ready for a family."

"But I'm terrified of having kids. I can't imagine being stuck in a slum, worrying about my kids with gangs and drug dealers and—"

"I don't live in a slum."

"I didn't mean that you did," she said. "Your neighborhood's getting better . . . not nearly as many shoot-outs."

I stared at my array of appetizers. "Carole, I'm not a loser. Don't judge me just because you don't like my originals."

She blotted the tablecloth around my overflowing plates.

"I quit The Out House gig, you know," I said.

"I hope not because of me . . ."

"I've got a very special job now."

"Really? In what field?"

"In music. Is that so hard to believe?"

She winced.

"I'm playing four times a week for a family in Sheepshead Bay."

"On saxophone?"

"Yes. Someone actually wants to hear me play the saxophone."

"That's great, Shawn. Do you play your originals?" The wince was still there.

"Sometimes, but everything is different now. My teacher Wendell died."

"I'm sorry. He meant a lot to you."

"He did. But before he died I went to visit him in the hospital. I don't think he even knew who I was. He was raving to himself. But something he said, something he'd always wanted me to understand, hit me all at once. I'm now better than when you heard me at The Out House. I pay more attention to tone and phrasing and—"

"A single family in Sheepshead Bay hires a band four times a week?"

"I think Wendell had always wanted me to feel the core of the music, you know, to feel my own soul, to—"

"Who can afford to hire a band four times a week?"

"There's no band. It's just me."

"Seriously? Isn't it rare for people to hire a screaming atonal saxophone to—"

"I told you I pay a lot more attention to my sound now, and phra—"

"Are these people deranged?"

"Actually, one of them is, but he's my fan." I told her about Jimmy's illness and how his parents thought I was helping him. I stressed the music therapy angle, and Carole's eyes widened, her face opening up to me.

"Wow!" she kept saying. "This is so amazing!"

She was elated for me, not because I had a job playing my instrument, but because I was helping someone with schizophrenia. When I told her that the previous night was the first time in years Jimmy had had a semi-normal conversation with a stranger, she started bouncing in her chair.

I paid the bill, and though I'd be leaving soon for the Bells, we strolled and talked while I yearned to kiss her. Then she brought up Mark again.

"He's got this dashing way about him," she said.

"Why, is he in a rush all the time?"

"He's a heart surgeon."

Yes, I thought, that would account for the sudden pain in my chest.

As we ambled the mile toward her apartment, she vented about Mark's moods, his ongoing divorce, his obnoxious cell phone voice—their day-to-day problems that should've been *our* day-to-day problems. I forced back a tear and said, "Carole, I'm not good at this kind of advice. All I can say is he sounds like a turd."

"That is so rude. What *happened* to you? Mark is a brilliant, hard-working, important—"

I told her I couldn't be her token male point of view.

When we reached her building, she sobbed on my shoulder and wouldn't let go. For that moment I *knew* she loved me—I could feel it, but an obscure jazzer with crazy music could never keep her. If only I were an important anything. It was official—it was over, I was free to find someone else. But holding her quivering body, I never wanted anyone more.

CHAPTER 9

Out of His Shell

OF ALL THE TIME I spent in Sheepshead Bay, the Fall of that year was my happiest with the Bells and their limitless circle of friends. No one brought up asylums or nervous breakdowns, and I asked no questions. Four times a week I fled my private students and whatever dreadful gigs I still had, all the way to Apartment 1, my refuge.

I was Jimmy's only friend. To the elders on the southern tip of Brooklyn that made me a star. They'd watched from a distance since he was a boy, but now that he seemed less psychotic, they were anxious to engage him, to kibitz with him. Jimmy paid no attention to any of them—only Uncle Hen, his parents, my horn, and all the incomprehensible things he couldn't wait to tell me about my music.

Henry showed up often and with pals he'd want me to meet or another widow to parade. "Son, keep it up," he'd say in front of them. "Everybody's blabbing about the job you're doing here. Boy's almost out of his shell. Soon he'll be running for Congress."

Of course, the more Jimmy ranted to me, the less time I had to play, which made my job easier. I just had to pretend to listen. All I could discern was that he was grateful—annoyingly grateful. And he was preparing my "special reward." By December the reward would be ready, and whatever relief I'd derived from my visits to Sheepshead Bay would be gone forever.

On the first night of Hanukkah, while Sarah cooked, I played for Jimmy and Henry, attempting to merge free jazz with the most arcane Jewish melodies. It was safer to risk butchering something unknown than any of the classic hymns. During "Oy, You Sat on My Latkes," Jimmy stopped me with a speech that might've never ended: "It is so dazzling that you bring the jellybeans all the way to our Apartment 1 living room at 271 Denwood in Sheepshead Bay, Brooklyn, New York when you live so very far away and I have to paint what I feel which is not always so easy for me to do because my arms shake, but you bring the jellybeans when you ad lib the sax—I love the sax—I wish I played the sax—and I wish I could ad lib too but I have the shakes sometimes and I can't play but I wish you could see what I see about the other worlds and the jellybeans—my God, the jellybeans—and the plarps; you have to see the plarps—so I paint these things I feel not just for me but for you too because I want you to see what I can see but . . . "

He stopped. He turned and muttered toward the fireplace—not to me, and apparently not to himself either. It was another one of his quiet conferences and it lasted for hours. He didn't even pause as we sat down to the holiday dinner and he gorged one of Sarah's best meals.

Regardless, Sarah, Arnie, Henry and I relished the dinner and our banter about which of us had the nosiest neighbor. I won with Galicia. After the apple cinnamon cheesecake they walked me to the door. "*Mr. Shawn Lewis,*" Jimmy yelled, bounding after me. "You can't go yet. Your special reward is ready. I painted for you. I painted all the things I have to show you. That's your extra special reward. If you would come visit my most lovely room, it would be so dazzling to give you your special reward because I would like you to take it to where you live so very far away. Follow me," he said, his mouth twitching. "Follow me, follow me."

We were all so jovial, so content it never occurred to me it might be dangerous to go into his room.

"Shawn, don't," Sarah said, looking pale. "I should . . . tidy up a little first."

"Oh, it's okay," I said. "I told you about my old pad above the fish market—I've been through everything."

Jimmy flung open his door, urging me on as Arnie and Henry backed up.

The stench hit me in waves: ripe underwear, sour cheese, a cache of moldy Entenmanns. I coughed. My nose ran. I don't know why I didn't flee. Maybe it was the turpentine. The further I went in, the more it masked everything else.

"Follow me, follow me," Jimmy said.

I blew my nose, held my mouth, and stumbled over red clothes, cassettes, open bags of marshmallows, cookies and Fritos that hid the carpet. I bumped into his bed, and three black-marble composition books flopped over the side. A dozen more of the open notebooks littered the mattress—pages brimming with jet-black scrawl.

He motioned to me from the far side of the room, by his easel. I couldn't move. It was anarchy, a ransacked jungle topped with crumbs and paint splashes. "Over here, Mr. Shawn Lewis," he said. "I have so many to give you. But which is the special reward? That is the question." Canvases leaned on the windowsills and on his paints-and-brushes table next to the easel. "I think it would be most lovely to give them one at a time, don't you? I do, don't you?"

I took half a step, crunching and crackling something under my feet. I picked up a splintered cassette case labeled with the same black scrawl, "Mister Shawn Lewis." I had to peel the case from my hands that were now coated in yellow. The underside of the case, wet with yellow paint, had two raisins stuck on it.

Looking at the frantic abstracts wedged tightly on the walls and perched on the TV and wherever they could stand, the room appeared to shiver.

"Really," Sarah said, exasperated. "No visitors in here till I've had a chance to straighten up."

I turned to leave. "*This* is the one for you today!" he said, studying the painting on the easel. "Yes, absolutely, absolutely! The plarps pick *this* one. *This* is the one."

I rushed out gasping for air as Sarah darted in, closing the door behind her.

"I never go in there," Arnie said.

"The boy needs a place like that where he can spread out," Henry said.

Sarah emerged, carrying the painting from the easel. "Jimmy's having another conference now," she said, "but this was the one he intended for you." She held up the painting.

Tiny splatters in all colors encircled a gold blob. Somehow the blob reminded me a little of my saxophone. The splatters seemed to be twirling around it. The slop was so irritating I wanted to shield my eyes but I couldn't look away. And the more I looked, the more I was pulled in. I thought, *I* could be one of those splatters flying around the saxophone. Like a rocket I shot upward, straight through the ceiling, insulation and beams, through the two apartments above, the shingled roof, into the night sky and into space with the saxophone from the picture in my hands.

In a cold sweat I turned away from the painting. For five seconds I'd been miles above Sheepshead Bay.

"I don't know what it means," Sarah said, holding it, "but it's divine, yes?"

"The boy's a talent," Henry said.

"It's Jimmy's Hanukkah gift to you," Arnie said. "Take it home."

"It's special," I said, quaking. "Why don't you keep it here for me?"

I have no memory of my trip home or even how I got to my apartment, but I was okay the next morning. I should've never gone into his room, I thought. How could anyone expect to enter the lair of a lunatic and get away clean?

WHEN I ARRIVED the next afternoon Apartment 1 was already hopping. Sarah and Arnie were celebrating Jimmy's "progress." With two dozen seniors—three-to-one women—the Bells had even hired a caterer. I was the band. While Sarah and Arnie served drinks, basking in all the attention, Jimmy hid in his room. I weaved through the crowd, and parked on my chair by the fireplace.

Someone named Agnus rushed over to me. "We heard the news and had to come see for ourselves," she said.

"*Very* impressive, *very* impressive," Boris said, who seemed to be with Agnus.

A woman named Selma confided she'd feel safer if Jimmy were locked away. "He's got the look of pure evil," she whispered. "Reminds me so much of my second husband."

Mildred, Selma's friend, said the Bells should've never left me alone with Jimmy when they went shopping—very irresponsible. "One day they're going to find you strangled, stuffed in that fireplace," she said. "I've been on such tenterhooks."

The "shoes" couple arrived carrying Tupperwares of tuna and cheeses. As I took my saxophone out, they squabbled over whose fault it was they didn't know about the caterers. I played a couple of test notes, and they hurried over to pinch my cheeks. "No one can believe it! *You cured Jimmy.*"

"Oh no," I said. "He's not cured. I just—"

"What a magician you are!"

Frances Pinklestein overheard and got excited. "Really?" she said to the "shoes" couple. "Cured Jimmy?"

They nodded, pinching my cheeks again.

"Then you got to take a look at my niece," Frances said, leaning over me. "She's thirty-five and she thinks she's Dorothy from Wizard of Oz. I'm serious. All the singing wouldn't be so bad, but she's got a voice like a sea lion. She's driving my sister crazy." Frances insisted I take her number so we could set up an appointment.

My soft speaking voice—Carole used to called me her "Serene and Easy," I think, because she found me so easy to talk over—was no match for the seniors of Sheepshead Bay. These people bellowed at each other. And no amount of my feathery protest was going to stop them from hearing what they wanted to hear.

When Henry popped in with a bundle of fresh caught bass, barking orders to the caterers, I made my escape, edging through the mob to greet him.

"By golly, son," he said. "You've done it—done what no doctor could do."

"I haven't done anything," I said.

"It'll take a while, but Sarah says the boy's getting all better."

"Uh . . . I think, maybe . . . shouldn't we let a doctor decide that?"

"You can't see the difference because you're too close to the action." He cupped a hand over his mouth and said, "You don't realize how far gone we all thought he was. It's a good thing you're coming five days a week instead of four."

"Nobody said anything about—"

"It's all been decided. Now *play*. Let's get Jimmy out here." Henry had the New York talent of being bossy and endearing at the same time.

I began with an original slow blues I called, "Mark, the Heart-slicer." After four bars Jimmy, holding a large canvas, barreled out of his room and through the crowd. Shouts rang out: "My foot!" "Owww!" "Watch it!"

Jimmy sat and waited for me to finish the blues, stroking the top of the canvas that rested sideways against his chair. When I was done he spoke continuously for three minutes: He was glad I came, and so were the plarps. He wished I could play for him all the time, he discovered that sardines didn't go well with chicken liver, and he wanted to show me his newest, "most lovely" work.

"Maybe later," I said, and began the next tune, but he kept talking, so I stopped and listened. The crowd gathered around to listen as well.

"Why didn't you take my gift last night?" he said. "Why didn't you take the other gift I made for you? Why? I don't understand why you leave them here. Why do you do that? They're for you, for you to take to where you live so very far away."

"I wanted to, Jimmy, really I did. It's not easy to carry a whole painting on the subway. And I don't have the wall space, not an empty spot on my wall. I wish I did. I'll just have to enjoy them here."

He looked perplexed, but everyone applauded. Sarah came over to me and said, "That was marvelous, just marvelous."

"See, that's what I'm talking about," Henry said.

Then Sarah leaned down and whispered into my ear, "It's working; I can feel it. One day, with your help, he'll be independent. He'll be a part of things. God knows, our world needs someone like Jimmy."

"Would you like to see my newest portrait of you?" he asked me.

"Uh . . . " I said, trying to figure out what the hell Sarah was talking about. "No Jimmy, not just now."

"I wonder," she whispered, "do you know any nice girls he might like?"

I wondered, Was I the only one who still thought Jimmy was insane?

"Hey Jimmy, my boy," Henry said, "don't you say hello to your Uncle Hen?"

"I'm talking to Mr. Shawn Lewis now," Jimmy said slowly, glaring at me. He then hoisted the bulky painting above his head and held it there. I stared at my lap.

"Uncle Hen," he said, "Mr. Shawn Lewis comes from very far away to be here and now, right now, *right now*, he's going to see my new painting. Isn't that right, Mr. Shawn Lewis?"

"Okay, carry on," Henry said.

"How about if I play a tune?" I said to Jimmy.

"You're not looking," Jimmy said to me.

"Can you do five days a week?" Arnie said, squeezing between Henry and me.

"Sure, thank you," I said, keeping my head down.

"We'll give you your own set of keys," Sarah said. "It'll be flexible. Each week you can set a new schedule."

"I made this for *you*," Jimmy said to me, his voice rising. "Look at it."

"Can you think of a girl who would understand him?" she whispered to me. "He'll be ready soon, don't you think?"

"I want to know the real reason," he said, "the real real reason you won't look at this painting or any of my paintings I make for you. I want to know why you don't take them home where you live so very far away. And I want to know *right now*."

"I just don't have the wall space," I said.

"That's not true," he said. "If you wanted, if you really wanted, you would look at my paintings I make for you, you would bring them to your house—a lovely house I'm sure—and you would bring them there and look at them all the time."

"Jimmy," I said, pretending to examine my shirt pocket, "your paintings are fabulous—really, and I'm not just saying that—but perhaps, maybe, they're just not quite my style—"

"They make you sick, don't they?" he said.

"No, don't be ridiculous."

"I think they make you sick," he said, lowering it, and pushing it up to my face. "I think they make you sick."

"No . . . " I said, now staring at my nose.

"Look at it! Why won't you look at it?"

"With your help," Sarah whispered, "he'll make friends, lots of friends, he'll paint, he'll be a part of things."

"I WANT TO KNOW WHY YOU WON'T LOOK AT IT!"

No one made a sound. No one breathed. Even the caterers saddled with Henry's forty pounds of bass stood silent, waiting. My heart skipped several beats, but nothing could make me lift my eyes.

"I can't look," I said softly.

Frances and the shoes couple pleaded with me to look at it.

"You're right, Jimmy," I said. "Your paintings make me sick."

He nodded and rested the canvas on the floor. Then with a yellow knobby-toothed grin, he said, "*Dazzling.*"

AFTER THE SESSION the caterers fanned out to wait on the numerous tables throughout the apartment. I grabbed a table in a quiet corner by the coat closet, but Jimmy quickly glommed on, sitting across from me. Then Henry and his hot date Goldie, who was 75, joined us, and soon I was trapped.

"Soooo, where are you from . . ?" Goldie asked in a plodding, gravelly voice that rose at the end of each sentence.

"I'm from Philad—"

"You ever run into Moe Klepstein?" Henry blurted. "Used to work the docks in Philly—old army buddy."

"No jellybeans today," Jimmy said. "Most of your loops were wrong too."

"I've never known anyone named Moe," I said, and "I'm sorry, Jimmy."

"Ever serve in the military?" Henry asked.

"Didn't play very well today," Jimmy said. "The plarps were bored."

"I served in the big one, you know," Henry said.

"Soooo, how come you're not touching your fish . . ?" Goldie asked.

"I used to live above a Greek fish market," I said. "Jimmy, what are the plarps?"

"I saw a lot of action," Henry said, "45th Infantry. Army made a man a me though. Ever thought about a career in politics?"

"No," I said, "I can't speak in front of large—"

"Soooo, do you have a girlfriend . . ?" Goldie asked.

"No, I guess not," I said.

"Politics can be great," Henry said. "You help real people. You play sports?"

"I used to play stickball back in the neigh—" I said.

"It's good that my art makes you sick," Jimmy said. "Do you want to know why? Do you want to know why it's so very good?"

"Soooo, how come a nice Jewish boy like you doesn't have a girlfriend . . ?"

"It means my art is working," Jimmy said. "It means I painted it right. It means it's—"

"You knoooow," Goldie said, "my granddaughter—"

"If you could see what I can see," Jimmy said, "then you could play whatever you want because you would see the things that are always—"

"Soooo, would you like to meet her . . ?"

"I like to fish," Henry said.

"Why don't I bring her here one of the days you're playing . . ?" Goldie said.

"I was in the Battle of the Bulge, you know," Henry said. "Lieutenant. Ever play in the army band?"

"Ireeeene . . ." Goldie said. "That's her name. Such a doll . . ."

"If you could hear what I hear," Jimmy said, "then you would know how to—"

"Want to go fishing tomorrow?" Henry asked.

"Soooo, would you like her number . . ?"

I couldn't eat. You can't eat when you're the rope in a tug of war.

FIVE DAYS A WEEK Jimmy pressed me to take his paintings and willingly give in to their sickness. "This might sound a little weird," I told Sarah and Arnie, "but please tell Jimmy I can't play here anymore if I have to look at his paintings." They were dumbfounded.

"Shawn, his art is *remarkable,*" Sarah said, "ahead of our time."

"Why so kvetchy?" Arnie said to me. "Don't look if you don't like it."

~~~

On the last Friday of the year I arrived to find Arnie, Henry and a man named Max playing Poker and smoking cigars in the dining room. Jimmy was waiting in his chair at the fireplace—waiting with a two-and-a-half-foot square canvas in his lap, the front facing in. I sat in the other chair and slowly put together my alto.

"You're not going to play for me today, Mr. Shawn Lewis," he said. "Today you will look at the painting I made for you two weeks ago. Today you will look at it."

I needed help. I didn't want to hurt Jimmy's feelings, but I refused to surrender to the witchcraft he called his art. I hollered to Sarah, but she was in the kitchen chopping cabbage. I would've asked for Arnie, but when I saw the mountain of quarters in the poker pot, I knew I was on my own. "Jimmy," I said, rubbing my forehead, "every day we have this discussion and—"

"I know you say it makes you feel bad, but that is good, it means it's working. It means I painted it right, Mr. Shawn Lewis."

Sarah came out to help—I thought. "How could it hurt to just give it a chance?" she said. "One look. His work is so beautiful. Everyone loves it. And he made this one just for you."

There was a pause in the game—Henry had won the hand. While Max accused Henry of flustering him with dirty jokes, and Arnie charged Max with blowing smoke in his face, Henry got up, stretched, and trailed Sarah into the living room.

"Please, Shawn," Sarah said.

"What's the problem here?" Henry said. "Still won't look at the boy's art?" Arnie and Max put down their cards, and soon everyone was in the living room, scolding me.

"No," I said, "I can look at his art—just not the art he makes for *me*."

"Sounds pretty cold, if you ask me," Henry said.

"Sounds meshuga, if you ask me," Arnie said.

"What's wrong with you?" Max said to me. "These people are paying you to entertain their son. You can't look at the paintings he made for you?"

"I know it sounds crazy," I said, "but—"
~~~

"Don't you know you're more than a musician to these people?" Henry said. "To all of us—why—you're a *healer*. Now behave like one."

"Just oil paints," Arnie said.

"I'll give you a hint on who needs his head examined," Max said, twirling his index finger at his temple.

"I never said I was a healer," I said.

"Son," Henry said, "you've done more for the boy in seven months than—"

"Jimmy doesn't hide for days like he used to," Sarah said. "He's with us, he's involved, almost like when he was a boy. And he's painting all the time. It's always, 'When is Mr. Shawn Lewis coming? Is he coming today?' He thinks you and he are twins, the same kind of artist."

"Look," Henry said, "pay attention to the boy's art." Then he leaned down to my ear and said, "I'll slip you a couple extra bucks—even get you a date with my lady friend's granddaughter."

Max sauntered behind Jimmy, and winking to everybody, glanced down at the painting and said, "It appears to be safe . . . yes . . . definitely safe."

"This is my painting that will show you why I wear red," Jimmy said, "only, your color is not red. You have to look at it to know what your color is."

"Okay, Jimmy, fine," I said, still rubbing my forehead. "I'll look."

A giant blue blob sat in the middle of a cluster of yellow splashes and jagged black figures. What shit, I thought. I could've turned away and told Jimmy it was brilliant. I'd be done with it, and everyone would be satisfied. But I kept looking.

They all took turns lauding the blobs and splatters. As much as I wanted to tear away from them, I couldn't, especially the blue blob, which began to look a lot like me. But it *was* me—my posture in motion. It was more me than any photograph or video anyone's ever taken of me. Yet this "real" me was contorted, stressed. I scanned the other shapes and was drawn with terror to the pitch-black jagged figures. Something about them was familiar. I knew them. I'd already been a victim of their cruelty but I couldn't remember how or when—which made them even more terrifying. I pried my eyes away and looked up at Jimmy. He was grinning.

"See," Sarah said. "Was that so hard?"

"Don't you like it?" Henry asked me.

I pushed the painting down, out of my view. "Oh . . . of course," I said, wiping my palms on my shirt. "It's . . . nice."

Jimmy roared with laughter, and at that moment he frightened me as much as when he stormed the float.

Under Sarah's direction Arnie and Henry rearranged the wall paintings so they could hang Jimmy's blue-blob horror above the fireplace—a head-on dose for every time I came to play. Meanwhile, Jimmy droned on about his lovely, dazzling choices of colors and shapes for the painting, and how I lived so very far away. But I wasn't yet free of the painting's pitch-black evil, and as he blathered, my head and stomach whirled. I would've thrown up if he hadn't turned around for a sudden conference with one of his special friends.

"Play for him," Sarah said. "Play for him now; I'll bet he comes out of it."

I took a deep breath and played my latest original, an angry be-bop tune I called, "Hitting the Mark." I had to play three choruses before he turned back to face me. He smiled, gaping above my head. Sarah squeezed my shoulder as she left for the kitchen to finish dinner. Arnie and Max had missed it; they'd been arguing over which Brooklyn diners serve the best corned beef. But Henry was a witness, and when I finished the tune he slipped me a twenty.

"I would've never thought it possible, son," Henry said, leaning over me. "Sarah and Arnie know more than me about everything. Just do what they tell you, son. They know what they're doing."

"I don't understand," I said.

"They're champions, son. They can turn Hell into Paradise. They can make anything work."

"Shouldn't a doctor be in charge of this?"

"Trust me, son—do what they tell you. Those two are champions. Champions of life."

CHAPTER 10

Focus

My New Year's Eve gig in the Catskill Mountains paid double scale and was almost worth the 80-minute drive with the guitarist Wally Gonfman reciting every detail of his sexual conquests. Locations, smells, screams—nothing was off-limits.

I put in my earplugs, but the free ride in his cluttered old Volkswagen meant I couldn't object too much. Three times I said, "Wally, don't you think this is more than I need to hear—I mean, since we just met today?"

Wally's reply was always the same: "Oh, it's no problem, man," as though sharing his sleaze was a sample of his generosity.

I couldn't believe any woman found this short, hairy guitarist attractive, much less took part in his adventures. Even in his tuxedo he looked slimy. Yet as we parked and unloaded our equipment in the hotel lot, he still had more to say.

"Yeah, I'll be busy tonight," he said. "The band's not the only ones staying over, you know that? Hotel's putting up the dancers too. That means *babes*, man."

A night in the Catskills should've been a welcome break from Jimmy and his voodoo paintings, but Wally Gonfman had worn me down. Now all I could think about was the chasm in my own love life. His stories brought me back to high school and Elsie Slingerland and how I would've sold my parents to see her naked but never had the nerve to say more than a voice-cracking hello. Then I remembered the girls in my college trampoline class, and my early years in New York when everywhere I looked I saw actresses and models and unattainable Elsie Slingerlands. Carole had airlifted me out of all that. But now she was gone, and Wally reminded me just how much I wanted them all.

THE CEDARWOOD HOTEL no longer carried a band for their shows, but this was the biggest New Year's of them all, and to usher in 2000 they hired seventeen of us to accompany the Millie Grace Swing Dancers. The Cedarwoood was splurging on this one, hoping the dancers and big band could rev up their dwindling audience more effectively than their usual accordion player or ventriloquist.

The band played a quick run-through of the dance group's charts—without the dancers—and then was herded to a stifling locker room where we changed into our tuxedos and ate food especially prepared for us: parched slabs of roast beef and all the Diet-Pepsi we could drink.

Instruments in hand, we filed behind dark velvet curtains onto a wide stage, and sat in three rows. The curtains opened, showering cakes of dust over the band as we purred tranquil melodies for elderly couples working their bargain-price, full-course dinners. The band, a mix of working professionals and players who gigged only on New Year's Eve, sounded like soft mush, perfectly capturing the faded ambiance of The Cedarwood. I scanned the worn art deco house—once a pinnacle of the Catskill glory days—and spied on the waitresses as they pranced from table to table. They were easily fifty years younger than most of their clientele, and soon I was hypnotized by their short skirts. Little by little, Wally's stories needled me on the bandstand.

It was the great paradox of my life—so afraid of losing my sanity I could never surrender to drugs, booze, or even Benadryl, yet in jazz I'd freely hurl myself into the void. It was no wonder Jimmy identified with my music. He seemed to live all the time out of control—his paintings, psychedelic shortcuts to his madness—which is why I was so glad to spend a couple of days in the mountains. But there I was, in an uncontrollable trance I could've never anticipated.

Under the exhausted direction of Conrad Bolvis, a stout, retirement-ready conductor with a veiny nose, the band maintained its dusty mush—nothing to rattle the dining audience. But medleys from between the World Wars weren't enough to erase Wally's stories or my inspired fantasies for every waitress at the hotel. When Conrad pointed to me to blow a solo in the middle of "Charmaine," my thoughts couldn't have been further removed from the tender 1920's waltz. What he wanted was Guy Lombardo. What I gave him was a freeform guttural wail like a cab slamming its brakes into a bus. It might've worked at The Out House, but Conrad turned a shade of red I'd never seen on a human being before. The sax players to my right and left yanked me down to my chair before I could finish the chorus.

Our audience looked stunned while they picked at their desserts. We played one more tune, and the curtains closed in front of us. The Millie Grace Swing Dancers were just off stage, stretching. Conrad approached me. Just walking up to me seemed like a challenge. "Shawn," he said, "that's your name, right?"

I nodded.

"What the hell were those goose sounds?" he said, his beady eyes almost tearing.

"My double E isn't quite—"

"Listen . . . " he said, swallowing, "you've got a big solo . . . starting the second number of the show." He swallowed again. "We didn't have time to rehearse it in the run-through. You got a couple minutes now; look it over. And . . . uh . . . this is a '40's swing show, you know, like Johnny Hodges, Duke Ellington?" He cleared his throat. "Please, no more farm animals or jungle screams, okay?"

I assured him it would be fine, and I examined the music: an a cappella, bluesy cadenza that propelled the rest of the band into "Sophisticated Lady."

As we waited behind the curtains, a few of the guys straightened their bowties while others adjusted reeds, and the old guy playing second tenor swigged from an airplane bottle. Wally sat beside the grand piano several feet to my left, and pored through his music while he scratched a side-burn. Conrad, in his massive tuxedo, stood in the fold of the piano, leafing through the score, anxiously marking notes.

To hell with the waitresses, I thought. Somehow I'd landed the lead alto part—front and center of the band—and I had to collect myself, and fast. Jimmy would've loved my "Charmaine" solo, but the conductor and most of the band now thought I was out of my mind. It was a fluke, and I blamed Wally Gonfman for it.

The percussionist pounded on the timpani. The curtains opened as the rhythm section snapped an uptempo, swinging vamp, and I counted my measures of rest. I could feel it; I was climbing back into the music. I forced myself to count every beat—four beats to a bar, four bar phrases. The trombones wah-wahed, the trumpets bwopped. By the time the saxes entered in a bluesy swirl, my mind was with the band and free of Wally's curse.

Then six girls flew onto the stage. Their sparse threads glittered as they kicked and twirled their bare legs, flinging and being flung by their male counterparts. Six Elsie Slingerlands jitterbugged right in front of me. How could I play? Conrad, sweating and waving his baton, signaled for me to play louder; he couldn't hear me.

My solo was moments away, and the dancers and Wally's curse had nearly taken me over. Discipline, discipline, I thought.

We ended the overture, and the audience erupted. I turned the page, ready for my cadenza. But the Millie Grace Swing Dancers bowed. *Bowed.* From an arm's length I faced the most sculpted, nearly-g-stringed female rears ever created.

Conrad looked nervous. I could tell he wasn't sure I would play the cadenza. He was waiting for the applause to fade, his arm propped high above his head, his baton trembling in the air, about to drop the downbeat for my solo. I had only seconds to get control of myself. I tried to think of anything but sex. I studied the ancient audience but I couldn't look past the waitresses. I conjured the Bells and their friends, but that looped around to Henry and his filthy jokes, which led straight to the bowing dancers. I was worthless. Desperate, I thought of the one thing so insane it could never lead back to a human reality: Jimmy's gold-blob-saxophone painting.

I remembered it surprisingly well, so well that once again I could feel myself holding the gold blob that seemed to be my saxophone. Conrad dropped his arm. I couldn't make a sound.

There were two of me: one in a daze, sitting in front of a fat, panicking conductor, and another with a glowing alto in my arms, shooting up through the searing spotlights and musty rafters into the frozen starlit sky. While I could still hear the silence in the dim hall and see the dancers waiting offstage for my solo, I rocketed through the dark mountain air, holding the gold blob from Jimmy's painting. It felt more like my instrument than my alto ever did. I heard Conrad yell, "Play," but I didn't know which one of me should do it. I had never been split in two before. I wondered, What if we tried to play at the same time, would it be together? The part of me that floated above the clouds, far from gigs and girls, and much more confident than the one paralyzed on the stage, played, and it sounded to my ear remarkably smooth. It was effortless. The band entered and the dancers jazz-stepped back onto the stage.

I played with wild abandon. For the rest of the evening I alternated between the two of me, between the night sky and the low music stand. I missed key signatures, botched entrances, was largely out of control, and yet, I reveled in every note I played. I'd traded one spell for another.

After "Auld Lang Syne" and a few fox trots the gig was over and I collapsed in my hotel room, still shifting between the sky and the mildewy sheets. I recovered in the morning, hid from Wally, and begged a ride with the drummer.

JIMMY HAD the talent to create images that could somehow take over my mind. He could play with my sense of reality and he found the game hilarious. Any more of these diabolical paintings, I decided, and I'd quit the job. Then a solution came to me, so elegant, so easy, I couldn't believe I hadn't thought of it sooner.

On Sunday, January 2nd, I trudged down Denwood Street through high winds and flurries, ready for his next monster. I'd practiced my new technique all morning. Jimmy stood grinning by the fireplace, pointing up to his blue-blob-and-black-shadow nightmare. I blurred my eyes, half crossing them, and gave it a long, thoughtful gaze.

"Yes, Jimmy," I said. "I'm glad to see it there." His grin dissolved.

I played until he stopped me—about forty minutes. "I have another one I need to show you right now, Mr. Shawn Lewis," he said, and galloped to his room.

He returned with an oversized canvas, and stood the new painting directly in front of me—some new agony, I was sure. "You have to look at it, Mr. Shawn Lewis," he said. "You can't look away, you can't tell me—"

"Fine, Jimmy," I said, blurring. "I'm looking at it and it's very nice."

He kept holding the canvas. "Don't you see it?" he said. "Don't you see it?"

"Sure. It's very nice."

He took the painting back to his room and stayed in there until dinnertime.

The next day Jimmy greeted me with the same painting. "I fixed it, Mr. Shawn Lewis; I definitely fixed it. It's much better. Try it now."

"It's nice," I said. "I liked it before, but now perhaps it's even better."

"But, but, don't you see the field of blue soaring up through the ground?"

"I guess so, I'm not sure . . . Yes, I suppose when you put it that way I do see it. It's nice."

He left for his room. An hour later he returned with another painting. They were paying me to play or otherwise encourage Jimmy, so it didn't matter to me if he came or went. I had a book to read or I simply practiced. The new painting was no worse than any of the others, now that I was trained to blur.

"Good job, Jimmy," I said. "It's really coming along."

"But don't you see the lights? The dazzling lights?"

"Yes, nice job."

"You have to take this one home to where you live so very far away so you can see what I can see, Mr. Shawn Lewis. Indeed, you have to, you have to."

"Certainly. And I know just where to put it."

That cheered Jimmy, and our session was very pleasant after that. Of course, once I got three blocks from the apartment, checking to make sure I wasn't followed, I broke it in half, and stuffed it in a trashcan.

For weeks Jimmy gave me one new painting after another. I blurred my way to relative peace and harmony, throwing out the ones he insisted

I take. And Arnie, Sarah, Henry and all their friends were delighted with my new attitude. But Jimmy's frustration was growing.

By the end of February the Bells had replaced in their living room a third of Jimmy's paintings with the ones he'd made for me. I'd become adept at blurring anytime I picked my head up above the music stand. Sure, soon I'd have to get my eyes checked—the blur was starting to take—but Jimmy stopped making paintings for me, or at least, stopped showing them to me.

"I'm sorry, Mr. Shawn Lewis," he said. "I can't paint for you anymore."

"Really?" I said. "That's a shame."

"Yes it is, yes it very much is. My TD is so bad it gets in the way of everything. It must be getting in the way because you just keep telling me my paintings are nice when they're much more than nice. They are the worlds, and much more than nice. But my arms shake and maybe my painting shakes and you can't see what I can see."

"Well," I said, "maybe now we can just focus on the music."

"Yes, but I'll keep practicing even with the shakes, so I can give you paintings that show you the worlds."

"Sure, good, you do that."

"Because then you won't want to throw them all away."

It had to be a figure of speech, I told myself. But I felt a chill just the same.

CHAPTER 11

Kitsmeh

JUST BECAUSE I played solo sax five times a week for a crazy person in his apartment didn't mean I'd abandoned my goal to be a normal working class jazzer. I was only on a slight detour. Yet now all the Bells' friends were scouting nearby apartments for me. On March 1st, Arnie's seventy-sixth birthday, he and Sarah invited me to move in. "You're family now, yes?" Arnie said. "You sleep in the living room. I sleep good on that couch in front of the Mets." I couldn't do it. I couldn't chain myself to a seniors club in the boondocks, my fortunes linked to a jellybean-ranting lunatic.

When Sarah and Goldie set the table for Arnie's small birthday party, Goldie squeezed me next to her granddaughter Irene. While we wolfed buckets of Chinese food—Arnie's favorite—I didn't mind that Irene's left leg and bare arm kept rubbing against me. She was in her twenties, had long, straight black hair, and a generous shape. She didn't speak, except to make soft giggles that never quite stopped.

"Soooo," Goldie said to Henry, "don't they look nice together . . ?"

"Nice, shmice," Henry said. "The sax player's worked up like he hasn't sat next to a woman in years."

Irene giggled.

"It's my Ireeeene," Goldie said. "She's got a smart head on her shoulders."

"That's not what I meant," Henry said.

Irene giggled.

When we got to the fortune cookies Jimmy abruptly stood up, his arms shaking, and announced, "Thank you for a most divine dinner indeed, I go to my room. Mr. Shawn Lewis, will I expect you at three tomorrow?"

I nodded.

"Stay with your old man," Arnie said. "Birtday cake is coming. Stay."

"I will return when the noise is gone," Jimmy said, glancing at Goldie. "When the noise is gone I'll have cake, but for now, I have to write or maybe mom's maple cookies or a lovely *Twilight Zone* or some Fig Newtons."

Jimmy left, and Sarah unveiled her homemade dark chocolate cake with one tiny candle in the center. Henry pointed to the candle, whispering in Arnie's ear. Arnie belly-laughed, then whispered back into Henry's ear.

"Yes, Arnie," Henry laughed, "'*oyf tsonveytung.*' Arnie's favorite Yiddish curse: 'All the man's teeth should fall out except one . . . and that one should hurt.'" We all laughed except Goldie, who didn't get it. Arnie laughed so hard he broke into a coughing fit.

It was time for presents. Arnie tore through the wrapping papers like a little boy. Henry's gift, a deluxe heating pad, moved Arnie to tears. Goldie's gift was a green rugby shirt with fat yellow stripes, destined for the Goodwill box. After Arnie opened Sarah's gift, a handcrafted wood cane, the two embraced for a long moment. Irene giggled. I gave Arnie two caps—uncertain of his allegiance—one Yankees, one Mets.

"What," he said, laughing, "no Brooklyn Dodgers?" Then he hugged me with a firm hold—and fresh tears. "Tank you. Tank you for all you done for my Jimmy."

When the party was over I asked Irene if she'd like to go for a brief walk. She muttered Yes, and it wasn't until we'd left the building that I heard her real voice.

"Soooo, you play the saxophone . . ?" She talked just like her grandmother, only an octave higher.

I nodded, my jaw dropping. "Uh . . . " I said, "I have very little time. You should lead the way—I don't know this neighborhood—but just a block or two."

"Soooo, would you like to see where I work . . ?"

"Well, I guess, maybe, I don't know, if it's not too far."

She talked so slowly I found myself finishing her sentences for her. We stopped in front of an elementary school where she taught kindergarten. She said her apartment was a block away. "Do you want to see it . . ?"

"Sure, but then I've really got to get back."

Her one-bedroom, with her toy stuffed animal collection, Winnie the Pooh fixtures and orange shag carpet, looked like Goldie had decorated it. When Irene left for the kitchen, I sat on the plastic-covered sofa, wondering why the hell was I there. When she strolled back with the tray of tall Cokes and sliced Twinkies, her huge breasts nearly waggling out of her black silk suit, I knew exactly why I was there.

She sat next to me on the sofa, chatting about her love for big hats or miniature dolls or something, but I couldn't take the voice another minute, so I kissed her. She threw me down on the sofa, piling on top of me, kissing and kissing without stopping to breathe. I was willing to suffocate.

Though Irene had few friends and rarely ventured out of Sheepshead Bay, she knew plenty. I don't remember how we wound up naked writhing on her bedsheets but there we were, two desperately lonely people, her plump, creamy flesh enveloping me in the flood of our overdue, unpaid passion. We devoured each other. And then we lay still, exhausted—saturated in her strawberry rose perfume.

"I'd better get back to the Bells," I said, straining my head to see where my clothes had gone. "I've got to get my saxophone before I go home."

"Soooo, I'll be seeing you tomorrow . . ?" she said, sitting up, her straight hair now at all angles.

"Sure," I said, crawling out of the bed, trying to put myself together.

"And then you'll see me whenever you play for Jimmy?"

"I . . . guess so." For Irene my obligations were just beginning.

When I returned to the Bells it was 10:30, and Arnie and Jimmy had already gone to bed. "Henry and Goldie left well over an hour ago," Sarah said.

"I would've come back sooner for my things," I said, "but Irene and I went for a very long walk. She's a real talker."

"Yes, I can see that," Sarah said, lifting one eyebrow.

"Well, she wanted to know all about the music business, stuff like that."

"Hmmm . . . You smell just like her perfume."

As I opened the door to leave, Jimmy popped out of his room in his red T-shirt and red pajama pants, holding one of his scrawled-up notebooks, chocolate icing pasted to his beard and shirt. "Is it three already?" he said.

"No, Jimmy," I said. "That's tomorrow. It's 10:30, the night before."

"Tomorrow? Because I want to show you that I now know what I need to practice so that you will see the things that I can see in my paintings. I now know."

"Good, Jimmy. Good work."

"I need to paint bridges."

"Okay, sure," I said, "you do that."

"With the proper bridges you will be able to cross over."

THE NEXT DAY Sarah and Arnie were out shopping—Jimmy and I were alone. He was unusually jolly, often interrupting my music to rave about his bridges and worlds.

Then the door rang—it was Irene. "Don't mind me," she said to us. "I just came to listen. You won't know I'm here . . ." She dragged a chair next to me. I played one of my favorite bossa novas, but Jimmy had receded into himself or joined one of his special friends; I couldn't tell the difference.

"Did you like that tune?" I asked Irene.

"I don't really like jazz," she said. "Don't mind me; I'm not here." She inched closer, kissing my cheek and giggling. Jimmy closed his eyes and began to mumble.

"Irene," I said, "this isn't the best time."

"I'm sorry," she said. "I'm just so glad we found each other. Aren't you?" She nibbled at my neck.

Jimmy leaned back in his chair, mumbling at the ceiling.

"Soooo," she said, "tonight you'll stay over?"

"Well, I've got early teaching tomorrow, unbelievably early, then I have a rehearsal. The Canarsie Senior Center is doing *Hair*."

"You'll stay over," she said. "There's so much I want us to . . . talk about."

Just then, I heard low voices and the jingling of keys. Arnie, in his new Yankee cap, marched in first, followed by Sarah, Henry and Goldie. I didn't know about my mussed hair or the lipstick on my face.

While Irene and Goldie slow-talked at each other, Henry scooted over to me. "I understand things went very well last night, huh?" he said, winking.

"It was a nice birthday party," I said.

He handed me a handkerchief and murmured: "Son, wipe off the lipstick."

I wiped feverishly as Sarah came over. "I guess I can't leave you here alone anymore," she said.

In the commotion Jimmy had gone to his room, and though I kept playing, he wouldn't come out.

I skipped the dinner with the Bells that night; Irene wanted to eat out. I took my instrument this time, and it was a good thing I did. She changed the plan, offering instead, a home-cooked meal. But once we entered her apartment we forgot ourselves, and it was hours before we ordered in, too drained to cook.

Over dinner I suggested we be careful not to let our thing interfere with Jimmy's progress. And perhaps, I told her, maybe we shouldn't see each other *every* time I come to Sheepshead Bay. My feeble retreat had no chance against her soft giggles and juicy form, and I wound up spending the night.

It was a long night, and in my enthusiasm to keep going with the only thing we could do together, I made myself agreeable, too agreeable. It was the least insulting way to end her slow sentences. She was a dedicated teacher, devoted to each of her kindergarten students. So was I, I told her, jumping in—though mine were private students, a few years older. She believed there was no greater gift one could give than unconditional love to children. Absolutely, I said, before she concluded the thought. And she wanted at least three or four of her own. Why not, I blurted. She was inclined to think I might make the perfect husband. Of course, I said.

I was an idiot, a simple machine of reflex. When Irene imagined how blissful it would be if we could spend every night like this together, I said, Certainly. This was Carole's fault. I still loved Carole; I would always love her, and the only way to lift the pain was in the arms of someone else. When Irene said she and I were "kismet," I said I couldn't agree more, though I had no clue what she meant. Apparently, lost in the primal haze of my grief and longing, there was one other thing I'd agreed to.

When Irene rang the doorbell during the next day's session, Sarah took charge. "Young lady," Sarah said, "it's best you don't come around while Shawn is performing. This may look like foolishness to you, dear, but this work is serious."

"Oh, Mrs. Bell," she said, "you don't understand. Shawn and I are engaged."

"What?" Sarah said.

"What?" I said, yanking the saxophone from my mouth.

"We're in love," Irene said.

"Is this true?" Sarah asked me.

"Uh, I . . . What?"

"Do your mother and grandmother know about this?" Sarah asked Irene.

"Oh sure," Irene said. "I told everybody. They're on their way over."

Jimmy lurched up from his chair across from me, and without a word, tramped into his room.

"Don't you think you should get to know each other better?" Sarah said.

"What are you talking about?" I mumbled to Irene.

Irene put her hand on my shoulder. "We agree on everything," she said to Sarah. "We even agreed that there was no point in waiting."

"Uh, I . . . No," I said, shaking my head.

"Soooo, what's a matter, Shawnsy?" Irene said. "Remember? Kismet? Last night you were so sweet. You were just as certain as I was."

"Is this true, Shawn?" Sarah asked. "Did you propose last night?"

"I don't . . . "

"Oh, it's true," Irene said. "We think so alike—even that our kismet means we shouldn't wait."

"Love at first sight," Sarah said. "It's so romantic. Just like Arnie and me. The moment I met Arnie I knew." Her eyes welled. "My darlings, mazel tov. When's the date?"

"We haven't set a date yet," Irene said.

"What is kitsmeh?" I asked, my soft voice cracking.

"Arnie!" Sarah shouted. "Come out. Shawn and Irene are getting married!"

"Kismet," Irene said to me. "You said you couldn't agree more."

"Arnie!" Sarah shouted. "We have to celebrate!"

"Irene," I said, trying to make my voice firm. "We're not getting married. We've known each other three days."

Arnie now entered, still wearing his Yankee cap. "What?" he said. "You *not* getting married?"

"No," I said.

"Why'd you make me come out here?" he said. "And in the middle of *Oprah.*"

"Soooo," Irene said to me, "what about last night?"

"What is kipsmeh, anyway?" I said.

"Kismet," she said. "Fate—soulmates. Forever and ever, Shawnsy."

Sarah left for the kitchen while Irene recounted everything I'd agreed to in alarming detail.

That wasn't *me* agreeing, I wanted to tell her. That was a shell of me. Blame Carole.

Instead I said, "I didn't know what I was saying. It was instinct. I'm sorry."

"Oh," she said, "don't be sorry. It was my instinct too."

The guests started arriving. First, it was Henry and Goldie. Then it was a handful of Goldie's closest friends, Irene's mother, Irene's mother's friends, and Henry's poker friends, and everyone wanted to meet the groom.

"Son, take it from me," Henry said, "give yourself time. What's the rush?"

"Everybody's confused, Henry," I said. "I'm not rushing into this."

"You don't call this is a rush? You kids today think you know everything, but—"

I excused myself, and wriggled through the crowd, desperate to find Irene or Sarah, when Frances Pinklestein grabbed my arm.

"Congratulations!" she shouted over the noise. "When's the date?"

"No date. We're not getting married."

"Irene's a doll, isn't she?"

"Yes, but we're not—"

"Say, when you going take a look at my niece, Louise? Yesterday she let out the neighbor's dog, yelling 'run, Toto, run!' It's enough already with the braids, the apron dress, the puddles—"

"Wait—puddles?"

"Well, you scold her and you get a bucket of water on your head while she's screaming, 'Ding dong, the witch is dead, the witch is—"

"I'll let you know when my schedule clears up," I said, and wriggled further into the crowd.

I found Irene but got caught between her, her mother, and Goldie in a slow-talking analysis of temples, caterers, and halls.

Irene's mother paused to splatter a kiss on my cheek, then continued: "If we're going to get Avi's to do the food," she said to the other two, "we've got to book early."

"This is all a mistake," I said, interjecting. "Irene, tell them it's a mistake."

"Soooo," Goldie said to me, "what's wrong with Avi's?"

"Avi's Caterers," Irene's mother said to me. "*Everybody* uses them. Look, what does he know?" she said to Goldie. "He lives in the Bronx."

"Tell them, Irene," I said. "Tell them we're not getting married."

"Drinks for everyone!" Sarah shouted, as she and Arnie worked the crowd with trays of champagne. Someone handed glasses to Irene and me, and Henry pushed people out of the way so he could take pictures of the happy couple.

Irene's mother made a gushy toast—something about kismet and the two darlings living together around the corner. The room broke out in cheers.

"We're not getting married!" I yelled like the building was on fire.

Everyone stopped.

"Soooo," Irene said softly, "we can still celebrate, can't we? We'll live together first. It'll be perfect. You don't blow your sax that much, do you Shawnsy?"

"Irene, I play all the time. I play avant-garde, wild free jazz. It's really loud. Everybody hates it. I can't help it, it's what I hear. And also . . . I'm still in love with my ex-girlfriend."

At that moment Jimmy sprung from his room, pushing through the crowd to Sarah. "But I want Mr. Shawn Lewis to play sax for me," he barked, "and all they do is make a lot of noise and they don't know anything. They don't know *anything*!"

Never before had he made so much sense.

"They're here to celebrate Shawn's engagement, Jimmy," Sarah said.

"They all go," he said. "Right now. She makes the wrong lights for Mr. Shawn Lewis." Then he turned to the crowd and waved his arms, "Everyone gets out! Everyone gets out!"

Sarah begged them to stay, but people hurried for the door.

"I'm sorry," I said to Irene, in front of her mother and Goldie.

Irene looked bewildered. Her mother snarled, "You lied to my daughter."

"Gets out!" Jimmy shouted.

"Jimmy stop it," Sarah said. "Please stay! He doesn't mean it!"

Before Irene could say anything, her mother and Goldie, grumbling about liars and lunatics, whisked her out of the apartment.

"Good job," Henry murmured. "Next time date a while before you propose."

In just five minutes the apartment cleared. Jimmy was waiting for me by the fireplace. "I know why you like her so very much," he said, "but not her, Mr. Shawn Lewis. Not her. Her lights are not the right lights for you."

It was impossible to take advice from my mental-patient friend too seriously. "What lights?" I said. "And Jimmy, how would you know? Have you ever had a girlfriend?" I didn't mean to sound so heartless, and I wished I could take back the words.

"I know you think I have no friends," he said, his eyes tearing, "but I have a lot of friends, Mr. Shawn Lewis, a lot of friends. Friends everywhere."

"Of course, Jimmy, I understand."

"You say that, but you don't understand. I wanted to show you in my paintings, then you would understand. Then you would see the worlds. I have many girlfriends, but they . . . they live in the fourth and fifth worlds."

"Okay, sure . . . Anyway, you're right about Irene. But how did you know?"

"I can see it," he said. "You are each lost in your sex power before you have found your other powers, but when you each find your other powers you would be so different from each other, she would drown you."

Jimmy almost sounded profound, and just as I was gaining a new respect for him, he straightened his back, closed his eyes, cocked his head to one side, and hollered, "Oh, let us fly tonight! Together, we'll get the gripes!"

CHAPTER 12

The Right Lights

I NEEDED TO TALK face-to-face with Irene, but I couldn't tell her I'd only agreed with her so much to stop her never-ending sentences. Of course, seeing her alone could lead to her apartment and another engagement bash at the Bells. In my two days off from Sheepshead Bay I phoned four times—four withering conversations—the last one ending with her calling me a lizard.

That evening the Mendez kids were upstairs blitzing their armies, and I barely heard the call from Carole.

"I'm so glad I got you in," she said.

"Carole?" It had been six months since we'd spoken—the lunch at Peppers—and she thought she didn't have to say who it was. She was right. She chatted about her new neighbors and the rainy weather while I held my breath, waiting for the favor—like watering her plants or helping her move in with Mark.

"I've been thinking," she said. "I can't stand how we left things. I'm worried about you. Can't we see each other without it being—you know, serious. I mean, I don't want us to go out on the town or anything, but, well, do you want to just keep things as they are or—?"

"I didn't hear that—there's a lot of pounding from the floor above me. Did you say you're going out of town and you want me to keep some things in my apartment?"

"Shawn," she yelled, *"do you want to see me at all?"*

"You mean . . . get back together?"

"No . . . not exactly."

"Are you still seeing Mark?"

She sighed. ". . . Yes, but it's—well, I can't end it. I'm not sure what I want—it's a problem."

A huge problem. "If I were a success," I said, "we'd be together, wouldn't we?"

"You *are* a success. You're making the music you want to make. You're doing what you want. And you're still my serene and easy Shawn."

"Well, you want a family," I said, "and you don't want to starve and duck bullets and—"

"I'm not sure about the family anymore. I miss you. Can we get together, just . . . keep it slow. I'm dying to see how your music is helping the schizophrenic. Can I come watch you with that family in Sheepshead Bay?"

"Sure. But Jimmy . . . He's very odd, very shy. For two months all I heard out of him was gibberish. He could hide in his room the whole time you're there." I didn't mention Irene.

I CALLED SARAH for permission to bring Carole, promising my best behavior. Sarah said she'd stick around just in case.

I met Carole a few minutes before three, outside the building. It was drizzling, and though she wore a full-length raincoat and hat, she looked as stunning to me as the day we'd met. Her pull-away hug left no doubt she meant it when she said Slow.

As we entered the building, Jimmy was already waiting in the hall. He hugged me too, but unfortunately it wasn't a pull-away, and my shirt was now smeared with the mysterious goo that dripped from his beard down to his red socks. Sarah welcomed Carole, taking her coat, and Jimmy stood close by, studying Carole, scanning all around her.

"It is so nice to meet you," Sarah said. "Shawn talks so much about you."

Carole squinted at me, half-smiling.

"All *good* things," I said. "Really. I never talked about how you broke up—"

"Wild paintings," Carole said, surveying the walls. "By anyone I should know?"

"Perhaps," Sarah said. "He's famous around here." Sarah smiled at Jimmy.

"Wow," Carole said. "You did all these?" She seemed genuinely impressed.

Jimmy nodded, breaking into his gaping yellow-toothed grin. "May I call you Miss Carole Bonner," he said, "or Miss Ceebeeceebee or Miss Kettilux or—"

"Carole is good."

We all sat by the fireplace, and I couldn't resist playing my latest original, "Mark the Dashing Turdball." I closed my eyes and played—I could still get thrown by Jimmy's antics—and when I finished the tune, he was standing, his chair flipped over, his arms high above his head. He'd been dancing. Carole was riveted.

Jimmy held back his monologues this time, listening and dancing with one eye on Carole, who sat quietly, respectfully, the entire session. In the middle of "I'm in the Mood for Love" Jimmy arched his back and mumbled at the ceiling. No matter what he did, Carole exuded kindness, not a trace of judgment.

After the session she marveled at Jimmy's blue-blob-and-black-shadow hell world, the painting above the fireplace. "I really like this one," she said. "Jimmy, when you were making this, what were you feeling?"

"It was my gift for Mr. Shawn Lewis," Jimmy said, as they stood in front of it, his mouth twitching. "It didn't work because my TD shook it too many times."

"I've noticed your arms shaking," she said. "*I* think the painting's beautiful."

"Yes, it's nice," I said, blurring at it.

"It's important you take your meds for your TD," she said to Jimmy, "but did you know there are breathing exercises that could help?"

"Exercise breathings?" he said. "Dad makes me exercise arms and legs."

Carole guided Jimmy back to his chair, the goo still in his beard and clothes, his mouth still twitching, his swollen, dark eyes staring at her as she gently, patiently taught him the exercises.

She was perfect with him. I'll go slow, I thought. For her I would do anything.

THAT EVENING I skipped dinner with the Bells and escorted Carole five blocks to La Cucina di Bella. We found a secluded booth, and she bit her lip while she examined the menu, and I tried not to examine her. Her poufed brown hair was scattered from the wind and there was a new line under her big chestnut eyes. Her eyeliner was worn off on one side. She looked a little tired underneath her thin-framed glasses—the contacts must've been giving her problems again. But each flaw only added more depth to her fresh, pale beauty—her staggering beauty.

"It's great to see you again," I said.

"That was *so* interesting," she said, sipping a Merlot. "He reacts to every note you play."

"Except when he's talking to himself. Didn't he creep you out a little?"

"No, not really. I mean, I wouldn't want him sneaking up on me. He's like a big red whale with bulging eyes, but I see a lot of disfigured patients—with tics worse than his. I love that he's so *free*. He's his own creature."

"Okay, fine . . . But do you really like his paintings?"

"I do. They're very strange, but he is a schizophrenic, after all. Many of the best artists have been schizophrenics."

"So did my sax playing make you want to flee?"

"It's just that it's so 'out.' *You* taught me that word. And *you* taught me to love Bird and Cannonfield—"

"Cannonball."

"Right, Cannonball. Everything they played made so much sense."

"Was it as bad as at The Out House?"

"No," she said. "There were *four* of you playing your music then."

"Ouch."

"Please, I *love* that you're doing things your way. It's just that for me, Shawn, your music is . . . complicated. And weird, weirder than Jimmy's paintings. I'm just so glad you have this job. Believe it or not, I still worry about you."

Our waitress brought her chicken parmigiana and my seafood pasta. As we ate, Carole talked about Mark, the things she loved and hated about him. There was more hate than love, and my digestion went better with the hate. But she still wasn't ready to give him up.

"Can we *not* talk about Mark?" I said.

"Sorry."

"Unless there's more that you hate about him . . . "

"You were so cute," she said, smiling, "the way you closed your eyes and played that whole time. He loves it so much, but . . . what do you suppose his parents hope to achieve?"

"They think my music will stop him from talking to his imaginary friends."

"Hmm. I guess they don't know that schizophrenia is incurable. Isn't he on his medication?"

I told her the whole story, the years in asylums, the side effects, his relentless conferences. "Soooo," said an angry voice from above.

Shit, I thought, how did she find me?

"Who's this?" Irene said. Her mother stood next to her, glowering at me.

"Who what?" I said.

"You're shameful," Irene's mother said.

"Oh hi," I said. "I—uh . . . this is Carole. Carole, Irene."

"Soooo," Irene said, "You really *are* back with your ex—or is this a new one?"

"No," I said, "I mean . . . we're not *back* . . . exactly."

"My mother and I went for a walk," Irene said. "We watched you leave the Bells together. You were walking close together. I had to see who you left me for."

"Excuse me?" Carole said to her.

"You told me she was *history*," Irene said, raising her voice, pointing at Carole. "You lied to me. That's right, our first night together you said she was with some rich scumbag doctor."

"Shawn," Carole said, furrowing her eyebrows.

"I meant it in a *good* way," I said to Carole.

"Only five days ago we were planning a wedding," Irene said to Carole, as the waitress refilled our water glasses.

"You're nothing more than slime," Irene's mother said to me.

"He'll just do the same thing to you, you know," Irene said to Carole. "He's a predator." Irene stood with her hands on her hips.

Carole sat back and folded her arms, amused. "Have you been misbehaving?" she asked me.

"I don't know anymore," I said. Then I mumbled, "I should've known what the hell she meant by 'kismet.'"

"Well, don't worry," Carole said to Irene. "Shawn and I are close friends but we're not dating."

"Really?" Irene said. "In our last call he said you two were eloping to Nova Scotia. I knew it was another lie. You're history, then you're eloping? Believe *nothing* from him."

"Check, please!" I hollered.

"You lying lizard," Irene said, as they sped away.

Carole, arms folded and gloating, studied me without a word. I paid the bill. Then I played with the receipt. The more holes I could poke in it with my fork, the longer I could hide from Carole's gloat. "It's so uncanny," she said, chuckling. "Every time I get in a fight with Mark I tell him you and I are running off together."

AT EACH SESSION Jimmy wanted to know when Miss Carole Bonner would be coming back. "She has the right lights," he said. "The right lights that work with your lights. And she looks good."

"What lights?"

"I am making the paintings, Mr. Shawn Lewis, the paintings that will show you. I want Miss Carole Bonner to see them too."

One week later, after a full day on her feet at her Queens hospital, Carole would be joining us for the last half hour. Jimmy had worn his fanciest reds: new red sweatpants and a new red button-down long-sleeve each free of stains. He'd slicked down the loose hairs on the side of his head and removed the crumbs from his beard.

"I'm so glad Miss Carole Bonner is coming," he said, "because I made a painting I think she will like. I want her to come every day so she can look at my paintings."

"You have a crush on Carole, don't you?" I said.

"I'm not weak to my sex power like you. I want her to come here every day so we can talk about art and sit very close and she'll look at my paintings, and maybe I can touch her hair—"

"Right . . . " I said, as Sarah emerged from the kitchen, wearing her familiar cooking mittens.

"Shawn," she said, "there *must* be another girl you could introduce him to. All he talks about is your Miss Carole Bonner."

At five o'clock I was in the middle of my new blues, "She Left Me for an Asshole," when Jimmy rose and stood by the door. He moved into the hallway seconds before Carole entered the building. She responded to his monster hug with her classic pull-away. Then he showed her his latest paintings, occupying her the rest of the session with a tour of his works. She had no "problems" with any of his art.

I watched from a distance, amazed at the interaction—at Carole's unaffected encouragement and at Jimmy's easy, almost normal dialogue with a person he'd met only the week before. "Look," he said to her as they stood by a painting near the sofa, "in this one I make the blue lines merge with the bright yellow strands to pull you to the center of the galaxy where the orange spirals reveal the fiftieth link. I did the opposite with the one near the front door, where I pull you away from the center on the roller coaster of green and purple to take you to the Fourth Quadrant."

Jimmy led Carole into his room. I stood at the open doorway, and even from there, the smell was intolerable. He had a stack of paintings to show her, but he attempted another hug. Carole soon trotted past me, holding a kleenex over her nose and mouth. He tailed her with another painting in his hands.

"Jimmy," she said, coughing, "it might be time to have someone clean your room, maybe throw out your clothes, strip the carpets, start over."

"Mr. Shawn Lewis," he said, "I wish Miss Carole Bonner didn't live so very far away because I would really like to show her all my work and talk about my theories and maybe touch her hair—"

"That's another thing," she said to him, switching to her nurse-tone. "Watch out for the hands. I like the art, but I'm not okay with the grabbing, all right?"

The front door sprung open. "Fish weren't biting today," Henry said, hanging up his coat.

"We were hoping to add someting to Sarah's dinner," Arnie said, behind Henry.

After I introduced Henry to Carole, he quickly ushered me to the other side of the room. "Son," he said, in a low voice, "you have no idea the trouble you've started between Goldie and me."

"Because of Irene?" I said.

"Son, Goldie won't come here anymore. Says you're number one on her shit list. A 75-year-old woman who loves everybody started a shit list just for you. She says you not only reneged on the marriage but you're running around with your ex-girlfriend behind Irene's back."

"We never talked marriage—I'm almost positive. Anyway, we're through—I mean, she called me a lizard. Twice."

"Well," he said, leering at Carole while she and Jimmy discussed another painting, "I can see *why* you were . . . cheating on her . . . "

"Dinner's ready!" Sarah shouted from the dining table. In honor of Carole—though Carole wasn't Jewish—Sarah made the Bell family traditional meal: homemade chicken soup, kreplach, blintzes, potato latkes. Throughout the meal Carole never veered from her professional charm, even when Jimmy missed his plate, splattering sour cream over the tablecloth or when his arms shook and his knife hurled half a blintze through the air. And as Henry and Sarah and even Arnie peppered her with questions, she'd thank them for their interest—compliment them for their loving care of Jimmy. She was in control.

She and I hadn't had a chance to talk that night until we rode the subway together to the Village—the first leg of my trip back to the Bronx.

"You're astounding," I said to her.

"Why?" she said, her lips crimping toward a smile.

"The way you handle Jimmy—the way you handle everybody."

"It's not so astounding. I take care of everybody else—then I feel neglected."

"No, Carole, it's beautiful. You take care of people. It's what I love most about you. I just wish, you know, you thought a little more about *me*."

"Oh, I do," she said looking me in the eye. "I think about how with you . . . I can talk, I can relax, I can just be myself."

"Then . . . then why . . . "

"I think about how great it is that you love what you do," she said, now facing straight ahead, "that your music puts you in your own little paradise, and you dare the world to accept it. You're really brave. My dad loved his cello so much but he wasn't as brave."

"Then . . . then why don't—"

"The more I think about you, the more I worry. I worry about your music, your dreams, your bills, where it's all taking you . . . and I just want to run away."

CHAPTER 13

The Support Group

THE NEXT MORNING my friend Tommy Meehan called with the kind of news musicians wait a lifetime to hear. "I can get you on an in-town, open-ended gig," he said. "Six, maybe seven nights a week—starting the end of May." Our drummer friend, Gus DaLucci, had asked Tommy to help him assemble a band.

"Where?" I said.

"A new hotel wants a big band, can you believe it? In Midtown. They want us to play every night—ballroom dancing, variety shows, even jazz concerts."

"Wow."

"But before I remind Gus about you, I've got to know you'll be available. You'd have to give up playing for the nutcase."

"Completely?"

"Shawn, Gus says our days will be full with rehearsals or doing jingles plugging the hotel—for at least the first couple months. And they want us to cut an album. They're even talking about a fall tour. This is big, man. And since I'm recommending you, you can't show up fried from long commutes and psychos."

"I guess not."

"But you won't want your old gigs when you see the all-stars in this band. And the money's right, Shawn, but I'll let Gus fill you in on that.

You got two months to find a sub for the other thing. Do it, man. Don't look back."

My first thought was I could buy a car. But a gig like this could buy a whole lot more—like the future I'd given up on, the missing piece that brings me Carole.

I called her right away. She was excited for me, but not so excited she'd go away with me the next weekend to celebrate; she and Mark were still barely together. "How are you going to handle it with the Bells?" she said, changing the subject. "Don't you think they might feel, well, a little betrayed?"

"I wouldn't just drop them, Carole. I'd get them a player so great they'd forget all about me. A lot of musicians would love an easy job like theirs."

"But you yourself said it took months before Jimmy trusted you."

"And I'm the only one he ever saw with the jellybeans," I said.

"Jellybeans?"

"Never mind," I said. "You're right—this could be tough. From the end of May until August they'd have to do without me. After that I could drop by now and then."

"Do you think you'll have the energy? What about the tour?"

"I won't mention the tour. You know, this would be much easier if you were with me when I broke the news. Jimmy has a crush on you."

"I wish he didn't paw at me," she said. "Can't we just find him a girlfriend?"

"That's *it*. Sarah keeps bringing it up. Do you have any friends who'd—"

"Shawn, I was kidding. What Jimmy needs is a talented psychiatrist and a support group. If you like, I'll look into it."

"They've tried all that. He hates groups and won't talk to doctors."

"But you can't pass up a break like this one, Shawn. You've made it; you've finally made it. I'm so proud of you."

I'D PLANNED TO TELL them as soon as I arrived the next day, but when I saw the bustle of worried faces, I couldn't go through with it. Friends of the Bells streamed in and out of Apartment 1 the whole afternoon, carrying food, expressing sympathies and asking Sarah what they could do.

"The police were here," she said to me.

"What happened?" I said.

"Last night around 3 AM Arnie caught a burglar who'd cut his way through the front window."

"Is Arnie all right?"

"Not a scratch, but he nearly killed the burglar."

"Where is he?" I asked, unable to spot Arnie among all the neighbors milling around me.

"He's in our room. He told the police what they needed to know but now he won't talk to anyone and he won't come out. He hates violence, Shawn. In the movies it's one thing, but my Arnie—he can't . . . "

Henry came over and put his hand on Sarah's shoulder. "That's our Arnie," he said to me. "I'll bet you didn't think the old fogy had it in him."

"He must have heard the prowler in his sleep," she said.

"Then he went on automatic," Henry said to me.

"Automatic?" I said.

"I didn't even wake until it was over," she said.

"Burglar was a foot taller, fifty years younger," Henry said. "Arnie with that huge gut, surprised him, pinned him down, and just about twisted his damn head off."

"Incredible," I said.

"The cops think it was the same shmuck who's hit Sheepshead Bay three times this year alone," he said. "He had an M9 in his pocket."

"A what?"

"Nine-millimeter Beretta—fifteen rounds, accurate to fifty yards."

"A gun," Sarah said.

I didn't ask, but I wondered how it could be automatic for a fat seventy-six-year-old retired dry cleaner to sneak up on an armed prowler and crush him with his bare hands. And from a deep sleep.

Arnie refused to discuss the episode. It took a week and a half, but he gradually returned to his jovial self. Of course, in between it all I couldn't find a way to tell them my news.

WEDNESDAY, APRIL 5TH was Jimmy's fiftieth birthday, and I thought I'd found the ultimate present: a red polo shirt with red sweatpants, each double extra large. There were streamers and balloons, a "Happy Birthday,

Jimmy!" banner above the fireplace, and two dozen family friends, half of them bringing packages of red polo shirts with red sweatpants, double extra large.

Sarah had bought him a red silk robe—the kind Smokin' Joe Frazier might've worn—and Arnie had bought him a new set of paints. The only thing missing was Jimmy. All day they tried to lure him out of his room, and now the party hinged on my saxophone doing the job. After thirty minutes of blowing, he threw open his door, lumbered through the drink-spilling guests, and announced, "Mr. Shawn Lewis, it would be most agreeable if you would play sax in *my* room. I don't like these people. Indeed you'll now join me in my lovely room away from all the noise."

"I like it out here," I said. "Anyway, it's your *party*. These people love you; they brought you gifts."

"Love. Do people know what it is, Mr. Shawn Lewis? Do you know what it is?"

I didn't want to consider what he meant, so I just kept playing, and eventually he flopped down in the chair across from me. Everyone closed in with their gifts and Happy Birthdays, but he ignored them all. When Frances Pinklestein forced her way to the front, I stopped playing—I had an idea.

"Say Frances," I said, "how's Louise these days?"

"My niece?" she said. "When you going to take a look at her? Last week she started calling my sister's freezer her Tin Man. Now she's got everybody on needles because she says she intends to find him a heart."

"Oh, that's too bad . . . What do you think—could she be interested in somebody like Jimmy? Would they make a nice couple?"

"What, you kidding? My Louise and Jimmy? No no no. She's looking for a doctor or a lawyer. You couldn't get her near somebody unemployed like Jimmy."

I COULD THINK of only two ideal ways to part with the Bells: One, I could find someone else to play for Jimmy. This would require extensive auditions, with Jimmy deciding if anyone brought the jellybeans. It could take weeks, months, and he might choose no one. Or two, I could find him a girl. Sarah would love this option, and from the way Jimmy spoke about

Carole, I suspected a girlfriend who understood him could make him a lot happier than a daily fix of jazz, no matter whose it was. Of course, I didn't know where to begin to find someone compatible for the most peculiar person I'd ever known. Then it occurred to me.

"Wally Gonfman? Hi, it's Shawn Lewis. I'm calling to see if you could help me find a girl for a friend of mine. He's—well, he's kind of eccentric and unattractive and hates just about everybody. He's very attached to me—we're together almost every day—well, not *together*. We're straight. But I have to end it. Could we set him up with one of your ex-girlfriends? Hello? Wally?"

"What number you trying to reach?"

"Isn't this Wally Gonfman?"

". . . Maybe . . . I don't know anyone named Shonnal Oos."

"Shawn Lewis. You remember? New Year's Eve?"

"Which year?"

"Come on," I said, "you drove me to the gig and told me all about your . . . you know, all your affairs."

"Oh yeah! You're the bass player with that big rash. Did it clear up okay?"

"What? I'm a sax player. And I never had a—"

"Fine, a sax player. How's the rash—because if it's a herpes—"

"Forget the rash. I'm the one who played the atonal solo in 'Charmaine.'"

"Oh, man, that was *out*!" he said, squealing. "We never laughed so hard. It was like Sun Ra meets Paul Whiteman, like Dracula pounces on *The Waltons*, like—"

"Okay, you remember. You're the only guy I know with a list of hundreds of available ladies. I hate to bother you with this, but—"

"What's a matter, you can't get a date?"

"It's not for me; it's for my friend, I told you."

"Right, I get it," he said. "You know, everybody says it's for their friend. Hey, if you can't get a date, just admit it. You don't have to be ashamed—it happens. Own up to it, man."

"I would, but it's not for me. Look, do you know any soothing, intelligent, unattached women who are comfortable around big, sloppy messes? It's okay if they're psychotic. In fact, that would be a genuine plus."

"Man, you're into some kink."

"I keep telling you, it's not for me."

"Right . . ."

"It would be great if they lived in Brooklyn," I said.

"Okay, I'll check. I'll do it for you, for all the laughs you gave the rhythm section when you torpedoed 'Charmaine.'" Through the phone I heard the rapid clacking of his computer keyboard.

"Are looks important?" he said.

"Yes, but what counts is that she be open to the big, shy slob concept. He's an artist, if that helps."

More clacking. "What should she do for a living?"

"Doesn't matter."

"I'm running a search through three lists," he said. "'Brooklyn,' 'Desperate,' and 'Psychos' . . . Okay, I got two names."

"Are they intelligent?"

"Intelligent. I don't have a list for that."

"Are they soothing?"

"What do you mean 'soothing?' They'll soothe you, all right. Listen, the women I keep on file are pretty lonely. I'll give you names, but I want a full report."

"But it's for my friend."

"You just can't admit it, can you?"

The first one, Vicki from Ft. Greene, Wally called "an extreme sadomasochist. Lots of fun, but watch your back with this one." Maybe not. The second one looked promising: Mandy of Carroll Gardens "goes for hours without saying a word. Sees and hears voices." It was a little reckless—getting involved with Wally and his sordid lists—but everyone, especially Jimmy, would forgive my exit if I could make this work.

WE MET FOR COFFEE at Angelo's Diner in Carroll Gardens, at the booth nearest the entrance. Mandy Tarnov was fortyish, thin and very tall, and completely bought my line that Wally was in jail and I was his prison counselor reaching out on his behalf to apologize to one of the many women he'd mistreated.

She had nothing to say unless it was about Wally and what a sleazeball he was. So I did most of the talking, spicing my real life story with the heroic details on how I became a prison counselor in between my music gigs. I looked for a reaction when I described my favorite patient—who had nothing to do with my prison work—Jimmy Bell, and how he could see and hear the wildest things when I played my saxophone. But she just gazed at her coffee.

"Jimmy is becoming a good friend," I said. "He's an abstract painter—very prolific. And he's powerfully built. When you're around Jimmy you don't worry about muggers. And believe me when I tell you he's working very hard to lose the excess pounds. Sometimes he slides into his own world, but he's a great guy."

Silence.

"He just needs somebody to talk to," I said, "someone he can relate to."

Silence.

I was ready to give up, but when she lifted her eyes I saw a recognition, a gloom. I asked her out for dinner—for the following week.

MANDY CHOSE the Wellington House, the most expensive restaurant on the west side of Brooklyn. She wore a high skirt and slinky top, and over her filet mignon, potato leek casserole, and several vodka martinis, she let go a little, talking with a crisp, sexy Russian accent about being a secretary in Flatbush after the hardships of life in Omsk. But she quickly returned to her choice subject.

"Wally is despicable, you know," she said.

"Oh, I know," I said.

"I only agreed to see you because you said he felt so terrible about what he did to me."

"He does."

"You seem like an honest man." She batted her eyes a little.

"Speaking of honest men, that patient and friend of mine, Jimmy Bell, is an exceptionally honest man."

"Why do you say that?"

"Well," I said, "even though he sees things no one else can see, he doesn't try to hide it from anyone. Have you ever, you know . . . seen things?"

"What? Why?"

"Just asking."

"Did Wally tell you this about me? Did Wally tell you I was crazy?"

"No, of course not," I said, "just something to talk about. *I* experience things that no one else does."

"You do?"

"Sure, I'm convinced my neighbors are plotting against me. When I play jazz I'd swear I see the weirdest flashes out of the corner of my eye. And I always feel like there's a much bigger audience listening to me than the one that's there."

"I used to hear voices," she said. "I thought I saw people following me too. It was terrible, but I'm all right now."

"I didn't mean to pry; it's just that I'm worried about Jimmy. I'm his only friend. He needs more friends."

"Does he take his meds? Make sure he takes his meds."

"Medicine doesn't seem to help him," I said.

"It's hard. He has to tell his doctor. They could try doses and combinations."

"I think Jimmy would really like you. Would you care to meet him, see me play my saxophone for him?"

"I don't know," she said.

"I'll make it fun—I'll play whatever you want."

"I don't know."

"Here's the deal: Ever since I've been playing for him he's opened up, but now what he needs is to be understood."

Silence.

"He needs companionship," I said, "but more than that, he needs female companionship, and—"

"Is that why you asked me out? To be a girlfriend for your crazy friend?"

"Well, yes, but you don't have to *do* anything. Just meet him. Meet his parents; they're really wonder—"

"Did Wally put you up to this? Is this all a joke? Donate Mandy to your sick friend? Am I the piece of meat that gets tossed around?" She threw down her napkin.

"No, no. You come over, you listen to me play some music, you watch him dance a little, you have a nice dinner with his parents. All very tame.

Wait till you see his getup—very cute—he only wears red."

"So you're not even a counselor, are you? *Govno.* Wally and you have nice joke on Mandy, is that it?"

"No, you've got me all wrong—well, partially wrong. Just try it once. Jimmy's parents—everybody would be so appreciative, they'd welcome you right in—I mean gifts, loans, whatever you need. These people are very generous."

Then she stood up and yelled, "So you want a hooker for the sick, fat man who wears red, is that it?" Every head in the restaurant turned to face me.

"No, don't be ridiculous. And please, not so loud; come on, sit down."

"You get a hooker. *Govno*!" she screamed, and stormed out.

There would be no easy way to tell the Bells I was leaving.

ON MONDAY MORNING, April 17th, Gus DaLucci called to confirm the gig. The Royal Galloway Hotel, at 43rd and Sixth, after nine years in the making, would open on Friday, May 19th. It would be the first Manhattan hotel in decades to feature an in-house seventeen-piece jazz band backing up shows virtually every night. Wednesday, May 17th would be the first day of rehearsals. Gus hired me to play second alto to Freddie Cavanaugh. The other players were among the hottest names in town. I'd have never gotten in if it weren't for Tommy.

Gus talked like it was a gig that would run for years. The owner, Herndon Galloway, he said, was beyond loaded, and planned to make the hotel world famous for its luxury and cutting-edge entertainment. With all the jingles and extra rehearsals, the weekly pay could triple my current best.

First I'll buy the car, I thought, then I'll get a nice apartment in town—within a few years, a house in the suburbs. I'll finance my own band and make albums. And Carole would be there with me because she'd see I was right for her all along.

After the session that day I'd planned to finally give the Bells my news—it would have given them a month's notice—but it was Passover, and Sarah had cooked all day to prepare an authentic seder. They were in such a festive mood, once again I choked. Instead, I sent out probes.

"How would it be if now and then I skipped a week?" I said.

"An emergency we could work out," Arnie said.

"What if in a month I tapered it down a bit?" I said.

"That would be dreadful," Sarah said. "We're thinking of *adding* another day."

"Mr. Shawn Lewis," Jimmy said, "what about the bridges to the worlds? How will you see the bridges to the worlds if you don't see the new paintings I'm making for you? How will you cross over? When is Miss Carole Bonner coming back?"

"How about joining a support group, Jimmy?" I said. "Carole and I can pick one that's just right for you."

"No, no, no, no, no," he said, shaking his head from shoulder to shoulder.

"*You* are his support group," Sarah said.

I CHOKED AGAIN at the next session when before I could tell them, Henry dropped news of his own: He and Goldie were on the outs. "She's so anti-men now," he said. "Says we're all pigs. That or we're sissies. It doesn't help that her son-in-law bought a subscription to Gayboy."

"I guess she's still mad at me," I said.

"That reminds me," Henry said. "Irene had a message for you. Something about predatory lizards and how they sleep at night. She said you'd know what she meant."

I did know, and it threw me off—I couldn't break the news after that. I asked Henry if I could call him for some advice. That night and every day for the next week I dialed and re-dialed Henry's number with no answer and no machine.

I didn't see him at the Bells until the following Monday. Toward the end of the session, as I finished a somewhat screechy avant-garde solo—which Jimmy loved—Henry slipped me a five and said, "Play something sweet for an old man."

I played "I Let a Song Go Out of My Heart," and watched the now eighty-year-old retired Brooklyn power broker dance a slow, smooth jitterbug all by himself. When I finished, he applauded like I was the whole Duke Ellington Orchestra.

"Where have you been?" I asked Henry. "I've been calling every day, and—"

"Oh, I met a live wire named Lucille—only seventy." Then he put his hand over the side of his mouth and whispered, "Ain't been home much."

I coaxed him out of the apartment, down the hall, and onto the porch. I told him about the big band and that I hadn't yet mentioned it to the Bells.

"You can't take the job, son," Henry said.

"You're kidding, right?"

"I've never been more serious."

"But for the sake of the money alone, I have no choice—you can see that."

"Trouble is, son, Arnie and Sarah are counting on you. You can't leave them."

"But this job will help me launch a real career—a jazz career. I've been working for it forever, Henry."

"These are not ordinary people," he said.

"I know. Sarah was in the Philharmonic and Jimmy is . . . special, and—"

"I don't mean the boy. And Sarah's more than a fiddle player. Arnie's more than a fat old dry cleaner. A *whole* lot more. They have a story to tell, but it's up to them if they want you to know. Those two are not only my best friends, they're the best people I've ever known. Why do you think all the neighbors keep coming here?"

"I've been wondering about that."

"They're champions of life—I told you. Believe me, that boy was a suicidal loon—one of the worst—and they saved him, restored their family and made it look easy. Then Sarah discovered *you*. *You're* going to pull him out of his shell forever."

"Henry, there's no cure for schizophrenia—it's a fact. No one gets pulled out of that shell without continuous drugs and therapy.

"For most people, sure, sure. But if Sarah Bell says *you're* the drugs and therapy, that's good enough for me. Stick with them, follow through with her plan—whatever it is. They'll take care of you. Hell, the whole community will take care of you. Son, you can't walk out on them now."

CHAPTER 14

Heart

I HADN'T PRACTICED my horn all those years just to bait someone out of his room—or his delusions. But Henry had promised to tell the Bells my secret within days, if I didn't. I couldn't sleep that night. Tomorrow, I kept thinking. Regardless of birthdays or burglars, tomorrow I tell them everything.

On the gray morning of Tuesday, May 2nd, with my eyes half closed I taught five lessons at North Bronx Elementary before commuting to South Brooklyn. As I got off the B Train the clouds opened. Through the torrent, clutching my sax case I splashed down the stairs, then sprinted over the flooding sidewalk, past the shops and around the dog run, the small single homes, crossing the boulevard, then onto Denwood, washing up to the porch at 271. I sloshed down the short hall to Apartment 1 while Jimmy stood with the door open, watching me. He wouldn't let me pass without hugging—in spite of my soggy clothes—for a little too long.

"My, you're a sight," Sarah said. "Where's your umbrella?"

"I forgot it."

"You're soaked," she said. "Why I don't I get you a change of clothes? Jimmy has some—"

"No, no, please." The thought of his clothes against my body made my stomach turn. "Sorry about all the water," I said, observing the lake under my feet.

"I'll get you Arnie's beach towel," she said. "You can wrap yourself in it."

Arnie was stretched out on the sofa, snoring, his glasses and Yankee cap askew. She left for the towel, and with her back to me she said, "You're early."

"Yes," I said. "I need to . . . Before I play, there's something I need to—"

"I know, Mr. Shawn Lewis," Jimmy said.

Arnie's towel covered me twice around, as I sat on a stool by the front door.

Jimmy stared at me, motionless. Sarah dragged two upholstered chairs—one at a time—in front of my stool, and together they sat facing me.

"Let's wake Arnie," I said. "Arnie should hear this too."

"No, he needs his naps," she said. "Since the burglar."

"Oh, I'm sure," I said, drying my hair. "The guy did have a gun."

"That's not it," she said. "Arnie hasn't felt . . . The burglar's not going to make it; it's day-to-day. Arnie's our hero, but he can't stand to hurt anyone."

"Really . . . " I said. I needed to tell them already, but how do you segue from dying burglars to big bands?

"For all we know," she said, "he saved all our lives, but now he feels guilty."

I dove in: "I've been asked to play full-time at a Midtown hotel—The Royal Galloway—very fancy. I told them I'd do it. It starts in two weeks."

They each stared at me, silent.

"I can come back once in a while," I said, "if you still want me—and I'll bring Carole too."

Jimmy's eyes were tearing, and Sarah looked stunned.

"I'll come for the next two weeks," I said. "And maybe a day or two in August."

"I see," she said softly. "In a few months, if we're lucky, you'll drop in on us?"

"Yes," I said, "but for now, why don't we find a replacement?"

"Everybody wants you to play for them," Jimmy said, scratching his beard.

"Jimmy," she said, "musicians go wherever they're hired."

"I'm so glad you understand," I said. "I was up all night worrying."

"Worrying—why?" she said. "Because we gave you the best work you ever had? Because we welcomed you into our family? This is all the height of absurdity, isn't it?" she said, averting her eyes. "Whoever heard of playing saxophone to cure a schizophrenic?"

Her words hung in the air while I looked to Jimmy for help, but he'd already gone into one of his conferences, his head cocked to one side. I needed Arnie.

"Sarah," I said, "I've been told there is no cure for—"

"Ah, but what if there's *nothing* to cure? What if the things he sees and hears are really there?"

"Yes, yes, of course," Jimmy mumbled. "But did you talk to the Sheml? I'll be in Trob as soon as Sedgwick gives me the signal."

"Let's get Arnie!" I barked. Arnie was oblivious. How he'd ever heard the burglar was a mystery.

"We don't need you to cure Jimmy," she said. "We need you to *save* him."

"Excuse me?" I said, now drying my ears with a corner of the huge towel.

"Your music keeps him here," she said.

"Yes, I know," Jimmy mumbled, "but Mav is too proud to show him the gift."

"Each time you visit, Jimmy is more . . . Well, he's painting more, he's happy, he's talking to us. I want him to be independent one day, a man of respect. He has much to offer, much more than you know. Everyone thinks his mind is broken, but I tell you he's ahead of all of us."

"That's what I have been trying to say," Jimmy mumbled. "The jellybeans are very rare in this time field. The plarps have seen them too."

"His conferences are *real*," she said. "As real as anyone's. They're not just a jumble of misfiring synapses. There's nothing wrong with my Jimmy."

"Fine," I said, "then why do you need *me*?"

"Where is he right now?" she said. "How long will he stay there? He's not in our living room. Before you, he could disappear for days, even while he ate. What if he never came back?"

"So let's find someone great to play for him," I said. "We'll hold auditions."

"No, no," Jimmy mumbled. "The plarps can't deliver the message until they get back from the hunt."

"Impossible," she said, her eyes blazing. "You're the one. If you stop playing for him, something—one day something will upset him and he'll go away forever."

"Yes indeed indeed," Jimmy mumbled, his head still cocked. "But what should we do if we can't reach the Sheml and Mav never shows him the gift?"

"With our love and your music," she said, "he can go wherever he goes—but he'll *always* come back."

"I'll call Jimmy every morning. I'll play for him over the phone. Jimmy! Hey Jimmy! How about if I play for you over the phone?"

"It's up to Mr. Jula," he mumbled. "Mr. Jula could arrange it with the Sheml."

"He won't use the telephone," she said.

I should pretend to be a burglar, I thought; Arnie'd be here in a flash. I stood up, shook the water off the stool, then slammed it down, coughed, cleared my throat, and blew my nose. Arnie was stock-still. I sat back down.

"Turn down the job," Sarah said. "We'll make it worth your while."

"I appreciate that," I said, "but how could you match that kind of salary?"

"What makes you think they will either—for very long?" she said.

"They're sold out."

"We read the papers," she said. "That hotel has been under construction for years—labor disputes, bribes, kickbacks. The musicians will be the first to go when things get rough."

Jimmy straightened up and turned to face me, a tear rolling into his whiskers.

"Jimmy," I said, "how about if I play for you every day over the phone?"

"I don't like the phone, Mr. Shawn Lewis. I can't see the sounds."

"He's not going to leave us, Jimmy," Sarah said, stroking his arm while she looked at me. "We've come too far to have your jellybeans taken away. We'll pay you well," she said to me. "One more year, Shawn—one year, that's all it will take. After that, go play wherever you want."

"But Sarah," I said, "I don't know how to save anybody."

"Jimmy's talents are unlimited," she said. "His art is only a glimpse, Shawn. If he chose to help you, there's nothing you couldn't achieve. Isn't that right, Jimmy?"

"I'll paint for him the bridges to the worlds so he can—"

"Save him," she said to me. "Work with him, *learn* from him."

The Yankee cap fell off, and Arnie sat up. He stretched, yawned, straightened his glasses, and scratched his back. His saggy light blue pajamas clung to his potbelly as he trudged over to us, still scratching his back and yawning wide like a lion.

"Why the sour looks?" he said.

"Shawn wants to leave us for another job," Sarah said, staring at me.

"You *see*," he said to her. "How many times I tell you not to cut the grease? Fat is the flavor, the *flavor*. All of a sudden you cut everyting I like. No fat, no salt, no sugar. No *taste*. That's why the boy's leaving."

"It's not the food, Arnie," she said. "That fiasco in Midtown is hiring a band."

"You sure?" he said. "Because I been tinking of leaving. What if we always order in?" he asked me.

"It's not the food," I said. "I've never eaten so well."

"Even lately?" he said. "She cut out cake."

"Mr. Shawn Lewis has to play his sax very very far away," Jimmy said.

"I think we could match whatever they've offered you," she said. "But you'll have to earn it. You'll play here every day—twice a day."

"Listen to Sarah," Arnie said to me. "Very smart. One of the great musicians. You stay, we order in, we get back to the old desserts."

"Arnie, go in the kitchen. It's time I told him about, you know . . ."

"*No*," he said, waving his finger at her. "*No*. We agreed—it's too much, too much."

"It's time," she said.

"We *agreed*, Sarah, for *his* sake."

"He needs to know, Arnie dear," she said. "Jimmy, go with your father."

Arnie grumbled his way to the kitchen.

Jimmy started for his bedroom, then turned and said, "You'll play sax for me later, okay, Mr. Shawn Lewis?"

After Sarah took from me the damp beach towel, she gathered from her linen closet dry reinforcements. Then she directed me to the sofa. "This could take a while," she said. "Put these under you."

I squished onto the layers of towels on the pillowy sofa.

"Once you know our story," she said, settling into a leather armchair in front of me, "the miracle of Jimmy . . . the miracle of all of us, I know you'll want to stay."

"I've already taken the job," I said.

"We'd hoped to spare you this, Shawn, but you can't just push us aside. Like it or not, you're now family." She turned to look at the brick wall, at the paintings. "Jimmy was just a boy when I saw him do something no one else could do," she said. "It happened right here, forty years ago. But until two weeks ago I couldn't accept what I saw. It was—well, humanly impossible. Yet in the back of my mind I wanted to believe it, and each day that our boy sat in those institutions, I agonized: What if the only thing wrong with Jimmy is that he has powers no one has ever seen before?

"But you can't understand our angel unless you know how we raised him, and for that, I have to tell you about Arnie. How does a fat, old man wake out of a deep sleep, tackle a gun-toting burglar, and then nearly snap the man's neck in two?"

"I don't know," I said, shifting on the towels. I began to feel a chill under my sopping clothes. I was frustrated and spent. She seemed unreasonable. No one would've turned down the Galloway gig, to play solos in someone's apartment.

She told me Arnie's story. Arnald Lev Belitsker spent his childhood towing wood from the forest outside his town, Rezhnyky, in western Ukraine. The woods were his second home. Both his parents and older brother and most everyone he knew worked for the lumber mill in the center of town. When the Luftwaffe bombarded Rezhnyky on the morning of June 22nd, 1941, Arnie was deep in the forest, collecting wood. He was only seventeen. While German tanks were obliterating Rezhnyky, Arnie ran deeper into the woods. Within days the SS was paying mobs of Ukrainian men bread and vodka to hunt down the Jews, but Arnie knew exactly where to hide.

Over the months he came upon others escaping other towns, many of them families bringing stories of death-squads rounding up and shooting all the Jews. "My Arnie knew how to survive outdoors," Sarah said. "You see the way Arnie is—he's unflappable. He wins everybody over. He was the same way then, at seventeen. Everybody loved him. Even the people much older trusted him to be their leader. The Soviet Underground trusted him too, and taught them all how to be saboteurs. The Nazis slaughtered his family and all the remaining Jews of Rezhnyky, but for the next four years, 88 of Arnie's 127 partisans survived."

She said the Nazis couldn't tolerate Jews fighting back; it put the lie to the Master Race. Whole companies of Wehrmacht shifted from the Russian Front to the forests in the rear. The Underground, grateful for the diversion, smuggled guns and explosives to Arnie's partisans. Arnie had no choice but to become a killer. They all became stealth killers.

"The Nazis forced this on him," she said, "and now the thought of brutality makes him ill, not out of fear, but because he wants everyone to be his brother. He wants peace. We couldn't shout or raise a hand to Jimmy. Our child—born in Sheepshead Bay, America, would be *free*."

Sarah said Jimmy had been a shy but happy boy—with an uncanny knack for the violin. "He had the ability to play whatever he could hear," she said, "just like me. In my village I was *Di kishef-makherin fun musik*. The wizard of music."

She said Jimmy couldn't handle the stress of school or his schoolmates, but at home he was free to be as creative as he wanted, to paint or play the violin or do nothing at all. She paused, gazing at Jimmy's paintings.

"Teachers and principals were always calling," she said. "I never worried. Our boy was a virtuoso.

"Jimmy was still a child when the man from the Survivors Network came to tell me the Soviets had just released the records, the information I'd been requesting since the war had ended. The news about my violin teacher, my great mentor, Cezary Wiencek." Her eyes welled.

"Sarah, please," I said. "You don't have to put yourself through—"

"Cezary was so beloved," she said, "the founder and concertmaster of the Krakow Orchestra. He could've played anywhere but he stayed in Krakow for his orchestra and his students. He stayed true to his soul, Shawn, true to his soul."

She said Cezary had heard about the young wizard from the Durszka shtetl, the daughter of the cantor, the thirteen-year-old klezmer violinist with a cultivated ear—Sarah Topolowsky. He invited her to study with him, certain he was shaping a new talent for his orchestra. Cezary and Robynne Wiencek were in their sixties, their children long gone, proud Catholics welcoming a Jew into their home, an uncommon act at that time. And for her it was a huge risk to leave her parents and sisters for an eight-hour carriage ride to Krakow to live with her teacher. "That was the summer of '38," she said. "For one magical year I had lessons every other day with a world-class violinist. I learned more about music in that one year . . . Well, I got to hear his violin every day, even the concerto he was writing—his masterpiece tribute to Poland. Then the Germans came, and the lessons stopped forever—September 1st . . . 1939.

"For the next four years the Wienceks risked everything to hide me in their home. When word reached us that Durszka was no more, that my parents and sisters were gone . . . All I'd ever known and loved before Krakow was gone. Robynne and Cezary were now all I had."

She paused, looked at me, then back at the wall—the paintings—as though they gave her the strength to keep talking.

"Robynne caught pneumonia in the Fall of '43," she said. "She died in her bed. I soon lost touch with Cezary. After the war I contacted every agency I could to find him. The house was rubble and no one had information.

"On that June day in 1962 the man from the Survivors Network told me the Gestapo had arrested Cezary for being a courier in the Polish Resistance. They tortured him. He died just a few days after we'd been separated. You see, he'd stayed true to his soul right to the very end."

"Were you in the house when he was arrested?" I said.

"Cezary was like a father to me."

"Where did you go?"

"He never did finish his concerto," she said, gazing again at the paintings. "After the man from the Survivors Network left, I sat by the fireplace—too much to bear. Arnie was at his dry cleaners. Jimmy sat close by, his violin in his lap.

"I couldn't move; I could scarcely breathe, but Jimmy, twelve-year-old Jimmy, started laughing. What was so funny? I asked him, my eyes full of tears. Then I saw it. Until two weeks ago I'd believed what I saw that day was a mirage from tears. I'd doubted my heart—maybe Jimmy *is* a hopeless schizophrenic. But now I know what I saw was *real*. It lasted only seconds. I saw my teacher, Cezary—here, above the dining table." She turned and pointed. "He was hovering inside a glowing, yellowish field, playing his violin—his spectacular concerto as a solo, like he used to practice it, only better. It was perfect. But I didn't accept it—how could I? I didn't believe in such things. It quickly faded, but Jimmy, still laughing, picked up his violin, his eyes wild, and started playing toward the dining table right where I'd seen my teacher. The same concerto, Shawn. Jimmy played beautifully the same music, music from a ghost or a mirage or whatever it was, music that had vanished five years before he was born. It was violin mastery and it was impossible.

"I don't remember anything after that. When Arnie arrived from work he found me in the same chair, unable to move. He put me in the hospital, and they called it a nervous breakdown. Arnie told me he had to pry the violin out of Jimmy's hands while our boy conversed with a Cezary no one else could see. That's when the conferences began. And the medications. And the hospital stays—brief at first, but he never got 'better.' No drug or talk could stop Jimmy's secret friends from multiplying. The doctors put him in an institution. A few months later the TD shakes set in—a byproduct of the neuroleptic drugs. And his violin days were over.

"But Jimmy never doubted himself," she said. "His faith in our world was broken, yes, but no diagnosis or condemnation could break him away from his truth, his talents. Shawn, with your special help, we'll save him; we'll nurture those incredible talents. Do you understand now?"

"I'm sorry," I said. "It's all very sad, but—"

"Very well, follow me." She got up and walked over to the brick wall. I stood beside her as she examined a painting that had been there all along, a "safe" one: green and brown splatters. It took less time to paint this garbage, I thought, than we just spent looking at it.

"Jimmy made this for me eleven years ago," she said, "just weeks after we brought him home from the last hospital. Do you like it?"

"It's nice," I said.

She studied my eyes. "You only blur for the ones he paints for you."

"I don't blur . . . "

"This one wasn't meant for you; that's why you don't have to hide from it. I should've believed you when you said his paintings made you sick. They're very powerful. Two weeks ago I was looking at this one . . . and all at once I understood. I've told no one; only Jimmy knows. Shawn, this isn't a painting; it's a portal, a window to another realm. You see layers of green and brown, but I see my teacher Cezary Wiencek performing his concerto right now, just as he did above the dining table in 1962. Two weeks ago I saw this and burst into tears. Now I can look anytime and feel the exuberance my teacher had for music and life."

She glided along the wall, gazing into another one: sloppy multi-colored triangles. "Here," she said. "What do you see?"

"Triangles?"

"It's Durszka, not in form, but in feeling. The temple and the shops and homes are gone, but I see the Beskid Mountains, I hear the bustling carriages, the children laughing. I feel my home. How do you think Jimmy does this?"

"I don't know, but, are you sure you're not reading into it just a little?"

"I have to show you another one."

I followed as she strolled the length of the wall, toward the dining table.

Yellow streaks splashed across giant blue blobs. "This one is my favorite," she said. "Listen. Can you hear them?"

"Sorry?"

"My three sisters, my father and mother. Don't you hear them?"

"Well . . . uh . . ."

"Sometimes I see them too, but I have to be in a certain mood. The paintings have changed my life. I feel better than I have in years. Somehow, don't ask me how, Jimmy is the Albert Einstein of art and music. Now do you understand? Do you see why you must stay on, keep him returning to us, the rarest genius there ever was?"

"Uh, Sarah . . . the paintings he makes for me scare the crap out of me."

"All right," she said. "I have one last thing to show you. A genius like this shouldn't be alone in a room, Shawn. He was born to help our whole sad world." She rolled up the left sleeve of her white cotton sweater. For an entire year I'd never seen her frail forearms or the six blue numbers now searing into my eyes: 512378.

"Two days after Cezary had disappeared," she said, "the Gestapo came for me. In the middle of the night they tore up the house until they found my crawl space. Three hours later I was on a cattle car packed with other Jews on a one-way trip to Auschwitz/Birkenau. From that moment till fourteen months later when I was left for dead in the snows outside the camps, my life was worthless—but for one thing. One thing spared me from the gas chambers, the guards, Mengele's experiments. Can you guess what that one thing was?"

I shook my head.

"My violin. My violin was the only thing the Gestapo let me take from the house. It was *my* truth, the music in my soul that saved me. The women's camp orchestra had more than enough strings, but I was good enough that the SS made a place for me and my violin. While trainloads were marched into gas chambers, we played the victims' national anthems so they wouldn't suspect they were about to die—then Wagner and Strauss to entertain their murderers.

"By the time the Red Army was closing in, in January of '45, the guards rushed us out of the camp and through the blizzards. I could last only one day before passing out in the snow. This meant a bullet to the brain; they wanted no witnesses. But perhaps the SS guard liked the way I played Mozart—I'll never know. She fired twice into the snow, inches from my skull. I would've soon perished anyway if it hadn't been for the Jewish partisans trailing us just out of sight. It was a fairy tale, Shawn, my fairy tale. My prince was their leader—short, hairy, all beard and shoulders—Arnald Belitsker. My brave, young prince with the laughing eyes. After all the world had been through, no one else could've had such gentle, laughing eyes like those. They made me want to live. Now we squabble over everything—little things—but not a day passes that I don't look into those eyes, and remember my hero."

I thought I saw Jimmy emerge from his bedroom, but I couldn't turn away from Sarah.

"If you stay true to your highest nature," she said, "even in the depths of suffering a miracle comes. A hero with laughing eyes—or the birth of an angel. We're old now. Who knows how much longer we have? What will happen to Jimmy? Save him, Shawn, so the world will know his genius. Now do you understand?"

"Mr. Shawn Lewis!" he called from behind me. I turned around to face a canvas of yellow dots, pink stripes and black geometric shapes. My mind had been tumbling through the stark newsreels of concentration camps. And I forgot to blur.

The black trapezoid began to look like a piano. The other shapes then glommed into each other, taking human form. The form said, "Don't take the hotel gig, Shawn." The form was Wendell Rice, complete with thick bifocals and his false front tooth, and he was smiling at me from his Steinway.

"This one's better, isn't it, Mr. Shawn Lewis?" Jimmy said. "I made the right bridges, didn't I?"

"There's heart here, Shawn," Wendell said. "Can't put a price on heart."

For a moment I wasn't in Sheepshead Bay or Philadelphia or anywhere else I recognized. Wherever I was, I had to get out of there. I yanked my eyes away from the canvas, pain spiking through the top of my head.

"I really got it, didn't I?" Jimmy said, laughing with his knobby yellow teeth. "You see what I see, don't you?"

The pain was unbearable. "I have to go," I said. I staggered to my saxophone case, and there was Wendell sitting on top of it. I grabbed the case and lunged for the exit, and there was Wendell sitting on my wet stool in front of the door.

"How can you leave now?" Sarah said. "After all I've told you. Have you changed your mind? Are you coming tomorrow?"

"I'll call," I said. "I have to go."

"You have to take your painting, Mr. Shawn Lewis," Jimmy said. "Take your painting of your teacher." A teacher he'd never met or heard me speak about.

"I have to go." I barreled out of the apartment with Sarah trailing me down the hall.

"How can you leave now?" she said.

"I have to go," was all I could utter as I stumbled out of the building, and through the hard rain.

PART 2

CHAPTER 15

The Royal Galloway

FOR THREE DAYS it felt like someone was driving a nail through my skull. I didn't leave the apartment, let alone teach, or play for the Bells. Anyone else would've run to their doctor, but I knew the cause: Jimmy's haunted paintings. Something had sprung out of Jimmy's stripes and dots, but I refused to believe the ghost of my esteemed jazz teacher was chained to a canvas in South Brooklyn.

I wanted to call Sarah and Arnie but what would I say? Her dramatic appeals had sapped me of all reason. And I was furious with Jimmy for swooping in with a new hell world before I could remember to blur. Fortunately, the headache was just starting to ease when the Mediterranean Club called last minute for another gig of starts and stops cued by Izzy, the tattooed don. Jobs for goons had a way of making me forget everything else, and before I knew it, four days had passed without my calling the Bells.

I wanted to call on the fifth day but I had the early chills of a cold, and besides, it was Sunday; the Yankees were on with a double-header. On the sixth day I had the sniffles. I would've called anyway if the Tamsy twins hadn't been so obnoxious after showing up late to the lessons they never practiced for. I was in a snippy mood. Since my bank account would soon be overflowing, babysitting no longer made sense. After over a decade of it, in just minutes I passed all my students into the hands of the most available, motivated teachers: out-of-work sax players.

On Tuesday, May 9th, I picked up the phone to call the Bells, but I froze. Am I ready, I thought. Am I ready to deal with possessed paintings, Sarah's visions—the Holocaust, for God's sake? I stewed on this for two more days, all the while hoping to quash the sniffles and chills now gaining on me.

By Thursday my throat had a golf ball in it, and I had a full-blown cold. Now that it was impossible to be guilted into a trip to Brooklyn, I picked up the phone. There was no answer—which was rare for the Bells—and they had no machine. I tried each day to reach them, and by Sunday the 14th, though I was now on my back with a fever, I started to worry about them.

Early Wednesday morning, May 17th, the fever broke, but my head and lungs were so clogged, I couldn't breathe without sounding a chord. Still, nothing could keep me from the first rehearsal.

The Royal Galloway's towering teal glass blinked and flashed in the morning sun, and I nearly passed out on the curb. I blew my nose and wheezed deeply, triggering three minutes of hacking in front of the lobby. The red-carpeted main entrance, lined with fountains and gold cherubs, was off-limits to the band. But our entrance was easy to find. I just had to follow the yells and curses from the crowd of sweating men heaving giant wheeled cases through a side door. Inside, a bigger crew hammered and buzzed in a cyclone of sawdust and wires. Once I made it to the Grand Ballroom on the second floor, the thousand-seat theater and dining hall, I understood the ruckus. The Royal Galloway was opening in two days and its main room was half finished. Carpenters were still making tables. A dozen painters on ladders worked the walls while electricians on much taller ladders worked the ceilings, their black cables stretching to the bare concrete floor. I walked the length of the enormous room, flopped down on a plaster-dusted chair near the stage, and blew my nose.

"Up here!" Tommy shouted, with an armful of folders and music. "Come meet the guys." While two irate electricians in front of the Stage Left doors threatened to slash each other, I snuck around them and climbed the stage.

Tommy greeted me with a crisp-cut gray-haired man named Phil Manglio, one of the most recorded tenor sidemen in New York. The air, dense with paint and sheetrock, was no help, and I sneezed prolifically into a kleenex. "Forgive me if I don't shake," Phil said.

Tommy showed me to my seat while the red-haired, burly, first-call baritone player, Harold Koby, parked his instrument and sat nearby. "Nice meet you," he said, sorting his chair and equipment.

"Wow," I said, "Harold Koby. This is such an honor for me—after listening to you on so many of my albums."

"Yeah?" he said, still adjusting his things. "What shit you got?"

"What?"

"Which albums you got an shit?"

". . . What?"

"You know, what shit you got that I'm playing on . . . an shit?"

"Uh . . . I've got a cold and I can't hear too well, so . . ." I gestured we should just give up for now. I was soon amazed at how much of Harold's personality could wrap around one word.

Gus DaLucci said a quick hello as he handed out paperwork. I waved to Joe Terry; he was carrying his bass, searching for a safe spot to put it down. Half the band was loudly warming up while the rest tried to shmooze over the noise.

"Hi, I'm Chuckie," said Chuckie Bowman, the young black tenor master, one of the biggest names in the band.

I told him it was a thrill to be working with superstars. He told me it couldn't come at a worse time—he had to pull himself off his tour with Sting as well as some crucial record dates.

All the saxes were now there except Freddie Cavanaugh, the one I wanted most to meet. While Harold, Phil and Chuckie warmed up—a mellifluous blizzard of notes—I hardly played at all, conserving my energy for the first of two long rehearsal days.

Gus strode to the front of the band moments before the start, as Freddie darted in with multiple cases dangling from his frail shoulders. He said hi to Gus, and as he quietly set up his soprano and alto saxophones, his oboe, clarinet, flute and piccolo, I introduced myself.

"Hi Freddy, I'm Shawn. Great to finally meet you." I held out my hand.

He didn't notice me—just kept unpacking his instruments.

"I mean," I said, "after all those gigs Danny had me fill in for you . . ." Freddie Cavanaugh was short and gaunt, nothing like I'd expected, and he paid no attention to me. Well, I thought, even on a good day my voice is soft, and no one can hear a thing when trumpets are warming up.

I tried again, louder: "Freddy, I'm Shawn. It'll be great to work with you . . ."

He didn't even look at me.

Gus called for everyone's attention. He said we'd be featured as a jazz act but we'd also do private banquets, corporate parties, whatever the hotel needed. "And all those extra gigs," Gus said, "would pay on top of our scale for the nightly shows. Mr. Galloway, our British patron, wants this to be the next big thing in New York. So he asked for a big band, and to lead it, a New York star."

A lean, slick man with a jutting coiffure that reminded me of a head of broccoli, ambled in front of us, spreading his scores over three music stands. "Everybody," Gus announced, "please welcome our conductor, Renard Phisbin."

Most New Yorkers had heard of Renard Phisbin. He was the force behind the long-running Broadway hit, "Forever Boys," which produced the smash ballad, "How Long Will You Want Me." The critics loved it.

Among the clatters and clangs of hammers and power tools, the vapors of joint compound, sawdust, polyurethane and China White semi-gloss, Renard started the rehearsal with a Count Basie chart. A cathedral of sound powered through my bones, the band swinging so hard, I forgot my cold. But Renard looked desperate for us to stop, frantically shaking his arms at us. I was the only one who stopped. Everyone else was already familiar with Renard's conducting pattern.

As we rehearsed the celebrity acts, I had to blow my nose and cough more and more, drawing attention I didn't want. Harold Koby leaned over Chuckie and Freddie from the left side of the sax section to offer me encouragement.

"Man," he said. "Some nasty shit you got. Couple weeks ago I had some nasty shit. Throwin up an shit."

Phil Manglio, to my right, had a different take. "I haven't heard an alto played like yours in some time," he said in a low voice. "No one sounds like you anymore."

I thanked him. Phil's praise was always gushing, but you could drown in the undertow.

Renard had arranged a medley of old tunes: "Belle of the Ball," "Darktown Strutters' Ball" and "Woodchopper's Ball." He called it "Fabulous Balls from a Bygone Era." And I had a featured solo. When my moment came, a rising cough forced me to pause until I could stuff it back into my lungs. As the rhythm section vamped, waiting for my solo, another cough rose, so I trampled it again. Then with all my will I blew into the horn, the cough erupting through my mouthpiece in a barking squeal. I stopped, hacking, convulsing for the rest of the solo. Renard looked horrified; I'd debased his magnum opus. But Phil leaned over and said, "Yeah man, I hear what you're going for. I mean, why play notes when you can use bodily functions?"

I looked at him and blew my nose.

THE NEXT MORNING I entered the ballroom on fresh carpet under crystal chandeliers. Carpenters were finishing the tables, painters brushing their final coats, and technicians were testing microphones and spotlights. The room was nearly ready. I was too—almost healed, except for the cough.

By Friday, May 19th, I was nearly free of the affliction that had started on my last day with the Bells. And although tonight was the grand opening and I got Carole a free ticket, I kept worrying about the Bells. I tried calling every hour. They must be on vacation, I thought. But they don't do vacations. I felt guilty that I'd followed my career, and not them.

I arrived in my tuxedo at the service entrance on 43rd Street while klieg lights, stretch limos and a crush of photographers massed in front of the lobby on Sixth Avenue. In the Grand Ballroom white-tied VIPs nibbled hors d'oeuvres in advance of the advertised gourmet meal. I wondered if Carole would be at the 8:00 show or the 10:30. She'll go nuts for the band and the hotel, I thought. She'll want to see me after the show. The Out House is far behind me.

The band congregated silently on the stage behind the shut curtains. "No warming up," Renard decreed. "They're not paying us to hear lip exercises."

Phil wondered if maybe I should take some weeks off, really get that flu bug out of my system. "I'm okay now," I said.

"Better still," he said. "Take a whole month."

"Shit," Harold said. "I was moving my shit today and lost my neck strap an shit. Anybody got an extra neck strap? It can be a shitty one, it doesn't matter."

Chuckie complained that Renard wouldn't let him off to play a Stevie Wonder session. Freddie, as usual, said nothing to anyone.

While we waited hidden behind the tall drapes, Herndon Galloway strolled in front to center stage. In Oxford English he saluted the audience for participating in his maximal achievement. "It may have taken us far too long to fashion this majestic edifice," he said, "but I dare say, it will embellish this glorious city for decades to come. You, ladies and gentlemen, are now a part of history. You are the first audience, the first eyes and ears of what will surely be an illustrious New York City landmark. So without further ado, I enthusiastically bring you . . . Renard Phisbin and the Hotel Galloway Jazz Orchestra!"

Renard, staying off-stage, cued in the rhythm section swinging under Tommy's solo piano lines. The curtains slowly opened. I couldn't see Carole; the audience was pitch-black. As the trumpets, trombones and saxes joined the rhythm section, the vibrations bathed through me—a roaring machine of talent—and I was in the middle of it. After thirty bars we stopped dead—two beats silence. Out of the stillness little Freddie Cavanaugh, drenched in spotlight, stood up and played his alto, billowing notes as masterfully as any solo I'd ever heard. Soon the rhythm section was accompanying him, and then a trombone took his place, then a trumpet—all impeccable. Phil and Chuckie followed by trading fours, and a jazz history lesson washed over my ears. The whole band followed with the shout chorus, a perfect wall of sound, something I'd never had in my small groups, not to mention the solos for Jimmy.

Then Renard in a white tux with tails, leapt onto the stage, half-bowed to the cheering audience, and turned to conduct our last chorus like a madman waving down the Coast Guard. The swing stiffened, the sound pinched, the feel was gone.

The first act, a Hungarian acrobat troupe, called for an endless stream of czardas and gypsy music. While the audience ate their dinner, daredevils and gymnasts flew from swings and platforms above the stage and over the band—with no net. I was glad I wasn't eating.

The next act was a comedy duo pretending to be singing a concert of Beethoven lieder. They kept stopping to fight with each other or accuse band members of making up their own parts. Freddie was the perfect foil because he not only had solo woodwind lines to play, but no matter what they did to him his natural deadpan never changed.

The last act featured the headliner, a singer named Erica Swain, a six-foot, Swedish-looking stunner in a crimson evening gown slit up to her hips. She didn't actually sing; she whispered, but her charm and her songs—about the man who got away, the man she always wanted, or how any man would do—had at least half the audience on its feet.

The 10:30 drew an even bigger reaction: a two-minute standing ovation. The Royal Galloway and its band had all the earmarks of a hit. But Carole never showed.

I heard her message when I got home. "I'm sorry, Shawn," she said. "Mark and I got into a big fight just as I was leaving to see your show. It got really ugly. He says he's finalizing his divorce and wants me to stay away from you. I feel so bad. How did your show go? Oh, you better not tell me. He doesn't want us talking either."

I stood there over the machine, rubbing my eye into another pinkeye. I was a fool for expecting anything else, I thought, but at least I can cleanse my guilt for leaving the Bells. I traded playing wild solos to a psychotic—a job going nowhere—for the best big band gig in decades, the hit of the year. And this is just the beginning, I thought. With my accounts spilling over, I'll finance my jazz career. I'll perfect my compositions, make albums and tour the world.

I slept till nearly eleven the next day, waking to a duet of Lloyd Fetterman's snore and my phone ringing. The call was Izzy asking me to lead a band at the Mediterranean Club the following Saturday.

"I can't do it," I said. "I'm working."

"What's that?" Izzy said.

"I'm already booked. I have another gig."

"I don't think you understand."

"I'm working every night now. In fact, I may not be available for some time." Like *never*, I wanted to say.

"Not available?" he said, chuckling. "You think you can bow out, just like that?"

"No, it's just that I—"

"We've taken care of you, right? So when we need you, you take care of us."

"Theoretically. But you see I'm—"

"You don't understand. I'm not *asking* you to work for us next Saturday. I'm *telling* you, okay? Be here at 6 PM."

"I'd love to, really I would, but I've been hired to play at the new hotel, the Royal Galloway, and—"

"What's that?"

"The Royal Galloway. I've been—"

"Hold on a second." Two minutes passed with his hand over the phone and muffled voices.

"It's okay," he said. "We'll get somebody else. Yeah, Hernie's all right."

"Oh . . . good," I said. "What's—what's a hernie?"

"Herndon. Hernie Galloway is good people. Don't worry about it."

I tried not to worry about it, but what sort of things do you have to do to become one of Izzy's "good people?"

AFTER THE SHOWS Sunday night Herndon hired the band to play a party for him and a few friends till 4 AM—his own private opening. I felt like a star.

The next day Lloyd Fetterman's snores woke me around eleven again. I called the Bells right after breakfast—still no answer. It was my day off, so I went back to sleep, only to be awakened at three by the Mendez kids rehearsing the Battle of Anzio. I tried the Bells again. A trip to Sheepshead Bay was overdue.

On my way to the subway I bought the Times for the Arts Section. Our review was in. Damian Sheers, the most influential New York critic, led off with "*Royal Flop, Nine Years in the Making.*" It went downhill from there, slamming everything about the hotel, including Galloway himself and his court battles over bribes and contract and building code violations. Sheers went on to skewer the acts but saved his worst for the band: *"The only genuine musician among them is their conductor, Renard Phisbin, without whom, their self-indulgent racket might implode the Ballroom into the parking garage. But on second thought, the parking garage is likely more entertaining and certainly a good deal cheaper than an evening at the Royal Shallow Way."*

I bought four other papers at the stand. The Times review was the best one. At least Damian Sheers didn't get sick from the meal or the formaldehyde in the carpet glue. I stared at the subway entrance, then turned around. I couldn't visit the Bells now; they'd tell me to quit the flop and move in. No, I couldn't face them yet.

When I arrived for the rehearsal on Tuesday afternoon, management had tacked up our only unqualified rave—from the South Amboy Scuttlebutt.

No one said a word as we set up on the stage and Renard called us to order. We were in shock, and hungry for some reassuring words. "The reviews are disgraceful," he said. "Some of them describe an out-of-control band incapable of accompanying a show." He paused to look at each one of us. "I agree."

Chuckie rose from his seat, and said quietly, "Excuse me."

"I didn't want to raise hell before the opening," Renard said, "but damn it, I'm not going to let you all ruin my reputation."

"Excuse me," Chuckie said.

"The only reason this has happened is none of you are following my beat. I don't care how famous you all think you are, you have to look up and follow."

"Excuse me, Renard."

"If you learn to follow, in a month or two I can pull some strings, maybe get us re-reviewed. But I promise you, if you fight me, you won't get another job like this in New York. Not if I have anything to say about it."

"Renard."

"Yes, yes, what are you mumbling?"

"I just got paged for a record date, starts in half an hour," Chuckie said. "I've got a sub ready to come here. Since I couldn't get out opening night, can I at least—"

"You must be joking. Sit down."

Chuckie remained standing. "I can't speak for the rest of the guys," Chuckie said, "but the reviews about the band are just wrong. There could be a problem with the cheap sound system though. And if you don't mind me saying, you should—"

"I said, sit down," Renard said, flipping through one of his conductor scores.

"Have you ever videotaped your conducting?" Chuckie asked.

"How dare you."

"Have you ever used a metronome?"

"Gus," Renard said. "Isn't there something in the contract about this?"

"I'll bet if you got a video of yourself, you couldn't follow it," Chuckie said.

"Gus, I want an action brought against this person. Give me the papers; I'll sign them right now." Gus was sitting behind his drums, his hands over his eyes.

"Every show we save your ass," Chuckie said.

"I want those papers, Gus. Now!"

"Forget your papers," Chuckie said, slipping his tenor in the case, "I quit." In five seconds he hustled off the stage and out of the ballroom.

"Shit . . ." Harold said.

WITHIN AN HOUR Chuckie was replaced with a fine player—not his equal, but few were. And this exceptional band, now squashed, did all it could to follow Renard.

Every day I tried calling the Bells, even Henry, and no one ever answered. I wrote three letters but I never got a response.

By July it was obvious the hotel was failing. The "sold-out rooms" were mostly empty. Only two jingles and three parties had ever materialized. The two shows, six nights a week became one show five nights a week, then four nights. No one talked anymore about albums or tours.

The strangest phone call I ever got was on one of the days off, Monday morning, August 7th. It was Gus DaLucci, and he sounded nervous. "Shawn," he said, "I'm glad I caught you. Is your instrument or anything of value in your locker at the hotel?"

"No," I said. "Everything's here. Why?"

"Did—did you leave anything on the stage?"

"Just my sax stand. Why?"

"Do the other guys store their instruments in the lockers?"

"They might. I think Harold does, probably Freddie too. Why?"

"There's no rehearsal tomorrow," he said. "Just—just stay home tomorrow."

"But I have to come for the 8:00, right?"

"No."

"What happened? Did Renard fire me? I'm getting better on that 'Fabulous Balls' chart. Last time we did it Phil told me I played like I'd never played before. That's a quote."

"You didn't get fired. Just don't come in. And don't talk to the other guys."

"Gus, are you okay? You sound a little . . . stressed."

"This conversation never happened."

"Uh . . . okay . . ."

"Just stay home tomorrow. Don't talk to *anybody* about this. And we never spoke. Understand?"

"Well, do I come in on Tuesday?"

"I don't know," he said.

"Gus, what the hell's going on?"

"If they find out, I'm . . . toast."

"Who they?"

"Just tell me you understand."

"I think so. I'm not coming to work, I'm not telling anybody I'm not coming to work, and I haven't talked to anybody about anything."

"Good. I have to call Harold now."

On August 8th at 11 AM there was a four-alarm fire at the Royal Galloway Hotel destroying most of the second and third floors. No one was hurt. But the hotel was no longer sound. The city and insurance companies launched aggressive investigations, but eventually, millions were paid to Galloway Management Corporation.

My dream gig had come and gone in twelve weeks.

CHAPTER 16

My Horn

EVEN THOUGH the broccoli-headed monster had done his best to make us miserable, and my big break was torched in an insurance scam, I was still glad I took the job. I'd worked with some of the busiest players in town, and my future looked solid—if they brought me along. Though things were dismal with Carole, I was convinced she'd be calling as soon as her mistake with turdball had run its course. And when she did, I'd brag about all the jobs and connections I'd landed from the Hotel Galloway.

Most gigs don't end in four-alarm fires, and it took me a few days to believe the hotel was really dead. Then I made my calls. Tommy had already gotten a trio gig in San Francisco, and was packing to move. For weeks Chuckie had been in Japan or Jakarta or somewhere. Harold took ten days to return my call—with an observation: "You've got some shit together but your harmonic shit ain't always locked up with your technical shit. You dig?"

I left Gus alone. Most of his gigs were now with Danny James, and I wasn't ready to crawl. And I didn't even bother with Freddie, who'd only spoken to me twice, each time to pick up his mouthpiece cap that had rolled under my chair.

Phil Manglio was happy to take my call. If his recording people ever asked for a recommendation, he said he'd give them my name. "But they'll never ask," he added.

It had taken me years to acquire twenty-two private students, and because I was ill on the eve of my now-and-forever gig, in three phone calls I'd thrown them all away. Fortunately, I'd been able to save enough money from the hotel job to go without work for three months—if I didn't go anywhere and ate a strict diet of fruit, peanut butter and soup.

They'll call me a fool for not listening to them, I thought. They'll scold me for leaving in such a hurry after Sarah had trusted me with her life secrets. It didn't matter. I didn't care so much if they rehired me or not; I just wanted to be a part of their family again. There was no point in calling ahead because no one ever picked up the damn phone. With my set of keys I journeyed to Sheepshead Bay.

I rang the outdoor buzzer and waited in the summer breeze, remembering my first time at 271 Denwood—the gold tinsel, the yellow balloons, all those crusty elders blocking the doorway. I waited a few minutes, then used the key to the building and walked down the short hall, expecting Jimmy and his sloppy reds to leap out of Apartment 1 to greet me. Nothing. I knocked and rang their doorbell. Nothing. I tried their house keys, but the locks were changed. After living in the same place for over forty years, would the three of them just disappear?

The building had only two other apartments, each with its own floor. The one above the Bells was empty, soon to be renovated. But I found someone home on the top floor, a plumber named Aldo. He said he was terrified of Jimmy, and for the two years he'd been living there he stayed clear of the whole family. He had nothing more to say. When I walked back down the stairs, I noticed "Bell" was still on the hallway mailbox, and I slid a note under their door.

I never got a reply.

OVER THE NEXT FEW weeks I called and wrote music schools, band directors, principals, but no one from Staten Island to the Bronx needed another saxophone teacher. I called Izzy at the Mediterranean Club. He said he'd found someone who could follow his start-and-stop signals even quicker than I did, and for less money. So I crawled to Danny James after all. It was brief. After he relished describing what I should do with myself, I told him everyone knew the muskrat on his head was a toupee.

Then Irene called out of nowhere to tell me Carole and the heart surgeon were living in Scarsdale. They just got married.

"No," I said, "impossible."

"Oh, I keep in touch with things . . . " she said. "I talked with Sarah . . . after you walked out on her. I kept track on your ex. You too. I heard about your huge flop. You must be so ashamed and humiliated—"

"I've been trying to reach Sarah. When did you last talk to her?"

"Not since you dumped them. Soooo, did you hear that I'm dating someone? It's *very* serious. He's soooo gorgeous."

"May you be together always," I said.

Now I had no work and no audience and Carole had married Mark. I stuffed it all into my alto. I could play my avant-garde in my living room and still feel the sky opening up, the stars flickering to every beat, an audience of thousands. It was amazing: As long as the horn was in my hands I was on fire.

Lloyd Fetterman had had it with my practicing. "What the hell you doing?" he said, edging into my apartment in his sweaty tank top, his hairy brawn merging with cascades of fat.

"Just playing my horn," I said, staring right back at him, wondering if this was the dreaded moment—the neighbor uprising.

"Sounds like crows trapped in an attic fan. And I know what that sounds like. Colfield says you're giving him heartburn. Everybody wants you evicted. What are you, unemployed?"

I nodded to him, subtly reaching for my cordless phone, my finger over the 911 button.

"If you made some cash," he said, "you wouldn't blow that thing so much, right? Why don't you put something down on this week's games?" He opened his coat pocket, showing me five long cards—football pools. "We pay fifteen to one."

Lloyd's leathery face reminded me of a worn car seat. "I thought you drove a car service," I said.

"Yeah, yeah, every night, but for my friends I got this way to make serious bucks without lifting a finger."

"Well, I really don't . . . " I said.

"Okay, all right," he said. "How about baseball?" He lifted four more cards from his socks.

Lloyd offered me a job delivering football-pool betting cards, or dropping off extra large, full bags of—he wouldn't say what—that could be stored temporarily in the trunk of a car he'd give me to keep. I told him I'd think about it.

I wanted back my year in Sheepshead Bay. Despite my problems with Jimmy, I'd mattered to the Bells, and I missed them for it. The closest I could come was to form a trio to play for homebound people in hospitals, shelters and nursing homes. I knew it wouldn't bring me any closer to the Bells. Sarah and Arnie would never give up Jimmy again. Even so, I rounded up a keyboardist and bass player and made calls and sent notices to every nursing or homeless residence in the city. It would take months to get gigs, and as my money ran out I was lucky to find the perfect interim job for my decaying attitude, and only a block away. With my earbuds humming Bird and Cannonball from three to eleven, I stood blankly behind a counter, stuck in a blue T-shirt and cap, each inscribed with a clownish yellow "Super Duper Video." A jaded attitude was a plus at Super Duper Video, and I wound up cleaved to that counter for years.

At fifty-two dollars a man for the trio, I had to keep the video job even as we started playing a few mornings a week. It didn't matter that at Fieldcrest Nursing Home and Maspeth Home for the Aged the patients all covered their ears even before we started. Or that in the Van Cortlandt Medical Center psychiatric ward they were so medicated or in their own world they didn't notice us. I was finally in a band again.

We delivered time-tested melodies with less edge than a warm pillow, but I couldn't help pushing the music "out," tweaking our lullabies with a softened version of my avant-garde. I'm sure it kept us from getting more work, though it wasn't quite the wave without limits. Still, I'd lose myself in every solo, soaring through the flashes and crackles of an avant-garde ether I'd always believed was a fantasy.

PART

Five Years Later

CHAPTER 17

Parkview Manor

SO GLAD TO SEE YOU," said a smiling man in a navy blue suit and crew cut. "I'm Al Gazemsky, the director of the home. Allow me to escort you to the recreation room. Today it's our concert hall." I was flattered. I'd never gotten such attention from the director of anything.

The adult home was Parkview Manor, but the nearest greenery was a mile away and the only view from the window bars was East Brooklyn's smelly, bustling Connelly Boulevard. The 2005 mid-September heat wave was already in full sizzle even on this early Tuesday morning. My tapered shirt and slacks had melded into one wet rag clinging in all the wrong places by the time I'd entered the cool, immaculate lobby of the Parkview. Ferns, begonias and assorted cacti garnished the main entrance, while the walls shined with cheery watercolors.

"We're very excited about your concert today," he said, leading me down a shimmering hall. "For weeks it's all my staff has been talking about. I've already met your pianist and bassist. Where are the rest of you?"

"Well, we're only a trio," I said.

"But . . . what about the string section? We requested strings."

"Are you sure?"

"Oh yes. And the small choir. Are they late?"

"I think you must have the wrong—"

"No matter," he said, stopping in front of the swinging doors to the recreation room. The keyboard and bass players were inside, warming up. "If you'll just make the payment now," he said, "you know, before the concert, that would be best."

"What payment?"

"Yes, didn't my secretary remind you? The fifty dollar performance fee?"

"No . . . You're supposed to pay *us*. You know, a hundred and fif—"

"Those are your wages—from the State of New York. There's still the matter of the performance fee. You're required to contribute fifty dollars to ensure your ensemble remains on the list . . . All right, you didn't know. How about forty-five dollars? I'll see to it you and your orchestra get most of the concerts. Just bring the strings next time."

"My whole share is only fifty-two dollars."

"Okay, thirty dollars then."

While he nagged for his kickback, I pushed through the swinging doors, greeted the guys, and set up my alto. Even though it seemed like a decent place, it was a far commute and I didn't care if he never asked us back. Five minutes later two young and very bored-looking nurse's aides entered the glistening linoleum room followed by a tottering army of about fifty mental patients. The nurse's aides had to work to get a few of them to obey, cajoling, even physically planting them into the rows of steel fold-up chairs. But I wasn't going to wait for them all to be seated. I wanted to play, to make enough noise so I wouldn't hear the guy now hassling me for twenty-five dollars. I counted off our waltz medley, which started with "Fascination."

He kept pestering even while I played through the melody twice. "All right, look," he said, as the keyboard player lightly improvised around the tune, "just give me ten bucks and I'll see what I can do." A barrel-chested orderly stepped toward us.

"Gordon," the orderly said, "you pretending to be Mr. Gazemsky again?"

"I'll have your job for that tone," Gordon said.

"Take your seat!" the orderly yelled, muscling him into a chair in the front row.

We segued into the waltz, "Bluesette," and a low voice murmured from the front row, "Five bucks. Just five bucks and I'll see what I can do."

A man in the back row began to yelp, and maintained the yelp even as the nurse's aides rushed to him, stood him up, and walked him out of the room. Three minutes later they returned him—now quiet—to his chair. His eyes were closed, his head cocked to one side. In fact, except for a woman in the third row having convulsions, the whole audience looked sedated. At least three or four were moaning or chanting—I couldn't tell which—but most were asleep.

While I blew free-jazz lines over "Fly Me to the Moon," one of the chants got louder, an insistent rasp out of the fifth row. A scrawny old man with large sunglasses duct-taped over his cheeks was slowly croaking, "Yeah . . . Bee . . . Yeah . . ."

We're not in B, I thought. You want B Major? I spun some B Major lines over the C Major tune, winding through a maze of soft avant-garde.

"*Yeah,*" the man roared. "*Bee.*" He got louder as I played, even louder than Gordon's current offer of three dollars.

One of the nurse's aides weaved quickly through the rows toward the "yeah-bee" man. The orderly circled around from the other direction. "Mi-ha-shawoooo," the yeah-bee man rasped, "mi-ha-shawoooo." We were playing "Tenderly" when he stood up and tugged at his sunglasses. His gray sweatpants and white T-shirt were so grimy he looked like he'd been sleeping on Connelly Boulevard.

"Sit down!" the orderly barked, glancing furtively at our trio. Then softer: "Take your hands off the glasses." But the yeah-bee man yanked until the tape ripped, and the glasses dropped. Both eyes were swollen purple.

The nurse's aide and the orderly hurried toward him from each side of the row.

I put my saxophone down, and the keyboard player took over the tune.

The orderly clutched the man's skeletal arm from one side while the nurse's aide pushed from the other. The man was staring at me as his arms began to spasm, his mouth twitching violently. "Mi-ha-shawoooo."

I climbed over Gordon, and forced my way to the fifth row. Yeah-bee.

Jellybeans.

They started dragging him from the aisle, yet he kept his battered eyes on me. "Come on," she said to him. "If you don't behave, you're getting the new needle, and you know what it did to you last time." The patients around us quickly hunkered to the floor.

I hugged him. He was all bones.

"You know this man?" the orderly asked me.

"Jimmy," I said to my friend.

They pulled him, but he resisted. I blocked their arms, and yelled, "Shit!" It was all I could think of.

"Sir," the nurse's aide said, "let me do my job."

"Mi-ha-shawoooo, dra," Jimmy said. "Dra dra dra."

"I hear 'Mister Shawn Lewis,' Jimmy," I said. "But . . . 'dra?' Drugs?"

Jimmy nodded.

"Stay out of the way, sir," the nurse's aide said, "or I'll page Security."

The orderly, who looked big enough to be anyone's "security," put his arm on my shoulder.

I ducked. "You touch me or my friend again," I said, "and I'll sue. I'll quit my shitty job and live off *you* assholes for a while."

They backed off, and the aide used her walkie-talkie to call for help.

I led Jimmy out of the rows of patients, and up to the duo now plunking "Oh, What a Beautiful Morning." The dark eyes and twitches were the only resemblances to the man I knew in Sheepshead Bay.

"Guys," I said to the keyboard and bass players, "split the money today. I'm done. I'm taking my friend out of here."

They looked bewildered.

"Seventy-eight bucks each," I said. "Just keep playing."

I guided Jimmy toward the swinging doors. The orderly blocked the exit, both nurse's aides surrounding us from behind.

"You won't get anywhere," one of the aides said.

"This man is a patient here," the other aide said. "You'll go to jail, and your friend will come right back."

"Fine," I said, "who do I see to make it legal?"

Within seconds a tall and armed security guard and a squat, smiling man in a dark business suit swung through the doors. "Come on out," the smiling man said, leading us into the hall while he sent the aides and orderly back to the concert.

"Is there something we can do for you?" the man asked me.

"Are you in charge?" I said.

"I'm Al Gazemsky," he said, straightening his tie, "the operator of Parkview Manor. Please, just call me Al." He smiled and shook my hand.

Jimmy, eyes half-shut, began to sway. I held him upright and said, "This is my friend—"

"We all know Mr. Bell. You're the sax player—Mr. Lewis, right?"

I nodded.

"Do you realize what you're doing?"

"Yes, I'm getting him out of—"

"Mr. Bell is one of our most disturbed residents," he said. "And that's saying something."

"Well, he's going home today."

"Hold on, Mr. Lewis, it's not that easy."

"I think it is," I said. "Take us to his room."

"Uh . . . all right . . . if we take you to his room, will you finish the concert?"

I didn't answer him. We slowly climbed up a flight of stairs, then turned down another lustrous hall with more ferns and watercolors. A nurse hurried in front of us to our left, through a different set of swinging doors. For an instant, before the doors could shut, a sweltering reek wafted over us. No more than fifteen feet down that side hall a patient in his underwear lay in a fetal position on the floor. The nurse raced around him without even slowing.

We came to another set of doors, and Al paused, then stepped in front of us.

"Look," he said, his face jumping with a sudden tic, "we're short on staff at the moment, and I have other things to do, so let's cut the bullshit: You're getting fifty-two dollars, right? What if I add just for you, you know, just for you right now, an extra fifty?" He smiled and held out his hand to shake. "That'll do it, right? You'll leave this very sick man alone and go back to your concert?"

"We need to get his things," I said.

"Okay, all right, okay. I like musicians. I'll give you the money and you can just leave. You don't even have to finish the concert."

I said nothing.

"But we can't let him go, Mr. Lewis," he said. "Other than that, tell me how I can put your mind at ease."

"Who's beating him up?"

"It's not our staff, if that's what you think," he said, crooking his neck. "Mr. Bell is not very popular with the other residents."

Nothing he said made me feel better. "Why does he look like he's starving?"

"Is it *my* fault he won't eat?" Then he pointed to my chest, nodding and smiling. "I know some very influential people, Mr. Lewis. I could get you a *real* job—you know, something with full benefits in a state home. Would that interest you?"

"I'm going to guess his room is somewhere beyond these doors," I said, steering Jimmy through the swinging doors and into a barely lit hall as putrid as the one we'd just passed. The floors were sticky with garbage and I could only imagine what else. We stumbled into each other, getting used to the dimness. Al and his guard kept close behind us as we hobbled by closed rooms with TVs blaring and people arguing.

Jimmy called out when we got to his room. He collapsed onto his single bed, his eyes closed, mumbling, pleading with me, I thought, to take him home. His cubicle looked out through a small, filmy window with iron bars. A blank and dirty canvas sat in the corner of the floor, on top of the remains of a broken easel and next to an overflowing wastebasket. There were no paints or brushes or writing tablets. No red clothes. The only things resembling red were the bloodstains on his sheets and within the dirty laundry piled on the floor.

"We're short on—"

"I know," I said. "You're short on staff at the moment."

"But you'll be glad to know this is his *private* room," Al said, smiling in the doorway, the guard behind him. "His first year he had to share."

"It's just like the Waldorf," I said.

"Well, his roommate was Pavel McElroy, a violent paranoid."

"A killer," murmured the guard.

"Jared," Al said to the guard, "no one was charged for those murders. Point is, Mr. Lewis, we protected your friend. We gave him his own room, a rare privilege in a Medicaid facility."

"May I have a trash bag so I can pack his things?" I said.

"Jared, get a bag from the janitor closet. We're happy for you to clean his room, but I hope you don't expect to walk out of here with Mr. Bell."

"He needs his family, Sarah and Arnie."

"Who?"

"His parents! Who brought him here?" I repeated the question to Jimmy, but he was already asleep.

"All I'm permitted to tell you is Mr. Bell has been with us for four years."

Jared handed me the garbage bag, and I stuffed it with a few of the less-soiled items. Jimmy's wallet had only a social security card and a photo ID. The more I sorted through the squalor inside the stifling cell, the more I felt like strangling Al Gazemsky. "Damn it," I said, "who committed him here?"

"That's confidential," Al said.

"You son-of-a-bitch, what the hell does that mean?"

"Keep it civil, Mr. Lewis."

"This is *America*. You can't drug people and hold them against their will."

"We have a discharge procedure. Perhaps you'd like our social worker to explain it. You're in luck because she's only here on Tuesdays. Mr. Bell is not going anywhere. But I'll tell you what, you and I work out a cash arrangement, you sign a few papers—I'll let you pick somebody else to take home for your good deed." He flashed his programmed smile, but another tic caught him by surprise.

Al paged the social worker, and he and Jared waited in the doorway while I strained to open the window. It wouldn't budge. It was painted shut.

When Marjorie Schnipp, with Brillo-gray hair and a prominent brown wart over her right eyebrow, entered carrying a file under her baggy arm, she blabbed as casually as if it were a dinner party. Although she made the rounds for three adult homes and a hospital, her sunny indifference made it all seem very part-time.

"We'd like to go now," I said, trying not to look at the wart.

"Is Mr. Bell your father?" she asked, ruffling through Jimmy's file.

He looks old enough to be my grandfather, I thought, but the difference is only nine years. "No, I'm just a friend."

"I see," she said. "Hmm . . . And your name is . . .?"

"Shawn Lewis. Look, he doesn't belong here."

"And you are now his legal guardian?" she asked.

"No . . . "

She closed the file with a snap. "Our medical team has determined this man needs strict monitoring," she said.

"I can't say I have much respect for your medical team," I said.

"Mr. Lewis, I have a Master's in Social Work. I'm the treasurer of the East Elmhurst League of Certified Social Workers. Trust me when I tell you Mr. Bell is a disorganized schizophrenic with prolonged periods of acute hallucinations."

"It could be dangerous to let him out," Al said.

"You're kidding, I said. "He barely weighs a hundred pounds."

"I *know* he's dangerous," Al said. "Four nurse's aides have quit because they said he was playing games with their minds. One of them is now a patient here."

"Good," I said.

"I told you about Pavel MacElroy," he said. "Mean, mean as they come. His neighbors think he ax-murdered his boss and his landlady and tossed their remains in the river. After one year with Mr. Bell he stopped talking and only made chirps. He'd run down the halls naked, flapping his arms, chirping. He's in Bellevue now, in a padded cell."

"And this is Jimmy's fault because . . . " I said.

"Because I know what I see," he said. "He's manipulating our minds, all of us, *all of us*." His face ticced wildly.

"Al . . . " Ms. Schnipp said. "You need to relax."

"Ohhh," Al said, glaring at Jimmy sleeping, "*he* knows. Mr. Bell, call them off!"

"What?" I said. "Was Jimmy committed here or not?"

"Mr. Bell is involuntarily committed at this time," Ms. Schnipp said. "I think what you want is a re-evaluation, our Safety/Competency Assessment."

"That's it!" I said. "Let's do *that*. Thank you."

"Oh, you're most welcome," she said, "most welcome. Mr. Bell is very fortunate to have a friend like you. He hasn't had a single visitor in all these years—has he, Al?" She opened her pocket calendar. "Now let's see . . . this is September 13th. I'm gone next week . . . After that, the psychiatrist is off for three weeks in Corfu . . . Mr. Lewis, the doctor's not here on a Tuesday until October 25th. So how are you with Tuesday, October 25th? Shall we say . . . 10 AM?"

"I thought we could do it *now*," I said.

"Mr. Lewis," she said, "everything has to be scheduled."

"But I'm a witness," I said. "I've seen how you treat your patients. My friend is evidence. I want the Safety/Competency Asshole *right now.*"

"*Assessment*," Al said.

"I'm sorry if you're feeling upset," Ms. Schnipp said to me. "You have some trust issues. Are you seeing a therapist? You may need to talk to someone."

"I plan to," I said, "like the Department of Health. They'd be fascinated with how Parkview Manor spends our money. Problem is Jimmy can't wait for them to close you down. So let's have the Safety Asses now—"

"Don't make threats," Al said. "I don't take well to threats."

"You have to play by the rules," Ms. Schnipp said to me. "Or do the rules not apply to you? For a full re-evaluation both the psychiatrist and I are required to be present and we can't be until October 25th. It's that simple."

"Do you honestly think he'll still be alive by then?" I said.

"Of *course*," she said, chuckling. "You really need to talk to someone."

"Call the psychiatrist *now*," I said, "or maybe we should see what the Fire Marshal says about fused windows covered in bars, and what the Times would say about beatings, patients over-medicated, airless rooms in a heat wave, all in a state-funded home. Doesn't that sound like the front page in the Metro section?"

"Mr. Lewis," Ms. Schnipp said, "we have limited funds. Our residents are destitute and severely ill and would otherwise be living on the streets."

"Enough," Al said, flipping open his cell phone. "I'll call the psychiatrist. Just stop with the threats. We'll get it done today." He loosened his tie, removed his suit jacket and scratched his arm. "Mr. Bell is going nowhere. Don't you think I'd like nothing more than to be rid of his goddamn Mr. Jula?"

"Did you say, 'Mr. Jula?'" I said.

"Did I say that?" he said. "W-well, what I mean is . . . we're always hearing him rant one name or another, always manipulating us. They're all—I mean, he's dangerous. Look, *we're* the ones who'll pay if your friend goes out and kills somebody."

Al roamed into the hall, bellowing into his phone. He had another maggot on his hands, he told the doctor. "You have to come *now*," Al shouted. "No I can't reason with him . . . This *is* an emergency . . . Yes . . . No . . . Look, if I can't count on you . . . Sure, Jared's here . . . Fine . . . "

"Dr. Dorfmann will be here in ten minutes," he said, walking back into the room. "Your friend will flunk. After today, you show your face again, and I'll have you arrested."

While Jimmy slept, Ms. Schnipp recommended Al take baths instead of showers. More relaxing, she told him. And she suggested scented candles. Then she chatted about her upcoming week off in Cape Cod while he held his forehead. All I could do to contain my fury was to pace back and forth in my half of the stuffy cell, my clothes getting more and more soaked. I kept wondering, Whatever happened to Sarah, Arnie and Henry?

The patients here were the ones nobody cared about. Even if I left to get an army of officials—which could take days at least—anything could happen to Jimmy between now and then. I needed to get him out *today*. But his speech was so slurred, would anyone find him competent? And we couldn't just barrel out of there. Beyond the doorway Jared's hand rested much too comfortably on his holstered sidearm.

There are levels of empathy. You identify with your old friend laying twisted on filthy sheets because you care about him or you feel guilty for not having helped him more when you had the chance. Or because for one moment you see no difference between him and yourself. In that moment you'll do whatever you can for him. You'll risk everything to save the one-of-a-kind, wild man schizophrenic . . . as you would a discarded jazzer ignorant of his own true power—the wave without limits.

CHAPTER 18

Beeom of Spirarus

TEN MINUTES turned into an hour before a man in a white lab coat with hulky black shoes squeezed around Jared, and into the room. Dr. Dorfmann, even with his hunched shoulders, towered over us, and with deep-set eyes that never seemed to blink, he looked as frightening as any of the patients. He coldly introduced himself, glanced at his watch and said, "Wake your friend."

"Jimmy, it's Shawn," I said. "Mr. Shawn Lewis." I nudged his bony shoulder, but he groaned and wouldn't come to. "Wake up, buddy. We need to show them you're not crazy." I kept nudging. "Come on, I'll play sax for you. Mr. Shawn Lewis has come from very far away to play for you. Wake up, buddy."

His eyes opened. A tear rolled out.

"It's me, Jimmy," I said. "You're safe. I won't let them hurt you anymore."

He grasped my hand, and started to sob.

"If you can make the bridges to the worlds," I whispered in his ear, "then you're a lot smarter than *these* bastards."

Jared brought in three chairs, and Al and Ms. Schnipp sat on the other side of Jimmy's narrow bed. I stood over Jimmy while the doctor sat next to me, his legs crossed with one of his size-18 shoes brushing against

Jimmy's sheets. "Let's get on with it," he said, bouncing the leg and the shoe, and looking at his watch.

I propped Jimmy up with his pillow.

"Name, age, place of birth," Dr. Dorfmann said.

Jimmy struggled to answer him, his words sloshing together. The doctor scribbled something on his pad.

"Stop it, damn it," Al said. "*Stop it.*"

"I agree," Dr. Dorfmann said. "Mr. Bell appears to be on tranquilizers. Let's reschedule."

"No," Al said, "we can do this. I, uh . . . I didn't mean anything." Then I thought I heard him whisper to the floor, "Fucking plarps."

"Scented candles, Al," Ms. Schnipp said, nodding. "Very relaxing."

I mumbled into Jimmy's ear: "I've got to get you out of here, buddy. Breathe. The drugs are slurring your speech. Breathe, buddy. Breathe like Miss Carole Bonner taught you, remember? Breathe so you can speak really slowly, as carefully as you can. Do this right, and I'll play my saxophone for you every day. I'll even look at your paintings, Jimmy, every day, and we'll talk all about the bridges to the worlds."

He gazed up at me. Then he answered the three questions again, hoarsely enunciating each syllable. There was no doubt he knew who he was.

He whispered to me, "You'll look? You'll look at my paintings?"

I nodded and held his hand.

"Do you know where we are, Mr. Bell?" Ms. Schnipp asked.

He took several deep breaths, then said, "Room three three . . . Second floor . . . Parkview Manor."

"Very good," Ms. Schnipp said.

"One Four Six Connelly Boulevard," Jimmy said. "East Brooklyn."

"Excellent," Ms. Schnipp said.

"New York. New York. United—"

"That's enough," Dr. Dorfmann said.

"Northern America," Jimmy said. "Western hemis—"

"That's enough, Mr. Bell," Dr. Dorfmann said.

"Earth. Third planet."

"Okay, Jimmy," I said, "I think they get the point."

"Lugos Solar System. Orion Arm. Milky Way . . ."

"Doctor," I said, "What's going on in this place? Why don't they feed him? Why do they torture him?"

"Twenty-second Meridian," Jimmy said. "Fourth Quadrant . . ."

"I don't know anything about any torture," Dr. Dorfmann said.

"Give him a physical then," I said.

"Malkuthian Circle . . . "

"We'd have to schedule that," Dr. Dorfmann said.

"We could plan one for October 25th," Ms. Schnipp said, beaming, "after you return from your exciting trip to Corfu. Oh, I do hope it doesn't rain when you're there."

"Ninth Zendosphere . . ."

"Mr. Bell," Dr. Dorfmann said, "why do you keep talking?"

"How do you think he got all those welts?" I asked the doctor.

"A delusional patient is capable of extraordinary things," Dr. Dorfmann said to me, "even beating himself into a coma."

"Third Universe . . . "

"Jimmy, you can stop now," I said.

"Beeom of Spirarus . . . "

"Why do you keep talking, Mr. Bell?" the doctor said, bouncing his Munster shoe against Jimmy's sheets.

Jimmy stopped, looked the doctor in the eyes, took two deep breaths and said, "Wart Lady wanted me to tell her where we were."

"Oh really," Ms. Schnipp said, folding her baggy arms. "Can you tell us *why* you're here?"

"A bad man lied to me," Jimmy said.

"Shut your mouth, Jula," Al said.

"What was that, Al?" the doctor said.

"Uh—what?" Al said, hiding the tic, his hand jiggling over his forehead.

"Tell us about your mother," Ms. Schnipp said to Jimmy.

"And very bad people want to keep me here," Jimmy said.

"I'd say you have a lot of issues, Mr. Bell," she said.

"I'm not feeling very well," Al said, getting up. "It's the heat. I'll uh . . . I'll just go into the hall." His body shook and quaked as he wandered out of the room.

"Maybe we should talk about these 'bad people' you say are after you," Ms. Schnipp said.

"Money money," Jimmy said. "Al Gazemsky Clyde Dorfmann get more money from big New York State if—"

"We're getting nowhere here," Dr. Dorfmann said, "and I have to leave in a few minutes. Mr. Bell, do you know the medical reason why you're here?"

"Disorganized schizophrenia," Jimmy said. "And for every drug you order you get money. Money money. For every patient you get—"

"I won't sit here and listen to this," the doctor said to me.

"But I'll bet my team of lawyers would find it very interesting," I said.

"I heard that," Al said, his voice muffled from outside the open door.

"Who is our wonderful president—can you tell me his name?" Ms. Schnipp asked.

"Bushface," Jimmy said.

"See?" she said. "You don't even know the president's name, do you?"

"George Walker Bushface of George Herbert Walker Bushface of Prescott Sheldon Bushface who gave money money to very bad people to help Nazi Hitler take over and—"

"Okay, all right," she said.

"Call them off, Bell," Al said from outside the room.

"Al, what are you talking about?" the doctor shouted.

"Uh, what I mean is," Al said. "You—Bell. Like to kill someone off, wouldn't you?"

"No, I am nice," Jimmy said. "Mr. Jula, when can we go to the Sheml?"

"Jimmy, not now," I said in a low voice.

"Yes," Jimmy said, "but I'm too weak to fly . . ."

"Not now, Jimmy," I whispered. "Quiet."

"What's all this?" Dr. Dorfmann said.

"Who is Mr. Jula?" Ms. Schnipp asked.

"*I'm* Mr. Jula," I said, pinching Jimmy on the arm. "His nickname for me. The Sheml is the new bodega in my neighborhood."

"Do you think you can fly?" Ms. Schnipp asked Jimmy.

"Not anymore," he said.

"You're *lying*," Al said to me, standing in the doorway. "*Lying*. You're not Mr. Jula and the Sheml is no grocery store, and you know it."

"Well, why don't you take it up with Mr. Sheml?" I said.

"Okay . . ." Al said, nodding, patting his forehead with his handkerchief.

"I—I will . . ."

Dr. Dorfmann suggested Al get under an air conditioner. The doctor then asked Jimmy to count backwards by seven, starting from one hundred. Jimmy had no problem. He asked Jimmy about traffic lights, gas stoves and other safety issues. Ms. Schnipp asked if he ever had the desire to injure himself. Jimmy practiced his breathing, spoke slowly, articulating as best he could. Twice he went off about Sedgwick, the plarps or Mr. Jula, but I quickly covered for him. He answered all their questions.

"How would you get a job?" Ms. Schnipp asked.

"I will make paintings," he said.

"Well, will that support you?" she asked.

"Mr. Shawn Lewis will play saxophone for me."

"You promise not to have anyone killed?" Al shouted from outside the room.

"What kind of question is that?" Dr. Dorfmann shouted back.

"Just make him answer," Al said.

"Al wants to know," the doctor said, "if you promise not to—"

"Yes," Jimmy said. "I am nice."

"How do you feel right now?" Ms. Schnipp asked.

"My head hurts," Jimmy said.

"Don't you think you'd be better off here, where you can rest?" she said.

"My stomach hurts. Back too."

"You have a lot of complaints, don't you?" she said.

"Hands aren't so good either and—"

"If we discharge you," the doctor said, "where will you go?"

"Mr. Shawn Lewis. He is my friend."

"What does it mean to be respectful of others?" Ms. Schnipp asked.

"I am nice."

"But you called me the Wart Lady," she said. "Is that how you show respect?"

"I forgot your name," he said, "and you have a very big wart."

"If I recommend a discharge plan," Dr. Dorfmann said. "It would require you to take your meds and see my assistants two or three times a week. Will you comply?"

"Maestro C will have to show him the gift," Jimmy said. "Mav is too proud."

"What was that?" Dr. Dorfmann said.

"What? What?" Ms. Schnipp said.

"Okay," I said, pinching Jimmy hard. "Maestro C is Jimmy's *other* nickname for me. And he calls his medication 'the gift,' wouldn't you? So he's a little eccentric; that doesn't make him crazy."

"What *horseshit,*" Al shouted, storming into the room in his undershirt and scratching his arm. "First—first of all, you—you're not Maestro C."

"I'm not?" I said.

"Uh . . . " Al said. The doctor and Ms. Schnipp were gaping at him. "Well, we've all heard Mr. Bell's rants enough to know that Maestro C couldn't possibly be you."

"Why not?" I said.

"Hmm," Al said, stepping backwards and trying to smile. "It's clear to *me*, anyway . . . "

Dr. Dorfmann shook his head, scribbled on his pad, then turned to me. "If we were to discharge Mr. Bell today, we'd need from you a commitment, Mr. Lewis: He has to take his meds every day."

"Fine, sure," I said. "Every day."

"Do you understand what we're asking you to do?" Dr. Dorfmann said to Jimmy.

"You want me to take the drugs every day," Jimmy said.

"All right," the doctor said. "Let's consult in Mr. Gazemsky's office. We'll be back in a few minutes."

After they left, I asked Jimmy, "Where are your parents? Who brought you here? Why is Gazemsky so mad at you?" But he was already asleep.

It took fifteen minutes for the jury to return. Al waited outside the room while Dr. Dorfmann sat on the other side of the bed, crossed his legs and again unconsciously bounced his shoe on the sheets. "Since the legal guardian is not present for a transfer of status," he said, "we have garnered the proper materials to satisfy that concern."

"Huh?" I said. ". . . Did Jimmy pass?"

"Yes," Ms. Schnipp said. "Mr. Bell is deemed competent and capable of making decisions. After you sign the two affidavits, you can go."

The first document was a dismissal of prior legal guardianship and a court order of "special guardianship" in which James Bell is responsible for his own person, but all financial and legal liabilities are assumed by the undersigned, Shawn Lewis of 232nd Street, Bronx, NY. The second attested to Mr. Bell's exemplary care and improved condition at Parkview Manor, as witnessed by the attending psychiatrist, social worker, local magistrate and the undersigned special guardian—me. Both statements were predated August 23rd, and already notarized by the magistrate. If I brought charges of abuse, they could claim Jimmy had been away from their care for three weeks.

"Where'd you get the phony judge?" I said. "I'm not signing these."

"We have all your information, Mr. Lewis," the doctor said. "Since Medicaid won't be paying for my consultation today, we're holding you responsible. With the Assessment and Discharge fees the total is 650 dollars—to be applied *now*."

"I don't have it," I said. "I get paid in two days. But I still won't have—"

"I'll take care of it," Al said, from the doorway. "Sign the documents."

Signing would allow their lawyers to ruin me if I made any trouble. I signed.

Dr. Dorfmann led Al back to his office while Ms. Schnipp woke Jimmy so he could sign his predated Discharge Plan. She showed us the prescriptions clipped inside. As I helped Jimmy out of his bed, Ms. Schnipp said to him, "I do hope you'll come visit us. Come on a Tuesday."

"Ms. Schnipp," I said, gripping the garbage bag and Jimmy, "you *really* need to talk to someone."

My saxophone was still in the recreation room, and Jared accompanied us there. The guys were playing our '60s TV medley. Most of the audience was snoring.

Jimmy and I headed for the exit, and Dr. Dorfmann appeared out of nowhere. "I just left Al on the couch in his office," he said. "He swears Mr. Bell is dangerous—homicidal, actually."

"Well, don't worry," I said, opening the lobby door as Jimmy clung to me, barely awake.

"Just make sure Mr. Bell takes his meds and sees my staff at least twice a week."

~~~~~~

WE WALKED down the wide, busy sidewalk of Connelly Boulevard—Jimmy and I, the garbage bag and my saxophone. I'd gotten him out, the proudest thing I'd ever done. I glanced back at Parkview Manor, and savored our triumph. I wasn't watching where we were going, and Jimmy and I collided with a homeless man in rags, frantically waving his arms. The man was laughing with half his teeth missing, and waving giant beats in the middle of the crowded, overheated sidewalk—conducting—to no one at all.

"Mr. Shawn Lewis!" the man shouted and laughed, still waving his arms. "It's your turn!"

"How do you know me?" I said, glaring at him as I rushed Jimmy toward the subway.

"We all know you, Mr. Shawn Lewis," he said. ". . . Hey, don't leave me! It's *your turn*!"
~~~~~~

CHAPTER 19

Bird & The Starry Night

SO WHAT IF another lunatic knows my name, I thought, trying to calm my pulse inside the subway car. But all the old fears came storming back: about the madness, the recklessness of my music, about becoming another *man in red*—the man whose survival now depended on *me,* now dozing next to *me,* leaning on *me* in his soiled clothes and tattered slippers. What will happen if I can't find Jimmy's parents? *Chaos.* I can't take care of him. I can barely take care of *myself.*

He needed an Emergency Room, but that would certainly risk losing him to the authorities. A few slips about jellybeans or the Sheml and he'd be back in an institution, and for all I knew Parkview Manor was the norm.

It was close to 3 PM by the time we were walking down my street. I held Jimmy close, guiding him, while I called Super Duper and told them my "back spasms" were worse than ever, but I'd be in tomorrow. We got stares from the hoods loitering along the construction pile and the neighbors sitting out in their lounge chairs, among them, Colfield Dixon. He studied Jimmy and me a long moment, and said, "Interesting . . . "

I half-carried Jimmy up our stoop, past the mailbox wall in the vestibule, and up the stairs. As we turned for the second flight we walked right into Muriel Fetterman. "Hello Shawn," she said, grabbing my wrist with her pudgy hand. "Is this gentleman one of your jazz cohorts?"

"Uh . . . sort of," I said, holding Jimmy upright.

"You know," she said, gesturing for me to lean down so she could whisper, "management frowns on vagrants."

"Thank you, I didn't know," I said to her, pulling my groggy friend around her. But she held onto my wrist.

"I won't mention anything to anyone," she said, "about your homeless chums. But management also frowns on . . . shall we say, unusual relationships."

"How about if I stop by later and pick up some more detergent or something?"

"Oh, that would be lovely," she said, and let us go. Bribes were the fastest way around Muriel.

I opened the door to my apartment as Galicia jumped out of hers, shrieking, "Thank God you're all right!"

"Not now, Galicia," I said, shoving Jimmy through my door.

"The cards said you were in mortal danger."

"Good," I said, "have a nice day now." I slammed the door. Her muffled voice was still yapping, so I turned on the stereo. Cannonball always set things right.

I flicked the magazines and CD covers off the sofa so Jimmy could sit down.

"Thank you so much, Mr. Shawn Lewis," he said, stretching out. "So much, so muh . . ." He was gone again. With Cannonball bopping through the apartment, one last time I tried Sarah and Arnie. The number was no longer in service. I sifted for two minutes through the piles on my desk until I found my old datebook with Henry's number. *His* was out of service.

I didn't want to disturb Jimmy, but I had to know. I shook him awake, and asked if he knew where his parents were. His eyes half closed, he said Sarah was in the kitchen and Arnie was in front of the TV, then fell back asleep.

I returned to my desk, to my computer, and did my weekly search for the Bells, hoping for something new. There were the same decades-old albums Sarah had made with the Philharmonic, and the same six-year-old blurb about the closing of Bell's Cleaners—nothing else.

Other than Henry, I couldn't remember the names of their friends. The only first name I could summon was Frances, the woman with the crazy niece. The last name was hopeless. Frances Flicklicker? Beetlestein? Tinkleman?

Above the desk was a bulletin board so cluttered with receipts and urgent notes, it defeated its purpose. Bulletins couldn't cut through the noise. Still, I always made room for my superhero, a black-and-white eight-by-eleven of Bird with his alto. What would *he* do for Jimmy, I wondered. He'd play for him, since there was no way he could get Jimmy any more stoned.

Bird jogged the name: *Pinklestein.* I looked her up and made the call.

"Whatever you're selling," she said, "forget it. I've had it with you people."

"Frances," I said, "I'm not selling anything. This is Shawn Lewis, remem—"

"Lawnmowers? I live in an apartment! Don't you people check these things out?" Apparently, Frances had lost a little hearing, but that wasn't all she'd lost.

"No, this is *Shawn,*" I hollered, "*Shawn Lewis* . . . Remember the sax?"

"Slacks?"

"I played sax for Jimmy Bell!"

"Plaid slacks? For shimming felt? No, no, I finished with the felt already."

I was lucky she didn't hang up. After three torturous minutes she remembered me and the Bells. "Where are they now?" I asked her.

"Do you know where they are?" she said.

"No, I'm asking *you.* Do *you* know where they are?"

"Who?"

I shouted like I was at an airport hangar: *"Do you know where your good friend Sarah Bell is?"*

"Oh yes. I'd love to know where she is."

"What about Arnie? Do you remember where Arnie is?"

"Arnie? Of course. I used to know all about Arnie. Do you know—"

"What about Henry Felder? Any chance you might know—"

"Oh sure," she said. "Henry's at Greenburg Commons Assisted Living Facility in Coney Island. You get there on the D Train."

"Thank you, that's a big help. Say Frances, whatever happened with Louise?"

"Louise? Louise is doing great—married a corporate lawyer."

"He's okay with all the—you know, Dorothy stuff?"

"Well, she still sings like a sea lion, but he loves the braids and the outfit, says it makes her look fourteen."

". . . Fourteen?"

"Yeah, that worried me too," she said, "but my sister's family is all over him—always kissing his butt."

"You mean, because he's a big-time lawyer?"

"No, they're just so glad to be rid of all the singing."

I PHONED GREENBURG COMMONS, but Henry accepted calls only from his immediate family. A trip to Coney Island was now imperative, yet how could I leave Jimmy to wake alone in an unfamiliar space after years inside that nightmare? And there was no way to lock him in. I needed a favor from a trusted friend.

Julio, the super of my building, would've been my first choice. He loved music, and aside from Jimmy, was the only one who liked it when I practiced. Though he was the most affable person I knew, Julio had a temper. Complain too often and you'd find your malfunctioning radiator or spigot in pieces. He'd make everything work a month or two later, but you couldn't do that with a human being.

My friend Kelvin from the video store would do it, but he was only twenty and never left the house without smoking half a bag. I couldn't call him anyway. Because of my "back spasms" he was the one covering me at the store.

It had been over five years since we'd talked, and still, the prospect of calling Carole in Scarsdale and hearing Mark answer the phone made me cringe. But now I had no choice. I called Scarsdale. The number had changed to somewhere in downtown Manhattan. I called that number;

it had changed. I tried the next one, and Carole picked up the phone. I told her I was in a crisis; I'd rescued Jimmy and couldn't find his parents. I needed her help. Incredibly, she said she'd be right over.

Within an hour Carole was standing in my living room in a sleeveless gray pantsuit and short hair, looking a little older but with those chestnut eyes, smooth pale skin and that smile that drew me to her lips. *And no wedding ring.* After her pull-away hug, she ran over to Jimmy who was still asleep.

"Are you sure that's Jimmy?" she said.

"You look wonderful," I said.

"Shawn, this can't be the same man."

"Thanks so much for coming."

"Well, whoever it is, you did the right thing getting him out of that hell-hole."

"It's definitely Jimmy," I said, "and did I mention how wonderful you look? How's Mark?"

"Shawn, we've been divorced for three months—no children, thank God . . . You were right about him." She kissed me on the cheek and backed away.

"Well, I never said—"

"You called him a turd, and, well . . . I wish I'd seen it. Anyway, I'm in therapy about it. We talk about you too. I'm dealing with a lot of stress. I *love* therapy though—the whole process. How are you doing? Are you going to be able to take care of Jimmy if his parents are gone? I live on West 78th Street now. I'm a hospice counselor. My own therapy is teaching me how to help other people. Are you still composing? Are you in a relationship? That woman Irene calls me once in a while—really strange conversations. It's so great to see you. I still worry about you."

It annoyed all her friends, she used to tell me, but the excited way she'd dance through ten earnest thoughts in five seconds was the same way she'd skipped off with my heart. For me, not a moment had elapsed from the day we'd met. "Carole, I . . . I—"

She looked deep into my eyes. "I don't know, Shawn," she said, "maybe . . . you know, your friend should really be in a hospital."

"We should really be . . . " I said, our eyes still locked. "Uh . . . No, when he opens his mouth they'll just commit him again. We need his parents or Henry."

She urged me to find Henry.

It was almost 5:30 when I arrived at Greenburg Commons. I asked the guard for Henry Felder, and he sent me to the dining hall. Henry was easy to find. His table, with four other red-faced seniors guffawing at his jokes, was by far the rowdiest. At 85 he was still the sparkplug in the room.

"Excuse me," I said, standing across from Henry, "I'm sorry to interrupt your dinner. Do you remember me, Henry? I'm Shawn Lew—"

"Of course, son!" he said. "Hey, your rash is all cleared up."

"No. I never—why is everybody—"

"What brings you to our little haven?"

I told him all about Jimmy and how I needed to find Sarah and Arnie.

"Sorry, folks," Henry said to his friends as he got up, still chewing, wiping his mouth with a napkin. "First thing tomorrow—golf course, right? And let's lay some manly odds this time—none of that chicken shit, okay?"

He clasped my shoulders. "What a treat to see you, son," he said. "I'll give you the tour."

"Henry, I don't have time for a—"

"You've got to see this layout. We'll start with the exercise room."

"I'm sure it's great, but what's happened to Sarah and Arnie?"

"On second thought," he said, "let's start with the breakfast lounge. The food is terrific and it's included in the price."

I kept asking. It wasn't clear if he was evading the question or a little senile. His mind was on the tour: the ping-pong room, billiard tables, the indoor pool, sauna and steam room, the bingo club, the dance hall. I stopped him, seized his forearms, looked him in the eyes, and said, "Where are Sarah and Arnie?"

"They're gone now, son," he said.

"What happened to them?"

"You know, when they got married, Arnie made me his Best Man. I was the one who brought Sarah and Arnie to Sheepshead Bay. *I* did that. Me. They were mine—the only couple I ever adopted."

"Did they both die?"

"*Everybody's* gone now, son," he said. "Oh look, that's Building C over there on the left. That's where Jack and Shirley live. She has a glass eye. Over there, that's Gertrude Hammerman's pad. She's big and fat now, but I understand she used to be a cutie. We had something going before Milton Mazelli showed up. Such a blowhard."

"Who is Jimmy's legal guardian?"

He ignored me, leading me to his apartment, a three-bedroom suite with a view of the Atlantic. "Not bad, huh, son?"

"Best apartment I've ever seen. What about Jimmy?"

"I'd rather not to talk about him," he said, pointing around to his big-screen TV, his framed war medals, his Brooklyn Dodger table of programs, caps, baseballs, bats, autographs by Jackie Robinson and Gil Hodges. "I'll tell you how Sarah and Arnie met."

"I know already. Sarah told me."

"She tell you Arnie used to have hair? I mean, he was no Tom Cruises, but he had a mane of black hair, a beard like Rabbi Schneerson. He was tough. Fearless. But you know what I remember the most? The mischief, the twinkle. There he was, tragedy all around, and he'd have a great joke he couldn't wait to tell you."

"How did he die?"

"Did you know Arnie could live off shrubs?" he said. "And he was a crack shot. Saved almost all his partisans. The Underground wanted him to shed the slow ones—you know, the kids and grandparents; he wouldn't do it. Hey, take a look at my library."

After he showed me his rare book collection, his fishing rod and cuff links, he said, "I'm thirsty. Wait till you see this kitchen."

"How did Sarah die?"

"Say, I'll bet you didn't know her name used to be Sarah Topolowsky? Did you know she was a violin prodigy?"

"Yes, of course."

"Did you know she lived through Auschwitz? She played in the women's orchestra. They had to be perfect. A spot in the orchestra meant a chance to live, but if they plucked you out, you were a goner. The SS loved classical music—can you believe it? The orchestra was wired to loudspeakers while the Nazi lords of culture would strut around, cleansing the world of their 'inferiors.' For those devils great music went fine with mass murder." He took a sip of ginger ale.

"I need help for Jimmy," I said. "Who committed him to Parkview Manor?"

"Did you know I was a lieutenant in the 45th? We liberated Dachau. Changed my life. I saw mothers, fathers, little children, whole towns starved and gassed . . . stuffed into open wagons. I can't erase it from my mind. It's why I went into public service, son. After the war I went east, where the survivors needed the most help. That's how I met Arnie and Sarah. She was recuperating in a Red Army hospital. Arnie never left her side. Neither of them had anywhere to go—no family left."

"Jimmy's in my apartment right now."

"You have Jimmy?" he said. "No, the boy's in a home."

"Not anymore; that's what I've been trying to tell you."

"After you stopped coming around—I don't know, it must be over five or six years now—in the middle of one of his naps Arnie dropped dead right on the couch—heart attack. Jimmy found him. When Sarah and her friend Agnus came back from shopping and saw what happened, Sarah began to shriek. Agnus told me the boy was sitting next to Arnie's body and laughing. *Laughing*—can you believe it? What a putz. Losing Arnie, seeing Jimmy laughing must've been too much for Sarah. Her mind came apart. Soon she was talking to people that weren't there, just like the putz. There was nothing any of us could do except help her into a nursing home. She lasted only a year. I'm still not over them. My best friends."

"I'm sorry, Henry."

"I miss them," he said, blowing his nose into a handkerchief.

"I miss them too, Henry," I said. For a few minutes we stared at our warm ginger ales. Jimmy must've snapped when he found his father, I thought. No rational person could laugh at a time like that, but nothing about Jimmy was "correct." I couldn't judge him—not after what he'd been through.

"At least now we can help Jimmy," I said. "Have you seen how he's been living?"

"I haven't had a chance to visit him recently. Maybe I'll go next week."

"I've told you; he's with me now. He's lost a lot of weight. He looks—"

"That's good he lost the weight. He was a pig."

"They were beating him and keeping him unconscious, Henry. I can't believe Sarah would put him in there."

"She didn't," he said. "She wanted the boy near her nursing home, so first we moved him into South Shore—South Shore Medical Center, but he hated it."

"Wait—why would Sarah put him in a place he hated?"

"She wanted him nearby but she never left the nursing home. She never left her room. And they mistreated him there."

"So *you* moved him into Parkview. Do you have power of attorney? Are you his legal guardian?"

"What is this, the Third Degree?" he said. "Sarah needed me. She couldn't do the simplest things. She was talking to the walls half the time. And I didn't move the boy out until she was gone. South Shore was getting ready to discharge him anyway."

"He said 'a bad man' had put him in Parkview. Did he mean you, Henry?"

"He's talking about the South Shore administrator. What an asshole."

I hugged and thanked him. All these places must be snake pits, I thought, and it couldn't have been easy for Henry. After all, he was 81 when Sarah died.

WHEN I GOT BACK to my place, it was already 9 PM. Carole was sitting on a chair by the couch, spoonfeeding Jimmy a bowl of soup.

"Any luck?" she asked me.

"Jimmy," I said, "do you know about your parents? Do you know that—"

"Mom and dad are in the kitchen," he said, slurping a mouthful.

Soon he needed to sleep again, and Carole hustled me into the kitchen.

"Did you see all the needle marks on his arms?" she said. "Jimmy's an addict."

"Him? No, it was the staff over there. They saturated him with downers and painkillers. He probably fought back, and that explains all the—"

"Did you know you're almost out of food?"

"I was going to pick up some TV dinners and peanut butter and—"

"No way," she said. "I'll make a list. And when was the last time you vacuumed? Your whole apartment is under a film. You've got a patient in there. It took me half an hour of sorting through your stuff and vacuuming just to make the couch area tolerable." As she reached for the jug of "Monster Shine" off the top of the refrigerator, balls of dust snowed over us. "I've never seen a dustier apartment with so many unopened cleaning products," she said. "This one says it's 'the finest marble cleaner in the world.' You don't have any marble."

"I know, but I get everything half price. From my neighbor downstairs. She leaves me alone if I buy soap from her . . . It's complicated."

"Well, what's going on upstairs?" she asked. "Up until an hour ago it sounded like mobs of stomping kids. How do you live with it?"

"You know what? I just realized maybe that's why I took a job from three to eleven . . . Wow . . . Carole, it feels so right having you here. And I'm not just saying that because I could use your help for another day or two . . . But, could you help me for another day or—"

"My schedule's pretty full," she said. "And I'd have to get down to my apartment for some clothes and things . . . "

"You can have my room. I promise not to come knocking . . . unless . . . "

"You come knocking, Shawn—the deal's off."

I told her about my job in the movie business—the counter at Super Duper Video.

"What happened to all your students?" she said. "Your big music jobs?"

"Things kind of died when the hotel burned . . . and when you got married."

"Where are Jimmy's meds?"

"The prescriptions are inside the Discharge Plan."

"You didn't fill them?"

"I had to find Henry," I said, "and anyway, Jimmy doesn't want the drugs."

"Shawn, listen to me, *Jimmy is a schizophrenic*. He needs his medicine."

"I'm beginning to wonder. I'm not sure he's so mentally ill."

"The doctors don't know anything?" she said. "Take it from the nurse:

The meds maintain a balance in his brain. There's an all-night drugstore on White Plains Road, underneath the elevated. And if you give me a minute I'll make a grocery list."

Jimmy was still asleep when I returned with the drugs and the food. Carole had already made three place settings at my small kitchen table. While she cooked, I sat by Jimmy. He smelled like a rotting New York City dumpster. I'd never been so exhausted and distressed, the weight of it all dawning on me again. And then I remembered the psycho on Connelly Boulevard, waving his arms, yelling my name. What did he mean, It's *my* turn? I started shaking.

I stared at the noisy bulletin board, my photo of Bird and the framed poster above the TV, Van Gogh's *The Starry Night*. I loved *The Starry Night*. The moon and stars and the spaces between them vibrated and flowed in and out of the trees and hills. It jumped with the sense of possibility, almost like it was talking to me, comforting me. A few moments with that poster, and I always felt better.

Carole had made sautéed chicken breasts and a full salad, and we ate quietly in the kitchen. The dinner was perfect, but even from there I could smell Jimmy. Halfway through the meal he woke up. Disoriented, with rabid TD shakes, he cried out to his invisible friends.

"Never!" he shouted. "I told you, get them away from me! *Destroy* them."

"Jimmy," I said, rushing to him, "you're safe. You're with Carole and me."

"Destroy," he said, "destroy, *destroy. Now!*"

Carole calmly went to work on him, reassuring him, soothing him, telling him over and over where he was and who we were. She led him to the open chair at our table, where she demonstrated the deep breaths that had helped him pass the competency test. He relaxed, and began to weep. Carole served him a bowl of vegetable soup, and we sat next to him. "Thank you so much, so much," he kept saying, his mouth and arms twitching.

"You need gentle foods now," she said to him, "until you regain your digestion. They weren't feeding you. I'll make a list of the kinds of foods you can handle. Shawn, you'll have to watch him. He can't just eat whatever he wants. If he ate that whole bag of Fig Newtons you just bought, he could die. I'll stay a couple of days, but tomorrow you have to find out what happened to his parents' estate. Maybe they left him a trust. You'll need whatever's out there. Home health care adds up fast."

"Jimmy," I said, "did your folks give you a trust?"

"Mom and dad give me lots of trust," he said, slurping the soup.

"Thanks, great," I said, and turned to Carole. "You know, I think they *owned* that big apartment—two blocks from the bay, must be worth a fortune."

"Maybe Jimmy owns it now. Do you own your old apartment?" she asked him.

"No one owns anything," he said, "but people think like they do."

She handed him his collection of pills with a tall glass of water. He looked each of us in the eyes, turned the glass upside down over my rug, and hurled the pills across the kitchen.

"Hmm," I said. "Maybe we should wait before we rush him back to the pills."

"You need your meds, Jimmy," she said. She explained it to him in the clearest, most logical terms, referring to doctors, science, research. She handed him the pills again. He threw them on the floor. She kept telling him it was for his own good, but he'd have none of it.

He finished his soup, and Carole served him another bowl. Within a minute, he picked up the half-eaten bowl, looked at each of us, and turned it upside down over the floor. "No more drugs!" he yelled at Carole.

"I dissolved the pills in his soup," she whispered to me. "All right, Jimmy, you win. Tonight we'll skip your meds, but you can't just stop taking them. You'll go into withdrawals. Your heart could stop."

While Carole helped him with his soup, I took Muriel's "Gonzo Clean" and the garbage bag of his fouled clothes to the laundry room. Gonzo Clean was guaranteed to remove smells and kill anything near it.

I returned to find Carole still persuading Jimmy about his drugs. "The Risperdal is for the schizophrenia," she said to him, showing him the bottle. "Compazine is to help with the nausea from the Risperdal. Paxil is for the mood swings, and the Sennacot is so you'll poop when all of these clog you up. These could make you a little tired or dizzy, but I think you're confusing your meds with the sedatives those jerks shot into you. Their needles would've interacted with your meds. I promise, Jimmy, no one here will ever do that to you. Your drugs are good for you, the best treatment for what you have."

"No more," he said, shaking his head, "no more, Miss Carole Bonner."

"He's really stubborn," she said to me, then turned to Jimmy. "You remember how excited you were when I said I'd give you a bath?"

He nodded, his eyes flaming.

"Well, how about if we make a deal," she said. "I'll give you a bath tonight and tomorrow, and I'll make your meals, and I'll come visit whenever I can if you agree to a strict program for weaning yourself off the meds."

He slowly scanned the room.

"You could die if you stopped cold turkey," she said.

"The plarps," he said. "The plarps say I should do it."

"Shawn, this is way over my head."

I went back to the laundry room to transfer his sandblasted clothes—mostly pajamas and underwear—into the dryer, and ran back to the apartment. By that time they'd negotiated a ten-day weaning period. Carole had wanted three weeks.

While we waited for the dryer, for the first time in over five years I played the saxophone for Jimmy. It was close to midnight, so I played like a whisper, but I'd kept my promise to him. No jellybeans, he told me, but he liked it anyway.

When the basket of clothes was ready, I helped Carole with Jimmy's bath, testing the limits of my uneasy constitution. I couldn't inhale anywhere around him and my stomach buckled with every welt and needle mark. But Carole was in control.

Jimmy wasn't at all bashful. He groaned and called out a few times but mostly reveled in it, thanking Miss Carole Bonner and guiding her hand as she wiped down his body. We decided not to shave him—too many bruises on his face.

Carole never winced or changed expression. Two of his wounds were infected, she said, but none looked serious. After she treated them, bandaging the open ones, we dressed him in his clean pajamas.

We placed fresh sheets and a pillow on the sofa. Then she gave each of us pull-away hugs, and locked herself in my bedroom. Jimmy was out as soon as his head brushed the pillow.

But on the floor between my desk and Jimmy's sofa, as bone-tired as I was, I couldn't get comfortable. And it wasn't just the hard rug or the clouds of dust. How could I sleep knowing it was up to me to find Jimmy's money? Then I imagined Bird and *The Starry Night* just a few feet away watching over me, comforting me. That's when I realized something: With the love of my heart camped in my room and my only fan snoring on my couch, I'd accomplished more in one day than I had my entire life.

CHAPTER 20

The Celebrity of Greenburg Commons

I COULDN'T HAVE BEEN more wasted when Jimmy woke me at 3 AM asking for more soup. I heated him two cans, and while he ate, I slept with my head flat on the kitchen table. Then he wanted some saxophone. My tired words on behalf of Carole and my neighbors never got through to him, but when I told him I didn't have the air to play a single note, he gave up and returned to the sofa. And I collapsed on my sliver of rug.

At five he woke me again, this time throwing up the soup three feet from my head. I turned on all the lights, and despite my pledge to her, I knocked on her door. While Carole took care of Jimmy, I changed the sheets, and poured a whole bottle of Muriel's "Scuzz Gone" over everything within a six-foot radius of the sofa. Carole helped him out of his wet pajamas, served him chamomile tea, and then somehow convinced him to take another round of medicines.

As the drugs coaxed Jimmy back to the sofa, Carole left for my room without a word. He curled up, his face buried in the cushion, but something had been gnawing at me, and I had to know the answer. "Jimmy," I said, standing over him, "Who was the 'bad man' who—"

"Uncle Hen," he said, his eyes closed.

"No, I mean the 'bad man' you said had lied to you."

"Uncle Hen," he mumbled, nodding off.

I couldn't go back to sleep. You don't quickly recover from nearby vomit. I dimmed the lights, sat at my computer, and began the search for whatever happened to Jimmy's inheritance. I found plenty of links listing Parkview Manor's address and phone number but no reports on its operation. The South Shore Medical Center website displayed an expensive, carefully monitored private hospital boasting state-of-the-art care and had a dozen links saluting the psychiatric ward.

I learned as much as I could until Jimmy woke at 8 AM, screaming, "The gripes! The gripes!" I jumped to the sofa, expecting another mess, but there was nothing. Carole, in my bathrobe, which fit her like a full-length poncho, cracked the bedroom door, then hurried over to him. I thanked her for taking over, and returned to my computer. Within minutes she was spoonfeeding him oatmeal and fruit. Even first thing in the morning—no makeup, the baggy robe, her short brown hair in a scramble—Carole made my pulse leap.

In between Jimmy's slurps, I asked him, "What was wrong with South Shore?"

"I like South Shore," he said. "I like it here. Please don't make me go to—"

"You *like* South Shore?" I said. "Henry said—"

"Uncle Hen put me in Parkview," he said, gagging, coughing up some oatmeal.

"Now isn't the best time," Carole said to me, holding the spoon to Jimmy's mouth. "He's had a rough night."

I went back to my screen and ran a search on pensions. Why would Henry lie about South Shore? A long-term congressman, borough president, and decorated officer could rack up almost 150,000 dollars a year in benefits and not need to steal from anyone.

I then called South Shore and told the director of Psychiatric Admissions about Jimmy and my role as special guardian. She said there was a one-year waiting list for long-term, live-in care, and even after private insurance—which we didn't have—I'd pay over $50,000 a year. I made an appointment with her for later that morning.

Then I dialed all the real estate brokers in Sheepshead Bay and learned it had been over four years since Apartment 1 at 271 Denwood, a 2000 square foot bayside condominium, was sold by Henry Felder for over $800,000. I then called the Greenburg Commons sales rep and told him I was worried my father couldn't afford his ocean-view three-bedroom suite. "Henry Felder is his name," I said.

"You're one of Henry's sons?" the man asked.

"Yes," I said, "and he won't let any of us give him money for what must be an enormous bill. I'd like to help him. How much is his rent?"

"Oh, no need to worry about Henry," he said. "He's our celebrity. Even my grandparents loved him. He's brought in a dozen other residents, so we give your father special treatment. That big suite is his for the price of a studio."

Carole was ruthlessly vacuuming the apartment, and I couldn't think anymore over the noise. I grabbed a bowl of cereal, and sat next to Jimmy's sofa while he talked to my window about pink skies and striped kangaroos. I asked him more about Uncle Hen, but he wouldn't notice me until I put down the cereal and blew my saxophone. "I have to go to South Shore," I said. "Carole will keep you company."

"I like Miss Carole Bonner."

"Me too . . . " I said, wincing, as she tossed my magazines and business papers into a garbage bag. "Are you sure about Henry? Is it possible he really believed he—"

"Money money," Jimmy said. "I didn't want Parkview but Uncle Hen said it was good. I trusted Uncle Hen. Then they stuck me with needles."

BY 11 AM I was describing Jimmy's nightmare to the director of Psychiatric Admissions while showing her my copy of the guardianship order.

"He was obese when he was with us," the director said. "And most unusual; he only wore red. Colors, you know, were very important to him. I guess it had something to do with his love for painting."

"You allowed him to paint here?" I said.

"We encouraged it. When he was a resident we hung every painting he made."

"Was he happy here?"

"Gradually, yes," she said. "His mother helped a great deal, made sure he had a nice room, whatever he needed: notebooks—he loved to write in his notebooks—and of course, the paints and canvases, and crates of his favorite snacks."

"His mother? Wasn't she incapacitated?"

"She visited every day, all day."

"She wasn't in a nursing home?"

"Mrs. Bell was fragile. Her husband had died recently, and she moved into Hadassah House just down the street, but she loved to sit with her son while he painted. She wanted to make Jimmy a long-term resident. She even drew up a contract to sell her home—use the proceeds to guarantee him a room. But then her health failed. She set up a legal guardian, a family friend. His name is in the file."

"Henry Felder."

"Yes. And the day after she died, Mr. Felder discharged Jimmy and admitted him into Parkview Manor."

By 12:30 I was in Greenburg Commons tracing the celebrity to the walkway toward the indoor pool. He was in his bathing suit, heading for the water.

"Henry," I said, "I have to talk to you."

"Son, I'm about to swim. I've got to do it *now*."

"This is urgent, Henry."

"In another half hour Dotty Krinkler gets in and wrecks it for everybody. You haven't seen cellulite till you see the legs she's carrying around—like bags of doorknobs."

"What did you do with all the money, Henry?"

"Money? Which money?"

"Sarah never would've left Jimmy to those slimeballs."

"Can't you see I'm in my bathing suit? I told you, son, if I don't get my swim in now, Dotty'll ruin everything."

"This is a great place," I said. "And to think you get all these perks for the price of a studio. Not bad."

"What are you, snooping into my private business? What happened to you? You used to be such a nice boy."

"You've known Jimmy all his life. He thought you loved him. Is taking all his money the way you show it?" I blocked his path. "The sale of the apartment would've been enough to keep Jimmy where his mother wanted him. What happened to the money?"

"That was years ago," he said. "I was grieving—I can't remember all I had to do. I can't even remember if I moved my bowels today."

"You can't remember what you did with Sarah and Arnie's estate?"

"There were all kinds of bills from South Shore, I remember that. Constant. And Jimmy couldn't wait to get out of there. Practically begged me."

"He told me he liked it there."

"You taking that wacko's word over mine? I don't have to justify anything to you," he said, glancing at a surveillance camera. "Son, we've got a fella here named Dante—more than your typical security guy. Sort of a bodyguard bouncer all in one. I holler—ten seconds your face is pinned to the concrete. Now let me have my swim."

"Every hour of home-health care costs almost twice what I make," I said. "We need to set up a trust in Jimmy's name. It's *his* money."

"What are you on, speed?"

"I just want what he deserves."

"You're high, son. Look," he said, checking his watch, "I got only ten minutes before fat Dotty makes waves you could surf on."

"You once told me the whole community would stand with me for what I was doing for Jimmy."

"I don't remember that."

"You said Sarah and Arnie were champions of life. Well, Jimmy's a champion too. He just needs a chance to—"

"He's a *putz*. Why didn't you leave him in the booby hatch?"

"If you won't do it for Jimmy's sake, do it for Arnie and—"

"Shit! There goes Dotty." A seismic wave swallowed the edge of the pool, and soaked our ankles.

"Now that she's here," I said, "let's go to your home and sort this out."

"Damn it, you son-of-a-bitch," he said, glowering at the pool as it cleared of the white-haired swimmers. "You killed my afternoon," he said, his voice breaking. "Get out before I call Dante."

"Sarah's body wasn't yet cold when you had Jimmy tranquilized where nobody'd ever find him; isn't that right?"

"You got some nerve!" he shouted, as bathing-suited elders surrounded us. "South Shore would've drained the estate, and for what? For that putz?"

"Henry, is this guy bothering you?" asked a man with flabby breasts.

"He was on his way out," Henry said.

"I'm not leaving till I get something for Jimmy," I said.

"Want I should kick his ass, Henry?" yelled a tiny man in a massive bathing suit.

When the growing crowd started tugging at me, I shot Henry with everything: "I'll tell these people and every newspaper in town how the great Henry Felder stole from his best friends, *Holocaust survivors.*" They loosened their grip on me. "Your dying friend trusted you with all she had to provide for her son, and you locked him in a shit-hole and kept the money for yourself." Everyone parted the way for a large man with a neck like a tree trunk.

"What's the problem here, Henry?" the man asked.

". . . No," Henry said, looking at the pavement, "no problem, Dante."

Dante asked several times, but no one in the crowd said a word.

"It's okay," Henry said. "He's with me."

Henry ushered me from the pool area to his apartment. He was silent while he put on his robe, and poured himself warm ginger ale. We sat at his kitchen table for at least five minutes before he spoke.

"Okay," he said, looking at the yellow table, "I'll do something, but not for you, and not for the putz. Whatever I do, it's for Sarah and Arnie . . . " He sighed.

"I was thinking of a trust of about 4200 a month," I said. "That'll cover his South Shore expenses next year, and for now, while we're on the waiting list."

"You're delirious."

"You have a world class pension. What do you need *their* money for?"

"Can you see into my life?" he said. "My five children from three marriages? They're allergic to the old man. My grown grandchildren could care less if I live or die. My great grandchildren—forget about it. You want to know what happened to the money? It went to *them*, all of them. They get a check, I get a call. A big check, I get a visit. My best friends are dead. I want my family. I deserve that much."

"Sarah and Arnie were your family," I said. "You adopted them, remember?"

"I understand you finagled your way into guardianship. What the hell is a *special* guardian?"

"What? How did you know—"

"Well you won't finagle me out of the executorship of Arnie and Sarah's estate. 4200 a month—*bullshit*. South Shore—*bullshit*. Out of respect for Sarah and Arnie, I'll give you 3000 a month. Better take it. Fight me and we'll tie this up in court for years. He stepped to his refrigerator, removed the magnets around a list of phone numbers and picked up his wall phone. "You're making me into a thief, son. *You're* the thief. All I've ever done is serve people." He anchored the phone around his neck, and dialed.

He called his lawyer. The trust would be in Jimmy's name, and I'd have power of attorney. "The boy'll have to sign for this," he said, handing me a note with the lawyer's information. "Call my man tomorrow. It'll be ready within the week."

Henry sat down. We both stared at the table. I tried small talk. I asked about his fishing tackle, his Dodger caps, his favorite shirts. He just looked into space, sipping ginger ale. "Where are Jimmy's paintings?" I asked. "Are they in storage?"

"What?" he said. "Oh, I threw them out. They were all shit; you know that."

AS I ENTERED my dimmed apartment, I stumbled into a row of full garbage bags waiting to go out. Jimmy was asleep on the sofa, and Carole put down her book in the kitchen to come out and whisper hello. As we crept back to the kitchen, I noticed what she'd done to my apartment while I was working my three-to-eleven. Every surface was bare and shining, nothing out of place. I'd forgotten how much floor space I'd had. Of course, any loose papers, like my handwritten music manuscripts—if they'd sat in the wrong spot, they were stuffed in the bags now.

"I just couldn't stand it one second longer," she said when we reached the kitchen. "If Jimmy's going to get well—I mean, you know, back to the way he used to be—he's got to have a clean environment."

"Well, great job," I said, straining to remember which bills were now missing.

We talked for twenty minutes about Henry, the bank trust, and the home-health agencies Carole knew from her hospice work. She offered us one more day so we could sort out the trust and book a nurse's aide.

"Carole," I said, "you're a lifesaver."

"No," she said, "the way you rescued your friend—*you're* the hero. I always knew you had it in you." She peered down, and said, "I'm sorry . . . I wish . . . I wish I was ready for . . ."

When she looked up, I gazed into her inviting eyes and tried not to show my feelings. I had to put on quite an act. Then I thought of the full trash bags by the door, and the act got easier.

She kissed me on the cheek, and went to bed.

THE NEXT MORNING Carole whipped up another gentle but mouthwatering meal for us. She then left for her apartment while I walked Jimmy to the bank. We moved slowly; he shook with every step. He signed the papers, and I called Henry's lawyer. Our new joint account would soon have three thousand dollars in it, with another three to be deposited every month for just six months. Those were the only instructions the lawyer had. I'd have to fight with Henry all over again, but whether it was Bird or *The Starry Night* or whatever it was, I sensed it would work out. Maybe that's how you feel when you save someone's life.

I brought him home and watched him go to sleep. What the hell, I thought, he can be alone if he's asleep. And now that I could afford it, I went back out—this time to the closest mall. At Melman's Sports I found a red spandex workout suit—perfect for a midnight jog. Of course, Jimmy didn't jog and never would, but it was red. I bought four Mediums and an extra large red Phillies cap to go with them. I estimated his shoe size, added an inch, and got him a pair of red high tops. Pure red socks and underwear were impossible, but I got close.

At ArtyFlarty I bought him a dozen canvases and brushes, an easel, a brush tray and palette, turpentine and a set of oil paints. This is what my friend needs, I thought, and I didn't worry about The Elephant with No Eyes, The Rocketing Saxophone, The Blue Blob with Black Shadows, or worst of all, Wendell Jumping out of the Blur. As I wrestled the five cumbersome bags down the street, I didn't worry about bringing back the old hell-worlds. All that mattered now was the yeah-bee man.

CHAPTER 21

The Eclipse

THE FAMILIAR citrus perfume didn't register as I lugged the bags one-by-one through the doorway. It wasn't until I dropped the last one in that I noticed Carole, arms folded, had been standing over me the whole time. "Oh, hi . . . " I said. ". . . What?"

"I thought we agreed Jimmy wasn't ready to be left alone," she said.

"He's asleep," I said, looking at him on the sofa. "What's wrong?"

"I found him sprawled on the bathroom floor."

I guess I shouldn't have gone out, I told her, but I was shopping for *him.*

She said now she had no choice but to stay another week—and it wasn't free. She'd take at least what we would've paid the home-health worker. "You're so sweet, Shawn," she said, "but your head is always in the stars. What are you going to do when I'm not here?"

"Carole, it was only a couple hours. I got him his red clothes and some—you know, painting stuff."

"Painting stuff," she said, looking at the bags with the canvases spilling out.

"Absolutely, to give him something to shoot for."

"So you think exposing him to turpentine and oil paints is just what his body needs right now?"

"I didn't think about that."

"And where would you have him do all this—the kitchen? Next to my bed while I'm sleeping?"

"I didn't think about that either," I said. "How about next to his sofa?"

"With the paints dripping on the carpet," she said.

"I'd lay newspaper."

"So after all I did to clean your apartment, you're going to crap it up with wads of paint-splattered newspapers."

"No," I said, "I mean, not until he's a little stronger."

Carole arrived every day at 2:30, giving Jimmy baths in exchange for him taking the ever-decreasing meds. I couldn't help admiring his little bargain. She also insisted on constant fluids—water, juices, soups. Though he hated the drugs, he trusted the supplements she made me get for him—Vitamin E, lecithin and manganese—for their help with the TD shakes. Despite a few more 3 AM emergencies and the occasional incontinence, every day our patient showed progress.

At bedtime Carole would gab to me for half an hour. The subject didn't matter; it was the best part of my day. Then she'd say goodnight, go to my room, and lock the door. In the mornings I helped her make breakfast, which she had to gulp to get to the Lower East Side by 9:30. This week she was helping a mother and three children deal with a father dying of cancer. I'd never admired anyone as much as Carole. She was smart, got things done, and despite her nurse mode I knew we'd be a couple again, I was sure of it. If I could just survive her dark side.

She demanded I return the red clothes. "Too rough on the bruises and bedsores," she said.

I got him a pair of red pajamas.

"Still too rough," she said, feeling the material.

I washed them three times in the Gonzo Clean.

"No," she said. "I still don't like them."

"But they're for him," I said. "You don't have to like them."

"The last thing he needs right now is to fall back into his *red* thing."

There were the daily orders: changes to Jimmy's diet, his meds, his exercises, and always a ready shopping list. It was all for Jimmy's good, but every minute I was scouring something. I had no choice—if I wanted to avoid another antiseptic tirade and the trashing of the rest of my manuscripts.

She made me cram the paints, canvases and art supplies into one closet—all for the sake of her pristine floors. In fact, since I slept on the rug each night, I was sure one morning *I'd* wind up neatly bundled by the door.

But after she left for Manhattan each day, I played for Jimmy. He'd listen for hours, muttering about jellybeans and loops and links, just like in Apartment 1. He tried dancing once, and fell and hit a chair. Still, the old Jimmy was coming back.

After he swallowed his last slivers of meds on Friday morning, September 23rd, Carole, promising to visit, kissed each of us on the cheek, and said goodbye. "Keep this place *clean*," she said to us. "And be very nice to Maura." The nurse's aide would be arriving in a few hours.

Carole hadn't even exited the building when I unveiled the red clothes. Jimmy hurried to try them on. Everything was a little too big. He watched while I placed on the sofa a set of dark pencils and a blank notebook. Then I spread newspapers on the rug. Without saying a word I brought out the easel and a tiny bench, planting them on the center of the spread. I hauled everything out of the closet—the canvases, paints, brushes, brush tray, palette and turpentine, and stacked them on the bench.

"Mr. Shawn Lewis," he repeated softly, weeping and rubbing his nose and eyes with the new red sleeve.

"Go to it," I said.

MAURA, A plump and quiet hard worker, handled the three-to-eleven shift, cooking, cleaning, and avoiding Jimmy while he painted in the living room. When he took a break, he'd drape the canvas with my bathrobe. "The bridges are not yet right," he kept saying. I didn't worry about the bridges. I just wanted my robe back.

After seven weeks we let Maura go. Jimmy didn't like painting around strangers. And once he was strong enough to make his own dinners—heating soup and tea and scavenging through my kitchen—Maura seemed redundant.

Carole and I spoke on the phone every other day. I'd brag about all the healthy habits she'd instilled in us. I didn't mention the painting, the red clothes or letting go of Maura. But it wasn't all business. She was softening. "Shawn," she said, "I'm so glad that we're getting close again. My therapist thinks I could be ready to start dating, maybe in a couple months." Carole promised to go out with me in the first week of the new year. I was already planning the restaurant and counting the days.

By the end of November all of Jimmy's wounds had healed. He was still fragile and looked old for his age but he was getting stronger, filling out his new clothes. Now the cap and red workout suit with his growing white beard made him look less like a mental patient and more like a health-crazed ex-junky from the sixties. The neighbors rarely got a good look at him because he rarely ventured out—painting, writing in his notebooks, conferring with his "friends," and slopping up my apartment. His TD spasms had sprinkled every part of my living room with paint. I stopped eating at the bridge table when Cerulean Blue strafed my tomato soup.

In early December I forced Jimmy out of my stuffy building, away from our gray 232nd Street for a long stroll through the woodsy Bronx Park. After a while the cold wind sapped his energy. He was shivering and unsteady by the time we were heading back over the dirt trail. I added my scarf to his red scarf, and guided him up the hill and past the bare maples in front of Bronx Boulevard. But there we had to stop. A man at the edge of the highway was waving his arms like Toscanini to the passing cars—the same homeless man as before, wearing the same grimy clothes. But this time he was surrounded by pigeons, a dozen of them cooing and strutting around his ragged, open shoes. "The Conductor" laughed as he turned to face me.

"This is the music beyond all other music, Mr. Shawn Lewis," The Conductor said, giggling and still waving. "And it's *your turn*."

I hustled Jimmy away, while The Conductor shouted, "*Don't go, it's your turn*."

Jimmy and I hobbled quickly along the sidewalk toward my block on 232nd Street.

"Why are we leaving the nice conductor?" Jimmy said. "He's a very good conductor."

How could I tell him: Because the son-of-a-bitch reminds me of you when I didn't know you? Because we should avoid lunatics we've never met who know our names and are telling us it's our turn? Our turn for what? To go crazy and live in the street, waving our arms up and down?

It was too disturbing to contemplate how the man found me or what he wanted. But he called me "Mr. Shawn Lewis," and the link with Jimmy was inescapable. Maybe they'd shared a floor in the nuthouse.

"I don't know what that guy wants," I said to Jimmy, "but I'm not going to let him hurt you." I stood there and hugged him, unaware that Colfield had been watching us from our stoop.

"You two shacking up?" he said, as we climbed the steps. "You gay, Lewis?"

I wouldn't look at him, but Jimmy was riveted.

"Word is, you met in the loony bin," Colfield said.

I steered Jimmy around him.

"I'm getting you evicted," Colfield said. "I made a petition."

"Mr. Stallings," Jimmy mumbled to him as we passed. "Remember Mr. Stallings."

Colfield's jaw dropped, and he stepped backwards, glaring at Jimmy.

"Who's Mr. Stallings?" I asked Jimmy, when we reached my apartment.

"He forgot Mr. Stallings," Jimmy said.

"Right, who is he?"

"The one who tried to fix the anvil."

"Right . . . What anvil?"

"The life he could've had," Jimmy said.

". . . Whose life?"

"The life with falcons and eagles."

Jimmy's explanations always made my brain freeze.

APPARENTLY, my friend had been laboring over the same canvas since the day I'd given him the paints, and he demanded absolute silence while he worked on it. I also had to stay out of his way during *Twilight Zone* and *One Life to Live*. The living room was now, as Carole had predicted, coated in trash and paint-splatters. Every night I returned from the video store, trekked through the hopeless living room with my eyes closed, and worked to stem the growing crises in the kitchen and bathroom. I stopped asking for Jimmy's help when I saw him scrubbing pots with his turpentine.

Whenever Carole called to visit, I told her Jimmy had been bussed to his therapist—something I knew she'd love to hear. Our date was now just fifteen days, three hours and eight minutes away—depending on the trains—and she'd kill it if she knew how we were living. But she wanted to cook for us for the holidays. I had to think fast. I told her I had an upcoming gig of my latest originals and was practicing day and night. She said she was proud of me, but she and I both knew the threat of her hearing my jazz guaranteed a mighty force field around the Bronx.

I needed my apartment back. Every day I scanned the Classifieds to find Jimmy a nearby studio. I rehearsed how I could break it to him: You won't be alone—not really. I'll stop by every day. You won't even miss me. I'll bring my saxophone. Nothing's changed. I'll buy your groceries, paint supplies, whatever you need. I'll even bring in Maura to cook and clean until you get settled. This is the independence your mom always wanted for you. And the rent will be taken care of because I'll settle things once and for all with your Uncle Hen.

On Tuesday morning, December 27th, while Jimmy painted in the living room, I found an ad for a space only two blocks away. "Hey buddy," I said, entering the living room. "The studio above Rollo's Shoe Repair is now available."

He stared at his canvas.

"It's just two blocks away," I said. "Got a great view of Poong's Market."

"It's ready," he said, his eyes still on the canvas.

"You damn right it is—it says in the paper."

"It's ready, Mr. Shawn Lewis," he said, and turned the easel to face me.

In the center of the three-by-three white canvas was just one small black circle with a yellow halo. An infant's impression of an eclipse, I thought. This is what the poor guy's been slaving over all these weeks. How sad, but I looked at him and forced a smile. He was grinning, his knobby teeth now a darker shade of yellow. I studied the painting again, searching for something positive to say. Then I noticed the black had subtle textures and shadings—the same with the yellow halo, which seemed to be moving. I was drawn in—drawn into the black circle. Time stopped. I forgot everything I was going to tell him. My mind emptied. Yet I was perfectly conscious. I melded into the yellow halo. I wanted to turn away, to resist, but I was trapped. I could hear Jimmy's muffled voice: "For you, Mr. Shawn Lewis . . . I made it for *you*."

I was in flames, but it didn't hurt. Then I merged with the pure white of the canvas. I had looked at this painting far longer than the ones from the old days. I don't know why—perhaps because I'd promised Jimmy I would, or maybe because the painting was stronger than the old ones. "I . . . " I said, "I need to sit."

As I stumbled for the sofa, the last thing I heard was, "Much better than the old bridge, huh, Mr. Shawn Lewis? It's a good bridge, huh?"

I fell asleep, soaring through a winding, checkerboard tunnel.

PART

CHAPTER 22

Between the Newsstand & the Downtown R

SNOOPER DOOPERS, Snooper Doopers!" he shouted.

"Leave me alone," I said, and rolled away from the noise.

"Almost three!" he said, poking at me.

I burrowed into the sofa, but Jimmy kept shouting. Slowly I turned around and opened my eyes. The easel and newspapers and overall mess existed only as a vapor underneath an entirely new scene. A Victorian ballroom with dark wood ceilings, flickering chandeliers and marble floors had usurped my living room. Behind Jimmy, strange, smiling people in tuxedos and long gowns waved hello to me as they slow-danced the fox-trot to a live big band and string orchestra playing "Embraceable You."

"Jimmy," I said, straining to wake up, "what did you do to my apartment?"

"Snooper Doopers!"

"Will you stop the yelling already? Who are these people? Where am I?"

"Almost three!" He handed me the dorky cap and shirt. That's when I woke just enough to realize I was going to be late for the video store.

~~~~~~

In front of an array of customers the manager abused me for walking in a half hour late. It was not my finest moment when I said, "Big deal." I wouldn't have been so late—my commute was a two-minute walk—but I got lost. The whole night I never gave one person the right change or pulled out the DVD or video they'd asked for. I was still halfway inside the eclipse, dangling in a soft web of multiple realities.

At ten o'clock with an hour yet to go, I was fired. Before leaving, I took the opportunity to rent a five-volume set of *Twilight Zones* to watch with Jimmy.

We watched the tapes till almost four, when the eclipse's hold started to wane. But I was a different person now. My terror at losing control, at going insane, had been temporarily buried by an overwhelming desire to be free, and the more I looked into the eclipse, the more I wanted its freedom. I went to my room, carrying the canvas with me, and propped it on the dresser.

All night I dreamed I was playing gigs. The first one put me in the front row of the Benny Goodman band. Gene Krupa bashed and kicked his drums behind us. I wanted to tell him he was too damn loud, but he'd been dead for thirty years, and that demanded a certain amount of respect. Later I was backing up Billie Holiday at Café Society, trading fours with Prez—Lester Young. Billie kept pointing to Prez while looking at me, mouthing, "Let *him* take it." They'd all been dead longer than Krupa, but I played anyway. I woke exhausted. It was two in the afternoon.

I looked into the eclipse for a few minutes, then checked out the living room. Jimmy was painting, deep in concentration. I poured myself cereal and black coffee. Usually, the lightest coffee hurled my pulse into a merengue, but this was black and had no effect. After my sixth cup I went back to the living room. "Jimmy," I said, "your painting screwed up my brain."

"Shhh," he said, as he flicked dots of red onto the canvas, his eyes bulging in excitement.

I went back to my room, stared at the eclipse a while, circled back to the kitchen, made more cereal and coffee, took another look at the eclipse, then ambled to the rear of Jimmy's easel.
~~~~~~

"Look," I said, "if what you're making's going to make things worse, I'm not—"

"Shhh."

"Unless you're painting an antidote. Hey, that's funny—a painting as an anti—"

"Mr. Shawn Lewis," he said, still absorbed in his canvas, "even at Parkview I practiced in my mind . . . the bridges. You'll see, you'll see."

I didn't feel well. The eclipse was colliding with a half gallon of black coffee, and I needed a doctor. But first, a little nap.

I dreamed about more old-time musicians and gigs and woke at 5 PM in a panic to get to the video store. Then I stopped, half dressed, not sure if getting fired was one of my dreams or not. I called the manager. "This is a little embarrassing," I said. "Am I supposed to be at work right now?"

Silence.

"Assuming I am," I said, clearing my throat, "I'm sorry I'm late. Let me explain: All the coffee I drank conflicted with my roommate's new painting . . . I know how that sounds, but you have to see this painting. Just don't drink any coffee. I'm having the oddest dreams. I even dreamed you fired me." I chuckled. "Anyway, we're good, right? I mean, in general, you and I, we're—"

He hung up.

I was starved. The smell of melted cheese, garlic and tomato from Jimmy's just-baked frozen pizza pushed back my qualms about the fresh paints on his fingers as he tore off a slice and handed it to me. I devoured half of the pizza before I began to wonder, Just what are Van Dyke Brown and Hansa Yellow made from? Then he led me to the easel and his new work.

It was a mishmash of geometric shapes, splashes and dots, nothing about it remotely artful. Perhaps I could've blurred my eyes and told him it was flawless, maybe clung a little longer to my old life. But it was too late; that life was already gone. The eclipse had already opened the worlds, and the bridges in his new painting were too strong.

I stared into the painting. I could hear the drums first, then the bass, then the piano. Squiggles of tan and gold looked like a sax player standing in front of a black splotch—the piano. Gray and white circles were the drums, a brown oval—the bass. I felt like *I* was the squiggles of tan and gold playing in front of a band bathed in yellow light for a nightclub audience of dark red, blue, and black dots. Jimmy laughed with his knobby teeth as I heard the clinks of glasses and silverware, the applause, the stomping of the rhythm section. My playing had never felt so natural—the saxophone, just another part of my body.

"Mr. Shawn Lewis, play the sax. Play now. Play now, Mr. Shawn Lewis."

All right, what the hell, I thought. I'd lost my stupid job and I'd taken in this guy who just made me dinner with wet, toxic oil paints and God knows what else on his hands. Okay, I'll play a blues for a few minutes, then call the doctor.

I took a deep breath and played. The notes spilled out so easily it startled me. Jimmy laughed, pointing to the canvas. I looked at it again. I played but I felt like I was playing for Jimmy from within the club inside the painting. I could feel the audience looking at me. I could hear the drive from a rhythm section of an oval, circles and a splotch. I played with more confidence than I'd ever had, my sound filling the club—and my apartment. While Jimmy carried on about jellybeans, I played well past the New York noise curfew.

We never heard Muriel Fetterman's pounding broom, Colfield's shouts or Galicia's buzzing, though I later found out that most of the building was massing for an assault. The police had come and would've broken down our door if they hadn't been sidetracked by a violent scuffle between Lloyd and one of his clients.

By three in the morning Jimmy collapsed on the sofa and I went to my room and continued to play. I played as softly as I could—not for the neighbors, but out of respect for my friend, who had now become my very weird teacher. I couldn't put the instrument down. I played almost without pause every set of chord changes I knew, every tune I could remember, every solo I'd ever memorized. How could I stop? Playing the alto had become the easiest thing I'd ever done.

At almost ten the next morning I could hear a faint knocking while I was in the middle of playing all the Charlie Rouse solos from my Thelonius Monk albums. I'd never memorized them—Rouse was a tenor player—yet now I knew them all and was playing them one by one in every key when Jimmy asked if I'd like him to make breakfast. The threat of us eating whatever poisons were stuck on his hands was enough to get me to put the horn down. I made us a quick breakfast and returned to the bedroom to practice while he went to his easel to work on what I assumed was another mind-slaughtering present for me.

Then all at once I felt the panic: *Shawn, what the hell are you doing? End this now. At all costs get your mind under control.* You want to wind up like *him*? You want people to call *you* the lunatic?

I was so unnerved, I blew into my horn to settle down. But the inspired music that flooded the room reached so far into the wave without limits, I thought: to hell with my fears. For the music, for the mastery of sound—isn't it worth just a touch of madness?

But what about Carole? Our date was just nine days, five and half hours away. Would she still want me—if I went the tiniest bit psychotic?

At two Jimmy knocked, asking which soup I wanted for lunch, the blue label or the red and yellow one. That got me to stop again. I left the room, walking straight into the large canvas he held below his grinning, bearded face. Five and a half years ago this trick would've put me in a rage. Now it didn't faze me. A big blue splash of paint was surrounded by rainbows of droplets, and beyond them lurked several angular jet-black figures—an updated version of the Blue Blob with Black Shadows.

"What do you think, Mr. Shawn Lewis?" he said, giggling. "It's better indeed, isn't it? I think it's better, don't you, don't you?"

I stared into it. I took a step back, a step forward. When I leaned back again I felt like I'd splashed into the blue of the painting. Then I slipped into the field of droplets. The angular shadows raced toward me like sharks. They were hungry. My instinct was to run, but where do you run when you're stuck inside a painting? I stumbled back into the big blue splash. The shadows turned and floated away.

"Do you see?" he said. "Do you see what I see?"

"What—what were those . . . " I tried to catch my breath.

"You know them."

"I do?"

"They're yours."

As we hung the painting by the doorway I began to recognize some of the shadows: my first-grade teacher Mrs. Klaviks; Gruber, the school bully; my Aunt Freda before her rehab. Just thinking about them terrorized me. That's when I realized the painting was Jimmy's way of telling me to wear blue.

At Melman's I bought the last pair of neon blue basketball sneakers for a fortune, but their Purdee brand blue polyester jumpsuit was only ten bucks; they were overstocked. I bought five. Rayz Phat Hats sold me a blue silk do-rag, and though I could never be an authentic bro from the hood, the scarf would keep me dipped inside the big blue splash.

I walked home in my new clothes under the brisk December sun, past the body shops, the high school just letting out, and the pot-smoking gang at the construction pile—conscious of each passing stare. No one had ever seen such a Gomer-looking jumpsuit underneath a gangsta do-rag, yet I was impervious. In fact, I'd forgotten all about the black coffee and painted pizza. I'd never felt better. When I got back, I asked Jimmy how he knew about Aunt Freda, how he could guess my color was blue.

"In my mind," he said, "I practice. I practice in my mind and then I practice with my paints."

"But, how do you . . . Okay, how did you make that nightclub inside a canvas?"

"Oh, I didn't make that place, Mr. Shawn Lewis. It's been in the Lower Second World for years and years and years."

"What?"

"I've been painting the worlds forever, but you were the first on Earth One to see it, Mr. Shawn Lewis. And I knew that you would."

"Uh . . . what?"

"Until mom started seeing. Before then, it was only you. That's why I had to paint for you. Remember?"

"But how . . . how did you—"

"The paintings made you sick because you saw what you didn't want to see."

"What?"

"You saw the other worlds," he said.

"Uh . . . but those paintings that were already in your living room—you know, when I first showed up, when I first met your family—I didn't see *anything* in those."

"Indeed," he said. "Those were not meant for you. I had to paint for you, just for *you*, and then you would see what I see. And I knew that you would."

"But, *how* could you know?"

"Oh, that's easy, Mr. Shawn Lewis. You bring the jellybeans."

AFTER A FEW more days and a few more gigs inside Jimmy's paintings, it was time to get out of the apartment. Late December in New York is too cold for standing on the street, but the subway stations are warmer—and full of people with loose change. I'd played in the subways before but it had left me discouraged and no wealthier. Everyone is so high-strung and in such a hurry, I was just another obstacle in their day. But now that Jimmy's paintings had blunted my self-consciousness, I wanted to try again, this time inside the busiest station in the country.

It was the evening rush hour on the Friday before New Year's at Times Square, the convergence of five swarming subway lines and a stampede in every direction. We chose to set up along the wall between the newsstand and the Downtown R. I asked Jimmy to watch over my open case that lay on the concrete, and I started playing whatever popped into my mind. It must have been a novelty even for the most hardened New Yorkers: One, wildly twitching in red spandex, a light gray beard and a Phillies cap, guarded an empty saxophone case. The other, a blue clash, stood behind him, his back against the soiled white brick wall—blowing avant-garde jazz.

A throng gathered. Money started flying into the case. Jimmy carried on about jellybeans and loops and links, and to my surprise, he wasn't alone. One or two in the crowd chimed in. After an hour and a half we'd made $140.

I kept playing even as we rode the subway home. We made another twenty.

When we got home, Jimmy offered soup—the blue label. Instead of taking over, certain he'd poison us, I was happy to let him serve me. And though the pot had been soaking under a stack of old dishes, and he barely rinsed it, I didn't flinch when he told me the meal was soon ready. I felt invincible.

After dinner I couldn't stand to wait another moment. I called Carole with the good news: "You've got to come over as soon as you can, sweetheart. You've got to see what Jimmy's done. It's changed my life. The man's a genius!"

An hour later she showed up with a full shopping bag. "Hello, hello," she said to us, marching in. "I've missed you two. I brought you my favorite, most nutritious—" She stopped, her jaw dropping. She put down the bag, stared at me, then Jimmy, then the apartment, then back to me.

"Sweetheart," I said, with Jimmy behind me, "before I show you Jimmy's work, I have something to tell you, something really important. It's urgent."

"Have you completely lost it?" she said softly.

"No, I feel great, sweetheart. I have something I have to tell you now."

"Do you realize you look like a freak?" she said. "Since when do you wear a scarf on your head? And what's with the bozo jumpsuit and day-glow sneakers? Did you lose a bet?"

"Miss Carole Bonner," Jimmy said, "would you like to give me a bath tonight?"

"You need one," she said. "You both need—"

"You are so funny, sweetheart," I said. "Here's what I have to tell you: You are so bright and giving and perky and—well, *gorgeous* . . . I absolutely more than anything else just adore you. You're my life."

"What happened to Maura?" she said. "This place is—is—"

"Did you hear what I said?" I said.

"This place is a *catastrophe*," she said.

"Yes," I said, "it's gotten a little out of—"

"A zoo smells better," she said.

"Yes," I said, "I'm sure it's time to do the laundry."

"Are you drinking?" she said, leaning toward me, sniffing.

I shook my head. Then I wrapped my arms around her.

"What are you on?" she said, pulling away. "You're *on* something."

"Jimmy's paintings," I said.

"Would you like some soup, Miss Carole Bonner?" Jimmy asked. "I made the blue label."

"It's the paintings, Carole," I said. "Look at them. They're alive."

She glanced at the walls, then turned back to me. "This is *so* irresponsible," she said. "What is it, coke? Heroin? You got into Jimmy's meds, didn't you?"

"I like Coke better than Pepsi," Jimmy said. "But Pepsi can be very nice with—"

"Let me take you into my bedroom," I said, reaching for her arm. "This is a masterpiece like no other."

She yanked her arm away. "How could you?" she said. "After all I did to help you two. How could you let it all go to hell?"

"Carole, I didn't," I said, reaching for her hand. "If you'll just follow me, I'll show you what it's all about."

"Don't touch me," she said. "What happened to your job?"

"I'm not sure," I said. "My guess is I was fired."

"Miss Carole Bonner, a bath would be very lovely." Jimmy belched.

"You two are living like goats. What will you do when Henry's trust runs out?"

"I just made $160 playing in the subway," I said.

"I don't believe it," she said.

"It's true, it's true, Miss Carole Bonner. A thousand dollars."

"Hundred-sixty, Jimmy," I said.

"Thousand million," he said.

"Shouldn't you be looking for a job?" she asked me.

"That's the beauty of it, Carole," I said. "Jimmy has shown me that I don't need to care about the mundane shit anymore. His paintings have taken me to a whole other level. Come on, let me show you the eclipse."

She backed away.

"Sweetheart," I said, "I got us tickets to the Met for our date next week—La Boheme. But that story doesn't even come close to the love I feel for—"

"It's too much, Shawn," she said, grabbing her stomach. "This is all too much. I can't go out with you next week. I can't handle this."

"Miss Carole Bonner," Jimmy said, reaching out to give her a hug, but she quickly skirted out the door.

"No, Carole, don't do this!" I yelled after her.

"My fault, Mr. Shawn Lewis. I should've offered her the red and yellow label."

CHAPTER 23

Visitors

I BLEW IT. I'd told her how I felt, and wrecked everything. I blew it. The phone rang.

"Soooo, I heard about you and your ex." It was Irene.

"How—how do you find these things out?" I said.

"Oh, I have ways . . . I also heard you've gone nuts, completely mental."

"Irene, I can't talk; this isn't a good time."

"See? You're being punished. You've gone craz—"

I hung up. Was she right, I wondered. Am I now a lunatic? Did my music push me over the edge? I had to make a choice—my crazy music or Carole. But I wanted both. Without the hope of Carole I couldn't imagine being happy, but how could I give up my life's work—now that it was easy? The choice was impossible, so I plowed into my horn each day, into the most complex tunes, theories and patterns.

Sleep was my other refuge, and my dreams were all gigs, lately in a duo at the Five Spot with Thelonius Monk. He let me blow all the solos, never saying a word, until one night. "Music is not about theories," he said. "Music is now."

The next morning Jimmy showed me his latest: a cyclone of bright and dark lines and specks that twirled my mind until once again, I fell over in a heap. I woke a moment later to his cackles of laughter as he held the painting in front of me.

My eyes now had a new and unusual kind of blur.

"Do you see it?" he said, still laughing.

The painting's bright and dark lines had merged and even extended beyond the canvas. Now wherever I looked, curls of transparent energy radiated upward, like the distortions off a pavement in the summer heat. I could choose to focus them away but otherwise, the paint-splattered newspapers, the lamps, the piles of mail, the cluttered desk—everything I looked at gave off the curls.

Jimmy pointed to *The Starry Night*. At first I was blinded by the energies flaming out of my poster—laminated cardboard radiating curls of blue, yellow and white. And Jimmy was far from done. Every few days came a new painting, a new perception, another quirk to push me further away from Carole's sense of normal.

I called her, left messages, begged her to pick up the phone. Jimmy knew I was hurting, and advised me to call the plarps.

"Yes, you've mentioned them," I said. "Who the hell are the plarps?"

"They'll fix your heart," he said. "They helped me with the girls from the Terriyon Zone. I never ever again got stuck between fields. And no one had to die."

In lieu of calling the plarps, we jammed all his paintings onto the walls. The effect was breathtaking. They were either the most original mediums for expanded awareness or the world's most peculiar form of psychedelics. And as long as I looked at them or played my horn or hung out with Jimmy, I felt great. I even felt hopeful again about Carole. I'd play my horn without sleep for days, then spend days on my back. I could forget to eat, then sit with Jimmy for hours devouring TV dinners, watching *Twilight Zones*. It was one long holiday.

And yet, at rush hour we'd somehow find our spot in Times Square between the newsstand and the Downtown R. We even developed a following, people going out of their way just to hear the weird blue man and see his even weirder friend in red. And each time we'd make enough cash to forget Jimmy ever had an Uncle Henry.

As the weeks passed, I was extracting more and more out of the paintings. I gave Jimmy my room in exchange for the sofa, so I could wallow in them even as I slept. For Jimmy it was just as ideal. He could close a door, spread out his notebooks and write and talk to his friends without interruption. And of course, his painting space by my new bed, the sofa, was sacred and never disturbed.

On Sunday, February 12th, I played all morning and afternoon for Jimmy until I couldn't hear myself over Colfied's wall-quaking gospel music. I left for his apartment—saxophone in hand—and buzzed the door. Jimmy stood behind me, mumbling, "Remember Mr. Stallings, remember Mr. Stallings."

"Yes?" said a smug, muscle-bound Colfield Dixon standing in his doorway, his speakers erupting with a blues organ and screaming choir: *". . . Open up. Open up your heart. Open up . . ."*

"Would you please turn it down?" I said. *"For our Lord, our Lord is the start. Open up . . ."*

"Can't hear you, prick," he said. *". . . Your love, give of your love . . ."*

"I said, turn it down!"

"Wish I could help," he said, "but my stereo's too loud. Can't hear you."

"Mr. Stallings," Jimmy said in my ear. "Remember Mr. Stallings."

Just as Colfield started to close the door, I shouted, "Remember Mr. Stallings!" He backed up, his eyes riveted on us as we ambled into his apartment. *"Open up. Open up your heart. Open up . . ."*

"Remember Mr. Stallings," I said.

He slowly turned around, lowering the stereo. Then he stared at us, silent. A moment passed while he flexed his right hand.

"You been checking on me?" he said.

Jimmy whispered in my ear, "Tell him you know about Mr. Stallings."

"But I *don't* know about Mr. Stallings," I whispered back.

"I asked you a question," Colfield said. Now both hands were flexing. He looked like he might end his neighbor problems once and for all.

"I know about Mr. Stallings," I said. "All about him."

"No one around here knows," Colfield said. "Except my wife."

"Tell him he should think about Mr. Stallings," Jimmy whispered.

"Think about Mr. Stallings," I said.

"Mav is not coming," Jimmy whispered.

"Mav is not coming," I said.

"What was that?" Colfield said.

"It will have to be Mr. Jula," Jimmy whispered. "Definitely Mr. Jula."

"It will have to be Mr. Jula," I said. "Definitely Mr. Jula."

"If you don't tell me what you know about Mr. Stallings," Colfield said, "I'm going to wrap that horn around your neck."

"The Sheml is too busy," Jimmy whispered. "What about Professor Thel?"

"The Sheml is too busy," I said. "What about Professor Thel?"

"You are one crazy motherfucker," Colfield said. "First you ruin my Sunday, blasting your bullshit horn all fucking day, and then . . ."

I detected sparkling lights within the transparent curls rising off Colfield's shoulders. If I looked at the curls out of the corner of my eye, the tiny lights streamed like living snap-shots, a multiplex of Colfield's life: his parents, brothers and sister, an orange sign that read, "Bowling Green State University, Home of the Falcons." I saw Perry Stadium and a young Colfield Dixon in his football uniform making one punishing tackle after another, the scoreboard heralding the linebacker known as "The Anvil." Two men from the Eagles, scouts, wanted to know if he would play in Philadelphia if the team drafted him. Then I saw parties, drugs, fights, fights with teammates, his coaches shouting at him. I saw him drinking alone in his dorm room, a campus minister visiting him, bringing home-cooked meals, helping him back to his classes, even back to the field. The minister's name was Reginald Stallings.

"You ain't leaving here," Colfield said, "till you tell me about Mr. Stallings."

"Uh, well, you see, it's like . . . " I said.

"I believe if I pummeled you two crazy motherfuckers, the whole Bronx would give me a medal." He held his fist up to my face.

"Don't hit me," I said. "I won't be able to play the saxophone if you hit me."

His eyes lit up, never more excited.

"I'm psychic now," I blurted. "I can see your whole life. You were a great football player. You had a little trouble. Mr. Stallings was a hero who gave everything—asked for nothing in return. You loved him. You miss him. I guess Jimmy thought you'd be less angry if you remembered Mr. Stallings."

Colfield dropped his fist and stepped back, his eyes welling.

"We'll just be going now," I said. "Thanks for turning down your stereo."

"Thanks, thanks a lot, Jimmy," I said when we were securely behind my three deadbolts. "Some convenient getaway you have. Things get dicey, and you start babbling to your friends. Where the hell are you now, anyway?"

"I can't fly now," Jimmy mumbled. "Maestro C is ready. The gift—it's *time."*

THAT NIGHT in the darkness of my living room I awoke to the thumping sounds of someone very big, moving furniture. I clung to the sofa and listened—motionless—hoping it was another dream. Heavy footsteps rustled over Jimmy's newspapers.

"Jimmy?" I said.

"You awake?" said a voice that was definitely not Jimmy's.

I fumbled for the nearest lamp, inches from the sofa, knocking a glass to the floor before I could turn on the light.

A portly black man in a brown silk suit and tie studied me from a chair he'd moved near the sofa. He held my saxophone in his lap. *"You awake?"* he said.

"I'm not sure," I said, rubbing my eyes. "Who are you?"

"You're not sure you're awake? They made me come here. I didn't want to come here. Why should I waste my time on a doofstick who can't tell if he's awake?"

The man looked just like Cannonball Adderley.

"How'd you get in here?" I said. "And what are you doing with my horn?"

He pointed my alto at me and played "Sack O' Woe," his sound popping with the same juice-of-life as my idol. It was spectacular but it couldn't be real. This is a warning, I thought—time to cut out the midnight pastries.

"Your horn plays like shit," the man said.

"Fine, shit, whatever. I'm going back to sleep now."

"Your mouthpiece is not even good enough to be called shit."

"Goodnight."

"I'm going to do you a favor," he said, standing up. He carried my alto over to the trashcan by my desk and examined the receptacle. Then he walked to the other side of the living room, staring at the can. He aimed my alto like it was a basketball.

"You can't be Julian Adderley," I said, now sitting up. "He died in 1975."

"Do I look dead, Einstein?"

"Cannonball died of a stroke. I cried my brains out."

"They call me Mr. Jula now."

This is it, I thought, the crisis point: when an addict or a lunatic looks at his out-of-control life and stops everything—turns it all around. I'm throwing out the paintings, cleaning up my diet, rehiring Maura and getting Jimmy and me to some counseling. The whole jazz mastery fog was nice; now it's time to wake up. This will win Carole back. It's a sure bet. Jimmy and I are starting over, and I can't wait to tell Carole—first thing in the morning. I turned out the light, and pulled the blankets over my head.

"Yoohoo?" Mr. Jula said in the darkness. *"I don't personally care what you think. I got much better things to do, but you saved the Majib, and now I have to help you. My colleagues say I'm bitter.* ***Assholes****. Well, not all of them. They want me to work with you, so turn on the goddamn light. I'm real. I should know if I'm real. And who are you to tell me I'm not real?"*

I turned the light back on. Now I was scared. "Uh, Cannonball—I mean, Mr. Jula, let me get my roommate, okay?"

"No, this is between us. Majib needs his rest."

"Who?"

"Majib. Master Artist Jimmy B, one of the superstars. I did my best to get him out of there. I fucked up Gazemski but good. The nurses too. Pavel McElroy thinks he's a birdy now. But I couldn't save the Majib. Only you could do that."

He yanked the neck and mouthpiece off the horn, and with a flare he threw them from behind his back—a bank shot into the trashcan. Next he made a two-handed overhead shot of the instrument, slamming it into the can. The basket now holding the ruins of my creative dreams wiggled convulsively, but stayed upright.

"I don't care if you are Cannonball," I said. "If you really hurt my horn, I'm going to . . . No. I'm going to thank you. When I look back on this you'll be the psychotic mirage that turned my life around."

"You're a doofstick." He handed me a notepad and a pen. *"Now listen to me: Tomorrow I want you go to Davenport, Iowa. There's a pawnshop on Kelly Street. In the back room on the second shelf from the top there's a piece-of-shit alto even worse than yours. I want you to buy it."*

"I'm not writing this down."

"I know your type. You think you're living clean, working hard, and you clutch to what you call real. Then you blow your jazz and another dimension opens, a place where you belong but refuse to stay, and you can't figure out why you're life's not working."

His words were like lasers. But how could I stay forever inside the wave without limits? The farther I'd gone the more I'd scared Carole away. I wrote down the info on the pawnshop. "Why should I go to Iowa for a horn that's *worse* than the one you just wrecked?"

"I want you to get the mouthpiece in the case. You can't just buy the mouthpiece. You've got to buy the whole horn to get it. And that piece, well, that baby's one of my all-time favorites." He smiled and nodded, his eyes closed. *"I traded it away in the '50s. I always missed it. No one knows about it. It's got everything in it—most beautiful-sounding mouthpiece ever made for an alto."*

"But why did you wreck my— "

"Forget it. There's something much better for you in Memphis in an old white lady's attic—a King Super 20. I sold it decades ago, another mistake. This horn is as great as that mouthpiece and the lady has no idea it's worth anything. Her name is Schtickly and she lives on Underwood Drive. Offer her $300—she'll be tickled."

"Wow," I said, "the ghost of Cannonball Adderley is sitting in my living room."

"Don't you go calling me a ghost."

"Mr. Jula, you said my jazz opens some sort of dimension. I think I know what you mean. The problem is if I ever stayed there, my girl wouldn't be with me. Her name is Carole. I've never met anyone like her; I can't shake her. She's good for me. Around her I never feel lost or confused; I feel alive. But she hates my jazz; she thinks I'm a freak. She wouldn't believe in you or any of this. But I just love her. Do you see my problem? If I can't win her back—"

"Do I look like I'm interested? Do I? Huh? Okay, here it is: When you're living fully as yourself, not through the girl or the Majib or anybody else, you'll get the girl. But for now, get the right horn and mouthpiece. Say," he snickered, *"that was some doofstick move of yours, taking that Mafia hotel gig, huh?"*

"What? Hey, how was I supposed to know?"

"Lord Wendell warned you, didn't he? My friend Lord Wendell told you specifically not to mess with that gig, did he or did he not?"

"You mean my teacher, Wendell Rice?"

"Now what other Wendell do you and I both know? Come on, wake up already. Majib painted the outside line, Lord Wendell answered the call and spoke to you. He said, and I quote, 'Don't take the hotel gig, Shawn.' Was that a little too vague?"

"I just couldn't believe it."

"Well, just in case you try not to believe this, I trashed your horn." He laughed. *"Now you have no choice. Get the new stuff and practice. I'll be back."*

In an instant he was gone, vanished. Yet the chair he had moved was still facing me, the notepad still had his instructions, and the remains of my alto still peeked out of the trashcan. I laid awake the rest of the night, struggling to make sense of what was happening to me. Early the next morning Jimmy bounded out of his room, and asked if I understood "Mr. Jula's mission." I showed him the notes.

"Go right away, Mr. Shawn Lewis. Everybody's saying, go right away."

I was too shaken to ask who "everybody" was, but I couldn't help trusting my idol now known as Mr. Jula. While Jimmy stayed home, painting, I jumped in a cab to La Guardia and tossed out a wad of cash for same-day tickets to get to Davenport and Memphis and back home that night. I had no bags, nothing, just cash.

The first flight had a brief layover in Cincinnati, then a connection to Moline, where I hired another cab—just a few miles through a sleet-storm—to Davenport. I studied the cabbie's residue lights the whole ride to Kelly Street and Monroe's Pawn Shop. I asked him to wait a moment; I'd be right out. As I opened the door, I told him to forgive his wife; she's been sour only because of the piss-poor economy in Moline these days.

"What?" he said. "How did you—"

"Be right back," I said, slamming the door.

Buck, the owner of Monroe's, had four other saxophones he wanted to show me. "Much newer and shinier than that old thing," he said.

I grabbed the small, dark gray case with a $75 tag off the second shelf. With Buck standing over me, I opened the case, ignored the corroded saxophone, and found the decomposing, rolled-up sock that held Mr. Jula's gem. The mouthpiece said "Thayer Brothers" on the front, "New York" on the back. Light blue sparkles twirled around it as I put it in my pocket. I paid Buck for the instrument yet I couldn't help noticing a problem in his lights. "Go ahead, have the operation," I said, "but find a new doctor. Your guy's a quack and drinks too much."

He asked me why I was intruding in his affairs. I tried to explain about the residue curls and lights, but he didn't take it well. As he chased me out of the store, cursing, I realized I could beat him to the cab only by leaving the old gray case on the pavement. I had the mouthpiece, after all. I leapt into the cab while he picked up the case, scratched his head, and shouted, "No refunds or exchanges!"

The cabbie got me back to Moline in time for my 11 AM shuttle-flight to Chicago. From there it was off to Atlanta to catch the 4:10 to Memphis.

At Memphis International I called 411 to get the address for a Mrs. Schtickly on Underwood Drive. I took another cab, but before long I was telling the driver he should've stuck with the guitar and singing the blues—not because he was so talented, I said, but because his driving was terrible. After he dropped me off in the worst part of town and nowhere near Underwood, I called for another cab.

The next driver was unflappable, a Vietnamese immigrant who understood none of my brazen advice and managed to get me to Underwood Drive by 6 PM. The street was lined with bare elm trees in front of a row of crumbling, turn-of-the-century homes. I paid the fare with a hefty tip and asked him to wait. That he understood.

I worked the rusted door-knocker for five minutes, wondering, Why in the hell didn't I call ahead? Eventually, a tiny, white-haired Mrs. Schtickly appeared—her first words, "Are you here for the saxophone?"

I asked her how she knew, and she said she just had a feeling. Then she offered me tea and biscuits. "Please make yourself at home," she said.

"My son-in-law won't be here till about eight. He'll get it for you from the attic. Steps are too steep or I'd get it myself."

I told her I couldn't wait. I had a 7:46 flight. I gave her the $300 and asked her to point me to the attic. I climbed the staircase. She asked me to look around, see if there's anything else I'd like to buy. Just the saxophone, I told her. While she shouted from below, I sifted through cob-webbed piles of bags and debris inside the suffocating attic.

"Do you need a blender?" she called up. "I've got a wonderful lawn-mower. Hundred-fifty and it's yours. Hundred-seventy-five and you can have 'em both. How about a dinette set?"

While I rummaged, she called up, "Take your time, young man. Pick out anything you want to buy, but the saxophone's leaning there against the newel post."

I coughed, wiping the webs and dust off my face and picked up the filthy plywood case. The handle snapped off. The latches were stuck, and when I forced them open, they came loose. But there it was: a pitted, tarnished-brown alto with the inscription on the bell, "King Super 20." I attached the alto's silver neck to its body, and picked up the horn. There was a spark, and I felt a shock. I decided to leave the useless case. The naked alto would be my carry-on.

Mrs. Schtickly thanked me, inviting me for an extended visit, but I couldn't help telling her the only reason her son-in-law stops by so often is to steal nips from her bourbon. She said I reminded her of a strange word she'd been hearing recently: "doofstick."

The return flights were uneventful. Sure, people gawked at my do-rag-jumpsuit getup and my carry-on—a bare, rotting saxophone—but I was too exhausted to care. When I finally got home, I laid the King Super 20 and the Thayer mouthpiece on top of the junk mound on my desk, and passed out on the sofa.

That night I dreamed of private lessons with some of the greatest legends of the saxophone. Coleman Hawkins said I played "too vanilla" and lacked imagination. Sonny Stitt said I needed to go back and master basic harmonic tenets before I could break rules and play free jazz. John Coltrane told me to rise above individual notes and play from the highest part of my being. Lester Young, "Prez," seemed to say the opposite: "Appreciate your notes. Nurture them, each one like little flowers."

Voices only a few feet away woke me out of the dream. I half-opened my eyes and saw four legs—two in red spandex, two in white linen. I sat up. A man that looked like Charlie Parker in a white, almost-translucent suit and tie, was examining the latest painting on Jimmy's easel. *"I love what you did here with those rays,"* the man said softly. *"Perfect light-to-dark ratio."*

"The bridges have to be just right for Mr. Shawn Lewis," Jimmy said.

"Well, he certainly has the gift, and none of us would ever know it if it weren't for you, my friend."

"But he doesn't know he has the gift. Mr. Jula calls him a doofstick."

"Only your artistry will bring it out of him, Majib."

"Mav could do it," Jimmy said.

"Who is Mav?" I asked.

"He's up!" the man said.

"I'm sorry we woke you, Mr. Shawn Lewis," Jimmy said, "because we know you were tired after going so very far away yesterday and—"

"Twelve hours seemed like a long time to sleep," the man said, *"but I would've waited another twelve to meet you."*

"Are you . . . are you Charlie Parker?" I said.

"Everyone calls me Maestro C," he said, *"but you call me anything you please, Mr. Shawn Lewis."*

"Forgive me," I said, "but is this a dream? My dream time and my awake time—I can't tell which is which anymore."

"Excellent," he said. *"You have no idea how profound you are."*

"Maestro C has visited me for years and years and years," Jimmy said.

"We're all indebted to you, Mr. Shawn Lewis," Maestro C said. *"You did something very powerful when you rescued the great Majib. I was at many of your concerts for Majib. I've been guiding you. What do you think of the lessons so far?"*

"Lessons?" I said.

"The lessons. Your teachers you call The Hawk, Stitt and Prez are just the beginning. Who do you think brought you to Professor Thel—uh, Thelonius Monk?"

"Jimmy," I said, "why didn't you ever talk about this?"

"You never believed about my friends," Jimmy said. "You used to think I was very very sick. Everyone thought that. I could never tell you about Maestro C or the others, but I knew I could paint for you and show you more and more because you could bring the jellybeans. That made you different. That meant you had the gift."

"Do you realize what a coup it was to get The Listener?" Maestro C said. *"The Listener—you call him Coltrane—is our foremost medium. He sits on top of Grord Peak, tuning in to the Epsilon Hierarchy. He's very busy. But because you helped the Majib and you have the gift, everyone wants to help."*

"What gift?" I said.

"Mav could've shown you but he's too damn proud," Maestro C said.

"Who is Mav?" I said.

"Master Artist Vincent, of course," Maestro C said. *"Van Gogh. The one who painted your Starry Night. He speaks to you through the painting. But he's very proud and says no one who has the gift should need to be told."*

"What gift?" I said. "And what the hell are the jellybeans?"

"You would've found out a whole lot sooner," Maestro C said, *"if you'd only listened to Lord Wendell. Didn't he tell you not to take the hotel job?"*

"Yes, yes, I know. I just couldn't believe that—"

"Well, now that you and the Majib are working together again, it's not too late. I've been examining Mr. Jula's alto and mouthpiece. I didn't want to wake you. May I try them now?"

"The horn's in bad shape," I said. "All the upper pads are shredded. I think the case had moths."

Maestro C removed from his suit pocket a reed that glowed like a flashlight.

"Maybe you should wait until I get it to my repairman," I said. "All the rods are wobbling and that dent in the neck can't be doing it any good."

He assembled the horn, slapped on the glowing reed, and tied it with a string. Then he blew. Maestro C—*Bird*—standing next to Jimmy's easel no more than six feet away, poured out the most beautiful, unmistakable, Charlie Parker shower of notes on his famous tune "Confirmation," and soon branched into harmonic directions I'd never heard on his albums.

Then I saw them. Hundreds of tiny, multi-colored oblong lights formed above his head and filled the air with indescribable joy. Every cell of my body was tingling, dancing with the lights, consumed with the fever of the glowing jellybeans.

Maestro C softened his tone, and the jellybeans turned blue and purple. When he brightened his sound, they turned red and orange, some sparking through the living room. Then a rainbow of them spun around on the ceiling, as if in ecstasy.

The door buzzed. Jimmy answered. It was Carole, with another nurse's aide, and their timing couldn't have been worse. Maestro C was putting on the greatest show I'd ever seen or heard, and I couldn't turn away from him. Carole was telling Jimmy, "Eunice will get you guys back on your feet." But while Carole pointed to the piles, handing a box of jumbo trash bags to Eunice, the world's greatest saxophonist was blowing furiously over his tune, "Koko." And golden jellybeans streaked through my apartment.

I was so spellbound I hadn't realized the woman I love had been sitting next to me on my sofa, yelling my name.

She grabbed my shoulders: "Shawn!"

"Wait a minute, Carole," I said so softly she didn't hear me.

"What's happened to you?" she said, taking my pulse. "Jimmy!" she shouted. "Did he get into your meds?"

"It's okay okay," Jimmy said. "Mr. Shawn Lewis is learning about the gift."

"Damn it!" she said, burrowing through her pocketbook. "I can't find my cell phone! Jimmy, where's your phone?"

Jimmy told her he didn't know about phones, but she couldn't understand him. The apartment was so cluttered it would've been a challenge to find it anyway. Carole snatched a cell phone from Eunice and called 911.

Now Maestro C was blowing over "Body and Soul," and the jellybeans turned shades of violet, blue and burgundy. Carole held my hand, kissing my cheek. She had no idea what was happening, and the words to tell her wouldn't leave my lips.

"Shawn," she said, "I'm sorry, *so* sorry. I should've never left you after that last visit. You needed me. I should've stayed with you, nursed you back. I'm sorry. This is my fault. You were so sweet to me; there's no one who makes me feel special like you do—and I walked away. Please come out of this. I'm sorry about the whole mess over your music. It doesn't matter. You'll always be the one. I love you, Shawn."

Maestro C finished the tune, cradled the instrument back on my desk, and even as the jellybeans and the rest of it began to fade, I still couldn't shake their grip.

"You've been attracting the jellybeans for years," Maestro C said. *"They come through your music. Majib can't help but dance in their presence."*

Carole was hugging me, weeping, but my eyes were on the Maestro. I wanted her so much, but I couldn't move or say a word.

"The jellybeans are from many star systems away. The enlightened ones say they've been visiting Earth for millennia. They zip through the outermost creative dimension. We call that dimension the Outside, the force of pure invention. Humans ignore this force, but it's all around us: Particles of inspiration spin beyond time and surround every being, urging us all to create forms never imagined.

"When a rare artist with the gift to merge with the Outside enters their creative state, the hidden loops and wormholes of the universe, the hidden tunnels between the Earth worlds, all the secret passageways open. The jellybeans are always waiting for such an artist, so they can leap through space to join the art, to celebrate another passageway. And wherever they go they bring the harmony of the Outside."

Though Carole couldn't see or hear the Maestro, she heard Jimmy when he muttered, "Everything is very alive, even thoughts are so very alive, and everything is making art all the time, speaking and speaking to everything else all the time."

"What are you trying to say?" Carole said to Jimmy. "Take the deep breaths I showed you. Speak slowly. Can you tell me what happened to Shawn?" She continued to hold me tight.

"Go into any rain forest and listen," Maestro C said. *"At first the sounds seem random: a macaw, a waterfall, a swarm of bees, an owl, a family of monkeys, a downpour. After ten minutes you're listening to the most beautiful symphony ever written. Interdependent chaos. Unified free invention. This is the universe.*

"For eons people have ignored the interplay of the cosmos all around them, even within their own skin. They push away whatever threatens their version of order. Don't you think the Earth and all her worlds suffer as well, from the gluttony and pain of billions of people?

"Majib has more paintings for you, more openings. The enlightened ones hope people will listen to your music and feel their connection beyond the tribe. Most

won't see jellybeans but they'll feel the Outside. Music will be the tool that finally smashes the old code. Now's the time."

The door buzzed again. Eunice answered it, and two paramedics rushed in with a fold-up wheelchair.

"I have to go now," Maestro C said, *"but there's one more thing."*

The paramedics picked me up and settled me into the wheelchair. Carole held her hand over her mouth.

"Take the horn to my friend, Cameron Cooke," Maestro C said. *"He's a Jamaican fellow, 91-years old—lives in Harlem. He used to fix all our horns. Nobody goes to him anymore. They think he died twenty years ago. Sometimes* ***he's*** *not sure. Tell him Maestro C sent you. He'll make the horn play better than ever."*

Maestro C vanished as I heard Carole utter, "Catatonic."

"Catatonic?" I said, standing up.

"Shawn!" she hollered.

"I'm fine, sweetheart," I said.

"But for half an hour your eyes were open and you weren't responding."

"Sit down, sir," said one of the paramedics. "You're going to the hospital."

"No, no, no," I said. "I'm not going anywhere."

"Calm down, sir," the other man said to me. "You're in a state of shock."

"I've never been more calm," I said. I convinced the men to do their tests in the apartment. Jimmy snuck to his room and locked the door, just in case they were there for *him*. After twenty minutes I satisfied them I was going to survive, signed a release form, and they left.

"You sure you're all right?" Carole asked.

"I feel unbelievable," I said.

"You had me so worried."

"I know," I said. "I heard all those wonderful things you said."

"You what?"

"That you love me, that you're sorry, that you—"

"You mean you were conscious the whole time? What kind of act are you pulling?"

"Carole, I was having the most amazing experience."

"Is that what you call it? Pretending to be a statue while someone's shouting your name in your ear? I'll tell you what's amazing: It's amazing I come over here. It's amazing I give my time to try to help you, that I even give a damn, the way you behave. I mean, look at yourself. That do-rag has got to go." She reached for my head, but I backed away. "You are a real shit for just sitting there when I thought you were dying. Do you even realize how cruel that was? Can you see what you're doing with your life? You're living like a bum, a derelict . . . "

A blob above her head started materializing into a bloated older man in a gray business suit. *"My name is Gerrybubbles,"* he said, floating in the air. *"I used to be Gerald Bonner, Carole's dad. Better not respond to me right now. She can't see or hear me and she's already upset with you enough."*

". . . and after all that buildup, I hear you and your band in that—that Out House crap hole, and I'm telling you, subway brakes sound more like music . . ."

"Just let her get it out," Gerrybubbles said. *"You're the one for her."*

". . . I worked so hard to make this place clean and safe for your friend—your friend. Maura told me you fired her. Why? And this is how you're living . . . Hey! Hello? Hello? What are you staring at? I'm talking to you . . . "

"Look at her lights," Gerrybubbles said, *"the ones Majib showed you."*

"That's better," she said. "Now at least you're listening. I've hired Eunice for today, but it's going to be your responsibility to make sure she . . . "

I saw the flash movie of Carole's life: her mother dying young, her father mostly absent, her ease with me right from the start, and her successful but cold husband.

"I wasn't a great father," he said. *"I loved the cello but I couldn't work, so, unlike you, I gave up my dreams. Money became my dreams. I wound up on the road as a sales rep for AcuTray plastic gauge holders. Can you imagine a more meaningless waste of a man's life?"*

". . . Hello?" she said. "What is so fascinating about the ceiling?" She glanced up. "Will you at least look at me when I'm talking to you?"

"That's my little girl," he said. *"Isn't she marvelous?"*

". . . Do I need to remind you that you have a schizophrenic patient . . ."

"I want you and Carole to wind up together," he said. *"But she's mixed up about you. Just tell her you're going to bring the little heavens back into her life*

through your music. And tell her I said so." Gerrybubbles then floated away through the ceiling.

"Carole," I said, "don't fret. We can be together now."

"Have you heard a thing I've said?"

"You never should've married the doctor. I understand. Ever since you lost your mom you've needed security. So you married Mark and screwed things up a little. I forgive you."

"You condescending—"

"No, Carole. I'm here to bring the little heavens back into your life—through my music. Your dad told me to say that."

"What?!" she shrieked. "Through your—what?"

Eunice emerged from the kitchen. "Uh . . . sorry," Eunice said, looking down. "We all out of cleanser."

"Dad's been dead for ten years, you freak," Carole said.

"No problem, Eunice," I said. I scrounged through a pile near the easel, and found Muriel's bottle of "Grime Gone." As I handed it to Eunice, I noticed Jimmy's latest painting.

Seven swirling ribbons—the colors of the spectrum—all connected to a central fireball. I slipped, tumbling into the fireball. The ribbons now attached to *me*, to my *ears*. I was ablaze, seven colors streaming in and out of my ears. I could hear *everything,* even conversations in other apartments. The Mendez kids really *were* playing war, half launching Pickett's Charge at Gettysburg, the other half mowing them down before they could get to Cemetery Ridge. Muriel Fetterman was demanding Lloyd deal with his foot odor problem; she was having trouble holding down her food. Galicia was talking out loud to her cats, giving them a reading. Jimmy was muttering to himself as he scrawled in his notebook: "If the lovely Green Bilgars of planet Horus use the tenth dimension's 38th link to get to Earth Four, could a man wearing red, fly to Planet Horus through the . . ." I collapsed to the rug.

"It's not going to work this time, Shawn," Carole said. "I'm sorry I yelled at you, I really am, but acting sick again is not going to make me . . . "

I fell asleep, and dreamed of lessons with Maestro C, Professor Thel, and The Listener.

CHAPTER 24

Blue Light Bar Jams

I BLEW IT again. She was professing her love to me, and still I blew it again.

"You've got to forgive me," I said when Carole finally picked up the phone.

"My stomach hurts," she said. "My therapist told me to avoid you."

"I'm sorry about your stomach. Just believe me, I wasn't faking. I would never deliberately—"

"Oh come on, Shawn, pretending to be in shock is unforgivable."

"Give me another chance, Carole. Sometimes, lately, I get distracted. But I'll get over it, I promise."

"That was 'distracted?' No, that was either you manipulating me or a total breakdown. When I see how you and Jimmy are living . . . I get so worried it makes me sick. And I can't turn it off. I've got a full load at Midtown Hospice and I can't afford to show up every day with a stomachache. I need to be away from you—at least a couple of months. After that, prove to me my sweet, easy, normal Shawn is back, really back—and he's responsibly caring for his friend Jimmy. Then we can talk . . . That's when I'd love to talk."

Okay—a couple of months. I just had to prove I was normal. Unfortunately, that wasn't so easy anymore. Normal is hard when everything around you is bursting with life and sound and curls of energy, while spirits are floating by.

Jimmy made all the arrangements with Cameron Cooke, which is incredible since he never used a phone or left the apartment. Cameron worked on the instrument for seven days. When I picked up the horn, it was re-padded, polished, oiled, and the neck was perfect. I put on the Thayer and the combination blew so easily and with so much character, it almost felt like Mr. Jula was playing it for me.

My dreams were stacked with lessons. Maestro C was teaching me how to move my fingers while scarcely touching the keys, and Professor Thel showed me how to listen to the rhythms in my body, the pulses in every organ.

On March 2nd, as Jimmy and I set up between the newsstand and the Downtown R, someone from the gathering crowd requested "Stardust." I improvised around the long, slow intro, and the crowd grew. But the scene at the station faded away, and though I was still blowing, I now stood in a grotto lit by giant red candles. Mr. Jula, in a burgundy robe and flanked by three-foot toadstools, sat on a pink-granite throne.

"What'd I tell you?" he said as I improvised over the tune. *"Your old horn was nothing.* ***This*** *is the sound. Only problem—you don't move your air. Blow. Nursery school is over. No more candy-ass wimpdom. Blow, doofstick. Blow that horn like it's the last thing you're going to do. 'Cause it just might be."*

As I finished the song, Mr. Jula's grotto receded, and I was back in the subway.

"A thousand million," Jimmy said, pointing to the open case piled with ones, fives, even a few tens. People with moist eyes thanked me as they ran for their trains.

That night Irene called again. "Soooo, I heard about the whole ambulance scandal," she said. "Your ex hates you now."

A typical Irene bomb, but I was ready this time.

"That's *nothing,*" I said. "You don't know *half* of what's going on. Like, I'll bet you don't know what time Carole boards her Times Square train to go home every day. I'll bet you don't know *that*."

"4:30 . . . By the way, my awesomely cute boyfriend is taking me to Bermuda."

"May you have a fabulous time—and even decide to move there."

Every day Jimmy and I planted ourselves in Times Square at 4:30. If

Carole could see my devoted fans, I thought, she'd see I was successful, normal. Or at least worth another chance.

While Jimmy turned out the paintings—about two a week—the lessons in my dreams got more bizarre each night. By April Maestro C was teaching me "Rain Forest Counterpoint," and The Listener was teaching me "The Art of the Solo with No End and No Beginning." At Times Square I got used to playing any fragment of a tune or piece that popped into my mind, and stringing them together for a few hours, all the while certain that Carole was somewhere noticing it. Mr. Jula would often drop by or pull me into his grotto, pushing me, demanding I be worthy of his instrument and mouthpiece.

After a few weeks the crowds became a problem for the Transit Authority. People were in no hurry to make their trains, clogging the thoroughfare. The T-shirt guy and the flower vendor would fight over who could set up closest to our wall, pissing off the newsstand guy. The police would try to push everyone along, but soon, even a few of them joined the party, which I used to my advantage.

When we showed up on May 5th, our bogeyman was already working our spot. Between the newsstand and the Downtown R, The Conductor stood with his back pressed against my white wall, maniacally waving his arms toward the throng. A mouse scurried around his feet. I approached with my saxophone.

"We shouldn't bother him," Jimmy said to me. "He's a historigantic conductor."

"No, no way, Jimmy," I said. "He's a nutcase."

"The Kloik Kleks!" The Conductor yelled, waving his beats. "The music beyond all music, Mr. Shawn Lewis, beyond all things, beyond life itself. You must know that it's your turn. Can't you see it's your turn for the Kloik Kleks? The world cannot wait!"

I didn't even have to consult my new friends in the Transit police. Within two minutes they were forcibly whisking him away—still waving his arms—as he pleaded to me in front of a gawking crowd, "Mr. Shawn Lewis, *please*. Don't let them take me! *What about the Kloik Kleks?"*

Already, my new talents had translated into power—at least with the Transit police, who asserted the lowlife wouldn't be bothering me anytime soon. But still, no Carole.

〰〰

ON MAY 8TH, as we finished that evening's performance, a tall man in a Baroni black pinstripe suit pushed through the crowd and dropped a twenty in the case. "I'm Dalton Popley," he said, handing me his card.

I gave it to Jimmy.

"You may have heard of me?" the man said.

"Huh?" I said, distracted by his gold tie, his sharp haircut, and some ominous shadows floating up from the tracks of the Downtown R.

"Tell me you haven't heard of Dalton Popley," Mr. Jula said from his cave. *"Number one jazz impresario of the last fifteen years. Where you been? At least tell the man you know him."*

"No matter," the man said. "I've been hearing about *you*. You're even better than what they say. I'd like to listen to you with a rhythm section. I'll pay you well. Come tonight around ten—the Blue Light Bar on 23rd. It's jam night."

23rd Street was only a twenty-minute walk, but we were soon lost, wandering the sidewalks while Jimmy asked everyone we saw, "Blue Light Bar jams?" He seemed to think we were looking for a special jelly—perhaps blueberry.

Eventually people guided us to 23rd Street and a blue-scripted neon sign. A piano, bass and drums on a small bandstand in the rear swung quietly for a few couples eating dinner. Jimmy walked up to the bar and asked for the jams. The bartender told him we were three hours early.

As we sat at the bar, eating pounds of wings and fries, I got sleepy. When I asked the bartender where I could take a nap, he told me to try my home. I threw down a slab of freshly-donated bills from the sax case, and while Jimmy stayed at the bar, working on a basket of fried shrimp, the bartender led me to a cot inside a cramped office that smelled like sour cheese.

I fell right asleep. I dreamed I was sprawled on top of a flying piano, the wind swirling around me as I peered into a cloudless sky. Delicate bebop to the changes of "Cherokee" tickled through my body. A yellow, nine-foot Steinway was the only thing between me and oblivion. And sitting at the piano was Wendell Rice.

"Wendell, it's you!" I said, lifting my head, hanging onto the closed piano lid. "Where are we?"

He smiled and kept playing.

"Are you all right?" I said.

He didn't answer.

"How did you climb through Jimmy's painting?" I asked.

He just smiled and played.

"Wendell, I need your help. I'm playing better than ever, but I think I've gone insane. I've lost all control of my life. It terrifies me to even say it."

"But Shawn," he said, "why would you want to control your life?"

"Uh . . ."

"It's like I told you: Find your one thing, the thing that makes you special. Why, you're a bridge between the worlds. Put that in your music and your life, Shawn. But don't ever control it. Just let the Heavenly Voice sing through your voice."

"I don't know how to do any of that," I said.

"Sure you do," he said, moving the tune up a half step. "You already bring the jellybeans. Very few people do that."

"Wendell, I'm insane. This right now—this is evidence."

"Relax. No one's going to lock you up for flying on a Steinway, now will they?" He laughed as he segued into "Just One of Those Things." "You'll be playing in a moment. Remember, all things are tones of the Heavenly Voice. Everything is the Voice. Now you'll not only hear the sounds of the rhythm players, but you'll hear their thoughts before they make the sounds. Don't just listen to their music, Shawn—listen to the music in their minds."

The piano started rocking, and I lost my grip. "Mr. Shawn Lewis!" bellowed over me as I fell through the sky and woke to Jimmy shaking me, yelling my name. "Mr. Shawn Lewis! Mr. Ploppy is here! Time to eat the jam."

"That's *Popley*," the man said, standing behind Jimmy. "Just call me Dalton."

Jimmy handed me the alto. As I sat up on the cot and rubbed my eyes, I could hear Dalton whisper to the waitress, "Has he been drinking?" She didn't know.

I climbed the bandstand, and well before I could situate myself, the trio ignited into "What is This Thing Called Love" at breakneck speed. Jam night or not, they didn't want me there. Jimmy and Dalton sat together, a few tables back, and watched as I let chorus after chorus blaze by without playing a note. But I was listening. I could hear every choice the musicians made. I soaked in the pianist's voicings. I observed the subtle language between the drummer and bass player. I *understood* all three of them. And as they returned to the melody to finish out the tune, confident they'd intimidated me from playing, I jumped in. I spun through the chord changes and added whole sets of my own. As the pianist switched into fourths harmonies, I darted through a field of fourths. When the bass and drums staggered a three-against-four pattern, I leapt into six, doubling up on the three. I could superimpose any chords or any meter I chose and make it work. Then I saw the glimmer of the jellybean lights all around me. I could feel their euphoria. Soon the trio was grumbling, Let's get out of this already, banging out the melody to force an ending. I played out the tune to applause from the nine people still in the club.

I asked the pianist why we had to cut it short. "Cut it short?" he said, leaning back with his hands palming his eyes. "You played thirty choruses."

"Mr. Popley better double that tip tonight," the drummer said, wiping his face with a towel.

Dalton was smiling and still clapping as he walked up and handed me a hundred-dollar bill. "That was the single greatest performance I've heard of that tune, since . . . well, since I heard Sonny Stitt in LA in '73. We have to talk."

I followed him back to his table, where Jimmy was drinking an extra-large Coke, his face and beard dappled in barbecue sauce. "The Outside indeed, Mr. Shawn Lewis," Jimmy said, laughing and biting into another wing. "Historigantic."

"You're too good to be playing subway stations," Dalton said as he ordered us cocktails and more bar food.

While Dalton laid out plans for an album, I could overhear the waitress and bartender from across the room, mumbling about Mr. Popley and his two weirdos.

"You need a good manager," Dalton said, "someone who'll guide you through the . . . " But now that I could hear so well, I chose to eavesdrop on the sexy waitress.

"That guy in red gives me the willies," the bartender said.

"Oh," she said, "the blue guy's much creepier. Look, he keeps staring at me."

"Yoohoo?" Mr. Jula said, materializing in the chair between Dalton and me. *"This is about the* ***album****. Pay attention to the man, doofstick!"*

"Will you stop calling me that?" I said to Mr. Jula.

"Uh, I'm sorry," Dalton said. "Did I say the wrong thing?"

"Not you," I said, *"him,"* pointing to Mr. Jula.

"Oh . . . " Dalton said.

"Dummy!" Mr. Jula shouted. *"He can't see me—you know that. Now stop staring at the waitress . . . Stop it . . . Turn your head."*

"A sharp manager and PR team could work miracles with you," Dalton said.

"Okay," I said, turning to Dalton. "But, don't you think the first step should be to hire a hospice counselor?"

"What?" Dalton said, wincing.

"Doofstick. Screw this up and I'll kick your ass."

"Don't speak to me like that," I said to Mr. Jula.

"Uh," Dalton said, "are you talking to *me* . . . or . . ."

"When do we get the jams?" Jimmy said.

"Okay, okay," I said to Dalton, "forget the hospice thing. She also doubles as a nurse. I say we get a full-time nurse for the—"

"Shut it, doofstick," Mr. Jula said to me. *"I'm not going to let you shit this up. Just smile, say Yes and nod your goddamn head."*

"Don't worry, Mr. Ploppy," Jimmy said, "you can tell *me* all about the sharp manchair for Mr. Shawn Lewis."

"Are you," Dalton said to Jimmy, "are you a friend, a relative? What is your—"

"Well," Jimmy said with a wide grin, "Mr. Shawn Lewis and I live together."

"Yes, yes," I said, smiling and nodding.

"Oh, I see . . ." Dalton said. "You're, well, you're partners. I understand."

"You're not helping me," I whispered to Mr. Jula. "Go away." I smiled and nodded to Dalton.

"I have just the right manager for you two," Dalton said to Jimmy. "He's cutting edge—too edgy for some—but I think you'll like him. His name is Renard Phisbin. Do you know him?"

Jimmy shook his head.

"Wait a second," I said, still nodding, "did I hear you say, 'Renard Phisbin?'"

"Do you know him?" Dalton said.

"Know him?" I said. "He's a real piece—"

"Stop right there," Mr. Jula shouted. *"Don't call his friend a piece of shit."*

"I was not going to say that," I whispered to Mr. Jula. "I was going to call him a piece of work."

"Well, don't say that either," Mr. Jula said.

"Hmm," Dalton said, "should we discuss this when you're . . . feeling better?"

"I was about to say," I said to Dalton, "I worked with Renard years ago and thought he was a real . . . peaceful fellow." I smiled and nodded.

"'Peaceful' is not the word I think of for my brilliant friend Renard Phisbin," Dalton said, chuckling, "but I'm glad you know each other. I'll arrange everything."

"Okay, we're in business," Mr. Jula said, and vanished.

"When do we get the jams?" Jimmy said.

"Could we do a big photo shoot for the album?" I asked Dalton. "Get Jimmy, all the producers, everybody onto West 78th Street—onto my ex-girlfriend's stoop."

"Sure, we'll make a splash," Dalton said. "Show her you don't need her anymore, right?"

"No, what?" I said. "I just want her to see I'm a success and I take good care of Jimmy. I'm as normal as I ever was."

"Of course you are," he said. "It's high time we all thought that was normal."

"*What* was normal?" I asked.

"Jam," Jimmy said. "A jam would be lovely."

"Do you have a card?" Dalton asked me.

"No," I said.

"Well, what's your home number?" Dalton said, pulling out his cell phone. "I'll log it in right now."

"I can't remember the latest one," I said. "It's unlisted. Five numbers in the last three months just to keep Irene from needling me. My stalker. She finds me no matter what I do," I said, rubbing my right eye for three seconds.

"How about your cell?"

"I think I lost it running out of a pawn shop in Iowa," I said.

"How about e-mail? You've got e-mail, right?"

"They cut it off when we stopped paying. Eunice threw out the bills."

"You still get regular mail, right?"

"Of course . . . Well, we forgot this week. Jimmy, make a note to check the mail."

Dalton took down our address. I couldn't remember the exact street, but Jimmy gave him every detail, including our position on the planet and solar system right up through the Beeom of Spirarus.

CHAPTER 25

The Meeting

"I'M WORRIED they won't go along with my idea, Jimmy," I said, after we got into the back seat of the limo. "Renard has a monster-size ego. He might not cooperate."

"Everybody is happy, very happy about this," Jimmy said.

"Renard too? He hated me. He hated the whole band."

"The Sheml is very happy about this," he said.

"Who the hell is the Sheml?"

"The enlightened one who made the nine big works."

Dalton's limo driver pulled up to the posh corner of 63rd and Central Park West in front of the home office of Phisbin Productions. A caterer answered the doorbell, offering us our choice of goat cheese-stuffed mushroom caps or hoisin-dusted crab squares. I declined, but Jimmy took several of each in one hand, and dumped a few more inside his red spandex jacket. We wandered into a spacious living room with abstract bronze sculptures, floor plants, and lots of glass. A dozen guests were clustering around two terrified Chihuahuas while a sound system piped in Midler and Streisand.

"Helooo," Renard said, rushing to greet us. I instantly recognized the broccoli-shaped hairstyle.

Right behind him was Maurice, a slight, soft-spoken man whom Renard introduced as his personal assistant. "You must be Jimmy, Shawn's partner," Renard said. "All in red—wow. And you, Shawn, all blue—how interesting."

"Uh, Jimmy's not really my partner," I said. "I mean, we're very close friends, but I wouldn't say he's my—"

"Such unusual outfits," Renard said. "Did you mean for the colors to clash like that? A bold statement about the world, yes?"

Jimmy nodded and grinned.

"We handle all sorts of talent," Renard said, "mostly vocalists, but when a jazz player comes to us through Dalton Popley, well, we know we have a winner. Of course . . ." He looked us up and down. "We're not committing to anything yet. That's what this meeting is about. You know, Dalton says you're the next big thing. So I ask myself, 'Renard, how come *you* didn't see all this talent at the Royal Galloway?' All I remember is your enthusiasm when you played on my 'Fabulous Balls.'"

"I don't think so," I said. "I'm straight."

"'Fabulous Balls,'" he said. "'From a Bygone Era?' The chart I wrote?"

"You must be thinking of someone else," I said, distracted by Jimmy grabbing more crab squares from a passing tray.

"A CD is no small investment," Renard said, watching Jimmy stuff one in his mouth and two more inside his jacket. "Still, Dalton holds a lot of sway, and he suggested we manage you because—well, around us you can be *comfortable* with who you are. In some ways we are just like you: unafraid to buck the tide."

"Fantastic," I said. "You understand us."

"Oh yes," he said.

"Then you'll love my idea for selling the album," I said.

"I can't wait to hear it," Renard said, smiling. "But first, a toast. People!" Renard signaled to the caterers to hand out the champagne. "People," he announced, "Let us toast Dalton Popley's next superstar, Shawn Lewis—the one in blue. And this one here is Jimmy, his partner. May our project—if we should decide to go forward—be a grand success with years of beautiful music and with any luck, a little bit of green, right?"

Everyone cheered, and circled around Jimmy and me.

"Uh, Renard," I said. "You're not going to conduct for this album, are you?"

"Oh no, Shawn," he said. "For this I wear my producer hat, unless you *want* me to conduct. I'd love to conduct, if you—"

"God no," I said. "I mean, *someone's* got to do the producing, right?"

Several of the guests introduced themselves, including Renard's A&R man and his public relations guru. Renard then led the two of them, Maurice, Jimmy and me away from the other guests and into his thick-carpeted, private office. Notebooks, pens, and glasses of Perrier with lime twists rested on a round mahogany table surrounded by black leather rolling chairs. The team sat close and opened their laptops while Jimmy and I sat at the other end.

"Gentlemen," I announced. "I have a breakthrough idea for selling the album."

"All right," Renard said, chortling. "I wanted to cover a few details first, but . . ." He swirled happily in his chair. "All right, do tell."

"Six words," I said, leaning forward on the table. Using my right hand to streak a headline through the air, I said, "Shawn Lewis Live at Midtown Hospice."

They gaped at each other while Jimmy nodded, grinning and bumping my shoulder in approval. Renard said he couldn't quite hear me.

"Shawn Lewis Live at Midtown Hospice," I said.

Manfred, the A&R agent, a sculpted man in a shimmering suit and tie, shook his head. "I'm sorry," Manfred said, "I just can't imagine Cool World Records or any other label recording in a health care facility."

"Precisely," I said. "It's a breakthrough." Jimmy was still nodding and grinning.

Renard and his team conferred. "We had something else in mind," Renard said. "We want this to be upbeat. A hospice is where, forgive me, people go to die."

"Exactly," I said. "Dying people are a completely untapped market."

They conferred again, unaware I could hear every whisper, including their unison hunch that I might be mentally ill.

"It could be beautiful," I said. "The first album ever made for dying people. All the profits could go to Midtown Hospice, and—"

"Just a second," Manfred said. "All profits? I thought we—"

"This is not a charity, Shawn," Renard said.

"I wouldn't know how to market an album made at a hospice," the PR woman said.

"Ah, don't worry," I said. "There's a counselor there, very hip, very—"

"Very very lovely," Jimmy said, still nodding. "Miss Carole Bonner."

"We feature her on the cover," I said, "the perfect image, the ideal caretaker—jazz as therapy for—"

"We have to go a different way, Shawn," Renard said. "Think 'lively.'"

"Lively sure, but I want it to be—"

"Shut it, doofstick," Mr. Jula said from his pink granite throne materializing inches behind Jimmy and me. *"This is more important than your sad sappy little love life."*

"For now, Shawn," Renard said, "let's not worry about what the album is called, where we do it, what's on the cover. We're not even ready to commit yet. Let's talk music. Dalton wants to feature you with a piano, bass, and drums. Does that sound agreeable?"

"I don't know . . . I guess," I said.

"He's nervous about you," Mr. Jula said. *"Show a little enthusiasm, for God's sake."*

"It seems to me," Renard said, standing up, pacing a few steps, "that what we need is a—"

"Yes, I would love that!" I shouted.

"Fine . . . " Renard said, glaring at me. "It seems to me, if we do this, your first album, we'll also have to do a promotional tour, and we'll need a big name, a headliner." He paced another step, gazing at the ceiling, his hand on his chin. "A big-name pianist. Yes, what would make me happy right now would be a very big pianist. Do you have any ideas, Shawn? A celebrated pianist, a pianist people will want to see. Let's make them take notice and say, 'Who is this Shawn Lewis fellow who was able to land that extraordinary pianist?"

"I just got another idea for the album cover," I said. "It's the two of us. I'm kissing her passionately; we're stark naked, the view partially blocked by an I.V. unit, maybe some oxygen tanks and—"

"We're discussing the music now, remember?" Renard said.

"Just smile, nod and say Yes, doofstick," Mr. Jula said. *"Leave your chick out of this."*

"You know," I turned to Mr. Jula, "I do a lot better when you're not around."

"Lovers' quarrel," Maurice mumbled.

"He keeps denying his relationship with Jimmy," the PR woman whispered to Manfred.

"Go away," I whispered to Mr. Jula. "Can't you see you're messing me up, distracting me? Aren't you supposed to be all-knowing?"

"All-knowing?" Mr. Jula said. *"I changed worlds, that's all. If I was all-knowing, would I be forced to work with doofsticks?"*

Manfred and Renard started calling out names of piano players while the other two typed into their laptops. Dave Latrelle won't do it. He's still on contract with Concord. Bill Gells is too expensive. Maury Golden is on tour in Malaysia. Manny Torber would be perfect if he hadn't tried to shoplift those socks in Colombia.

"Get Tommy Meehan!" I shouted.

Everyone covered their ears, grimacing.

"You remember Tommy?" I asked Renard.

"He's good," Renard said, slowly removing his hands from his ears, "but not a headliner."

"But he's who I want," I said, "with Joe Terry on bass and Gus DaLucci on drums."

"But you're an unknown," the PR woman said with a sympathetic smile. Sally, a sturdy, round woman with lustrous fingernails and burnished hair, not only directed Phisbin Productions public relations but also managed their bookings and touring company. "As far as I'm concerned," Sally said, "all of your back-ups should be household names."

"You're all very nice," I said, "but those are the musicians I want—and I want to record at Midtown Hospice."

"I think we have an impasse," Renard said. He sat down and swirled in his chair. "Too bad," he said, looking down. "Dalton will be disappointed."

"My associates will blame me for this," Mr. Jula said. *"Can't you forget the chick for five minutes? If I go down, I'm taking you with me, doofstick, and I'll kick your ass."*

"Can't you come up with a better threat than that one?" I said to Mr. Jula.

"Pardon me?" Renard said. "I didn't intend to . . ."

"I wish you would leave," I whispered to Mr. Jula. "I worshiped you as an alto player, but as a ghost you're a pain in the neck."

"You just call me a ghost again?" Mr. Jula said. *"I'm no ghost. I don't like ghosts. You're more of a ghost than I am."*

"Tell me how you're not a ghost," I mumbled. "You've been dead for thirty years."

"All I did was change worlds," Mr. Jula said. *"A ghost is someone stuck between the worlds. You're more stuck than I'll ever be."*

"Pardon me, Shawn," Renard said. "We need to wrap up the meeting . . . I mean, unless you need a few more minutes with your . . . imaginary friend . . . "

"Mr. Fishbins," Jimmy said, "Mr. Shawn Lewis can play his historigantic sax more dazzling with the lovely people that he likes."

"Thank you, Jimmy," Renard said. "It's *Phisbin*, by the way."

"If you're not dead," I mumbled to Mr. Jula, "how come no one else sees you?"

"Majib's paintings amplified your gift, your link to the Outside by nine times. The things you're experiencing have always been here. You just never knew it before."

"Do the clothes help?" I said to Mr. Jula in full voice. "Do you have any substance? I mean, if you didn't cover yourself in fancy clothes, would everyone see right through you?"

"So rude," Maurice whispered.

"Maybe this explains why he only works the subways," Manfred grumbled.

"Hmm," Renard said, "we can't agree on the musicians or the venue. And now you have some problem with *me*. I think Dalton will understand why we chose to . . ."

"What you see is my essence," Mr. Jula said. *"When I played your junk horn, I didn't play it with lungs, lips, and fingers. I played it with my essence, baby—essence—the same essence that's going to kick your sorry ass."*

I noticed the four of them scowling at me, waiting for my response. ". . . What?" I said.

"We're trying to decide if we should go any further," Sally said.

"Yes, I would love that!" I shouted, eyeing for Mr. Jula's approval. Jimmy grinned, bumping my shoulder again.

"Okay . . . " Renard said, slowly removing his hands from his ears. "Convince me you're worth the investment."

"Speak to Dalton," I said. "And just remember, if we use my guys, we barely need to rehearse. That'll save money. And if we record in Midtown Hospice, we save a ton on studio fees." I smiled while Jimmy grinned and bumped my shoulder.

The team groused about whether Dalton had lost his touch, bringing in such a pair of idiots—still unaware I could hear every word. Renard then asked Jimmy and me to wait outside the room while the team made a conference call to Dalton Popley.

Mr. Jula waited with us. He added a few more threats, and then he started to whine, almost sob. I felt sorry for him. He was sure if this fell through, he'd be demoted to guiding insurance agents. It was really true: Just because you're an angel from The Other Side doesn't mean you have any more of a grip than we do.

A few minutes later Maurice brought us back into the room. Dalton, promising to shoulder all fees, had persuaded the team to stick by me, to even use my musicians—on one condition: We record in a proper studio. Now *I* called for a conference. I quickly nudged Renard and his three associates out of their office, so *we* could discuss their counteroffer. We being Jimmy and me—and Mr. Jula. I thought we should play hardball, but Mr. Jula threatened to give me a disease that would cause my organs to dissolve. And then he said he'd probably screw that up and someone else would get the disease, but *that* would be on my conscience.

I brought them in, telling them I agreed—but on one condition: We schedule the rehearsals for Bruce's Sound Lab on West 79th Street, which happened to be a block from Carole's home. I'd bring up the photo shoot later.

Maurice, Sally and Manfred jumped on their phones, booking the rehearsals and sessions and laying out a plan for the tours. I consoled Mr. Jula that all was well. Within a half hour the recording engineer and the dates were locked in, and everyone breathed a sigh. A celebration of hugs floated around the room. Again, Jimmy didn't seem to know when to stop.

Mr. Jula was elated. As he was vaporizing, he gave me the biggest hug of all, planting a wet kiss on my cheek that so surprised me, I yelped, which caused everyone's head to turn.

Maurice handed me an appointment card with all the rehearsal and recording details. I gave it to Jimmy, who smooshed it into the crab squares in his jacket.

Renard asked about the music. I told him not to worry; it would be full of rain forest counterpoint and solos with no beginnings and no endings. I was excited. Finally, the career I always wanted. It was the big time, and I would make sure Carole knew all about it.

Before Jimmy and I could leave, Renard wanted to settle the phone problem. I told him it was no problem ever since we kept it disconnected. He issued us two cell phones. But I couldn't turn them on, I said; Irene would still find me. He said, Just use the caller ID and pick up whenever he called. I didn't like the idea. He begged me to keep them on. He offered us a hundred dollars to keep them on. A hundred fifty. It took ten minutes to hash out a settlement. Jimmy did the negotiating. In the end he guaranteed Renard we'd keep the phones charged, on and with us—for five cases of homemade jam.

CHAPTER 26

Plarps

IT TOOK THREE DAYS to lose the cell phones—just hours to lose the appointment card. And though Jimmy was determined to find the cell phones so he could get the jams, he hated phones. He'd convinced me that all electronics unrelated to food, TV or music were "molds on our freedom." We put aside our technological parasites—which explains how I shrank his reds. You can't throw spandex into the dryer and forget about it. Now Jimmy took control of the wash.

He stored his laundry and everything else in his room wherever it fell. But the living room was where *I* lived. And the canvases, newspapers, wet paints and our general mess had already been multiplying when it descended into a biohazard wrapped in blue laundry.

Late that evening I watched him uncharacteristically ransacking through the piles. He really wanted that jam. After two hours the apartment was more scattered than ever. And still no phones. But Jimmy did unearth the TV and VCR remotes, the brick of cheddar we never found, and $85 in loose bills and change. He was tired now, and armed with the remotes, he took a break from the dig to settle in for a *Twilight Zone* marathon. As I excavated through the layers of laundry, junk mail, bills past-due, leaflets, newspapers, magazines, books, receipts, notes, CDs, VCRs, boxes and bags of all kinds—some still with groceries in them—and everything splattered in paint, I had to do it all without making a sound. Jimmy's beloved *Twilight Zone* was on, and every move I made brought a "Shhh." I told him *I* wasn't the one who wanted the jams, but all reason melted away when the *Twilight Zone* was on. It's impossible to pick up an un-refrigerated two-week-old basket of strawberries without groaning.

"Shhh," he said, cupping his hands to his ears.

While I rummaged through the piles I got depressed. The jams didn't matter to me, but I wanted more than ever to find the phones, just to hear Carole's voice. "Jimmy, what am I going to do? I'm so attached to her. And she doesn't even want to talk to me."

"The plarps," he said, staring at the TV. "Call the plarps."

"With what?" I said. "And who the hell are the—"

"Just become feelings, Mr. Shawn Lewis. Stop thinking. Become your lovely feelings and your dreadful feelings. Then ask the plarps to come—but not too loud; it's Telly Savalas."

I had to do *something.* "Plarps," I said, "whoever, whatever you are, I feel—well, I feel kind of silly. My crazy friend here says I should—" My whole body began to tingle. I forgot about the phones. I just wanted to empty out my whole apartment or move. After that, I thought, a naked jog in the park might be nice. The thoughts were not my own.

Something rustled on top of my desk. I stared but I couldn't believe what I saw. Two small dogs, like smooth fox terriers but with folded wings, were slowly rotating, searching for a comfortable spot on my desk. Except for their tan faces and dark eyes, their bodies and wings were a glowing, cottony white.

"*Hello, Mr. Shawn Lewis,*" said one of the dogs, lying down on its stomach.

"Uh . . . Jimmy?" I said.

"Shhh," he said, "the Talky Tina doll just told off Telly Savalas."

"*The name's Sedgwick,*" the dog said. "*This here's my wife, Colleen.*"

"*We've been waiting for your call, sweetums,*" the other dog said as she scratched her right shoulder with her back leg. They spoke with an Oklahoma drawl that seemed to come from every direction.

"I can't fly now," Jimmy said. "It's *Twilight Zone,* and we should all be very quiet."

"Sorry Majib," Sedgwick whispered. *"Mr. Shawn Lewis, you need to know all about Earth Three. Of course, we don't call it that. We call it Plarpiana."*

"That's 'cause we're plarps," Colleen said, rolling over on her back.

"We've been hanging around Majib since he was a boy," Sedgwick said. *"Sometimes we bring over friends, party all night. Or else he flies over Trob Forest to meet us."*

"Jimmy, this can't be happening," I said.

"Shhh," Jimmy said, "Telly's getting his power saw."

"We're indebted to you, Mr. Shawn Lewis," Sedgwick said. *"We always will be. See, Majib is our great master. And you saved him."*

"And we're in awe of your great skill with the jellybeans," Colleen said.

"Are you," I said, "ghosts? Aliens?"

"Neither," Sedgwick said.

"Honey, we're as much a part of your planet as you are of ours," Colleen said.

"Talking dogs with wings," I muttered.

"Oh, Sedgila," Colleen said, *"the boy don't understand."*

"Earth has seven worlds," Sedgwick said, *"each with its own qualities and natural laws, and they all overlap each other. Qualities drip from one world to the other, feeding whatever they land on. Plarpiana is rich in emotion and feeds it to the other worlds. But we're just as sensitive to the qualities that drip back. Majib showed us all this or we'd never know."*

"Does it feel stuffy in here?" I said. "I feel like a midnight swim at Rye Beach."

"That's us," Colleen said.

"Huh?" I said.

"Those are the kind of things plarps do," Sedgwick said. *"Plarpiana is all about feelings—the rush to quench or break free. And we're in your space now."*

"You feel kind of excited now, right?" Colleen said, wagging her tail.

I nodded.

"Like you just won a prize," Sedgwick said, *"or you're about to go on a great trip, right?"*

"I feel like going for a run," I said, unzipping the top half of my jumpsuit.

"Plarps love to run and fly," Sedgwick said.

"And make love," Colleen said.

"For us, life is spontaneous," Sedgwick said.

"Maybe I'll run down Bronx Boulevard," I said, taking off my T-shirt.

"Everybody thinks their world is all there is," Colleen said. *"But when we sleep, all the worlds mix, and we visit each other like mad."*

"You should feel better now, Mr. Shawn Lewis," Sedgwick said. *"You know, we were at that meeting—the one with the Phisbins. Majib brought us."*

"We heard things y'all didn't hear," Colleen said. *"Majib and Mr. Jula say the album's more important—they don't want to know. But the head Phisbin can't be trusted, honey."*

"What—what are you talking about?"

"Don't trust him," Sedgwick said. *"We owe you this. You saved our Majib."*

"What's wrong with the head Phisbin?" I said. "He seemed reasonable—sort of."

"He thinks you're evil crazy," Colleen said, *"crazier than a pile a gerbils."*

The Phisbin may be right, I thought, watching Sedgwick lick his butt. All my life I've feared this. But a pile of gerbils can't make sense of things enough to be afraid.

"We'll check in with you soon," Sedgwick said. *"Majib, may we play with the paintings now?"*

Jimmy flicked his hand, showing it was okay, and without a pause the plarps flew off the desk and all around the apartment. They flew up to each painting, and like hummingbirds, hovered a moment, then darted to the next. Then they paused above the couch, flapping rapidly in front of the eclipse painting. Colleen turned to me and seemed to smile. One at a time they flew into the eclipse, and disappeared.

I would've been more rattled by the plarps if not for their carefree attitude, which was contagious. I scooped up the mounds of papers on my desk, whatever their importance, and filled a garbage bag. I stripped from the jumpsuit, and wearing only my blue boxers, I left the apartment for the dumpster. If it wasn't my sax, blue or related to Jimmy's art, I intended to get rid of everything I owned. I felt so free. A fictitious being just warned me not to trust my new manager, and none of it bothered me. Nothing was bothering me. I'd even stopped worrying about Carole. In fact, I felt a renewed confidence. After all, my plan to win her back was only getting started.

I climbed the stairs returning from the dumpster but before I could get to my door, Galicia leapt out of her apartment, her orange nightie swinging ever so slightly open. Luckily, her goth makeup and hair from *Night of the Living Dead* overruled her soft curves. "You're in mortal danger!" she yelled in my face.

In the eight years we'd been neighbors this was the first time she didn't startle me. After a pleasant and somewhat healing conversation with two flying dogs who'd disappeared into a painting, a mere zombie wouldn't seem so earth-shattering.

"The cards say you're dabbling in the affairs of the spirit world," she said.

"It's nice to see you," I said. "Would you like to jog with me in the park? I know it's a bit late, but—"

"You're not listening to me," she said. "Mortal danger."

"How about a cool dip at Rye Beach? It's closed, but I think I know where to—"

"I'm deeply concerned about you, Shawn."

The sparkling lights in her residue curls flashed a story of genuine loneliness, a grisly divorce and now poverty. For the first time, I felt sympathy for Galicia.

"Your actions are taking down the whole building," she said.

That ended the sympathy. "Don't you think the Mendez kids invading Normandy could take down the whole building?" I said.

"First, you bring home an insane homeless man and now, the cards say the two of you are dabbling in the black arts."

"I'm sorry your husband didn't appreciate the fortune telling," I said. "But maybe it was because of readings like this. Listen, if you're stressed about making the rent, I've made a few bucks in the subway. I can give you some cash if—"

"But I'm trying to help *you*."

"Well, my only problem is . . . I'm scared. I might be really bats."

"Let me do a proper reading," she said. "Come inside, sit down, relax."

"I insist on paying," I said. "And no discount just because I'm your neighbor."

"All right," she said. "Two hundred dollars. I don't accept checks."

"What?"

"An emergency reading after hours is two hundred."

The sympathy was long gone. "As you can see, I have no pockets," I said, pointing to the boxers. "I've changed my mind. I'd like to skip the reading."

"Nonsense, you'll pay me tomorrow."

I followed her and the orange nightie into her candlelit studio apartment. It was a bad mistake and I knew it, but I was still frisky from the Plarps.

"Would you like some kujungo tea?" she said, heading for her kitchen in the back. "It's okay to buy it now. The tribes that harvest it are no longer killing each other."

"No, no thanks."

She lit a stick of incense, but the cat food and litter were winning.

"Five cats, huh?" I said while she fixed her tea.

"Yes, well, they're my family now," she said from the kitchen.

Except for the cat scratching posts, there were only four pieces of furniture in the main room—two chairs, a dresser and a low circular table on a large area rug. On the table, four white candles formed a wide diamond around a deck of tarot cards.

She returned with the tea, and performed a quick reading. The cards told her I would soon be working in West Virginia as a sign painter for a shale mine. They also said Jimmy was an undercover agent for MI 5.

"I don't think so," I said.

She performed another reading, and this time the cards told her I was having terrible problems with my feet and needed an operation to make them smaller.

"Galicia, these aren't even close."

"I know," she said. "It must be you. What are you doing?"

She did one more reading that declared at last I'd be returning to China—after I had the baby. Before I could say anything, she said she knew. "There's something wrong," she said. "The vibrations are all mixed up."

"Are you sure?" I said. "Maybe you need a break. Maybe you've been working too hard. Why don't we go for a swim?"

She started to cry. I asked her what was wrong. She said that after all these years of urging me to get a reading, she'd failed me. I reassured her. I told her I'd never had any faith in her readings anyway, but that didn't cheer her up. When she started calling herself a failure, that's when I found her irresistible. I stretched across the table and kissed her on the cheek. She kissed me hard on the lips, her blood-red lipstick seeping into my mouth. I reached for her shoulder, and the nightie flopped down. In an instant we were rolling on the floor, her extended nails clawing my body, ripping my underwear away, her mop of undead, grayish hair clogging my nose and eyes. I knew it was all wrong—*wrong*—but as she tore at my body, and I caressed her full, smooth form, she pulled me inside her. And against my better judgment, I plunged into my next-door neighbor, the zombie fortune-teller. I plunged as deep as I could and for as long as I could into her bloodcurdling, screaming bliss until we detonated together, and lay smoldering in front of her staring cats.

CHAPTER 27

The Photo Shoot

EVERYTHING HURT. Even my teeth hurt. I'd been forced to sleep twisted on my side because of the deep scratches she'd carved on my back. The area rug—her bed—did nothing to tame the hardwood floor, and when I woke and tried to move, I thought my ribs were broken. Then I thought my legs were broken until I saw that two of her cats were sprawled on top of them. I squirmed in one direction, then the other, discovering a new pain every second. This was the plarps. This was *their* fault.

As I wrestled to extricate myself from the cats and the floor, she woke. We hadn't said a word since the combat. Now came the awkward hellos. I found my boxers across the room, and put them on. My fingertips hurt. She put on the orange nightie, and all five cats swarmed to her, crying for breakfast.

"Well . . . " I said, "thanks for the readings."

"Uh, yes," she said, moving slowly to the kitchen.

"I guess," I said, "maybe, I should . . . you know, get going."

"You don't have to pay me for the readings," she said from the kitchen, glopping food into cat bowls. "They weren't very accurate."

"Okay, uh, bye," I said.

"Don't you think we should talk about this?" she said, jumping out of the kitchen.

I nodded slowly.

"Don't you have something to say to me?" she said.

"I should explain," I said. "I wasn't myself."

"But you were very *much* yourself. The cards predicted this years ago. That's right," she said, nodding. "I've known. I've known a long time."

"No, Galicia, I mean it. I wasn't myself. Last night I had a dialogue with, well, flying dogs—they call themselves plarps. Out of nowhere they just—"

"There's no point in hiding your feelings," she said. "I care about you too—not in the same way, of course. But you need my guidance."

"I'm serious, Galicia, these plarps or whatever they were, they—"

"Shawn, I don't think we should see each other this way again."

"Oh really . . . Okay. I'm going to go now."

"Don't make me tell you why," she said.

"No, you don't have to tell me why."

"Last night can't happen again. I don't want to hurt you, so don't make me tell you why."

"Okay," I said. "I'm going to go now."

"All right, I'll tell you: I don't find you attractive."

"I understand," I said.

"But since we've had this experience together, I wonder, maybe I should rethink things, right?"

"No, don't do that."

"But maybe you were meant for me after all."

"No, I think you had it right before."

"Maybe I'm not meant to be with an attractive man," she said.

"I think you are. Besides, I told you, I'm bats. Every day I talk to people who've been dead for years, beings from other worlds, stuff like that. Everybody thinks I've lost it. Everybody. The only friend I have left is my roommate."

"Oh, Shawn," she said. "A moment ago I really wanted you to leave. I was desperate to put our disturbing night behind us. But now, hearing you talk about how you are so psychic and misunderstood makes me think, This is it, the depressed and forsaken man I've been waiting for."

"No, you were right before. Let me go, so I can put something on these scratches."

"But maybe I'm destined to be with a disgusting man—a forsaken, spiritual, disgusting man."

"Galicia, I'm in love with someone who thinks I'm a freak."

"Aren't we all?"

". . . Uh . . . well, five cats, whoa, I'm allergic to cats." I started fake wheezing.

"You're fake wheezing," she said. "Stop it. This is bigger than us. I don't love you, but sometimes we're meant to suffer for the greater good."

The door buzzed. It was Jimmy, holding up a fresh painting of flowers. "Hi, Mr. Shawn Lewis," he said. "This is for Miss Galicia."

"Oh, thank you," she said. "A painting of funny hats—how lovely."

"My name is Jimmy," he said to her, his mouth and arms twitching, "but you can call me Jimmy. Majib is good too. Or Jimmy."

"Okay, sure . . . " she said.

"May I call you Tomumda?" he asked her.

"I don't know," she said.

"I have so many paintings I'd like to make for you," he said.

"You have some tics, don't you?" she said. "I'll bet the cards would have excellent advice about that."

"Would you really really do that for me?" he said.

I stood behind her, shaking my head, waving my hands.

"Of course," she said. "It seems you need a great deal of guidance. Why don't I first make you both my special breakfast?"

I violently waved my arms behind her, mouthing a giant No.

"I would like that very very much indeed, Miss Tomumda," he said. "I've always thought you were very lovely."

"Uh, Galicia?" I said. "Remember the mortal danger? Don't you want us to go already?"

"No," she said. "This is the best way I can help."

She made cherry-okra omelets that made me gag, but Jimmy couldn't stop complimenting her. Then she led us to the circular table. I waited by the door while she read his cards. She said he would soon be leading an expedition in the Alps. She told him to hold out for more money.

For several days Jimmy occupied so much of her time with readings—which we had to pay for—she seemed to forget about our "disturbing night." When he wasn't in her apartment he was in my living room, painting for her. After throwing out the first three paintings, she changed her mind and took down her quilts and shaman capes in order to hang the many works that followed. On May 14th, he moved his easel, paints, and equipment to her apartment. They spent the whole day and night together. Her long moans and jarring yips were even more irritating than Lloyd's snore and the Mendez kids, and I couldn't sleep.

The next morning they joined me for breakfast, and Galicia stirred the okra and cherries into the eggs again. We were halfway through the meal when I noticed a shift in her mood. Her face dropped.

"What's wrong?" I said.

"I'm so, so sorry," she said.

"The cherries, right?" I said. "I thought I tasted something moldy."

"No, Shawn . . . " she said. "I didn't plan it this way."

Jimmy put his arm around her and grinned.

"I feel so terrible," she said.

"That's why you check for mold before you cook," I said.

"Will you forgive me?" she said.

"I don't know," I said. "My stomach hasn't started hurting yet."

"Jimmy and I are in love," she said.

"Oh *that*," I said. "Great."

"You're not mad?" she said.

"Well, a little," I said. "I didn't sleep at all."

"I must have really hurt you. Love is so unpredictable."

"What are you talking about?"

"That I'm in love with your friend and not you."

"You already said that. I'm very happy about it. Just keep it down a little."

"It's the ancient techniques, Mr. Shawn Lewis," Jimmy said, still grinning. "They have a lot of power."

"What techniques?" I said.

"My friends are teaching me," he said.

"Which friends?" I said.

"The fourth world tantric masters."

That morning Jimmy officially moved in with Galicia.

I got my apartment back, and guilt free. Jimmy was now his own man.

This was all Sarah had ever wanted. I would've rushed to tell Carole the good news but I still couldn't find the cell phones. It was easier to ransack the piles without Jimmy there, and after two hours I found both phones underneath a half-eaten pizza. They needed twelve hours to charge, and at 11 AM the next morning the rings woke me up. Jimmy and Galicia had been at it again; I'd slept maybe an hour.

"Where are you?" the voice said.

"I don't know," I said. "Where are *you*?"

"This is Renard Phisbin. We've been at Bruce's Sound Lab for an hour already. Everyone's here. When would you like to drop by?"

"Is it today?"

He sighed. "Yes. We've been trying to reach you every day. You must not have had the phones on until now. Didn't you write this down somewhere? Didn't you get our overnight letters?" He sighed again. "You probably don't look at your mail, do you?"

"I forgot."

"Of course. Well, a driver will be at your apartment any minute. When you hear him at the door, answer it. Bring your saxophone. Follow the man to his car. Sit in the car. When he parks, get out of the car and follow him into the building. Would you like me to go over it again?"

AS SOON AS I WALKED into the acoustic-tiled, fluorescent rehearsal room I sought my colleagues from the Galloway and Danny James days, especially my Philly friend, Tommy Meehan. We talked for only a moment when Renard and the team encroached, anxious to get started.

"Shawn," Tommy said, grasping my arm in front of all of them, "are you okay? What's up with the clothes? You don't—you don't look so well."

"I haven't slept," I said, "since my roommate started banging my neighbor."

"Oh no," Sally said, "Jimmy moved out?"

"Yes," I said, rubbing my eye. "He's got a girlfriend now."

"You poor thing," Maurice said. "I know just how you feel."

"You're much better off," Renard said.

"I never saw anyone with so many tics," Manfred said.

"Frankly," Renard said, "he was horrifying to look at. Now you can meet someone else."

"Stop," I said. "We were never a couple. I just want a good night's sleep."

"Such denial," Sally whispered to Manfred.

GUS ADJUSTED the height of his cymbals, Joe sat on a stool by his bass, Tommy noodled at the grand, and Renard and the team, bearing laptops, pulled up metal chairs around us. "Now that you've had two weeks to think about it," Renard said, "What will be your concept for the album?"

"I told you already," I said. "Even if we can't record at Midtown Hospice, we can still make them our theme. I've spoken to the administrators. They're interested."

"You really are deranged," Renard mumbled, staring at me.

"This can be jazz for dying people," I said, unpacking my alto, "folks who don't get to hear much music, and for the devoted, sexy angels who tend to them every—"

"We'll get back to the concept later," Renard said. "We have two full days of rehearsing. What's your agenda for today?"

"My agenda is to do a photo shoot of the band and everybody—you too, Renard—at my ex's building from about 4:30 to 5:30. If all works out, we don't need tomorrow. We can jam a little now, then relax over a leisurely lunch. We've got hours to kill before we need to be there."

"No one told me about a photo shoot," Sally muttered.

"It's all in his mind," Renard whispered.

"I heard that," I said.

"The music, Shawn," Manfred said. "Standards, originals? A mix?"

"I don't know," I said. "My jazz works better if I don't think about it." I turned to Tommy, Joe and Gus and started playing the first thing that came to me, a tune I sensed they'd like, "Bouncing with Bud." Immediately they joined in, and we popped and swung like a unit that had never stopped playing together. Renard tried talking over us. I played louder. He shouted; I played even louder. We blew multiple choruses apiece, taking half an hour to finish the tune.

I put the instrument away and embraced each of my old comrades. "Let's eat at Fava Bang," I announced to everyone. "It's on Forty-third, right across from Midtown Hospice."

"Uh . . . " Renard said. "We're still rehearsing . . ."

"No, we're done," I said.

"We're booked till six today, ten to six tomorrow," Renard said. "Surely you don't think you can prepare your CD without—"

"Renard," Manfred muttered, "I hate to interject, but he may have a point. They already sounded rehearsed. That solo he just took was some of the most original music I've ever heard."

"We have a job to do, Manfred," Renard said. "Shawn, we can't walk into the studio without a clue." He laughed nervously. "At least tell us what's going on the album?"

"I won't know until we do it," I said.

"The tune you just played—will that be on the album?"

"Probably not," I said.

"We—we have to know," he said, grabbing his forehead. "You must have *some* idea?"

"You asked me that already."

"I'm asking you again."

"Music for dying people," I said.

As the team deliberated, calling me several new names, Mr. Jula, in his burgundy robe and holding a glowing silver alto in his hands, appeared behind Renard and the others, and grinned. *"Music for dying people,"* he said, nodding. *"I dig it. I dig it. But my associates want me to kick your ass, so do me a favor—make nice with broccoli head."*

"I'm just so tired and beat up," I said to Mr. Jula. "I couldn't sleep because of Jimmy and his girlfriend."

"I'm sorry about your partner, Shawn," Renard said. "But look, I have Dalton on the line." He shoved his cell phone at me.

"Maybe we should postpone this," Maurice said. "He's obviously heartbroken."

"No," Renard whispered to him, "we don't take shit from sickos." Renard held the phone to my ear; Dalton was calling my name.

Dalton wanted to know why I was leaving the rehearsal. I'm not leaving it, I told him; we did it already. He asked me to be flexible. I am, I said; that's how I knew we we're done. Then I explained to him the hospice concept and the photo shoot. He asked to speak to Renard.

It took just one minute with Dalton for Renard to become gracious, even kindly. Renard hired his driver and two cabs to take us all to Fava Bang, where Renard treated us to lunch. And afterwards, he followed as I led the whole crew into Midtown Hospice.

I managed to get the head nurse, the administrator and the counseling supervisor to consult with me for ten minutes at the first floor nurse's station, the most conspicuous spot in the building. We arranged a concert to kick off the CD and the tours—to be programmed in the lobby of the hospice. Carole will see I'm not a loser, I thought. These people are deferring to *me*. Even if she doesn't walk by and notice my entourage and her bosses respecting me, she won't be able to avoid the flashy concert. She'll have to reconsider my music—*and me*. She'll have no choice.

"I'm apprehensive," the supervisor said. "I don't know about jazz in a critical-care facility—especially avant-garde jazz. We like things quiet here—library quiet."

"I understand, I understand," I said. "I play mellow when I need to. For years I played only hospitals. They were the only gigs I could get."

That didn't comfort them. But they saw the chance for a little publicity and some music, free of charge. After Maurice recorded the details, we headed for the doors.

Then I saw her. Her chestnut eyes could've fired missiles at me, but the sparkling lights around her in her sleeveless pantsuit felt just like home. I wanted to propose right there. Patience, I told myself, patience. She likes things slow.

"What are you doing here?" Carole said, in front of the exit.

"Hello sweetheart," I said. "I'd like you to meet my band and my management team; their office is on Central Park West. Anyway, we're producing an album, a series of albums, and tours, lots of tours all over the world. And we're dedicating it all to you and your Midtown Hospice."

"We are?" Manfred whispered.

"Just play along," Renard whispered.

"Where's Jimmy?" Carole said.

"He's fine, Carole, fine, well taken care of. He hooked up with Galicia.

He moved in with her. They're probably having sex right now."

"It just breaks your heart," Sally whispered to Maurice.

"The crazy psychic lady?" Carole said, holding her stomach. "He's better off alone. I'll bet your apartment's a catastrophe again, isn't it?"

"I haven't had a chance to call Eunice," I said. "But I have the phones now."

"You thought bringing all these people here would impress me, didn't you?" she said. "Do you see what's happened to you? Do you see how abnormal this is?"

"Would you like to be on the cover of our first album?" I said. "I have a particular hospital shot in mind."

"My stomach's hurting all over again."

I took that as a No.

We went back to Bruce's Sound Lab. It hadn't gone so well with Carole, but at 4:30, after several long breaks in between playing a few more tunes—none of which would be on the album—I ushered the group to her apartment building. Then I positioned everyone for the photo shoot: Gus stood on the top step to her building, holding his drumsticks in the air, with Tommy and Joe a few steps down, posing like they were playing their instruments. I asked Renard to look up at them from the bottom step, waving like he was conducting. Maurice, Sally, and Manfred sat on the bottom steps, smiling for the camera. Someone asked where the photographer was.

"Right," I said, "I guess one of us should've made the call, but I'm not blaming anyone . . . Sally."

Finally Carole walked up her block from the subway. She looked glorious in her raincoat, her quick, purposeful step.

"Okay!" I bellowed, as I ran up the stairs. "This'll be our dry run for the photographer tomorrow! Maurice, when I get to the top, snap some practice shots with your cell phone."

Carole marched around everyone and climbed the stairs.

I stood in front of the door to her building, just above Gus holding up his drumsticks. "Yes, with this album cover," I announced, "we kick off the campaign for hospice care all across the country . . . Oh hi, Carole, we just happened to be in the area. We're rehearsing across the—"

She walked past me, opened the door, and slammed it behind her.

I stared at the closed door. I blew it again.

Mr. Jula materialized next to me on the landing. *"You can't be happy or get the girl,"* he said, *"as long as you're living through what other people think."*

"She won't even give me a chance," I said.

"Hey, I really dig your dead people idea. Music for dead people. Nobody makes music for us anymore."

"Dying," I said, "dying people." Everyone watched as I talked to the air, to the invisible Mr. Jula.

"Okay, dying people. You know I'm in deep shit because of all your side-tracks? Just make nice with broccoli and do the album."

"The plarps told me to not to trust him."

"The plarps? What the hell do they know about the music business? Just make nice with broccoli. We need this album. The Earth needs this, baby."

He patted my shoulders, and as he was vanishing, kissed me on the cheek again. I yelped.

"You need some rest, Shawn," Gus said, "Would you like some, uh, you know, some pharmaceuticals. I got stuff on me that—"

"No, it's okay." I walked down the steps with my quartet comrades, ready for the Phisbin team scowl, but instead they looked sympathetic. First Sally hugged me, then Maurice. Renard said, "All in one day you lost your boyfriend and the woman too. Brutal. Brootull. Well, here's something that'll cheer you up."

On the sidewalk in front of Carole's building, Manfred presented me the contracts and publishing forms on clipboards and handed me a pen. "You're the most original jazz player in the world," he said, resting his hand on my shoulder. "Sign, Mr. Lewis. This is your golden calf. You don't need her. You don't need *anyone* anymore."

CHAPTER 28

Play On the Edge of It

I DON'T NEED ANYONE anymore. I'll make albums, play jazz, tour the world. She's nothing, just one more in a stream of groupies. How will I handle them all? My jazz comes first—that'll be the rule. They'll understand. Of course, it could get stressful if any of them turn out like Irene. Carole used to be great for stress. Around her I always felt grounded. But who needs "grounded" when they're playing out their dreams? Grounded is overrated. Beauty—that's not overrated. Carole is the ultimate unaffected beauty with a firm grip on the world. Now she avoids me—I'm a nuisance. Though it wasn't always that way. She used to say I made her special: No one else put her so at ease; no one else listened to her like fine music; no one needed her like I did. She must miss all that. Of course she does. Carole needs me too. She just doesn't know it yet.

WHEN RENARD'S DRIVER woke me, buzzing and knocking at the door, I leapt off the couch, determined not to keep anyone waiting this time. I threw on the do-rag, jumpsuit and sneakers and was out of the apartment. No shower, breakfast, nothing.

Jimmy and Galicia were already in the hall, chatting with Kabir, the driver. Galicia had painted her eyes and lips in thick, pitch-black makeup and added a blood-red streak to her graying jumble of hair.

"Doesn't Tomumda look extra exciting today?" Jimmy asked me.

"Hmm," I said, studying her. "You did that on purpose?"

"I'm sensing hostility," she said.

"No," I said. "It's just that I did the same thing a couple weeks ago when I tripped into Jimmy's paints."

"You're repressing it," she said. "Oh, this doesn't bode well for your album thing. We better talk on the ride down."

IT WAS BUMPER-TO-BUMPER, Kabir's full-size Buick weaving and lurching for every yard. I sat beside Jimmy and Galicia in the back seat. She propped herself on his lap, letting out soft moans every time the car jolted. I couldn't decide if I should be aroused or nauseated. At least she wasn't talking to me.

We were only a few miles from the Village and Smooth Trax Studios when I realized I'd left without the saxophone. As Kabir made the four time-consuming turns necessary in Midtown to reverse course, Galicia declared that my leaving the instrument behind was a subconscious ploy. "A clear act of hostility," she said. "I have a very bad feeling about this. Cancel the album."

Kabir had already made two calls to Renard by the time we double-parked in front of our building in the Bronx. It was 10:30, the time the session was supposed to begin. I ran up the stairs to my apartment only to realize I'd also forgotten my keys. I ran back down to ask if Jimmy had taken his set. He said they were in Galicia's apartment on the circular table. Galicia gave me her keys, and while the two of them necked, I raced back up to her apartment. I ran inside, right into one of the cat scratching posts, careened and fell headfirst onto the circular table, scattering tarot cards everywhere. I got up slowly, rubbing my chin, grabbed the keys and as I staggered out of there, at least four cats scurried through the open door.

Colfield and Julio the super, were in the hall. "Well, thanks for fixing our stove," Colfield said.

"My pleasure, my pleasure," Julio said. "Sorry it took nine months."

"Oh, hi," I said. "I think some cats just went in the hall. Did you see them?"

"Cats," Julio said. "You mean, like jazz cats?"

"Huh?" I said.

"You know," he said, "like, yo cats, whassup?"

"No," I said. "Galicia's cats. We've got to find them. I'm in a hurry."

Gerrybubbles then appeared below the hall light. *"Mr. Shawn Lewis, may I converse with you a moment? It's very important."*

"Not now, not now," I said. "I'm very late. Everybody's waiting for me."

"Where?" Colfield said. "The loony bin?"

I told him about the album.

"This all in your head, ain't it?" Colfield said.

No, I said. I had a driver and everything. But nothing I said could convince him anyone would actually want to record the noises that came out of my horn. If he helped me round up Galicia's cats, I said, he could go with us and see for himself.

"Can I get in on that?" Julio said.

"Now," Colfield murmured to Julio, "you're going to see what kind of spooky shit I've been living next to. Gig's probably at a tomb in Woodlawn Cemetery."

Using two cans of Friskies it took us fifteen minutes to get the cats back into her apartment. The three of us hustled down to the waiting car, but both Julio and Colfield refused to sit next to Jimmy and Galicia, who were still necking.

"Well, I don't want to sit next to them either," I said.

It was a standoff, and Kabir made another call to Renard. For Tommy and the trio's sake I relented, and squeezed in between Colfield and the obnoxious lovebirds. As Kabir started the car, he asked, "Did you forgetting your sax?"

I charged back up the stairs, but Muriel Fetterman wouldn't let me by, blocking me with her broom. "I'm going to hit you on the head with this," she said, "if you don't cut out all the running. What do you think, this is some kind of gym?"

"No," I said, "I'm supposed to record an album today but I keep forgetting—"

"You know," she said quietly and leaning in, "people have seen you talking to yourself—whole conversations."

"I'm in a hurry right now," I said, pushing her gently out of the way.

She clenched my arm. "They say you've become just like your insane homeless friend, maybe worse."

I tried to pull away, but she grabbed harder. "Apparently he's shacked up with the fortune teller," she said. "The other neighbors think you're forming a coven."

"Hey Muriel, I could use more Gonzo Clean. Here's a ten. I'll get it from you later."

"Oh, that's splendid," she said, snatching the bill and stepping out of the way. "Have a nice day now."

When we were finally heading south again, it was 11:30. They'd stopped necking, and now I was jammed next to Galicia, my alto in my lap. She stared at me. "All signs say you should cancel this immediately," she said.

"Fine," I said, "cancel it."

"Driver," she said, leaning forward, "we're canceling the album thing. You can take us home now. You won't regret this, Shawn." Kabir called Renard again.

While Jimmy explained to Galicia why we were in the Village and not back home in the Bronx, we pulled up to Smooth Trax Studios. Renard was waiting outside.

"I'm so glad you brought your instrument," Renard said, his eyes blinking rapidly. "I mean, who could expect you to bring your instrument to your recording?"

We moved through the doors and into the reception area while Renard strode next to me, yapping in my ear: "Only two hours late. Well, that seems to be your style, doesn't it? And a carload of friends. Let me guess: They're all coked up."

Julio asked for the bathroom. Colfield planted himself on the couch, flipping through a magazine while Jimmy and Galicia necked by the water cooler.

"I suppose it doesn't matter to you that you've seriously compromised the project," Renard said. "Doesn't it bother you that you kept your own trio waiting? Do you realize, at our expense we flew your pianist all the way from San Francisco? Don't you think Mr. Popley or my staff have better things to do than wait two hours for a street musician? Guess who else you kept waiting: Elgar Svarnson, New York's top recording engineer—and yours truly. What do you have to say for yourself?"

"I do feel bad about keeping the trio waiting," I said. "Say Renard, I'm starving, would you get me some waffles? Waffles and ice cream. Let me find out what the others want."

"This is a test, isn't it?" he said, his voice cracking.

"No, it's just that I'm hungry—thirsty too. Get me a large apple juice."

"Listen to me, you slimy little shit—"

"What's all the commotion?" Dalton said, emerging from the door of the recording booth. Renard, you're shaking. Relax, the star is here."

"Star," Renard said.

"What's two hours late among friends?" Dalton said, smiling. "Shawn, are you ready to start?"

"Sure, Dalton, I just need to eat something. Renard, I didn't see you write down the food order. Did you write it down? Because I also need a toothbrush and some toothpaste, okay?"

"Steady, Renard," Dalton said. "Have Maurice buy Shawn whatever he needs."

Renard swerved toward the recording room, bumping into Julio who chided him to watch where he was going. Then Julio laughed out loud, pointing at Renard's hair.

"Shawn," Dalton said. "Who *are* these people?"

"Well," I said, "Jimmy has a girlfriend now, and the others are—"

"Oh yes, I heard," he said. "We're all very sorry."

PRODUCERS DON'T LIKE strangers in the recording booth, but I wanted to take care of my guests, and this booth was spacious enough to squeeze in chairs behind Elgar, Dalton and the team. Renard, hunching in the corner at the far end of the sound mixing board, gaped as Jimmy, Galicia, Julio and Colfield filed in and made themselves comfortable.

On the other side of the glass, in the sound studio, I apologized to the trio, who'd been jamming for nearly three hours. They said it was fine; they were getting paid for the whole day.

As I took out the alto, an assistant positioned my microphone and handed me a headset so I could hear Elgar or anyone else speaking to me from behind the soundproof glass. Elgar asked us to play a little, to test the levels. Then he said, "Renard tells me you're not using written music, is that right?"

I nodded.

"How many tunes will be on the album?"

"Probably one," I said.

"If you do just one tune," he said, "you realize you'll be playing straight through for about sixty-five minutes?"

"*I* have a question," I said. "Do we have a wireless feed? Can we beam this live into the Midtown Hospice PA system?"

Renard was now screaming obscenities, and Elgar clicked off the sound.

Dalton wanted to speak to me, and the sound came on. "I'll tell you what, Shawn," Dalton said, "you perform like I know you can, and I'll make sure every nurse at Midtown Hospice gets a copy. But I need your help right now." He cleared his throat. "A lot of cash has been spent. Can—can you tell us what you're going to play? If you're undecided, any one of us could—"

I spoke to the trio: "Guys, I have no idea what to play. I know it would be easier if I called a tune or gave you at least a roadmap, but my music just comes through me. So I ask you to do the same. Just let it happen. Trust your instincts."

"What a load of sh—" Renard said before they could turn off the sound.

I nodded that we were ready. They started the tape. Jimmy leaned over Elgar's shoulder and waved hello through the glass. Manfred kept pushing Jimmy away, but every few minutes my friend's melon face would bob up above Elgar's shoulder, grinning and mouthing hello.

They were all waiting. I was waiting too—waiting for the impulse to go in one direction or another. Snippets of melodies from every kind of music I'd ever heard swarmed in and out of my mind, but I still didn't know where to begin.

Finally, all I could do was to hold out a quiet F. I repeated the note. Soon I was softly syncopating F's, alternating accents and shades. Tommy joined in with free-form sustaining chords. Joe pedal-toned the F's, rooting the subtle meters. Gus started swishing on the snare, pinging lightly on the ride cymbal, following Joe's meters. We were like a one-celled organism slowly growing, adding more cells. I began to slither chromatically around the F's, the phrases tensing and releasing, all the while syncopating and snaking forward. The trio followed me, their eyes closed, attuning perfectly to the increasing life of the organism. And just like with the trio at the Blue Light Bar, I heard their musical choices before they made them. I moved inside their instruments, inside their minds. There were no mistakes. Anything they played, I could work with. I used everything.

Through the glass Jimmy was nodding, mouthing the word, Jellybeans.

It was free jazz—everyone improvising with no format, no agreed-upon structure—yet it felt directed. Like Maestro C's rain forest, each of our lines of notes was running and flying on its own yet mysteriously propelled by the others. Soon scales and modes could no longer contain it. I explored the cracks between the notes, the microtones now sounding as natural to me as any Western scale. I held the instrument, but something much bigger was guiding my fingers and wind.

That's when I became aware of the amphitheater. I was standing onstage under billowing white clouds and pure blue, playing for a vast audience while still hearing perfectly the music from Tommy, Gus, and Joe. My guys weren't with me on that stage, but Maestro C was there, smiling, sitting on a glowing white stool to my left—Mr. Jula to my right, on his pink-granite throne. Mr. Jula was nodding with his eyes closed—nodding to the wild rhythms caroming through a quartet in Smooth Trax Studios, a world away. Professor Thel was behind me on a wide black piano bench with no piano in front of him, his hands forward, fingers moving in mid-air. The Listener sat in front of me on the lip of the stage, his palms open in meditation as a golden beacon streamed from the sky through the top of his head.

The audience was packed with musicians. Prez, Stitt and The Hawk were among those in the front row. Hodges, Ammons and Henderson sat a little further back. I didn't see Wendell but I sensed he was there. It was a new kind of music and the composer was the Universe—with help from

Maestro C, Mr. Jula, Professor Thel, The Listener—perhaps the jellybeans and everyone in that exalted amphitheater.

Joe Terry stopped for a moment, exhausted. Gus switched to brushes while Tommy covered for Joe with a bass line. I slowed everything to a crawl, playing long, pure tones, exploring the subtle colors of Mr. Jula's magical horn and mouthpiece. The trio was worn out, so I stalled the organism, concentrating on simple, isolated calls. As Joe came back in, Gus and Tommy rested, and I used the walking bass as my anchor to softly float the microtonal bebop.

A bright light blazed through the amphitheater and everyone there. For a few moments I couldn't distinguish between any of the souls around me.

Gus and Tommy re-entered, and the music came alive again.

A fireball of even brighter light slowly descended from the clouds to the stage and took a male human form inside a sparkling blue and white robe. The form had a cleft in his chin and had hair made of white flames. He spoke without a sound.

"I am called the Sheml," he said, each word firing more energy into my fingers and sound. *"Supreme High Exalted Maestro Ludwig."*

Beethoven.

"Already, Mr. Shawn Lewis," he said in my mind, *"the enlightened ones are calling you The Facilitator. Did you know I was an improviser before anything else? The passageways of the Outside dimension manifest in only one place: the free, pure creation of the moment . . . this moment. Play, Mr. Shawn Lewis. Play on the edge of it."*

The Sheml vanished. Then the clouds turned dark and a broad shadow cast over the amphitheater. Maestro C and Mr. Jula glided toward me. *"The concert is almost complete,"* Maestro C said. *"You need to inhabit the darkness now."*

"Own it," Mr. Jula said. *"Blow through your broken heart."*

I felt them pulling me along, manipulating my sound, molding it like clay so the transition wouldn't be too abrupt. From microtones and superimposed meters the free-form jungle organism merged into "Body and Soul."

As I played the familiar melody, the trio grabbed hold with the chords and straight time. From free jazz we melded into a bluesy cry. I stuck close to the melody, playing it only once, finishing with an endless taper on the final D Flat. The trio recognized there could be no tidy ending to this and they didn't try to impose one. They faded and I faded as long as we could sustain it—a taper into no sound.

I looked up, and instead of the amphitheater I saw the glass.

"Sixty-seven minutes," Elgar said. "Unbelievable."

"Okay, take a break," Renard said. "Maybe we can keep a minute or two of that but we'll have to do a lot of punching in. Between today and tomorrow we'll run as many takes as we can. Hopefully we can patch together some—"

"Renard," Dalton said. "I don't think so."

Elgar shut off the sound while Dalton and the team huddled. Jimmy tried to huddle with them, but someone's hand kept pushing him away. Tommy, Gus and Joe were spent, unable to move, their eyes shut. I headed for the booth.

Julio stood in the doorway, smiling. "Wildest shit I ever heard," he said.

Colfield put his hand on my shoulder. "I shouldn't have doubted you. Forgive me. All this time you was speaking in Tongues after all."

Jimmy rushed over to give me a bear hug. "Dazzling, Mr. Shawn Lewis! They were all there, all there! Now the Sheml calls you The Facilitator."

Maurice spoke softly, his voice choking: "I'm—I'm—I can't say it."

Inside the booth the huddle disbanded, and Elgar stood up. "Apparently," he said, "that's it. You're done."

"Very original," Manfred said, shaking my hand.

"That and more," Dalton said. "You had us scared—I admit it—but you just validated all my instincts. What would you like to call the piece?"

"Call it 'The Wildman of 232nd Street,'" Julio said.

"I think you should call it 'Escape of the Tortured Soul,'" Maurice said.

"Too grim," Sally said. "Why not 'Dancing on Reality?'"

Renard had no suggestions. He kept his eyes down and stayed seated at his corner of the board, holding a small ice bag over his forehead.

Dalton then corralled me out of the booth and into the reception area. "You are an original," he said, "I think a genius. A genius doesn't see the world like anyone else." He handed me a wad of cash. "You're going to need this for the next two weeks to hold yourself together. After that you'll be in the clubs, and we're going to rush like hell to get this album out."

"And don't forget," I said, "we have to get copies to—"

"Yes Shawn, copies to Midtown Hospice as soon as we can. And more than that. We'll push this as far as it'll go. No more subways. We're not giving this away anymore. I'd like to call the album something like, 'Jazz Angel.'"

"No, call it, 'Carole My Angel, Who Needs Me Much More Than She Realizes.'"

"How about just 'Carole?'"

IN THE SOUND STUDIO Tommy had folded down the keyboard so he could sleep over his arms. Gus was sprawled on the floor. Joe hadn't moved. His eyes were shut, his mouth open, and his left hand still in the position for a low D Flat. I thanked them over and over, but they didn't hear me.

My neighbors and Jimmy and I waited outside for Kabir to take us home. Galicia approached me with a bittersweet expression, which I assumed was the zombie makeup. "I tried to warn you," she said, shaking her head. "I really tried."

"About what?" I said.

"It didn't go very well, did it?"

"What didn't you like?"

"Well, Shawn, it took you and your group a whole hour to find the right key and rhythm for that song at the end. Maybe you should try again tomorrow."

CHAPTER 29

Sledge

JIMMY SLEPT the whole return ride from Smooth Trax, freeing Galicia to hammer me with dire predictions for an uninterrupted hour. I climbed up to my apartment, exhausted, and the last thing I needed was another guest.

He sat in the dark, facing me. I turned on the light but the man still looked dark. He was dressed in black. After the plarps, it was going to take more than a dark stranger in my living room to faze me. But the black ski cap and gloves should've been a tip.

I waved hello, walked past him, took off my sneakers and got ready for a nap.

"You know," he said, "you really should take better care of this place."

"You're right," I said, lying down on the sofa, closing my eyes. "After my nap you can clean it up."

"Don't you know who I am?" he said.

"Help me narrow it down," I said, yawning. "Are you an elemental, ghost, or inter-world transient?"

"I'm surprised how casual you are. I mean, if it was me, I'd be pretty upset."

"I'm too wasted to be upset," I said.

"Wasted. I like that word. Dated though. These days I prefer 'whacked.'"

"Good, good for you. Later on we'll chat about words. I sleep now, okay?"

"No, it's not okay," he said. "How come you don't pick up the phone?"

"I didn't know ghosts used the telephone," I said, yawning again.

He grabbed my elbow and twisted it. I yelled out.

"How come you don't pick up the phone?" he said, letting go of the elbow. "You forgot me. Izzy. Mediterranean Club?" He twisted my elbow again—any harder, the joint would've snapped.

"I—I guess the ski cap threw me off," I said. "When did you call?"

"I been calling for weeks. Nobody answers. And no machine. I get the feeling you're avoiding me. Now I have to make a special trip out here just to give you the fucking message I wanted to leave so courteously." He let go of me.

I sat up, rubbing my elbow, trying to straighten it out. My closest weapon was the music stand, which was currently a rack for a pair of jumpsuits. I was helpless.

"Don't take it personally," I said. "Our phone is disconnected. I have a stalker. Funny when you think about it, right? Me with a stalker." I faked a laugh.

"I don't think it's funny. We need you to play tonight. The regular leader just had a tragic accident."

"Oh, tonight . . . " I said. "Oh, that's impossible. I've got two gigs. I'm sorry to hear about the regular guy though. I hope he's going to be all right."

"Didn't make it. You sticking with the two-gig story or you coming with me?"

"It's not a story. It's for real. Both gigs—they're in Texas. In fact, I should be getting to the airport as soon as—"

In a flash I was in a headlock smothered in tattoos. As he twisted my head like the lid of a pickle jar, the pain tearing though my neck, I said a very muffled, I'd love to play for you tonight.

The next thing I knew, I was in the back seat of a black Cadillac sedan with Izzy staring at me and a muscle-bound elephant named Beppe at the wheel. In the forty-five minute ride to Bensonhurst Izzy spoke only once: "You used to be good with the starts and stops. You be that good tonight, capisce?"

The other four musicians—a trumpet player, keyboardist, electric bassist and drummer, all in tuxedoes—were bunched in the middle of the giant stage, terrified and barely twenty. It didn't matter that I didn't have my tux or I'd never worked with the musicians I was supposed to lead.

We'd played only a few warm-up notes when Izzy gave me his instructions: "Play loud and make sure you stop when you get the signal."

A moment later he made circles with his arms, his sign to start. But I couldn't decide on a tune. The trumpet player, Gary, begged me to start "before they kill us." I told him to just pick something, and I'd follow. Gary started with "Misty." I accompanied him, but I was sidetracked by the murmur of the thirteen finely-dressed thugs at the long table in the back. If I played softly enough, I could hear everything.

". . . I know, Sledge," one of them said to the man at the far right end of the table. "Jay Jay's asking to get popped, but—"

Gary was pouring all he had into "Misty," his trumpet muting the long table.

"Shhh," I said to him. "It's a ballad—keep it down."

". . . See, if *I* do it, then Lewie's bound to know it was you who put out the—"

The drummer thumped a fill, and I couldn't hear anything. I told him to switch to brushes. "It's a ballad, damn it," I said.

". . . not if you make it look like Donny the Weasel's work," another one said, glancing for approval from the man at the far right end.

"You think they would fix the Weasel, Sledge, if they thought he popped Jay Jay?" another one asked, looking at the man at the end.

"Lewie's out of his fucking mind," another one said. "He'll go to the mattresses if—"

"No, no," said the man at the far right end of the table. "Here's how it's all going down—"

Gary wanted me to play the bridge. I waved him off, then pretended to quietly play along.

". . . Jay Jay's history," said Sledge, the man at the end. "We just won't do a message job, that's all. We'll get Pluto to drop the pellets in his food—you know, the amyl nitrate shit. Nobody'd ever figure on Pluto. It'll look just like heart failure. Not so common for a guy in his thirties in his shape, but it's been known to happen."

"Specially in this part a Brooklyn," one of them said, laughing. Then they all laughed.

Izzy walked up to us with the finger-across-the-throat signal to stop. Gary and I sat down and didn't move. No one spoke, and it was easy to hear the long table. The waiters, who'd been absent while we were playing, skirted around the table, pouring wine and piling the food high, while the capos bragged about their volunteer firefighting and donations to the orphanage.

I remembered reading about "Sledge," Jackie "The Sledge" Torzelli, the don of the Brooklyn mob, a frequent target of the DA. Somehow there was always a shortage of witnesses.

When a man entered the club and marched straight back to the long table, the waiters disappeared, and Izzy gave us the signal to start again. The man was none other than the bionic snorer of the Bronx, Lloyd Fetterman. I called the tune "I Thought About You," telling the guys, "This one sounds best when you can barely hear it." After four bars I passed the melody to Gary and listened in again.

". . . Was a great couple of weeks," Lloyd said to Sledge, handing him several thick envelopes. "Everybody and their grandmother wants a piece of the basketball playoffs. As for baseball, as you know, we lucked out big time when a certain superstar caught the flu last week."

"Yeah, flu," one of them said, laughing.

"Lloyd," Sledge said, "how was the little, you know, blister we talked about? Did it heal?"

"Oh, sure, Sledge. Ugo was a big help. Thanks for that."

"Good, good, good," Sledge said, nodding slowly, then waving at Izzy.

Izzy ran up to us, signaling to stop. "What the fuck is with you?" he said to me. "You the Sisters of St. Cecelia's? I want loud. When I signal to play again it better be fucking loud!"

All the men at the long table now stared at the trembling band. "Hey, I know that guy," Lloyd said. "The guy in blue. My upstairs neighbor."

"Really."

"Mental case," Lloyd said. "Pain in the ass with the saxophone at all hours."

"He used to be one of our regular bandleaders," Sledge said, looking at me. "You can't blame a musician for playing at all hours, Lloyd. How else you going to get good? But we got something else to discuss, don't we?" He waved a hand at Izzy, and we got the signal to start again. Izzy then held up a fist, mouthing the word Loud.

Without counting off, I started wailing through the horn the first swing tune I could think of. Gary and the others fumbled to find the key, but soon we were all honking a raucous, frightened version of "On the Sunny Side of the Street."

I felt what must have been the Outside current spinning around me, and my fear went away. Between everyone else's panicked sounds I weaved in the microtonal bebop. Soon I was using my comrades' terror, inserting ornamental squawks and squeals into my multiphonics.

After a few minutes Izzy rushed the stage with his finger-across-the-throat sign. "You really suck tonight," he said to me. "Just cause I want it loud, you don't get away with bullshit."

Apparently, we only played when they talked business—and they wanted it loud. We were indeed the show, but not for them—for the FBI eavesdroppers they were faking out.

When Izzy quieted down, I could hear the long table again.

". . . His playing's really gone downhill," one of them said.

"Ain't that the subway guy," another one said, "Blue Man a Times Square? He made the crowds that made Paulie late for that thing we had. People go nuts for this guy."

"I don't get him," Lloyd said. "Sounds like rats caught in a turbine. And I know what that sounds like."

"I disagree," Sledge said. "I liked what he just played. I thought it was fucking beautiful. Izzy, tell him to do more of that."

When it was time to start again, Izzy asked us to "keep doing the bullshit." They were all watching us now. The only one smiling was Sledge. I gave the jittery twenty-year-olds the "trust your instincts" speech, and took off. While I grouped my atonal lines in a five-eight pattern, Gary and the others—after numerous attempts—couldn't follow any of it. But even their stumbles provided fresh material for me to use. After five minutes they stopped trying so hard, the group panic morphing into music. And our transformation escorted me into another world.

The stage and the club itself dissolved into a fine mist—replaced by a rolling field under a pink sky. I ran uphill through the grass toward a row of full-leaved trees with dark red bark. I'd never felt freer.

On the stage my fingers were spinning out whole phrases. Like the Sheml's amphitheater in the clouds, the overlapping scene ignited the music.

As I reached the crest of the hill, I saw two white fox terriers perched on top of one of the trees. *"Did you call us?"* Sedgwick asked.

"Sedgila," Colleen said, *"he's playing his horn now. Don't ask him no questions. Of course he called us—when he opened up the worlds. Why don't we give sweetums the tour?"*

"Did Majib teach you to fly yet?" Sedgwick asked me.

"Sedgila," she said, *"no questions. You keep blowing your horn, Mr. Shawn Lewis."*

"Yeah, you keep playing," he said. *"But if you want to fly, you got to lighten yourself, every part of you. Feel your aliveness, your pop—right down to your claws, like when you were little and you first noticed the pink sky. In Plarpiana, if you feel it, you can do almost anything."*

Sedgwick and Colleen lifted off from the tree, calling me to follow. I tried to float but I was weighed down by my fingers and lungs still working a saxophone in Bensonhurst. Then I gazed at the enchanted sky, trees and hills all around. I felt all of it alive and buzzing through me, and the whir hoisted me out of the tall grass. Soon I was above the trees. In a moment the three of us were bathed in pink, soaring above a dark red forest. We passed over green hills so green I felt the essence of green circulating through me. Purple cows grazed. Striped kangaroos with tiny horns were playing tag. Blue bats and huge yellow doves flew by us, even flocks of plarps. The more we flew, the more affection I felt for everything I saw. Sedgwick and Colleen's glowing white fur stood out against the pink sky as we flew above an indigo lake pierced with silver boulders. The sky, the white fur, all of it then collapsed into a cold and rigid pockmarked face.

"Gary," Izzy said. "All a you's! Lay out! Boss wants just the blue man."

For the first time I was conscious I'd been improvising around the melody of "I Love You, Sweetheart of All My Dreams." How or why

I'd landed on that tune I didn't know, but it was clear my feelings from Plarpiana were crystallizing through my horn.

I kept playing as Sedgwick and Colleen led me over an endless dark valley that looked like it could've been on the moon, for all its craters and gray barrenness. It took several minutes to pass over it and reach a stretch of blue-green woods. Then came our descent. *"Just glide,"* Sedgwick said. *"Hold your arms straight out. Nothing to it."* We landed on soft, black earth between a maze of piles—piles of straw, bones, rocks, bark, seashells. Beyond us was a group of plarps frolicking and digging tunnels.

"This here's our village," Sedgwick said.

"You're welcome to stay awhile," Colleen said. *"We've got lots of bones to chew on."*

"Our cockroach farm is just the other side of the haystack," Sedgwick said. *"Go for em."*

"But be careful of the tunnels," Colleen said. *"We got lots of tunnels."*

"Unfortunately, we have to leave," Sedgwick said. *"Time to hunt gripes."*

"He don't know about the gripes, honey," she said.

"Oh, they're dumb as hell and taste just awful," he said, pulling out a carcass from under a rock. It was the size of a large lobster, black with gray splotches and twelve hairy legs.

"They're winning," she said. *"No matter how many we get, they keep coming. Millions of em."*

"So far, we've kept them away from our village," he said, *"but they're coming. They eat everything—animals, trees, rocks, the ground itself."*

"They eat until their stomachs rip," she said. *"We don't know how they multiply so fast. Majib says they're the overflow from Earth One—from people."*

"Remember I said qualities drip from world to world?" he said. *"Oh, don't answer—keep playing. Majib says Earth One is so full of hate and greed it's flooding the other worlds—fueling the gripes. One day all of Plarpiana could be like that valley we just flew over."*

"Hey sweetums," she said to me, *"you better go. Someone's calling you."*

"We got to hunt gripes now anyway," he said. *"Plarpika to you."*

"YO!" Izzy shouted, as I ended the tune, holding a low E. "How many times do I have to ask you to stop? One more, I'm on that stage. What the fuck is with you?"

Sledge charged forward, his crew close behind. This is it, I thought. I'm going to die on a stage in Bensonhurst, Brooklyn.

He put his arm around Izzy and said softly, "You ever talk that way to him again . . ."

"Sorry, boss," Izzy said. "You wanted him to stop, and he kept playing."

"Ever talk that way to him again, and I'll feed your balls to my Dobermans. Understand?" Sledge patted Izzy's cheek. "You're a good boy, Izzy. You don't mean any harm, I know that."

Sledge looked up at me. The band had already stopped breathing some time around "I Thought About You."

"Did Izzy or Beppe give you a hard time when they brought you here?" Sledge asked me.

"Well," I said, "Izzy came on a little strong. First it was my elbow. And my neck," I said, rubbing and stretching it, "well, it still isn't right from the headlock."

"Okay . . . " Sledge said, nodding. He gestured for me to come forward, to lean over the stage so he could whisper.

"What would you like done with him?" Sledge said softly.

"Huh? Oh, I don't know."

"Name it," he said. "I've known Izzy since he was a boy. But you say the word and—"

"I'm—I'm fine now," I said. "My neck—feels great. Really."

"I'm going to make an announcement," Sledge said.

He slowly turned around to face his gaping collection of soldiers and capos, including my neighbor Lloyd. "Old man Glot made only one," he said. "It stays in my vault. Comes out only on special occasions." The goons all swallowed, turning pale. "Anybody," he said, his voice breaking, "anybody lays a finger on this . . . this genius—no, this *saint* . . ." A tear rolled down his cheek. He whispered, "They get the 'Glot' . . . the twenty-pound sledgehammer . . . Capisce?"

Everyone nodded vigorously—even the guys in the band. Even *I* was nodding vigorously.

"Your grace," Sledge said to me. "May I climb the stage to speak with you?"

I was still nodding.

The only sound in The Mediterranean Club was the clacking of his Rogani shoes as he walked across the gleaming stage. I'd never seen an expression like his. He had the iron bearing of a despot yet he was weeping and smiling at the same time.

"What you did," he said softly, "what you played . . . it's a miracle. My back, which has ached for twenty-five years—it's all better. Hundred percent. That's only the beginning. I've had like a sore throat now for six months. Six fucking months. I's afraid to get it checked, you know, what with the fact that I been smoking cigars since I was eight. But my throat—it feels fabulous. I feel like I could sing fucking Puccini. But that ain't everything. While you played I was on another planet or something. I saw these—these mythological beings. Sacred flying dogs. Giant yellow pigeons. Rocks of silver. Colors more beautiful than anything I ever seen. Your playing did that. I always loved music, but this—only an *avatar* could do this. I'm cleansed. I'm forgiven for all my sins; I'm right with God. And I swear to you, anybody—anybody bothers you at all, I'll personally smash their fucking skull in for you. What is your name, your grace?"

"Uh . . . " I said.

"Shawn Lewis," Izzy said, from below the stage.

"Right," Sledge said. "Do you mind if I call you Holy Divine Grace Shawn?"

". . . Please don't," I said.

"All right. You are so humble. What can I do for you? Name it."

I shook my head.

"Do you have a place to live? You need cash? I'll have my tailors make you a suit, okay? Frankly, your grace, you look like you've been sleeping on the street."

"I'm good," I said. "I actually prefer these clothes."

"Of course, your grace. I can see that, I can see that. Would you do me the honor, oh Great One, and play here every day until further notice—just for me?"

"I appreciate the offer," I said. "I do, but I'm going to be busy soon with jazz clubs and a national tour. Then we're going to Europe for a few months."

"Whatever you say, your grace. I will attend your jazz clubs. In the meantime, may I come to your home and hear you play there?"

"I'd rather you didn't," I said.

"Of course. I understand. I would pay you handsomely, you know. Look what you've done for me." He stood tall and wiggled his back, then stroked his throat, beaming. "I would never overstay my welcome. I promise."

"I don't know," I said.

He handed me two of Lloyd's envelopes stuffed with hundred-dollar bills.

"Oh, all right," I said. "Just not every day."

"Thank you, thank you, your grace," he said. "I have to make another announcement. Gentlemen," he said, walking to the lip of the stage. "This humble saint has cleansed my soul. I'm going to ask each of you to open yourself to his wisdom." Then he whispered so the FBI couldn't hear: "We have a new direction now—a path of peace . . . and love. Of saintliness." He turned to face me, put his arm around my shoulders and walked me slowly to the rear of the stage.

"Your grace," he whispered, "are you sure there isn't anybody—anybody that you need, you know . . . out of the way?"

CHAPTER 30

Lewisanity

WHEN COLFIELD AND JULIO brought their family and friends to my morning concerts, there were more than enough people sitting on my living room floor. But when the Sledge, his bodyguard Z and the Brooklyn crew piled in, it was standing room only, even in the kitchen.

Sledge's men were unmoved by my music or anything to do with Divine Humble Shawn, the don's insistent name for me, but at least I didn't have to go back to The Mediterranean Club. I never saw Izzy again, and my neck and elbow felt better every time the don ordered his gorillas to vacuum and scrub my apartment. If they ever made me uneasy, I had only to check the shoeboxes of accumulating cash on top of my now clean-and-organized desk. Sledge gave generously.

Jimmy never missed a concert, often dragging Galicia into the crush. He had no room to dance but that didn't stop him from trying. No matter how crowded it got, I could always pick out the red spandex and wide smile, and the irritated people next to him.

Before the concerts everyone would cluster around me, expecting a sage word. I stopped giving advice off their residue curls; it was too blunt—like a blunt guillotine. So I simply told them to donate in my name to Midtown Hospice. Sledge's gifts had put Carole's facility in the black, the hospice now planning a Shawn Lewis wing. I called Carole with the news.

"You need psychiatric care, Shawn," she said.

"No, you don't understand," I said. "I've made it, Carole. I'm *in.* And I'm sharing it all with you. I'm going to make Midtown Hospice a—"

"Very impressive," she said without feeling. "Do you even know what we do here? Do you have the slightest idea about hospice? Or are you just manipulating me all over again?"

"How could you say such a thing?"

"Well, your photo ops in the hospice lobby with you and The Godfather and my bosses, while you paged me every few seconds—that was a clue. I was with a patient. For some reason I still care about you, Shawn, but you need meds. I've got to go; my stomach is killing me."

Each time I reached out to Carole it was a mess. Nothing I could say or do would convince her I was normal—because I wasn't. Even in front of my audience of fans, Mr. Jula, Maestro C and Lord Wendell would still visit. There was also Julio's dead dog Cheech usually somewhere in the background, barking for Julio's attention. And Gerrybubbles was always hanging around. He needed me, he said, because all his *spirit* friends found him too boring. I didn't have the heart to tell him. And a spindly widow named Delores who lived in my apartment fifty years ago, apparently still did—and she hated jazz. But the scariest was a cold mist named Jay Jay with two words for the Sledge: *Just wait,* the mist kept saying. *Just wait.*

My senses were on fire, yet the further out my experiences took me, the more I yearned for Carole to pull me back in, to settle me down, and I kept calling her.

"I knew you'd call today," she said. "I got you an appointment with Dr. Peltsit, one of the best psychiatrists in the city. He says he can help, but first you have to admit you need the help."

"Carole," I said, "I've never felt better. I mean, if we were dating, it would be a whole lot better, but I'm not ill. I just have some—"

"Irene says you talk to ghosts and flying dogs and you slept with the crazy fortune teller."

"How does she do it?" I said. "I mean, that's not entirely—well—I think I can explain—"

She hung up.

I was devastated, but before I could wallow, I took Jimmy's advice: I "became" my feelings, good and bad. Then I "called" the plarps. Within minutes Sedgwick and Colleen arrived with plarp friends, all of them cackling with laughter, smashed on a fermented brown dip they kept offering me, while they took turns swooping in and out of Jimmy's paintings. My heart quickly eased, and I renewed my plan: There'd be no way to show Carole I was normal, but I could make her hear about me. Soon she'd be intrigued by my fame and goodwill. By the time I performed at her hospice on July 27th, less than two months away, she'd be longing for her serene and easy Shawn.

ON JUNE 6TH, the morning concert had stretched deep into the afternoon, and the usually composed don cried out, "No! No more! What is that racket?"

"You mean the Mendez kids," I said. I listened: galloping, yelps, gunshots. "I think I know this one . . . yes . . . 'Custer's Last Stand.'"

"I can't take it!" he yelled. "Beppe, get up there. Do what you have to do."

"Wait," I said to Beppe, "I'll go."

I rested my horn on the shoeboxes of cash and charged up the stairs. Beppe, Sledge, Z, Lloyd, the rest of the crew and even Colfield and Julio, followed behind me. Jimmy and Galicia took advantage of the quiet, sidling back to his old bedroom.

As I knocked on 4C, I wondered how kids that were running and screaming ten years ago could still be at it today. In all this time I'd never had a face-to-face with the Mendez's. The two titans of noise had never visited, never said hello, nothing. Any contact might've forced one of us to back down. And now was the moment.

A woman named Lucita answered the door. I introduced myself, told her about the concerts and asked if she could "calm" things a little. About thirty children with tomahawks and cap guns stared at me. Sledge and Beppe edged their way in.

"Just one threat should do it," Sledge mumbled to Beppe.

"Wait," I said, "it'll be okay."

Lucita, a Mendez cousin, said she'd heard about me, El Corno Silvestre,

The Wild Horn. She said she'd come down to listen but she couldn't leave the children. It was an immense, open living room, hardly any furniture or rugs, now filled with kids ranging in age from nursery to middle school. The few girls were sequestered off to the side while the majority were boys in dark blue or bare-chested with war paint.

"Which are the Mendez kids?" I said.

"They're grown up," she said. "These kids all from around here. Their parents working. After school no one watches them, so Mr. and Mrs. Mendez pitch in. They're running this many years."

"Why are they dressed like that?" I said.

"Well, years ago we saw we couldn't control the children—especially the boys. Lot of fighting, breaking things. But Mr. Mendez—he's a revolutionary actor and he had this idea—"

"Wait," I said. "Revolutionary *actor*—like in plays and movies?"

"Very committed," she said, nodding. "He goes in costumes all over. Valley Forge, Yorktown. Next week Bunker Hill."

"You don't mean revolutionary actor," Sledge said. "You mean Revolutionary War *re-enactor*."

"That's it," she said. "He's really an auto mechanic—best one in the Bronx. But he likes the battles—not for the war, he says, but for the history. Boys love it, and it's less broken windows than with the football. Some of the girls play too, but most of us—we make the costumes."

I invited them all down to hear the concert. Without enough room in my apartment I stood in my doorway and blew—the children cramming the hall and stairwell. "Divine Humble Shawn," Sledge said, nodding. "Such wisdom."

The next day he and his soldiers arrived wearing Purdee jumpsuits, Melman sneakers and Rayz Phat Hat do-rags—all in blue. Colfield and Julio had ordered sets for themselves, but the stores were already sold out.

On Monday morning, June 12th, while Gerrybubbles had been droning about the challenge of selling plastic gauge holders to machine shops that used compartment boxes, there was a buzzing and pounding at my door. I welcomed the interruption.

"It's time to go," Renard said, as I opened the door. Kabir stood behind him.

"Go?" I said.

"Did you lose the cell phones again?" Renard said.

I shrugged.

"You never opened the Fed-exes, did you?" Renard said. "Get your things. Dalton wants this done today."

"Wants what done?"

"We're moving you to The Granton Arms—across from the Blue Light Bar—where you're playing this week . . . You forgot the gig, didn't you?" He sighed. "Anyway, after this week you're at Bloomdido's for two weeks. It's all the same neighborhood, so get what you need for three weeks."

"I can't leave, Renard. I've got people coming in a few minutes."

"Oh really," he said. "For what?"

"I play for them. They think I'm some kind of guru."

"You need help, Shawn. I've got it: Why don't you bring your imaginary friends and you can *all* move into The Granton Arms? You see, we don't trust you. We just don't think you'll show up unless you're living across the goddamn street."

"Renard, you worry too much. Relax."

"Right," he said, chortling. "No need to worry. You play horseshit for an entire album that everyone likes but me. Because of you, Dalton is questioning my judgment, Maurice and I aren't speaking, and I can't sleep because a psycho has conned everyone I know. And there's not a damn thing I can do about it . . . Or *is* there?"

"Say, you guys should find a comfortable spot. Pretty soon the crowd's going to pile you into the kitchen or out the door."

"The crowd," Renard said, smirking. "Are you listening to this, Kabir?"

"What?" Kabir said. "When? Who?"

"Listen to me, you slimy little shit," Renard said to me, "you may have tricked the others, but I have everything I need on you. You're finished without us—a *nothing*. You're leaving now, if we have to drag you out of here!"

Just then Lloyd, Z, Beppe and Sledge—all in blue Purdees and do-rags—stormed into the apartment, barreled over Kabir, and pinned Renard to the floor.

"Say the word, Divine Humble," Sledge said. "Just say the word."

I introduced Renard as my manager. Sledge helped him up.

Renard, trembling, stood up slowly, and apologized to me, then apologized to them for any wrong impression he might've made, then apologized to me again, his hand now on his forehead. I asked Z to get Renard some ice for his migraine.

Sledge wanted to know which form of discipline I now required. I told him it was only a scheduling problem, so he suggested we at least break his wrists. As Colfield and his prayer group entered, followed by Julio and Julio's cousin's family, I convinced Sledge that solving the schedule was all we needed. Sledge then volunteered a bus and driver to come each day to take us all to the jazz clubs.

Soon Lucita arrived with a group of pre-schoolers, wedging all of us further in. The kids wore blue—some in Purdees and do-rags, even the four-year-olds.

After the concert Renard waited for everyone to clear out. "The world's upside down," he whispered to me. "But *I'm* not fooled. You—you'll get yours."

SLEDGE'S BUS showed up every evening to take me and my fans to the Blue Light Bar. He sat next to me, waiting for any words from Divine Humble. In case he missed something, he had one of his men jot down everything I said, which is why I always talked about raising funds for Midtown Hospice, the West 78th Street Neighborhood Association and the nurse's union. My plan was in full motion. The July 27th concert was now just a month away, and by then Carole would know I had the power to be her champion. But there is such a thing as too much power. On the overcrowded bus rides I couldn't comment on a sunset without a chant going off: "Oh, the sunset. Oh, the sunset." At the Blue Light Bar I made one passing remark about the dim light, and Sledge led the crowd: "This place darker than shit. This place darker than shit."

The bar had never done so much business in one week, and the audiences were dressed like me. Tommy, Gus and Joe loved the steady work, but away from the bandstand they avoided me, unable to relate to the Blue Man and what I'd become.

Bloomdido's swirling bar and saucer-like fixtures alongside photos of

Bird and Diz evoked the bebop of the early space age, and now it was one of the hottest jazz clubs in New York. Sally had worked overtime to get us the two-week stint, though it would've never happened without Dalton's shrewd pay-offs, bumping a band that had been scheduled for over two years. The sell-outs and reviews—and more pay-offs—persuaded Bloomdido's to extend us another two weeks.

New Blue Wave at Bloomdido's: I must admit, upon hearing that The Blue Man of Times Square would be appearing at Bloomdido's, I expected him to wither like a sidewalk banana peel tossed under the lights of Alfred Hall. I was pleasantly surprised. I found myself so engaged in every note played by Shawn Lewis and his able rhythm section, I intend to return each night.

At first listening it is just a free-form, rambling flood of notes. But soon the flood is a mass of colors overwhelming you with the sense he is speaking directly to you and you alone—speaking a language beyond personality that can only be understood with a new kind of consciousness. I felt changed upon listening to Shawn Lewis. I entered the new blue wave.

—Damian Sheers, New York Times

By the end of the Bloomdido's run reviewers like Sheers had joined the fanatics and were spreading the Blue Man myth—and I encouraged it. The louder the buzz, I thought, the greater the attention to July 27th, the day Carole comes back to me. After beholding her Serene and Easy's moment of triumph—all dedicated to her—what choice could she have?

We billed it "The Concert for Carole." It was a glittering celebration of Midtown Hospice, and the first time avant-garde jazz had ever come to an end-of-life care facility. The lobby and hallways were packed, and a mob stood outside the main entrance under the July sun, peering in. While photographers flashed, we played our most hushed, gentle, free jazz, ninety minutes of music stretched into three hours—with all the breaks I took to shmooze and scope the room. But Carole never showed. I called the plarps, and they comforted me even as I'd pop in over the next few days to check out the drawings for the new Shawn Lewis Wing. She'd just stepped out, the nurses would say. The plarps kept me from facing the disaster. And I sharpened my plan.

The "Carole" release party on July 30th was a jammed, VIP affair in

Dalton's East 52nd Street penthouse. I brought Jimmy and Galicia, but between all the celebrities, marketers and distributors, I lost them at the party. The five-foot speakers boomed "Carole" while caterers handed out free CDs with the hors d'oeuvres. The music didn't sound as good as I'd remembered it, maybe because that was from an amphitheater in the sky. The Outside dimension was too subtle for a CD.

As I squirmed through the crowd, I was quickly surrounded by tabloid reporters. "How did you come upon your unique style?" someone asked.

"Forget style," I said. "All you need is love."

"But what about the new sound you've created?" one of them said.

"Well," I said, "you also need for them to love you back, to get in touch with you, especially when they need you more than she thinks she does."

The reporters scribbled. "Who's Carole?" somebody asked.

"Carole saves whole families from the brink but can't see her serene and easy back to normal right there waiting for her all the time." My answers might've been a little cryptic, but the message was just for one.

The Post called me "a wacky savant ripe for our time." *Now New York* said I was "both a mystic and a madman, and everyone should own a copy of 'Carole.'"

The worst fanatic was Sledge Torzelli. He appointed himself Grand Duke of Lewisanity and led the weekly meetings rife with incantations, secret handshakes, the blue garb and the incessant playing of "Carole." His Imperial Scribe was Damian Sheers, who felt so drawn to the music he quit his job at the Times. Their reaction couldn't have been what the enlightened ones had in mind, but I didn't discourage it. I spoke and played at the first three meetings.

I never specified who she was, but everyone knew her identity. My plan was spiraling out of control by the time they were choking Carole's 78th Street foyer every day with flowers, gift baskets and invitations to join the cult. They were especially delirious about the upcoming meeting, the one celebrating Imperial Scribe Sheers's engagement to a Brooklyn woman half his age, a new member of the cult—a woman named Irene.

CHAPTER 31

Bluto's Hideaway

IT WAS THE PERFECT TIME to get away. But that didn't stop my disciples from following me. Cool World Records used the eight-week tour to plug the CD, while Sledge and his crew and scores of Lewisans filled our clubs, fomenting jumpsuit madness in each city. Renard and Manfred stayed in New York, but Sally and Maurice, always at hand, were elated with the extra business—even if it had sprung from the Grand Duke and his Imperial Scribe. Irene was there too. After the concert in Chicago, wearing the jumpsuit-do-rag getup, she confronted me: "Soooo, isn't Damian gorgeous and hot?"

"Hi Irene," I said, rushing off the bandstand. "I thought you didn't like jazz."

"I like jazz now," she said, and then softer, "just not the noise you play. I *hate* what you play. But when you're in love, you take the really bad with the good."

I hurried to the greenroom, but she was fast behind me.

"Soooo," she said, as I packed up Mr. Jula's horn. "I heard your ex is furious with you . . . Carole. Pathetic to name an album for someone who hates you . . ."

No, I refused to believe her. No! But in my hotel lobby in St. Louis Irene cornered me with a bigger dart. "Soooo, I'll bet you didn't know

Carole was thinking of moving and changing her name. Too many mobsters and blue maniacs hanging around her building and her hospice. She *hates* them. But not as much as she now hates you."

A thousand miles from the Bronx, and Irene had gotten to me again. If she was telling the truth, then I'd have to end the cult—and fast. But that night and every night I watched the tables fill, people packing around the bar, standing wherever they could squeeze, sixty percent of them clad in blue Purdees and Rayz do-rags. They were paying to see *me*, to hear *my* music, but they'd gone too far. I would disband them, compel them to leave Carole alone, and as soon as I got back to New York, I'd tell her what I'd sacrificed for her—for love.

ROOM SERVICE carted in my dinner to the table by my window view of the beach. It was the last two weeks of the tour, and I had a fine room—in Santa Monica—just across from our club, Bluto's Hideaway. I sat back in the leather recliner, sipping tea, gazing at the waves in my blue velvet jumpsuit custom made by Bo Purdee himself. How could I fix what the Lewisans had broken? I sipped more tea. Now that I've made it, I thought, I can finally give Carole the future she needs . . . if I can just fix what's broken.

Just as I sliced into my salmon steak, Z and Beppe and a third man all in blue Purdees and do-rags paid me a visit. The first two hulks stood just inside the closed doorway. The third man removed his false eyebrows, beard and sunglasses and the curly brown wig from underneath his do-rag. I already knew from the violence in his residue curls it was Sledge. He was "wanted" in Los Angeles.

"Your grace," he said, his voice rasping. "I'm sick all over again, worse than ever. Some shit going on in New York—all the stress. I got to go back right away. Can you play for me now?"

"I need you to end the cult," I said.

Z and Beppe edged forward. Sledge, without turning, held up his hand, and they stopped.

"Why do you call it that, Divine Humble?" he said, touching his throat. "All I ever do is serve you and our cause, which is why I let Lewie Six Toes get away with making a lot of threats to my, you know, my family. My back has gone to hell. I got fluid in my lungs. My throat—it's like I got wasps in there. You got to play . . . like you did when you cured me."

"I know how Jay Jay died," I said. "He told me. I need you to end the cult—and then turn yourself in."

"Jay Jay? But your grace, he died of a heart attack."

"I want you to make sure nobody bothers Carole Bonner."

"That's what we been doing," he said.

"I heard that you and your boys—the whole cult's harassing her."

"Harassing her? Making sure no strangers talk to her, watching her apartment, protecting her every time she leaves, making sure her bosses treat her nice, listening in on her calls to make sure nobody's rude to her—that's harassing? She's like our Mary, don't you understand? Divine Humble, your inspiration requires protection."

"It's over. No more cult, you leave Carole alone, and you turn yourself in."

Z and Beppe took a step toward me; Sledge held up his hand again.

"Your grace, I can't do that," he said. "How's three G's to play for me now?"

I sipped my tea, gazing at the beach.

"Five G's then. Ten G's—I don't care. I'm dying and you could fix it. Why won't you play for me? I would do anything for you. Anything at all."

THAT WEEK Lewie Six Toes Boriglio and his bodyguard were found in a scrap pile inside Maspeth Rubbish and Recycling. Within days Jackie the Sledge was arrested after a twenty-pound Glot sledgehammer mysteriously found its way to the 10th Precinct sergeant's counter. The blood on the hammer contained Lewie's DNA and a microscopic artifact: a blue polyester fiber from a Purdee jumpsuit.

IT WAS MY LAST DAY in Los Angeles, last day of the tour, tonight our final two sets at Bluto's Hideaway. The audiences had still been good, though not standing room since I'd publicly disowned Lewisanity. Damian and a few other zealots still showed—Irene always with a well-timed grenade—but now it was primarily jazz fans. The mania was tempered, the godfather already in a Riker's Island holding pen, and tomorrow I'd get home and tell Carole what I'd done for her. I had plenty of money coming to me, a bright future, and I didn't want to spend one day of it without her.

I sat on the floor of my hotel room with my usual crate of mail—letters, CDs from hopeful jazzers, gifts from the remaining Lewisans, and today, a huge flat box. I opened that one first. It was a painting from Jimmy with a letter:

Mr. Shawn Lewis, I asked my spectaculous Tomumda to send you this. Your lovely sax is not bringing the Outside in the way we all wanted but you are still The Facilitator. I love Tomumda. She is a bridge to many things indeed. Everyone carries a bridge to something, even everyone. You will always be a dazzling bridge to the Jellybeans and soon you will play the Kloik Kleks. When you play the Kloik Kleks the Outside will come in much better. I learned today not to eat bananas with herring.

The three by two canvas was a stew of gold and dark brown swirls, blots of white and red. Within seconds I was sitting inside the swirls, rotating slowly, rotating on a marble floor inside a Victorian ballroom with dark wood ceilings and flickering chandeliers—the same place I'd dreamed about after The Eclipse. Gradually I came to a stop. People in tuxedos and gowns glided around me, waltzing to a full orchestra. A couple in their mid-twenties drifted over to me.

"Shawn," the tall, delicate girl said softly.

"Look at you," the broad-shouldered young man said, his eyes twinkling. "You going to sit on the floor the whole premier?" His mischievous smile made me laugh.

I stood up. "Who are you?" I said.

"You can't miss Cezary's concerto," she said, "*Cezary's concerto,* Shawn."

"I know you," I said. "Who are you?"

"Stay true to your highest nature, Shawn," she said, "and even in the depths of suffering your miracle will come."

"Sarah?" I said. "Arnie?"

"When you saved the Majib you saved a part of yourself," the young Sarah said.

The waltz was over, and the elegant crowd now faced the orchestra.

A man with bulging eyes and a beard in a white tuxedo with tails, the back of his head under a red silk yarmulke, held a violin high as he strode to the front of the orchestra. Jimmy bowed, perfectly poised—no twitches, no shakes.

The concerto began with the low strings, bassoons and tympani bouncing gently to a minor-key mazurka, covered and mysterious. Muted trumpets followed with a dissonant ascending line. I could picture a mountain climber at the start of an imposing climb—dense fog masking the lush, natural beauty. With each step came higher instruments. When the English horn and trombones teetered along a descending line, it was as though the climber was looking down to see how far he'd gone. Now the clarinets and flutes welcomed the climber past trees and birds while the fog of the low strings, bassoons, and tympani persisted. Then all at once the fog switched into a storm, Jimmy searing into the violin with jagged arpeggios like bolts of lightning. He paused in between the volleys of notes, to wade in his masterful tone and vibrato while the orchestra swirled beneath him. And then hundreds of brightly colored jellybeans showered over him.

Jimmy led us through the storms up to the mountain peak. His violin was both raw and refined, a tone of pearls and broken glass—like his life. It was a striking display as commanding as any violinist I'd ever heard. In the finale he carried us into the clouds, and concluded the piece under a bittersweet sun, warm and fading.

The jellybeans were still dancing as Jimmy bowed, and the audience went wild. Sarah grabbed my hand.

"We're standing inside of one of Jimmy's paintings," I said to her. "I'm not dreaming this. What does this mean?"

"You got to get ready for the Kloik Kleks," Arnie said.

"What's a Kloik Kleks?" I said.

"A music beyond all things," Sarah said, "the music you *should* be playing. The music you *will* be playing. It's your turn, my dear. But you've got to get ready. The ones who weren't ready were destroyed."

"Will someone tell me what the—"

My hotel phone rang, wrenching me out of the painting. It was my half hour warning. It would soon be time to cross the street to Bluto's for the last night of the tour. But I wanted to understand, so I took another gaze into the painting. Nothing happened—just swirls and blots. Oh well, I thought, I'll study it after the gigs, and stood up. My knees buckled, my back twinged. For the first time, my body groaned about what had been a relentless schedule. I looked in the mirror. Why did I look so ridiculous? I tore off the do-rag. I called Maurice, gave him my sizes, asked him to find me the same uniform as my trio—black dress pants, a black button-down short-sleeve.

Between the swirls and blots, between the ballroom and Jimmy's concert and Sarah's Kloik Kleks, I'd emerged confused and drained. In fact, Jimmy's painting had single-handedly ended that chapter of my life. I trudged in my new blacks through the freezing lobby and loud muzak and into the piercing sun, feeling old and used up. I saw no curls, no residue lights, heard no extra sounds—just the aggressive whoosh of traffic across Wilshire Boulevard.

"Ladies and Gentleman!" the man hollered, "Bluto's Hideaway is proud to present the one, the only, Shawn Lewis and his quartet!"

The club erupted. I blew into the horn like I'd been doing every night, but nothing came out. Tommy and the guys vamped behind me, and I blew harder. Harder. I mustered all the air I could, and out came, "HAAAWNK," like a cruise ship. The audience looked stunned. I blew lighter, nothing. Harder, the cruise ship. I studied the mouthpiece, repositioned the reed. Tommy and the guys kept vamping. Everyone gaped except Irene in the front row. She was smiling, her arms folded. The whole set was either silent air or a docking cruise ship.

"What the hell happened?" Sally asked afterward. Maurice wondered if I needed a doctor. I told them I felt a little groggy and sore. How could I tell them it had something to do with a painting from my old roommate?

The second set went better: In between the honks I managed some notes—a quartertone flat—along with some fuzz and chirps. It was as though my reed had been long dead and I hadn't played a horn in years. I struggled the whole set while the audience heckled me. I'd gone from the great Blue Man to a traffic accident in just one day.

No one sat next to me on the flight home. I'd always cared for Mr. Jula's saxophone and mouthpiece like they were my children, yet sometime between arriving at LAX and landing in New York, they'd vanished—gone. I didn't panic; I didn't care if I ever found them. And I never did.

While Kabir drove from La Guardia to my apartment, Sally promised she'd get me an instrument. She asked if I thought I could handle tomorrow's Town Hall concert, the two weeks at Bloomdido's, the European tour. I told her I didn't know.

I climbed the stairs toward my apartment. Galicia's door was open. She was sitting in her kitchen with a few of the neighbors huddled around her—Colfield, his wife and son, Julio and his wife, and Mr. and Mrs. Mendez.

"Jimmy?" I called.

Their heads turned. Julio came over to me. "Happened last night," he said.

"*What* happened?" I said.

"They were uh . . . you know, together. In bed. Galicia's not doing well."

"What are you talking about?"

"I heard about Bluto's Hideaway," he said. "What the hell happened?"

"Julio, what's wrong with Galicia? Where's Jimmy?"

"He's gone."

"Where?"

"In flagrante," he whispered.

"Where's that?"

"Shawn . . . Jimmy's dead."

PART 5

CHAPTER 32

The Conductor

I STARED INTO the black dot . . . then the yellow halo. I stared five minutes into The Eclipse—no shadings, no flames. I went to the first nightclub painting. The black splotch that had become a piano was now just a black splotch. The squiggles that felt like me playing my saxophone were now only squiggles. The dots that had once created a living audience were now just random flecks. I studied each painting, one after the other: sloppy, abstract meaninglessness.

I'd lost much more than a close friend. The bridges to the worlds and my extra talents were all gone. I sat surrounded by his paintings. They had changed my life. Now they were cold and empty. And there was no one to help me, no Mr. Jula, no Maestro C, no Lord Wendell. No Jimmy. Without him his paintings and their secrets were dead.

Sally and Kabir had arrived early to take me to the sound check for Town Hall. I told them I couldn't play anymore. Sally talked about my commitment to them, about how this could ruin my name, ruin a lot of people's names, including hers. I repeated, I couldn't play anymore.

They left. At least I've still got the shoeboxes of cash, I thought. But I didn't. The desk was bare except for one post-it note: *We moved out. No time for goodbyes. You understand. Wherever we wind up, the shoeboxes will help. The boss sure loved your music. Muriel says it sounds like monkeys getting their backs shaved. And she knows what that sounds like. Yours, Lloyd and Muriel. PS: We heard about Bluto's Hideaway. What the hell happened?*

I still had a few thousand in the bank, but that wouldn't last long. And I had no plan—other than to sit with the paintings.

The phone rang, jolting me. It was Renard.

"So what's it going to be?" he said.

"I'm glad you called, Renard," I said.

"What's it going to be? You going to dry out or whatever your problem is in time for Town Hall?"

"I can't play anymore . . . I'm sorry."

"Ah . . ." Renard said. "Of course."

"But we have to talk money," I said. "I need the money you owe me."

"What money?"

"Renard, we've sold 400,000 CDs and downloads. At $1.10 a unit the royalties alone—"

"I can't tell you how long I've waited for this. I kept asking myself, Renard, when will the blue fart ask about his royalties? I'm his manager. Doesn't he care?"

"Could we do without the weird tone?" I said.

"You signed contracts. You're screwed out of your royalties and anything else we could owe you."

"I'll take you to court."

"But you quit on us," he said. "Don't judges have a term for that? Hmm . . . How about 'breach of contract?' Just an aside, I heard about Bluto's Hideaway. What the hell happened?"

"What about the ASCAP royalties? The jazz stations play the CD every—"

"You transferred all publishing rights to Manfred Keldrake. Did you mean to do that? It was in the contract you signed. Guess who you made the composer? Yes, yours truly. I conceived the piece that morning when I moved my bowels."

"Dalton will straighten this out," I said.

"Really? When you walked out of that first rehearsal so you could embarrass us all at your girlfriend's place of work, a hospice of all things, and that humiliating photo shoot, I mean, it was *Dalton's* idea to have you sign over the rights. He knew you wouldn't check. Of course, I was delighted to comply."

"I won't see another dime, will I?"

"Uh, let me think . . . No. I knew you'd pull something. For weeks I've had Freddie Cavanaugh on hold. Good luck with all your blue idiots. I wonder what they'll do to you now. They're liable to do *anything*."

I WOKE JUST AFTER DAWN, and put on my black clothes with the Melman sneakers. I couldn't take another second of the paintings. I raced down the stairs. "Hey Shawn!" Colfield said, chasing after me. "I heard about Bluto's. What the hell happened?"

I ran out of the building into the early autumn air, the sun peaking through the clouds. I ran across 232nd Street and down Bronx Boulevard between the zooming traffic and the tall maples, past 220th, 213th, Gun Hill Road—past the already congested Pelham Parkway. The more I ran the better I felt, the further I was from the paintings, the Blue Man, the craziness. All I'd ever wanted was to be a normal working class jazzer playing in my own style—with Carole by my side. Was that too much to ask? I turned on Tremont Avenue, the stark cubes of fire escape and brick getting meaner, the trees long gone. I ran down Boston Road, in the dust and shadow of the elevated, exhausted by the time I reached 161st and Gerard, standing in a sea of gray between parking lots and turnpikes, a block from Yankee Stadium and eight miles from home. I couldn't run another step, so I walked—past burnt-out factories, graffiti-sprayed warehouses, gargantuan housing projects. I walked through Harlem alongside strings of faded, jazz-age apartments, junk piles, littered lots, and schoolyards with scampering children arriving for the day. On 125th Street I hobbled between the shops and bustling commuters, all the way to the west side.

I collapsed on a bench, resting my battered feet and legs. No matter how far I'd gone I couldn't escape the turmoil in my heart. I sat there for half an hour before I realized I had only one place to go—and took the subway straight to Midtown Hospice.

Without the do-rag the nurses didn't recognize me even as I strolled past the Shawn Lewis Wing. They led me to the lounge where she was holding a paperback, eating a sandwich. I stood there, gazing, not as the stalker she must've thought I was, but in amazement that after all the success, all the creative super-highs, it wasn't enough without her. Yes, the music was in my soul, but Carole was my life.

She slowly closed her book, and glared back at me. "Blue jumpsuits go out of fashion?" she said coldly. "What you've put me through—you and all your freaks." Still glaring, she put down the sandwich and the book.

"I need you, Carole," I said softly. "I'm so tired." I braced myself on the top of the chair across from her, barely able to stand up after all the miles, and all the grief. "Please, Carole," I said, "the craziness is over. "I'm back to the way I was. You're the only thing that matters."

"Do you understand why I've been avoiding you?" she said, folding her hands on the table. "It's not just your illness. It's all the denial. The denial's what really gets me, Shawn. It's one thing with a patient, but when they're someone you know, someone you care about—"

"I was out of my mind," I said. "I'm through with the saxophone, with jazz, with all the things that stood between us. Jimmy died. He died, Carole. Music no longer matters to me."

"I'm sorry," she said, rising from her chair, her chestnut eyes opening with sympathy. "So sorry, Shawn. But you can't give up music. Jimmy wouldn't want you to do that. I don't want you to do that. How will you earn a living? You're a musician. You just need a psychiatrist. We all need someone to talk to. I've become a therapist myself, mostly grief counseling but all kinds of therapy. I'm leaving here next week—starting my own practice . . . in my apartment."

"But music—that's what came between us."

"No," she said. "I love that you're a musician—like my dad. It's the *crazy* stuff that came between us. And your refusal to get help." She walked right up to me. "But I have to admit, no one's ever named an album after me. No one's ever made a concert just for me. And that time my boss screamed at me . . ." She whispered with her hand over her mouth: "I got a secret thrill when the godfather threatened to set her house on fire." Her eyes were warm and sparkling. "Maybe now you can play show tunes and normal music and do your teaching."

She hugged me. It was no pull-away, and it was priceless. "My Serene and Easy," she whispered. Then she backed away. "I think I can help. You've lost your friend, you've changed, I can see it. You just need a little help. Come see me at my apartment tomorrow evening—around six. I'll make us dinner, and we can talk. Plan to stay awhile. You need someone who's learned how to listen—the way you always listened for me."

She had to return to her patients, and I strutted out onto Forty-third Street. I had no gigs, let alone a saxophone to play them, but a bright-eyed nurse angel had swooped down and healed me from every concern I'd ever had. I was giddy. No subway could contain such joy, so I walked, almost skipped under the autumn sun. I thought I might dance the whole twelve miles home, so happy I wanted everyone to share in it. I even went out of my way to cheer the very people I'd always avoided: the street people. They were easy to find, broken and with nowhere to go, sprawled on the sidewalks or trembling in the alleys. I wanted them all to feel the hope I now had for the world. I'd buy them food and give them a few dollars and keep moving north, looking for more as I walked. But ten yards from 55th and 8th I froze. A skeleton in rags was standing at the corner, excitedly waving his arms to no one at all. An old black mutt lay curled by his tattered shoes. People were rushing by, stepping over the dog, some even bumping The Conductor, but no one paid him the slightest attention. All right, fine, I thought, as I crept toward him, I'll even help The Conductor. But there was no cup or hat for money.

"Mr. Shawn Lewis," he said, waving his arms. "It's still you're turn, you know. Way past due."

"Can I get you some food?" I said.

"Just wait a few minutes," he said. "We'll soon be on break."

I stood there while he waved his arms and made cues like he was in front of the Philharmonic. After ten minutes he dropped his arms and laughed, displaying his missing and rotting teeth.

"How about a big, soft muffin?" I said.

"Nah," he said, "I'd like a real lunch. Besides, I have to brief you on the Kloik Kleks. You can't take over without getting briefed. You don't want to get yourself killed."

"Maury's Deli is across the street," I said. "Why don't I bring you some soup?"

"Nah, you and I need a real sit-down."

"But they won't let your dog in Maury's Deli."

"He's not my dog," he said. "He just likes the music."

Nothing, not even this latest, most alarming lunatic could dim the glow I felt for tomorrow night. I got us a booth in the deli. The booths behind and in front of us cleared out. He ordered two hot roast beef sandwiches, three baked potatoes, and three strawberry milk shakes.

I nursed a bowl of soup while he gobbled like he hadn't had a crumb in days. As he was gorging his second sandwich, he started conducting again—with his free hand.

"What's your name?" I said.

"Narman," he said, leaning forward to give a dramatic cue above my head.

"Why don't you give your arms a rest, Norman?"

"Narman, it's NARMAN. Get it right."

Another booth cleared out.

"Sorry . . . Narman. Tell me, why do you keep, you know, waving your arms?"

He laughed deliriously, his body convulsing, roast beef slopping out of his mouth, as he kept waving his arms. "They," he said, still laughing, "they need me. Well, they really need *you*."

"They?"

"The music beyond all music, Mr. Shawn Lewis, beyond all things, beyond life itself. You left me there, time and again, you walked away. Time and again, you abandoned your responsibilities. Your responsibilities!" More food spilled out of his mouth. "Damn you for leaving me there. It's your turn for the Kloik Kleks."

"I'll bet I can get you into a shelter, but you really need a clinic. I think you need attention from a trained prof—"

That's when I heard the sounds from the empty booth behind me. It's his bony, waving arms, I thought. They're hypnotizing me. Some kind of bat shit crazy voodoo. But that thought didn't stop the sounds. I refused to look. If I just don't turn around, I thought, the clucking voices will stop. Whatever's there will go away—if I don't look. It has to. The booth is empty. There's nothing there to make the sounds. I'm normal now, very normal, forever finished with haunted paintings, spirits, flying dogs, sounds no one else can hear. I've got Carole; I know it. She's giving me another chance, and this time I'm not going to blow it. I've got my life back.

But I *had* to look. Slowly—very slowly—I turned around.

Six of them sat in the booth. Three more stood next to their table. And all of them were ranting in the direction of The Conductor: "GLOOK GRAK KLOHK KREK KROTALAK GLARK KLEEK KLELKLEK KWEEK . . . " They were each three-feet tall with greasy black hair, naked gray skin, and round staring eyes. They were almost indistinguishable—pale gray versions of Peter Lorre.

"If you ask me," Narman said, "we've been incredibly patient. You ready to take over?"

I turned back to face him, unable to process what was happening.

The waitress came, cleared two of Narman's plates and asked if I wanted more soup. She never even glanced at the Peter Lorres.

"I've been conducting them for two years," he said, "music beyond all things. It's nice, but come on, fair is fair. I'm exhausted. It's *your* turn."

"Huh?" I said. "I don't know how to conduct, and anyway, conduct what? There's nothing there. Nothing!" I started to get up.

"Hey, sit down, Mr. Shawn Lewis The Facilitator, son of the sons of Facilitators of the Outside dimension. Music beyond all things waits for no one."

I dropped back into the booth. "Who *are* you?" I said.

"The Kloik Kleks have no rhythm. That's why they're here. They need a conductor."

"What? Wh—what are they?"

"They're from another planet—who knows where? They have no technology—no more, say, than a pack of wolves. But they live free of our third dimension. And they sing. Their group singing turns their puny voices into the music of the heavens. They improvise together, telepathically. This taps the Outside, and they skip between worlds. But they need a conductor. They have no rhythm. Without a conductor it's just noise and the cosmic grid lines won't open. They're here for our rhythm. Plus, I think they like it here; it's a beautiful planet."

"This is absurd," I said, turning around with a jolt. The nine of them were still there, clucking. Two of them smiled at me, showing their sharp little teeth.

Just then, the faint outline of Maestro C in his white suit materialized next to The Conductor. *"It'll be all right, Mr. Shawn Lewis,"* I thought I heard him say. Then a dozen more ghostly images, each holding what looked like instruments, appeared behind him. They were hazy but all too familiar—Mr. Jula, Lord Wendell and The Listener among them. And floating in the background was a fireball in a sparkling blue and white robe. The Sheml? I wondered.

Between the aliens, the wack job waving his arms and now the ghost of Bird and his big band, I wanted to scream, my head spinning worse than from any of Jimmy's paintings. But Bird had more to say.

"You need this, Mr. Shawn Lewis," the Maestro said, his voice muted, distant, as if from another room. *"**We** need this. Now that the paintings are dead, you've lost the bridges—but not your gift for the Outside. You just need a new teacher. We worried you might not save the Majib from that asylum, or that he might not even survive. As perfect for you as he was, we've been planning his successor. The Kloik Kleks will give you **their** bridges to the worlds. Just do as they ask. For months The Conductor has been anxious to show you. It'll be all right. Better than all right. You'll learn to be your **own** bridge, and we're hoping you'll show people the magic all around them. You'll do more good than you can imagine."* He turned around, kicked off his ghostly band, and before they all faded away, for one glorious moment they blew a ferocious bebop free-for-all right in step with the gray Peter Lorres squawking behind me.

"You see?" Narman said, as the Maestro and his band disappeared. "You can't live in just three dimensions—now that you know about the tenth."

I wanted Carole. She would nurture me and tell me what I wanted to hear, that after years of counseling and meds, and her love, I could be free of these visions once and for all.

"You heard the Maestro," Narman said. "We're on a mission. If it wasn't Kloik Kleks, it'd be something else. The Earth, spirits, aliens, people—we're all coming together."

"These—these Kloik Kleks—they sound God awful."

"They can read your mind, you know. Be a little sensitive. Just remember: You tap into the Outside dimension, you tap into everything. The Greeks tried. They called it the Music of the Spheres. The Hindus made ragas, the Buddhists, chants. None of them could do what the Kloik Kleks do without even thinking—the sound of creation itself. Only, they need a conductor or their songs fall apart."

"Why not just get a drummer?"

"Now you're being silly," he said. "Only people like us, with the gift, can even see them."

"This makes no sense. All I wanted was to help a homeless person."

"No you didn't," he said. "You came because you can't resist the music of the heavens."

"Good luck with the choir." I slid out of the booth.

"You won't get away; you were chosen."

I took the check, but before I could move toward the register, two of the Kloik Kleks were at my ankles, growling like pit bulls. "Tell them to back off," I said.

"They won't hurt your body," Narman said. "They'll just eat your electromagnetic life force, that's all. Take you five minutes to die."

"Tell them to back off." Now all nine surrounded me, smiling and growling.

"All you have to do is wave your arms with a steady beat," he said. "You'll get the hang of it. You'll learn to love it—even crave it. This is the next step in your evolution, the next step for all of us, fella. Bring in the Outside. Bring it here. They like five beats to the bar in three bar phrases, but it varies. Start conducting—they'll back down."

In the corner of Maury's Deli I started waving my arms up and down while the waitresses, manager and the few remaining customers gaped at us: one psycho training another. But the Kloik Kleks that only we could see or hear followed my beat, croaking even louder as they scurried back to their booth. They looked ecstatic.

"You're right," I said, "they really have no sense of time."

"They like *your* rhythm."

"They sound like car alarms in a hen house."

"Shhh. Don't hurt their feelings."

"You seem to think I'm going to just keep doing this—like I'm going to stand on a corner waving at aliens the rest of my life."

"A year or two—three tops," he said, and guzzled the last of his milkshakes. "Maybe four . . . It's only six-to-eight hours a day."

"Impossible. I've got a date tomorrow!"

"This is bigger than that. I keep telling you. The Sheml is involved. Once you've been recognized with the gift, you can't get away. Even if you escaped the Kloik Kleks, the enlightened ones would just try something else. See, when you power up the Outside, you link the galactic grid lines, you bring the universe together. If you're lucky, you even bring the jellybeans. I don't know if you've noticed, buddy, but humans and the Earth are not totally getting along. This work heals all the blocks to who we really are. Plants and animals love the Kloik Kleks. People will too, someday. You—you're The Facilitator. I was never a pro musician like yourself. I was at Lockheed for over twenty years designing aircraft tail assemblies. I never played an instrument. But my whole life, I could read a line in a story or see a dance or hear some music, and it was as if the sky opened and everything about the universe was revealed to me. There are no words for that, but that's how I got chosen for the Kloik Kleks—because I understand the Outside. You're the same. Deny it, but it'll catch up to you. I lost it all—my wife, my home, friends, the job. I may look like I have nothing, but I live in the open air of aliens, spirits, interdimensional beings, unfathomable paradises, all because the Kloik Kleks and I make the music beyond all things. I live in the *real* world while the rest of our sad humanity circles inside a fish tank. But I'm tired. It's *your* turn."

"Tell them to pick someone else," I said, still conducting.

Like a streak Narman slid from the booth and out of the deli. I threw a twenty on the table, and ran after him. Just as I got out the door, the nine of them, all giggling, tackled me to the pavement. The deli manager followed with his cell phone.

"You okay?" he said. "You took a nasty fall. You want 911?"

I started conducting from the pavement, and the Kloik Kleks sang along, all of them helping me up. "No," I told the manager, dusting myself off with one hand, conducting with the other. "I'm fine—just . . . just practicing my conducting."

I marched away from Maury's Deli, still waving a beat with one arm, the nine close behind me. When I rested my arms for too long, they bit me on the knee. It wasn't really my knee, it was the deep life flow within the joint, and it was terrifying.

"What do you want from me?" I said, rubbing my knee.

Broik, Graik, and Torndig giggled while they lifted my arms up and down. I surrendered—temporarily—waving beats to them as they joyously sang at the corner on 58th Street. But I knew that busses came every fifteen minutes, and I was only five yards from the stop. If I outrun them to the bus, I thought, I'll go straight to Carole. She'll take me in. I'll pretend this never happened. We'll still have our dinner. I'll never tell her, *never*. I'll never tell a soul. My shattered nerves will be because of Jimmy. Sure, that's it, Jimmy.

The bus pulled up, and Screg bit my knee. I kept conducting. I waited for the next bus. No matter how many people walked by, even though they couldn't see the little grays, no one crossed their path. Only in Midtown could you wave your arms up and down and get nothing, not a smirk. Though the black mutt had now curled around *my* feet while a family of pigeons cooed on the lamppost above me. Still, I never got even near a bus or a cab because one of the giggling beasts was always on me just as I moved.

I soon realized the Kloik Kleks were following every musical choice I made. If I wanted them softer and held my hands close together, facing down, they sung more quietly. If I raised my hands, they got louder. If I sped up the beat, so did they. I was their prisoner, but musically I was their leader. We were co-creators of a new kind of art. By 6:30, after countless failed charges into the crush of busses and people and cabs, I found myself almost enjoying the Klok Kleks' shrill clucks. And just when I started to feel the tingling all around my body, the high power of their otherworldly music, as we stood by the lamppost at 58th and 8th across from Columbus Circle, the twilight sky sprinkled rainbows of jellybeans.

CHAPTER 33

917

Four Months Later

ALL MORNING, as if they were at a football game, three patients from down the hall clapped and cheered at the unearthly performance. It was exhilarating work, though I didn't even have to get out of bed to conduct the aliens. Glenda of 935, Darnell from 914 and Zig of 922 were still whooping and shrieking when Carole entered the room. I dropped my arms to the sheets. The Kloik Kleks couldn't sing without me, and though we were on good terms, they wouldn't wait long. Still, I refused to acknowledge them when Carole or any of the staff were around. Waving beat patterns from my hospital bed several hours a day to creatures only the most disturbed patients could see had stuck me on the ninth floor, the floor of the "gumbo-brains." Even if the music *was* bringing in the Outside dimension and the jellybeans—galactic harmony rippling through the ninth floor—*I* was no gumbo-brain. And I needed Carole to believe me.

"You here for the alien concert?" Darnell said to Carole.

"Darnell, stop kidding around," I said, rolling my eyes to Carole.

Darnell Fortesman never missed his daily hour of Kloik Kleks. He was sure the alien concerts had cured his obsession that his ex-wife was a vampire and following his every move. For the first time in years he didn't have to walk backwards while holding a cross high in the air. Though now he suspected she was after Glenda and Zig.

"You must be so proud of your talented boyfriend," Glenda said to Carole. Glenda Biggs was a new patient and already she'd lost two of her ten phobias. "You know his magic concerts fixed my fear of bathing? Next week I think I might try it."

Carole hovered around the door, debating if she should turn around.

"Say Carole," Zig said, "what's a Carole? Do you know, does anybody, I didn't think so." Zig Abramowitz maintained nine distinct personalities. Four concerts with the Kloik Kleks and he tossed them all away. Now he swore *everyone's* identity had been programmed by a cabal in Zurich. Okay, he still had a long way to go. But when the nurses couldn't find their ninth floor patients, they didn't bother with the TV lounge. They came to my room.

"Come on, guys," Zig said, leading them toward the door. "Let the man give her one of his fancy-trancy concerts. You ain't lived till you fly out your body on the vibe of the Kloik Kleks. Out your body, baby, out your body. You ain't lived till—"

"Stop it, Zig!" I shouted.

Carole watched the three of them shuffle out of the room. Darnell paused at the doorway. "Shawn's got the shit down," he said to her. "*Down.* Old Charlie Parker's helping him. Cannonball too. You got to hear it. It's so out, it's *in.*"

Carole smiled faintly as he left.

"He's heavily medicated," I said.

She turned to me, her face growing sad. "I can't do this anymore, Shawn. I've come to tell you it's over."

THE LITTLE GRAY Peter Lorres would follow every nuance of my beat—the nine of them spontaneously singing the same clucks and patterns, timed with my hands. It wasn't easy. They had just two emotions, rage and glee. How do you hone a musical unit without pissing off *somebody*? Murkduk sang consistently flat and was the most temperamental of them all. Two or three life-force-draining assaults to the knees and you learn how to be tactful to a near-mindless alien. Fortunately, I had lots of help. Mr. Jula demonstrated proper conducting technique. Lord Wendell gave me lessons on musical telepathy. But most crucial were Maestro C's teachings on the Outside dimension, and how the Kloik Kleks triggered it with instinctive, sudden, unison shifts in pitch, tone and meter. For the enlightened ones, the choir was just an extension of Jimmy's paintings, merely the latest means for learning about the Outside. The goal: to bring the knowledge of our interconnectedness to all humanity. Or at least to the ninth floor gumbo-brains.

"IT'S OVER, Shawn," Carole said, sitting by the bed, still in her jacket and flowery scarf.

"Oh come on, Carole," I said, "you can't listen to the gumbo-brains. They're my friends, but they're psychotic. Zig has had so many personalities, he used to swear his wife was cheating on him every time he slept with her."

"When I came in," she said, "it was just like after the ambulance brought you here. Four months, and you're still waving your arms at the wall."

"I've told you about my arm cramps." I sat taller on the bed, shaking my arms.

"The doctor says you think you're conducting a choir."

"I was very tired when I told him that," I said. "You see a choir anywhere?" Murkduk was now at the foot of the bed. It was not an official break. In another moment he'd be draining the life force out of my knee. "My only problem is Restless Arm Syndrome. Nobody talks about that one. I shouldn't be here; you know that. And I don't mean to sound ungrateful. I know it was because of you I got my own room. They'd keep me in a coma if it wasn't for you. But, well, do you think you could talk to Dr. Schmielkin again, maybe get me another hearing?" I flapped my arms. "See? It won't go away. There are no aliens. I just can't shake this goddamn cramp."

"I never mentioned aliens."

"Right . . . there aren't any aliens . . . OW!" Murkduk bit me on the knee.

~~~~~~

NO ONE LIKES being forced into anything. It's natural to resist. But what if you're resisting your destiny? When I rescued Jimmy and encouraged him to paint, I didn't know it, but that was the end of my insulated world. There was no going back after that. Few people would *choose* to lead an alien choir six to eight hours a day, and it was my big secret from Carole, but I loved every minute of it. The ninth floor was my laboratory on the mechanics of the Outside dimension—917, my workbench. And as I lay on my bed, waving my arms to the unblinking little grays, when their cryptic clucks clicked just right, the sound would vacuum me into other worlds—*and I was learning how they did it.* The only problem was, if I was ever going to leave there, if I was ever going to prove to Carole I was sane, I needed the whole clucking diversion to be over with.

CAROLE SHOOK her head, frowning. "When we first met," she said, "you inspired me. You reminded me of my dad when he was at his best. You distracted me from my life of charts and needles and put me in a special dream. I knew the dream couldn't last—nothing like that could last—but you, my Serene and Easy, I felt more at home with you than anyone I'd ever known. That's how I want to remember you."

"Remember me? We should move in togeth—"

"Damn it, Shawn, *look* at yourself! You're in bed all the time waving your arms to a wall across the room! We have this discussion every other day. I've gotten nowhere with you. When will you *look* at yourself?"

"I do," I said. "I got a little confused when they brought me here, I admit it, but this is all a misdiagnosis. My real problem is this chronic Restless Arm Syn—"

"You deny *everything*. I can't take it anymore," she said, standing up, her hand over her stomach. "I'd hoped you were getting better. I have to go, Shawn."

"Carole, you can't go. I'm still the old Shawn, you know . . . special dream? Don't go."
~~~~~~

"Are you even aware of what you put me through every day?"

"Do I call too much?"

She glared down at me, speechless.

"The lounge phone is the only phone," I said. "There's always somebody on it, but if it's free I'll think, Hey, I'll call Carole. The problem is I forget if I've left a message and I call again. It's the meds; they kill my memory. I'm done with meds."

"You called five times yesterday. You called six times the day before, twice to tell me you were going back to school to become a lawyer."

"I must've seen an episode of Matlock. Either that or I wanted to sue the nurse again."

"I'm not taking any more of your calls," she said. "You told me you were through with the craziness, through with all the shit that stood between us. You said I was the only thing that mattered—your words. I've tried, Shawn. I've tried to believe you could get better—that maybe, maybe we could have a life together, but my stomachache never goes away. I'm getting an ulcer. I'm not coming back—*ever*." A tear rolled down her cheek. "You'll never get out of here, Shawn, not if you can't be honest about *why* you're here." She wiped her eyes. "I tried. I failed. I have to go now."

The Kloik Kleks were growling, losing patience. My thoughts were in a scramble. If this is all in my mind, why does every gumbo-brain see and hear them too? If it's all make-believe, why does it feel like the most important mission of my life?

But what if she's right and I'm never getting out of here? Or worse, what if 917 is exactly where I belong—everything before it just an illusion, a tease of sanity I never had? My brain was swirling. For four months I'd been living in two contradictory realities—one, drafted for an assignment blessed by the Sheml and the jellybeans to usher in the Outside dimension—and the other, longing for Carole to rescue me from its absurdity. She's never coming back, I thought. My hope for a normal life is never coming back. Am I now a gumbo-brain? Is there any point to living if you're a gumbo-brain?

"Stay a few more minutes," I said, holding my hand over the flashing lights inside my eyes. "Please, you have no idea what you mean to me."

She sat down again, and loosened her scarf. "Two more minutes," she said softly, her eyes still welling. "But for once, just for now, let's drop the lies. You're in a dreamworld of alien choirs and ghosts of your dead idols. Admit it."

"No . . ." I said. I've got to stop her, I thought. I've got to prove to her I'm sane—a little confused, that's all. Think, I told myself. Think. But my two realities were speeding toward each other.

"Damn it, Shawn," she said, "there are no other worlds. This is *it*. Better get used to it. And just for the record, no one has ever had an out-of-body experience. No one. The people who thought they left their body suffered from lack of oxygen to the brain. It's a medical fact. And for God's sake, Shawn, there are no aliens, no UFO's, no spirits of your favorite sax players or anyone else. I feel for you—I really do. You lost your friend Jimmy; you feel responsible; you feel guilty and you're in denial. But you were in your own world well before that. You were ill when you got together with the mob, when you formed a cult, when you destroyed my privacy. Now you've just upped it a notch, with alien choirs and planets, and busying yourself waving your arms, all so you won't have to feel your guilt or your grief." She stood up. "Before I go, will you at least examine what I'm saying?"

"Wh-what?" I said. "Because of Jimmy?" Everything in my brain collided. It was Carole and Reason versus the enlightened ones, jellybeans, giggling aliens.

"But—but Carole," I said, summoning all my energy to grab one last look at her through the violent blur in my eyes. "I won't make it without you."

She walked to the door, paused, and with a sob in her voice she said, "Then don't make it."

From anyone else it would've meant nothing. But from her, it stabbed like an icepick.

Then don't make it.

Half of my reality just blew away. In a flash there was no chance of Carole in my future, nothing to dream for, no hope of this detour to the madhouse being called a misdiagnosis. The collision was over; the aliens had won. The vertigo cleared.

All at once I understood my life. "You're right, Carole, you're right!" I said. "I've been denying it, minimizing it since I was a boy. Jimmy had tried to show me—the Conductor, the Maestro too. I have a rare gift. I've never accepted it. Even now I have trouble admitting it."

"Well, I wasn't referring to any sort of—"

"Whenever I played my horn I thought they were optical illusions—long before Jimmy and his paintings. I thought they were tricks of light or just plain old fatigue. I ignored the jellybeans. But the air really *was* shimmying, the stars really *were* flickering with every note."

"All right, Shawn, good," she said, blowing her nose. "At least now you're owning up to your delusions."

"I only wanted to be accepted—especially by *you*. Yet I couldn't help blowing on the wave without limits the wildest free jazz—even as it pushed you away. Why?"

"You've needed professional help for a long time. I should've—"

"Because my gift was to create music so fresh it activated the Outside dimension. The Outside is real, Carole." I stretched my arms, and sent the thought to the Kloik Kleks to get ready.

"Okay, I'll play along," she said from the doorway, heaving a long sigh. "What's outside again?"

"The Outside is the connective tissue of the universe. It flutters at the edge of our awareness as a wave without limits. You just have to create something from the freest part of your soul, and the wave floods over you and opens all the grid lines and folds of space-time. Maestro C is teaching me how the Kloik Kleks do it. But there's nothing like the jellybeans, the master healers, when they show up and amplify the energy."

"You sound very disturbed now, Shawn. I hate to leave you like this, but my conscience is clear. I tried."

"I needed you," I said, "just the hope of you to keep me from floating out on the wave without limits. Now it doesn't matter if I float away, so here goes." I faced the wall from my bed and started firmly, never more confidently waving my arms to a beat pattern of five to a bar, the accent on three.

"GRICK GROCK **GLOWTLE** GLOCK GRICK, KRECK KRAK **KITTLE** KROCK KLUCK . . . "

"My God . . ." she said, frowning, shaking her head from the doorway at what must have looked like my final meltdown.

The Kloik Kleks matched my assertive beat with their most piercing squawks, as if they wanted to be heard by every gumbo-brain in New York State. Euphoric, they bobbed up and down, giggling while they clucked. So what if I'm a lunatic, I thought, if that's how others want to see me. I have my job to do.

"You just graduated, my boy," Mr. Jula said, sitting on a dark red log in the woods, his shiny saxophone draped over his brown silk suit. *"You are officially no longer a doofstick, Mr. Shlewf . . . Shawn Lewis the Facilitator."*

While I conducted high and wide beats from my room, the Kloik Kleks reveling, Mr. Jula blew fiery licks in a distant forest around each GRICK and GRACK.

Carole was leaving; she wanted my attention, but how could I turn away from my art, my calling, the facilitation of the Outside into Earth One?

I could feel the soft black earth under me, yet I was still fervently waving from my bed in the psych ward. In a clearing deep inside a dark red forest smelling of raspberries and sweet pine, I sat cross-legged on the rich soil between patches of blue moss and three-foot toadstools. Behind me I heard chord changes: a glowing yellow Steinway. It was Lord Wendell playing a bright golden vapor in the shape of a piano, but his chords were as bold as Mr. Jula on the log and the Kloik Kleks in my hospital room.

"Keep going, Shawn," Wendell said as he played, *"you've got it now. Hear the phrase before they sing it. Shift the beat patterns just ahead of them, the way I taught you. Let the Heavenly Voice sing through your arms and hands. You've got it now."*

As Carole opened the door to leave, Glenda, Darnell, Zig and a herd of other patients pushed to get in. She slammed the door on them, holding them back.

An angelic stream of notes higher than Mr. Jula's lines flowed down from the trees, melding with the jazz on the ground and the alien song in 917. Sedgwick and Colleen swayed on their branches in rhythm to the sacred bebop from the high limbs above them. The man making the sounds was nestled near the crest of the tree, content and cozy, as if on a lounge chair. It was Maestro C blowing his alto, his white linen suit shimmering against the pink sky of Plarpiana.

Across from my bed the Kloik Kleks were giggling and grinning so hard their voices were breaking. I gave cues to Broik, Torndig, Gork and Vowelik to follow my beat, and to match the others. Murkduk, I said in my thoughts, picturing daffodils and kittens, Would you be so gracious as to consider raising your pitch?

"YEKEK VILK BLUK VLELK VARTIK GDIC GOTIKIK . . ."

Sedwick and Colleen danced in the air. It was our best concert ever, and out of the sky thousands of multi-colored jellybeans rained over Plarpiana to celebrate it.

"Mr. Shawn Lewis," Colleen said, *"it's amazing. The gripes have been disappearing! Do you hear me, sweetums? Disappearing. Plarpiana's saved."*

"That's right, Mr. Shlewf," Sedgwick said. *"You made the bridge for the jellybeans. The jellybeans came and the gripes quit eating."*

Soon I wasn't alone sitting cross-legged on the soft black earth. Next to me was Darnell Fortesman, gazing at the jellybeans, his mouth wide open. Then, next to Darnell both Glenda and Zig arrived already sitting cross-legged, gaping at the sky. I was proud, moved by my fellow gumbobrains. Just then, hundreds of narrow tunnels with no more substance than the clouds—faint but clearly visible—crisscrossed through the air and the world around me. One of the cloud tunnels appeared over Maestro C's head, streaking down to the clearing in front of Mr. Jula. Music was pouring out of it, a lively minor key adding to the jam in progress. Emerging out of the froth was a man in a red yarmulke and a white tuxedo with tails, a Klezmer violinist bowing furiously into the mix. I wanted to run to my old friend, to make sure I wasn't dreaming, but just as I was about to stop conducting, Jimmy shouted: *"No, Mr. Shlewf, keep the beat going! Play the Kloik Kleks!"*

As Darnell, Glenda, and Zig sat entranced, another sixteen gumbobrains from the ninth floor materialized on the moss and earth in between the toadstools, all of them sitting cross-legged, mouths open, and riveted on the jellybeans in the pink sky. I thought I saw Carole among them, leaning against one of the giant mushrooms, shaking her head, still condemning me. My soul wanted to touch each one of my comrades, to hold them, to love them all, to say to them, We, we of the ninth floor, we don't care if *no* one believes in us, we are all gumbo-brains together—and God damn it, we're just fine about it.

All at once the Kloik Kleks stopped singing. We were on break.

"Excuse me, Glenda, Zig," I said as I rose and stepped gingerly around my colleagues still glued to the sky. I strode over to Jimmy, who was talking to Mr. Jula.

"All I'm saying," Mr. Jula said to Jimmy, *"is you got to learn how to knit your Polish shtetl minor thing into the Cannonball minor bebop thing, 'specially when it's laying over the Kloiks. Just cause it's all upbeat minor doesn't mean your shit is going to work flawlessly over my shit."*

"But Mr. Jula," Jimmy said, *"it was good, most lovely shit indeed indeed. It increased the dazzling loops and links. Look around, Mr. Jula."*

"All I'm saying, my dear Majib, is you got to practice more with **me** *instead of prancing around in your duds with your Terriyon dancer chicks. I mean, really man, when do you get tired?"* He chuckled.

I cleared my throat.

"Mr. Shlewf," Jimmy said, *"thank you for your most splendid conducting."*

I hugged my old friend. It was like hugging a mirage, a vision in a dream, intangible, yet somehow it still felt like him. "Jimmy, is it really you?"

"Your concert was historigantic," Jimmy said.

Mr. Jula, Lord Wendell and Maestro C were now bickering over which inter-world bebop grooves and meters were most appropriate for Kloik Klek jam sessions.

"What's it like, Jimmy?" I said. "Where have you been?"

"Oh, I can't tell you too much, Mr. Shlewf. You'll want to come with me."

"Do you still see Sarah and Arnie?"

"Most often, most often indeed. But you need to go back now, to Miss Carole Bonner."

"I can't, Jimmy. Tell me, does Sarah still cook? I mean, is there food wherever you go?"

"Dazzling food. It's not so very solid; it's the energy, but it tastes the same. And no one just makes a meal; you have to meet and talk with all the lovely ingredients and ask them how they would like to be prepared. It's very democratic indeed. Mom is an expert. Yes, we gather for splendid dinners most often."

"Do you still paint?"

"Oh yes, oh yes, but I do a lot of other things you would not understand."

"So, you paint, play music, have dinner with your parents—and there are dancer chicks?"

"Oh, I really cannot tell you too much. You need to go back, Mr. Shlewf. "

"Your tunnel," I said, "it's fading."

"Yes, Mr. Shlewf, I have to go now."

"Can I go with you, Jimmy? Please."

"But Miss Carole Bonner— "

"It's finished, Jimmy. On Earth One I'm a psycho. My one consolation is they call me 'non-violent,' but even Carole thinks I'm the biggest nutcase in New York. My life is over. Take me with you."

"All right, Mr. Shlewf, if you insist. It's slowly slowly at first, but once you pass the lower level, it's speed of light—even faster when you know how. Follow me, follow me."

Holding his violin and bow in his right hand, he drifted into the cloud tunnel he'd come out of, and began to leisurely float up, like on an escalator. With his left hand he waved for me to follow. I took a step upward and fell down onto the blue moss. I tried again and fell backwards.

"Remember how you flew with the plarps, Mr. Shlewf?" he shouted, now ten yards above me. *"Same way, same way indeed."*

I tried to remember it. I looked around: My idols were still debating inter-world bebop, the gumbo-brains still spellbound, and Sedgwick and Colleen were in the trees, licking each other's faces. Wherever I looked I felt enchanted, jubilant, and the high feeling lifted me off the ground and slowly up the cloud tunnel.

"Not so fast," she said. Carole was standing at the bottom of the tunnel, eyeliner running down her cheeks, her denim jacket soiled and torn at the collar, her arms outstretched to me.

"I don't belong in your world anymore," I said to her. "It's no place for someone like me."

"Then I'm coming with you," she said, wiping a stream of tears from her eyes.

And as I lazily floated upward, she fell down onto the blue moss. She tried again and fell again. Over and over she tried and fell. "Please, don't go!" she shouted, reaching up to me with her arms. "I saw everything!

I heard everything! The whole ninth floor saw. You're not crazy! Or we're *all* crazy! Come back, at least so I don't have to shout like this!"

But I couldn't make the ride go down. No thoughts would reset the motion. Jimmy was two hundred feet up, gesturing for me to follow. I could already smell Sarah's maple walnut cookies. I'd risen above the Plarpiana sky, now immersed in blackness and flickering curtains of green and gold like the aurora borealis. Then I heard the words.

"I LOVE YOU, SHAWN!"

My heart tugged for her and in that millisecond I was standing at the bottom of the tunnel, her arms tightly around me, her lips all over mine. My god, I thought, now I know I'm dead.

"You're not dead," she said. "I heard your thought. You're a hero to all those people. Look at them—so happy. You made paradise for them. Look, there's even Nurse Blemm sitting under the orange mushroom."

The whole ninth floor had been transplanted to Plarpiana, and everyone was sitting cross-legged, transfixed on the sky.

"If you float away," she said, "we won't be together. I'll wind up on the ninth floor, because every bit of science I ever knew just got trashed. Without you, how will I square this in my mind? No, I'm taking you home. We'll set up the living room for you and your Choiklets."

"Kloik Kleks."

"MIKTER MIKTER,"—the sound of Murkduk's thoughts. *"MIKTER MIKTER MIKTER."* His way of calling me for another concert.

"Is that one of the aliens?" Carole said. "I hear it too."

"Just keep holding me," I said.

"MIKTER MIKTER. WE HAVE REPLAKEMENT FOR KYOU. WE MOKT KRATEFUL TO KYOU, MIKTER MIKTER. NO ONE BE AK GOOD. MAY CALL AGAIN. WE LOVE KYOU, MIKTER MIKTER."

My three idols approached Carole and me.

"Time for graduate school, Mr. Shlewf," Maestro C said to me.

"You'll need your saxophone for this, son," Lord Wendell said.

"I'll help you get a horn," Mr. Jula said. *"I'm sure I got another beauty sitting in some lady's attic."*

"The point is," Maestro C said, *"now that you know how the Outside works, you can never go back to the way things were. The gift will only grow—as will*

your responsibilities. The Sheml has put out the call: All artists are to use the Outside."

"To sing the Heavenly Voice back to the Earth," Lord Wendell said, *"to all living things. Will you help him, Miss Carole Bonner?"*

Carole stood motionless.

"When you play your jazz," Maestro C said, *"the Outside will open the passageways and point you to the people you need to guide—the way the Majib guided you. Will you help him, Miss Carole Bonner?"*

The Kloik Kleks were singing again. Darnell Fortesman was their new leader. For the first time since Maury's Deli, I wasn't their conductor. It felt *good*.

Lord Wendell, Maestro C, Mr. Jula, the jellybeans, Sedgwick and Colleen, the dark red forest and the blue moss all faded into a mist as Carole and I held on tight, and were now clinging to each other on my single hospital bed. She kissed me while Darnell stood beside us, holding a crayon for a baton, and waving at the nine Peter Lorres clucking in front of us. His beat was way off, but this was a giant step up from his days of walking backwards wrapped in garlic and waving crosses. And it was good for Glenda and Zig too, as they sat at the foot of my bed, struggling to mimic Darnell's ragged beat patterns.

"This is so weird," Carole whispered, between kisses. "I see them; I hear them. Is this what it's like to be psychotic?"

"Maybe," I said.

Carole helped me off my bed, and holding my hand, led me around the sixteen other patients stuffed in my room, all sitting cross-legged on the floor, some overlapping each other, all waving their arms and facing Darnell and the Kloik Kleks. It took two minutes to reach the door and another two to get around fat Nurse Blemm who stood in the doorway, unblinking, waving at the Kloik Kleks.

Carole held my hand like she'd never let it go, escorting me down the hall. I wonder if she means it this time, I thought. Or is she just going to crush me again?

"I don't blame you for doubting me," she said. "Not one bit."

How is it that all of a sudden she can read my thoughts, I wondered.

"I'm not sure," she said. "I think I even still hear the aliens. It started after everyone trampled me to get into the room. I watched you sitting there—so determined. You looked really crazy, but there was this strange power in your motion; I could feel it, a tingle buzzing all around me. The more I watched, I started to wonder if there really *was* someone in front of you I couldn't see. As soon as I had that thought, all nine of them instantly appeared. It was horrifying, but they looked so happy, focused on *you,* their leader. I heard instruments—incredible sounds. I couldn't figure out where it was all coming from. Everything I'd ever believed in was blowing up in my face. A moment later I was leaning against a mushroom the size of a bush, crowded in by the same patients from your room, all of us watching *you,* the leader of this thing, and those lights in the sky. You brought us to paradise—a paradise on another planet."

"It was *this* planet, Carole. Earth Three, Plarpiana. The Outside brought us there.

Carole grabbed me again, kissing me passionately just yards from the doctor's office. Then she gazed into my eyes. "How could I have been so cold to my Serene and Easy?" she said. "But if I tell anyone about this I'll lose all my clients; they'll call me a fruitcake."

"Let them."

"Listen, whatever happens," she said as we approached Dr. Schmielkin's door, "let me do the talking. We're never going to be apart again."

We stood outside his door. "No, Carole," I said, "I have to do this myself."

I knocked.

No answer.

I led her through the door as the doctor quickly dropped his arms to the desk—a pen and some papers flying off the side. He turned to us, nervously crossing his legs.

"How-how nice to s-see you, Dr. Bonner," he said. "Are you all right? Did this patient force you in here?"

"Of course not," she said.

Discharge papers and a file entitled "Shawn Lewis" were lying in front of him.

"Mr. Lewis," he said, "whatever this is about, you know you can't barge in without an appointment from Nurse Blemm. I'll be happy to talk to you personally when you've made the appropriate—"

"Just sign right there," I said, pointing to the line. "Then you can get back to your . . . your conducting or whatever you were doing." I wondered if Maestro C had laid out the papers.

"No," Carole whispered in my ear. "I think it was Mr. Jula."

"This is quite ridiculous," Dr. Schmielkin snickered. "Besides, where do you think you're going in your pajamas?"

"I'll get Shawn something from the—"

"I have to do this, Carole," I said. "Please, doctor, just sign. My pajamas won't break any laws. I'm leaving today."

"You need to schedule a Sanity Hearing," he said, pulling out his datebook. "For that you need Nurse Blemm, myself, the social worker, the magistrate and the head doctor, Dr. Gouritz." He thumbed through the pages. "Unfortunately, Dr. Gouritz is skiing in the Alps for the next three weeks, which dovetails with my own vacation. Hmm, the soonest we could evaluate would be—"

"Wait a second . . . " I said. It was faint, but I could still hear the Kloik Kleks.

"You hear them too?" Carole said.

"If I can still hear *them*," I said, "maybe they still hear *me* . . . Murkduk . . . "

"Please, be fair," the doctor said. "Don't call *him*."

"Oh, Murkduk . . . " I said.

"Please," he said, "schedule the hearing. I could lose my job otherwise."

"The doctor's giving us a hard time . . . "

"Hard time? No. No—I'm not . . . OWWW!" He rubbed his knee, and signed the papers.

"I GUESS WE'RE QUITE A PAIR NOW," Carole said as we walked down the street arm in arm. "You with the superman music, me with the Amazing Kreskin all of a sudden."

I didn't know how to tell her, but graduate school had already begun, a new adventure now whirling in my mind: a lonely sixteen-year-old girl painting watercolors in her basement, her tears dripping onto the sketch pad. An eighty-four-year-old ballerina with no functioning hips but with a perfect imagination. A twenty-year-old trumpet player who hears harmonies no one has ever played before. Somehow, I was going to have to find them; I'd have to play a saxophone or conduct another alien choir or find another magic painting to get to them, but I'd have to get to them, to make for them the bridges to the other worlds.

"I saw them too, you know," she said, after we got in the cab. "The painter, the lady in the wheelchair, the trumpeter. Who are they? What do they have to do with you?"

"I hope I won't scare the hell out of them the way Jimmy had scared me."

"So what will you do? How will you help them?"

I thought for a moment, then said, "I'll show them the jellybeans."

She smiled at that, then laughed. She took my hand, looking happily out the window. "You'll be playing your sax a *lot,*" she said. "I might—I might like it this time . . . I guess . . . Of course, you won't do any show tunes . . . I wonder, do you think your spirits or your Kloiklets could print me a schedule, say, a daily planner? Maybe I can work around it."

New problems were on the way. What did they matter next to this astounding woman who just threw away a lifetime of beliefs to make a new life with me?

"I'm flattered," she said. "It's just that avant-garde alien music might not go so well in my building. I can still read your thoughts, you know . . . Oooh, I *like* that one . . . *That* one was positively filthy . . . Now you're making me blush; we're in a cab, for God's sake. All right, based on this new information, as your therapist I'm prescribing for you at least several weeks recovery in bed. And I know just how to help you with that."

We clung to each other the whole ride like we'd waited forever for this moment.

"I think I can support us a little while," she said as she unlocked the door to her building on 78th Street. "But . . . there aren't any paying jobs for the sort of thing you do, are there?"

There were no stipends for Maestro C's grad school. I had no idea how I'd share the bills.

"I know," she said, leading me up her stairs. "How can you think about bills when less than two hours ago you were floating away with Jimmy just to have some maple walnut cookies? I have an idea: Why don't you lead one of those tours to the Caribbean, you know, siphon everybody's cash to send them to other dimensions?"

I would never do that, I thought.

"No, you probably wouldn't," she said, searching for her keys outside her apartment. "You're too ethical. It's just that I don't know how long I'll be able to keep my patients once they start calling their therapist a loon."

We walked in, and she threw her purse to the carpet, wrapped her arms around me and kissed me for three minutes. In the middle of her living room of suede chairs and bookcases—a haven compared to 917—she opened her big chestnut eyes—serious, then afraid . . . then a twinkle. "If you get back with your fancy aliens again," she said, "maybe don't conduct them in the waiting room or the office. And please, you have to keep them away from my sister when she visits. She already hates you. Oh, could you get Murkduk to go after Mark when he's late with the alimony? And could you teleport my neighbor's rottweilers? They drive me crazy. And my upstairs neighbor with her Square Dance Fridays. Just once in a while zap them all to Blarfiana."

Every soul has its art. It didn't matter—a horn, a painting, an alien choir. It was my nature to link with the Outside wave without limits—or the Outside would link with *me*. Of course, the soul never fits neatly into "real life"—until it's the *master* of your real life. Then there's an opening, and a miracle comes, like a stunning caretaker with a revolutionary change of heart. The look in her eyes when I looked at her—this, I thought, this is better than jellybeans, better than paradise.

"Yes," she whispered. "It's dazzling . . . "

ABOUT THE AUTHOR

Scott Shachter has played his flutes, clarinets and saxophones in groups ranging from the *American Symphony* to *Manhattan Transfer,* as well as in nearly seventy Broadway shows. *Outside In,* his first novel, is a finalist in the 2014 Next Generation Indie Book Awards. It also reached the quarter-finals in the 2011 Amazon Breakthrough Novel Award and received Honorable Mention in the 2011 Leapfrog Press Fiction Contest.

www.ScottShachter.com

Made in the USA
San Bernardino, CA
10 May 2014